Advance Praise

"Not many novelists have the courage to place today's political maelstrom into the center of the lives of her characters, but Kathleen Rodgers has done just that in *The Flying Cutterbucks*. When the history of this time is written, Rodgers will be one of those novelists who wasn't afraid to talk about what the late 2010s was really like. She tells her story with warmth, compassion, and a clear vision that satisfies John Gardner's call for today's writers to write 'moral fiction'."

—MARK CHILDRESS, author of *Crazy in Alabama* and *One Mississippi*

"When national politics triggers a buried family secret, the Cutterbuck women do what they do best, persevere. Their story is the story of a resilient American family, fragile in its unmitigated loss, triumphant in the ties that bind. With a page-turning narrative and an authentic sense of place, *The Flying Cutterbucks* will make you laugh and cry, while never forgetting the voices of Jewel, Aunt Star, Trudy, and Georgia."

—JOHNNIE BERNHARD, author of *Sisters of the Undertow*

"In a world that's been turned ··· ············ ······· ne 2016 presidential elec ········ *Cutterbucks* pull togeth ························ r to find hope for the futur ········

—MICHAEL COLE, "P ················· ·· ·quad, and author of *I Played the*

"With a cast of strong women characters—mother, daughters, sisters, friends—this novel about truth-telling is set in a small town in New Mexico after Donald Trump is elected. It's the perfect backdrop to this exploration of ending the silence and secrets women keep."

—JILL SWENSON, retired journalism professor

"Rodgers draws the reader into the world of fifty-something Trudy Cutterbuck, who returns to her childhood home of Pardon, New Mexico—to help her aging mother, but also to figure out her own life, and grapple with some secrets she's been hiding for decades. Set around the time of the 2016 presidential election, *The Flying Cutterbucks* tells a compelling story that links the characters' personal lives to the larger events swirling around them. A wonderful book!"

—DEBORAH KALB, writer, editor, and book blogger

"Mixing raucous hilarity and rakish commentary with a deft hand, Rodgers introduces readers to *The Flying Cutterbucks*, a military family of willful, spirited women. Recently retired from her job as an airline stewardess, Trudy has returned home to Pardon, New Mexico, to see after her mother Jewel, an aging beauty queen whose husband, a pilot, has been MIA in Vietnam all these years. Readers will laugh and cry along with *The Flying Cutterbucks* as the women try their darndest to heal old hurts while remaining open to new adventures."

—KAREN SPEARS ZACHARIAS, Gold Star daughter, author of *After the Flag has been Folded*

"In our sad state of political discord and growing accounts of #MeToo, Kathleen Rodgers has an unflinching ability to write stories that matter. *The Flying Cutterbucks* is a WOW of a book. The Cutterbucks, a Gold Star family, have a major skeleton in the closet as a result of a sexual assault on one of the women when she was still a girl. As this internal wound continues to eat at their souls, the family also combats the ugliness of targeted racism in their community and a national administration devoid of progress toward inclusiveness. Kathleen, however, eloquently gives readers pleasure, too, as they get to know this family of strong women—including a bit of romance—and the beauty of New Mexico, their home."

—ANITA MARTIN, Postcards & Authors, book blogger

"Kathleen M. Rodgers' book, *The Flying Cutterbucks*, is a rousing, timely novel of hope and solidarity among women in a family wounded by the tragedy of war and the trauma of sexual assault. Their resilience gives testament to the power of forgiveness, and the heroism among sisters."

—KATHLEEN KENT, author of *The Burn*

"Settle in for an insightful, entertaining read! Accentuated with vivid detail, *The Flying Cutterbucks*, immediately draws the reader into the heart of the Cutterbuck women and their experiences. Current events are woven together with mystery, family history, and reassuring nostalgia. This is compelling storytelling that keeps the reader engaged to the very last line."

—ROSA WALSTON LATIMER, award-winning author

"Rodgers skillfully spins a poignant and necessary story about grief, buried memories, and the struggle to come to terms with the past. With sensitivity and an insider's awareness, Rodgers honors the resiliency of military wives and children. Moving and deeply affecting, *The Flying Cutterbucks* will make you cry, laugh, and salute the courage and strength of women. Rodgers' remarkable Cutterbuck family will stay in your heart long after you finish the last page."

—ANN WEISGARBER, author of *The Promise*

"Kathleen Rodgers weaves a story that is part mystery, part romance, part social commentary—and all heart. Readers will enjoy each twist of this compelling tale as it winds its way along the gravel backroads and small-town streets of rural New Mexico, pursued by the shadows of long-held family secrets."

—TERRI BARNES, author of *Spouse Calls: Messages From a Military Life*

"Whenever a writer with such skill and sensitivity as Kathleen Rodgers publishes a novel, we must, for our own sake, read it. *The Flying Cutterbucks* is a profound and moving portrait of family, friendship, and forgiveness."

—ALLEN MENDENHALL, Editor, *Southern Literary Review*

"In *The Flying Cutterbucks*, author Kathleen Rodgers has written the 21st century version of Louisa May Alcott's *Little Women* with a wonderfully engrossing updated twist. *The Flying Cutterbucks* is a testament to Rodgers' extraordinary skill as a writer, sweeping you into a compelling story with vivid characters that are so well written as to feel as if you are there with your neighbors and friends. Bravo!"

—DWIGHT JON ZIMMERMAN, #1 New York Times bestselling author

"In *The Flying Cutterbucks*, Kathleen M. Rodgers has created a family of close-knit, funny, wise, resilient women and the people who matter to them. If waiting is a kind of strength in this novel, action is another, and this book is a call-to-action for our current time: action through empathy, advocacy, and even simple presence. I loved spending time with the Cutterbuck women, who have the kind of strength, compassion, and humor that make Kathleen Rodgers a terrific writer and this novel a joy to read."

—ANDRIA WILLIAMS, author of *The Longest Night*

"*The Flying Cutterbucks* excels in depicting haunted lives and a renovation process that involves more than a house. It shows how the women reconnect and become closer as each recognizes in the other a different method of coping and survival. This results in a strength that finally moves beyond alienating each other and protecting themselves from the world.

The Flying Cutterbucks is a powerful story of women returning from the dead (in a manner of speaking) to finally recover not just from assault and secrets, but from the lasting patterns, habits, and the alienation that stemmed from it. It will immerse readers in a world of discovery, recovery, and revised family lives, and is highly recommended for readers seeking an evocative, compelling story of family relationships and change."

—MIDWEST BOOK REVIEW

THE Flying
Cutterbucks

THE Flying Cutterbucks

KATHLEEN M. RODGERS

Wyatt-MacKenzie Publishing
DEADWOOD, OREGON

The Flying Cutterbucks
a novel

Kathleen M. Rodgers

Excerpt from essay "No Place For Self-Pity, No Room For Fear"
The Nation, March 23, 2015 ©Toni Morrison.

Wyatt-MacKenzie Publishing
DEADWOOD, OREGON

Wyatt-MacKenzie Publishing, Inc.
www.WyattMacKenzie.com
Contact us: info@wyattmackenzie.com

"This is precisely the time when artists go to work.
There is no time for despair, no place for self-pity,
no need for silence, no room for fear. We speak, we write,
we do language. That is how civilizations heal."

TONI MORRISON
from "No Place For Self-Pity, No Room For Fear"
The Nation, March 23, 2015

Dedication

To the fearless women in my life:
My sisters, Laura Doran Gulliford, for letting me tag along to the
library early on where you devoured chapter books,
and Jo Lynda Doran Rivera, whose passion
for dance inspires all of us.
We come from a hardy line of women who persisted
and took risks.

In loving memory of author Drema Hall Berkheimer.
When I butchered words, you gently corrected me and loved me
anyway. As Terry and Tom said, "You're a little girl again,
running down a Red Dog road with Sissy...into the sunshine."

And to Arlene Guillen,
Jo's best friend since second grade.
Days before Drema slipped away, the Muse whispered,
"When one door closes, another opens."
And now here we are, helping each other write our stories.

ELECTION DAY
2020

JEWEL CUTTERBUCK tried to control her trembling hand as she picked up the remote control and pointed it at the television. Mr. Grumples, her sister's cat, purred and jumped up on Jewel's lap. Instead of shooing him away, she welcomed his warmth on this chilly November night. As she waited for election results to come in from around the country, her thoughts hopscotched from who was going to be the next president of the United States to the dark and disturbing secret her eldest daughter had shared with her the previous day.

A noise came from the kitchen. Glancing sideways, Jewel saw it was only the big yellow dog pushing her food dish around. Nothing to fear there. Settling back into the sofa, Jewel turned her attention to the news and waited.

CHAPTER 1

Trudy Returns

Pardon, New Mexico
October 2016

"SISTER, DID you hear what the Orange Cheese Puff said? It's all over the news." Aunt Star's crotchety voice crackled from the tiny speaker of the cellphone into the stale air of Jewel Cutterbuck's cluttered living room. "He was caught on tape bragging about grabbing women's lady parts."

Trudy swiveled in the worn recliner and gazed across at her mother, Jewel, an aging beauty queen who'd let the contents of her household pile up around her like sand dunes. For Trudy, the sound of Aunt Star's voice functioned as both a welcome and a warning.

Jewel frowned at the cellphone in her hand like a stink bomb had gone off. "Good God, Star, what will the man say next?" Jewel sat on one end of the sagging gold velvet sofa, flanked on both sides by Spanish-style end tables from the seventies.

"He used the P-word, Sister! All the networks are talking about it."

Jewel's jaw dropped as she scooted forward and placed the phone on a stack of books on the ornately carved coffee table. "You mean like *meow*?" She covered her mouth with a delicate hand freckled in liver spots to stifle a giggle.

Trudy bolted out of the recliner, letting the back of the rocker thump against the textured wall. The song made famous by Tom

Jones crooned in her head. Bending over the coffee table, she cupped her hands on her knees and blurted into the cell, "What's new, Pussycat?"

Aunt Star roared with laughter on the other end of the line. "Lovey, is that you? When did you roll into town?"

"Hey, Aunt Star. About five minutes ago." Trudy glanced up at her mother and winked. "Momma Jewel and I were just discussing what to have for supper."

"You girls should splurge and go to Furr's Cafeteria. They serve everything but alcohol."

Jewel leaned forward on the sofa, jutting her chin toward the phone. "Star, Furr's closed two months ago. I'm going to miss their baked fish and banana pudding."

Star sighed on her end. "Sister, I sure hate to hear that. Next thing ya know, Pardon's going to dry up and blow away, especially since the base closed."

Was it Trudy's imagination, or did her mother's whole body change when Aunt Star mentioned the base? The place where Trudy was born, the last place they'd waved goodbye to her father after he crawled up the ladder to his jet and flew away into oblivion.

Jewel pulled off her knit cap and fluffed her crop of silver hair. "There's talk they're going to repurpose the base. Maybe move the municipal airport out to the old airfield. Turn the quarters into affordable housing."

"I'll believe it when I see it," Star huffed. "Heck, it took Pardon years to even get a McDonalds."

Jewel rolled her eyes and made a "yapping" sign with her hand. She lowered her voice and muttered under her breath to Trudy, "Just because she's the oldest by one year, that makes her the authority on everything."

Trudy hoped her aunt didn't hear her mother's snarky comment.

"Well, at least we finally got a Walmart," Jewel said, trying to humor her sister.

"And you call that progress?" Star shot back.

Ever since Aunt Star had moved to Las Vegas, New Mexico, a

quaint little town nestled in the foothills of the Sangre de Cristo Mountains, she got her digs in about Pardon.

While Trudy went to work tidying up the magazines and books, she leaned toward the phone and joked, "Aunt Star, the biggest problem with Pardon is it missed Route Sixty-Six by about a hundred miles."

A dry chuckle erupted from the other end of the phone. Jewel gave Trudy a big thumbs-up and mouthed "Good one" before she pulled her knit cap back down over her head and burrowed back into the sofa.

Aunt Star's voice burbled out of the phone again. "So how's my favorite stewardess?"

Her question caught Trudy by surprise. "Didn't Momma tell you? I retired." Trudy glanced at her mother who gave an exaggerated nod.

"Lovey, you're too young to retire."

Trudy straightened her tall frame and searched around the room for another pile to attack. There were so many. "I'll be fifty-eight the end of this month, Aunt Star. I've been flying since I graduated high school."

An assortment of rocks lined up on the windowsill caught Trudy's attention. The heels of her brown leather riding boots clicked on the terra-cotta tile as she ambled over to the large picture frame window facing north. She looked out across the straw-colored Bermuda grass stretching from the front porch to the four-lane highway that ran east to west in front of Jewel's place. A few pale blossoms still clung to the giant yucca plant in the center of the yard next to a black lamppost. Trudy reached over and flicked the light switch and nothing happened. Hopefully, it just needed a new light bulb. She would check on that later. A few feet off the porch, a New Mexico state flag along with a POW/MIA flag snapped in the October breeze, their metal clips clanging against the tall pole.

Picking up a smooth gray rock, she turned it over and read the inscription "Red River, NM Feb. 1958" scrawled in black marker. A souvenir from her parents' honeymoon, a treasure Trudy once cherished. But today, with a pang of sadness, she realized: *Even then, her mother was hoarding things.*

She turned when Aunt Star's breezy sigh filled the room. "Criminetly, Trudy. It seems like yesterday you moved to Dallas and started flying for Southwest."

"Tell me about it," Jewel piped up, flinging off a yellow and brown afghan from her lap and tossing it over the back of the sofa.

Trudy wondered when her mother had taken to wearing knit caps indoors and velour lounge pants instead of her usual tailored slacks and silk blouses, her trademark attire long after she'd sold her housecleaning business and taken up volunteer work at the hospital.

At the bookcases on the west wall, Trudy paused to stare at multicolored spines with too many titles to take in all at once and too many dusty knickknacks standing guard in front of the books. The whole house needed a thorough cleaning. Jewel may have owned her own business built from scratch in the late seventies, hiring single mothers like herself who needed to put food on the table. But when it came to cleaning her own house...well, she was like the plumber with leaky faucets or the cobbler with holes in his shoes.

After Jewel made a comment about how time flies, Trudy swiveled and walked back toward the phone. "How are you doing, Aunt Star?" Even after all these years, Trudy still pictured her aunt in a crisp white nurse's uniform.

"I'm creaking along. Knitting caps for the homeless and chemo patients. So, what are your big plans, Miss Gadabout?"

Trudy chuckled, her gaze fixed on the purple cap adorning Jewel's head, one of Aunt Star's creations. "My stuff's in storage for six months. For now, I'm going to bunk here with Momma and help her sort through stuff. Maybe haul a few loads to the dump or the Salvation Army."

Aunt Star snorted. "Good luck with that. It'd be easier to light a match to the place."

"I think that's called arson," Jewel chimed in. She pushed her frail frame up from the couch and handed Trudy the cellphone. "Where's the remote? Let's get the news on and see what Star's harping about."

"I heard that, Sister. Try any of the stations. It's made international news."

Jewel found the remote and aimed it at the flat screen television wedged between the bookshelves on a cheap metal stand. The image of a fancy tour bus filled the screen. In the background, the voices of two men bantered like teenage boys in a locker-room.

Trudy tucked one hand under her other arm and held the cellphone out in front of her. She stood glued to the screen, her mouth agape at the shock of what she was hearing on network television. She glanced over at her mother every few seconds to gauge her reaction.

Jewel's heart-shaped face, once smooth but now wrinkled, took on an amused look. All at once, she lowered the volume on the television and glanced toward the phone in Trudy's hand. "Honestly, Star, I heard Shep and his squadron buddies use worse language than that."

"Shep flew fighter jets, Sister. He wasn't running for president."

Still gripping the remote, Jewel sighed and placed one hand on her back and stretched this way and that. Trudy watched and listened as her mother breathed through her nose. "It's been forty-four years this month since his plane went missing."

Trudy swallowed, trying to ignore the panic swirling in her gut as if it were yesterday when her mother received the telegram. Trudy glanced at a large photo of her father in a flight suit next to his F-4 Phantom, his square jaw clenched in a tightlipped grin that said he meant business. She didn't need to walk across the room to read the words engraved on the small brass plaque at the bottom of the picture frame: United States Air Force Major Shepard Cutterbuck, MIA October 2, 1972 North Vietnam.

Aunt Star cleared her throat. "I'm sorry, Jewel. I know it still hurts."

Even in the waning light, Trudy could see her mother's blue eyes soften. Jewel scratched at something on the back of her neck and looked away, not bothering to answer.

Trudy hugged herself and began to pace. For a second, she regretted coming home.

In sequined slippers, Jewel padded toward the kitchen, the remote still in hand. Halfway across the room she swiveled and cranked up the volume. The offensive word blared into the room like an intruder. This time, Jewel's whole body stiffened. With a shaky hand, Jewel aimed the controller at the television like a mad woman with a gun. "I've heard enough of his crap," she snapped, clicking the power button.

"This election is making us all cranky, that's for sure," said Aunt Star.

Jewel spun and snatched the phone from Trudy's hand. Trudy flinched, surprised by her mother's sudden outburst and how quickly she could move when provoked.

Jewel held the cellphone up to her ear and mouth even though it was still on speaker. "Star, I just realized something."

"What's that, Sister?"

"The Orange Dude... it's the filthy way he talks about women. He reminds me of Cousin Dub."

Cousin Dub. All the air went out of the room.

Trudy shuddered and wrapped herself more tightly in her long cable knit cardigan. Even her winter leggings and flannel tunic couldn't stave off the sudden chill that crept through her body. She glanced toward the kitchen, half expecting to see him there. The sound of Aunt Star's labored breathing filled the room.

Then a long silence ensued between Trudy and her mother in Jewel's dusty living room on the outskirts of Pardon and Aunt Star in her little pink adobe several hundred miles away.

A freight train rumbled past on the railroad tracks behind Jewel's home. The whole house vibrated in its wake. A lone whistle sounded after a moment as the train drew closer into town and away from the women.

"We don't have to worry about Dub ever again," Aunt Star whispered at last. "Karma caught up with him."

After Star hung up, Jewel turned to her daughter. "Trudy...?" Her voice sounded odd, like she had something stuck in her throat.

Trudy swallowed and licked her lips. Her heart raced ahead

of her as she tried to appear calm. "Yes, Momma?" Her voice came out raspy.

Jewel took a deep breath and exhaled slowly. "Did something happen here that fall of seventy-four after I had to go away?"

Go away. Her mother couldn't even bring herself to say it.

Trudy gazed up at the ceiling, trying to dodge the question. *You mean when you had your nervous breakdown?* she thought. *It's okay to say it, Momma. Your husband got shot down and went missing and a year and a half later your son died. That's enough to send anybody to the funny farm.*

Funny farm: What Cousin Dub smarted right before he "bought the farm" as Trudy's father might've said, had he been there.

Trudy glanced down at her mother. She towered over her by several inches. "Aunt Star took good care of me and Georgia while you were away." Her dull voice drummed in her ears as she tried too hard to sound normal.

Handing Trudy the remote, Jewel walked to the kitchen sink and stared out the window. Dusk was settling. She turned and ran her fingertips over her bottom lip. "You know one of the last things your daddy said to me before he deployed? 'Keep that sorry cousin of yours away from my girls.'"

CHAPTER 2

Twirler Girl

October 1974

THE POWDER blue VW Beetle sputters away, heading east into town. Trudy waves to her girlfriends, all three upperclassmen whose daddies are civilians. She clops up the long gravel driveway in her chalky white majorette boots, the tassels swinging with each step. Gray clouds droop overhead, and she breathes in the promise of an early snow. For once, she doesn't wriggle her nose at the smell of cow manure from the feedlots south of town.

Her maxi coat flaps open, exposing her bare creamy legs and skimpy uniform, the stretchy sequined material the same shade of green as her daddy's eyes when they sparkle. So Trudy's momma always reminds her with a sigh of longing in her voice. Shifting her textbooks in the crook of her left arm, Trudy twirls a baton in her right hand. A few days shy of fifteen, she is aware that out of the six twirlers in the Pardon High School Band, she is the least talented. But at five feet nine inches with a slim but curvy figure and a shiny mane of reddish blonde hair, she is assured by the band director, Mr. Ennis, that her appearance more than makes up for her occasional fumble fingers.

"Hey, Daddy, I only dropped my baton once during halftime," she sighs as if he is standing by the side of the driveway in his green flight suit, both hands planted on his narrow hips, his long bandy-legs spread inches apart. "I'll never be as good as Momma the way she twirled her way into beauty pageants. And we all know

8

your youngest daughter, Georgia, got all the dance moves."

Trudy does whatever it takes to keep him alive, even if it means talking into thin air. She approaches the territorial-style flat-roofed dwelling her momma calls their adobe, but Trudy knows it's stucco. Halfway up the long lane, her gaze travels to the front door and the wooden sign her momma bought at the base thrift shop when they returned to New Mexico: *Mi Casa Es Su Casa*. "My house is your house," Trudy chants, switching back and forth between English and Spanish as she continues to twirl her baton.

Aunt Star's Plymouth Valiant is parked under the double carport next to Momma's Chevy station wagon that hasn't moved in weeks. Daddy's '69 silver and black Camaro sits out back under cover in the dilapidated barn, waiting for him to return and fire up the engine and drive ninety-to-nothing on the caliche roads outside of town, kicking up dust devils in his wake. Trudy reasons that if Daddy were here, he would brush a hand across his sandy-haired crew cut then let her take the wheel and teach her how to operate a stick shift. Instead, she must rely on some gum-chewing coach who teaches drivers education at Pardon High.

A fighter jet screams overhead at five hundred feet on its final approach into the air base a couple of miles to the southwest. Trudy pauses, filling the hole in her heart with the sound of thunder as she cranes her neck, gazing at the mighty war bird before it disappears out of sight into the setting sun, igniting the sky in tangerine and purple.

"Daddy," she calls, knowing her voice is lost to a jet engine that drowns out her plea. Knowing the sound will keep others from thinking she is losing her mind...like her mother.

Pushing open the side door under the carport with her right hip, she is expecting the savory aroma of chili bubbling on the stove, and Aunt Star's crispy corncakes browning in the cast-iron skillet.

Instead, Trudy's muscles go limp while her heart pumps like a fist in her throat. Her books scatter to the floor, but the baton... Oh, her blessed baton is still firmly in her grip.

Her mind scrambles to process the sounds and smells and the

terror in her own voice as she screams into the kitchen, "Aunt Star, Aunt Star, what's going on?"

Still in her white nursing uniform, Aunt Star's broad backside sways to and fro as she pelts a man with her purse. "Let go of her," Aunt Star yells in a strangled voice Trudy doesn't recognize.

To her horror, she realizes the man is Cousin Dub, the family drunk Daddy warned them to steer clear of.

How did he get in? Trudy scans the room. A half-empty whiskey bottle sits on the end of the counter by the back door.

The smell of liquor and sweat reeks from every pore of Dub's stocky body as he hunches over the back of a kitchen chair, pinning her sister Georgia beneath him. At thirteen, Georgia's terrified sobs fill the kitchen with sounds no sister or aunt should have to hear.

Dub clamps a beefy hand over Georgia's mouth while he shoves his other hand beneath the hem of her uniform, a short green and silver dress that swirls when she performs at pep rallies and games on the junior high dance squad. "You're a scrapper," he laughs, his crude gravelly voice sending shivers up Trudy's spine.

Aunt Star pivots, red faced and wild eyed. She is panting, out of breath, gasping for air. Trudy has never seen her look so scared. Aunt Star is the rock, the family caretaker, the keeper of them all. But at the moment, her frosted pink lipstick is smearing into the lines around her mouth, opened but silent, as if she has forgotten how to talk.

Dub's eyeglasses are askew on his wide glistening face, spittle spewing from his cracked lips as his head swivels in Trudy's direction. "Come here, twirler girl. Give ol' Dub a kiss."

Something primal roars through her body. Her guts twist, and Daddy's voice thunders in her head. "Get him, Trudy. Take that monster down."

Trudy dashes forward, the baton high over her head. She cannot disobey her daddy's orders.

CHAPTER 3

Talk About Town

October 2016

LUPI LOOKED up from slicing green chile and waved a meat cleaver through the air. "If a man tried to grab my VJJ, I'd chop his wiener off and grind it up for posole."

Trudy snorted coffee up her nose. She pulled a napkin from a dispenser with the words "Lupi's Diner" scripted in red. Trudy and Jewel were seated on barstools at the counter where they watched Lupi prepare their breakfast burritos.

Jewel tapped manicured red nails against the sides of her white mug. "So I take it you're not a fan of Mister Sweet Potato Head?"

Lupi went back to chopping chiles, her long black hair twisted in a topknot. The look accentuated her high cheekbones and slender face. "No way. The man is toxic...like agent orange." She mumbled something in Spanish and then glanced at Jewel. "Perdón. I shouldn't joke about chemical weapons. But that dude. He pushes my buttons."

Jewel shrugged and sat her mug down. "No offense taken. To be honest, I don't like either candidate. I'm seriously thinking of writing Shep's name on the ballot."

Trudy spun around, sloshing coffee on the counter. "You can't be serious!" She found her mother's comment sad and funny at the same time. Reaching for another napkin, Trudy noticed Lupi had set the cleaver down.

Lupi's dark eyes softened. "Miss Jewel. Can you do that? I mean your husband has been..." Lupi's voice trailed off as she retrieved two flour tortillas from a warmer. They hung flaccid over the sides of her small hands before she began stuffing them with her special mixture of scrambled eggs, Hatch green chile, and chorizo.

Jewel's ruby lips formed a wicked grin. "Well, they can't accuse me of writing in the name of a dead man." She batted her lashes at Trudy and Lupi. "Considering we have no proof. Considering they never found his body."

Trudy and Lupi exchanged glances. Lupi graduated high school the same year as Georgia, and both girls served as co-captains of the dance squad, the *Cougarettes*. After earning a couple of degrees and living abroad, Lupi returned to Pardon to run the family business, a tiny diner founded by her grandmother on the outskirts of town. Lupi was known for her homemade chile sauce, a secret recipe passed down from her grandmother. Customers raved how the heat opened their sinuses without leaving blisters in their mouth.

An older gentleman seated at the end of the counter pushed his plate aside and picked up a toothpick. "Good morning, señoras. I couldn't help but overhear your lively discussion."

Lupi flashed him a grin. "You're welcome to join us, Mayor Trujillo."

Trudy elbowed Jewel. "Is he the current mayor?"

Jewel shook her head and whispered, "No, a few years back. He lost the last election to that potbellied pharmacist who tried to kill me when he mixed up my meds."

Trudy smiled at the former mayor, a slim man with a pleasant face in his late sixties. He gave her a polite nod. "You ladies don't mind me. I'm a fly on the wall."

Jewel swiveled on the barstool. "Good morning, Mayor. If you don't mind me asking, who do you plan to vote for?"

Trudy nudged her mother. Was this the same woman who'd lectured Trudy and Georgia to never ask a woman her age, to never probe a person about his or her politics?

The former mayor slid off the barstool and grabbed his

cowboy hat. He strolled up to Jewel and placed a friendly hand on her shoulder. "To tell you the truth, Ms. Cutterbuck, I'm with *her*." He chomped on a toothpick and pointed his thumb at Lupi.

Then he placed his hat on his head and left. A little bell over the door jingled as he turned and waved.

"See you Monday, Mayor." Lupi picked up two plates and sat them in front of Trudy and Jewel. In the center of each plate rested a large breakfast burrito. "He's my best customer. Since his wife died, he comes by every morning for breakfast."

Jewel picked up her fork and knife and smoothed a paper napkin on her lap. "I think he's sweet on you."

"Or he's hooked on your special sauce," Trudy jibed with a knowing smile.

Lupi made a face and picked up a menu and went to wait on another customer. "The last thing I need is a man in my life telling me what to do." She paused in front of Trudy. "How long you in town for? We need to catch up."

"Um, I'm not sure." Trudy started to babble about how one day a few months ago after a long trip, she'd stepped off a 737 and rolled her battered suitcase through the jet bridge and thought, *I can't do this anymore. I need to retire.*

But something in Lupi's eyes stopped her from having to explain.

Lupi fanned herself with the menu and glanced at her waiting customer. "I'll be right there."

Trudy could feel the rush of air on her own face. "I'll tell Georgia I saw you. She'll be so glad to hear it."

Lupi's face lit up. "I bet that girl can still shake her booty."

"She's quite a tap dancer, too," Jewel tossed out, lifting a fork to her mouth.

Lupi dashed off and Trudy caught sight of Mayor Trujillo as he climbed into an older model pickup parked next to Trudy's 2016 silver Camaro. She pictured him holding open the door of his pickup for Lupi, and Lupi letting her guard down long enough to climb into the cab.

Trudy wished she could let her own guard down...

She shoved that thought aside and enjoyed knowing her

mother was inches away, still going strong at nearly eighty. And Trudy had the luxury, for now, to spend time with her.

Breathing in the delicious smells wafting up from her plate, Trudy picked up her burrito and savored the first bite, letting the spicy flavors of New Mexico welcome her home.

Jewel stuck a knit cap on her head. "How did the new mattress sleep? Your sister threatened to stay in a hotel next time if I didn't get rid of the old one."

Trudy drove, like her dad, with both hands on the wheel. Her smartphone sat on the console. "My back isn't killing me this morning if that's any indication." Trudy had slept in her and Georgia's old bedroom, surrounded by seventies rock band posters curled around the edges and a pair of green and silver pompoms tacked to the wall. Before going to sleep, Trudy texted a photo of the pompoms to Georgia and asked: Do you still want these? Ha ha. And Georgia had texted back: LOL! Sis. I'm surprised she hasn't bronzed them.

Jewel ran her tongue over her teeth. "Do you have any asteroids in your purse?"

Frowning, Trudy glanced at her mother. "You mean Altoids? Check the side pocket." Lately, some of Jewel's words came out all wrong. Just moments ago as they were leaving the diner, a young man held the door open for them when Jewel said, "Thank you, young fella. How's it hanging?"

Trudy had hustled her outside. "I can't believe you said that."

Jewel's eyebrows shot up. "Said what?"

Giggling, Trudy repeated Jewel's comment and held open the passenger door for her.

Jewel grabbed hold of a handle and eased herself into the low-slung car. "Must've been all that girl talk between you and Lupi." Unfolding her legs, she groaned as she twisted to reach her seatbelt. "Next time we take the minivan. I don't know how you manage to get in and out of this thing with your long legs." She paused, her eyes shining up at Trudy. "Like father like daughter, I guess."

As Trudy went to close the door and walk around to the

driver's side, she caught her reflection in the diner's window. Some might say she was too old to drive a sports car and wear hair past her shoulders, too middle-aged for tunics and leggings. But after wearing a uniform to work for years, and having to adhere to rules and regulations, Trudy dressed as she pleased.

Pulling open the driver's door, she tossed her slouchy purse in the space behind the bucket seats and plopped down bottom first. With one hand on the steering wheel, she kept her knees together, tucked her legs inside, and shut the door. Catching her breath, she inserted the key and said, "Where to?"

Jewel rifled through her wallet. "Can you run me by the bank before we head to the cemetery? I like to keep some cash on hand."

"Is it open on Saturday? If not, we can find an ATM."

"The lobby's open till one. And honestly, I avoid using ATMs. I've read too many stories about little old ladies getting robbed at gunpoint."

"In *Pardon*?"

Jewel gave her *the look*. "Oh, you'd be surprised what stuff happens in this town."

Trudy's stomach lurched at her own deceit. At the horror she and her sister had kept from their mother all these years. "Sometimes you have to block the bad stuff," Aunt Star had convinced them that night in the kitchen. "Otherwise it will wear you down."

Breathing deeply, Trudy banished the *bad stuff* from her thoughts, shoved the car into reverse, and focused on the backup display. Jewel's head swiveled from side to side as she told Trudy how to drive. Her mother had done the same thing to her dad. Trudy remembered how he would cock his head and waggle his eyebrows and say, "Jewel, it's amazing how I managed to get through flight school without your help." And she would reach over and pat his hand and say, "Yes, Shepard, but every good pilot needs a copilot."

The Camaro sped east on Seven Mile Road. At Coronado Street, they turned left and cruised by the old hotdog stand and the high school where a tall sign proclaimed "Home of the Pardon Cougars." As Trudy glanced out the driver's side window at the empty practice field, her mind filled with the sounds of snare drums rat-tat-tatting and the drum major's whistle piercing the air. Just as she tossed a baton high overhead, an earsplitting alarm jolted her back to the present. Her gaze shifted at once to the road ahead as her cellphone honked and vibrated beside her. A second later, her mother's phone squawked from the pocket of her velour warm-up jacket.

Jewel picked up both phones and squinted at the displays. "Silver Alert," she shouted over the racket. Glancing back and forth between phones, she announced the make and model of the vehicle, the license plate number, the height and weight of the missing senior citizen. Then all went quiet. After a moment, Jewel added, "Some poor old fool can't find his way home."

Trudy glanced at her mother as Jewel stuck her phone back in her pocket and placed Trudy's phone back on the console.

Shifting in her seat, Jewel clasped the red and white box of mints in her hands and stared out the windshield. "Too bad they don't have Silver Alerts for missing airmen lost over the skies of Vietnam."

Trudy caught her breath at her mother's remark. Jewel Cutterbuck might get her words mixed up occasionally, but there was nothing wrong with her mind.

Crossing her ankles, Jewel pried open the tin box and popped a mint into her mouth. "Here, have one." Trudy held out her right hand as Jewel shook mints in her palm.

Cramming a handful into her mouth, Trudy welcomed the refreshing burst of flavor, gnawing the coolness between her teeth.

Jewel stashed the tin box in Trudy's purse and they fell into a comfortable silence.

A short time later as they approached the intersection of North Main and Santa Fe Way, Jewel gestured toward the futuristic building to Trudy's left, the motor branch of The People's Bank of Pardon. "Bogey liked to pretend the Jetsons lived there."

Gazing at the concrete awning that stretched over the small nondescript building with one drive-up teller box, Trudy said, "Remember how he'd stick his head out the window of the station wagon and yell, "Look out for flying cars."

Jewel closed her eyes and smiled. "I wonder what he would think of drones. If your brother had lived..." Her eyes fluttered open and her words hung in the air, unfinished.

Trudy cracked her window as she broke out in a cold sweat. She hadn't had a hot flash in years. Looking away so her mother wouldn't see her tears, Trudy cleared her throat. "You want me to pull in there?"

Jewel was quiet for a second. "No, let's go to the main branch. It's always fun to visit."

They headed south on Main for one block, hung a left past the former beauty school turned electronics shop, drove one block and took a right at Estacado. As they passed the gas company on their right, Trudy remarked about going there on a field trip her junior year. "A nice lady in a hairnet served us warm cookies in the test kitchen while some kid kept bugging her about the energy crisis. That whole building smelled like snickerdoodles."

"I remember when your business class toured the slaughter-house. I couldn't get you to eat meat for a month."

Trudy chuckled, "Yeah, and guess what they served in the school cafeteria when we got back?"

"Hamburgers!" Jewel beat her to the punch line.

"Momma, I can still smell the blood and muck. See the men in their rubber aprons and boots as they strung up those poor cows on meat hooks and sawed them in half."

Jewel poked her. "Let's eat vegetarian tonight."

At the next block, a massive round building loomed into view. Trudy whipped a sharp left and pulled into a slot in front of the bank, a two-story structure that appeared made entirely of windows encased in a framework of white arched buttresses. "Aw, the mother ship." She pocketed keys in her purse and reached for the handle. "It always reminds me of *Close Encounters of the Third Kind*."

Straining against her shoulder strap, Jewel gazed up at the building and remarked, "Bogey would have loved that movie. It came out a few years after he died."

Seconds of silence passed before Trudy steered the conversation back to the building. "Have you ever wondered why the biggest bank in town resembles a giant spacecraft? Or why the motor bank looks like the cover from an old sci-fi novel?"

Shrugging, Jewel sighed as if she didn't have the energy to answer.

Pushing open the door, Trudy turned to look at her mother before getting out. "Maybe they're trying to piggyback off Roswell's aliens. Or when you're stuck out here on the high plains of eastern New Mexico, you have to have something interesting to look at besides windmills, tumbleweeds, and grain elevators."

"Are you making fun of my hometown?" Jewel raised an eyebrow, feigning hurt. "You're sounding like your Aunt Star."

Trudy shut the door and came around to the passenger side. "It's my hometown, too, Momma. But sometimes I get the feeling we natives are always apologizing for it. We're not quite west Texas and we're not the *sexy* part of New Mexico. Have you ever wondered why the founders named it Pardon?"

Jewel took Trudy's hand. "And here I thought it was something biblical."

As her mother struggled to get out of the car, Trudy wriggled her nose. "Get a whiff of that. I smell money."

"The bank you mean?"

"No, the stockyards. I don't remember them stinking this bad."

Jewel looped her arm through Trudy's and they headed for the glass entrance. "It's the dairy farmers who invaded this area. We're one of the biggest milk producers in the state, but they've drained the water table and the cows live their entire lives in pens in their own filth."

"Those poor cows," Trudy said, recalling several dairy farms she'd passed on her way into town yesterday.

Inside the bank, Trudy scanned the circular interior. Natural light flooded in from a scalloped skylight at the top of the dome. A wide spiral staircase led up to the second floor, and most of the outer offices appeared closed for the weekend. A handful of people milled about as Jewel made a beeline for the lone teller behind a round counter in the middle of the spacious lobby. Even the carpet carried a space theme, a pattern of gray and light blue circles of various sizes. Trudy hadn't been in the bank in years, and she marveled at the design, slowly turning as she took it all in.

"It's some building for a town this size," a man's voice rang out behind her. "Your first time here?"

Startled, Trudy spun and came face to face with a good-looking guy in his late thirties, his day-old beard and red cap setting off the merriest blue eyes. She tried not to stare at the campaign slogan stitched in white thread across the front of his cap. Her gaze shifted and she couldn't help but notice his broad shoulders and chest under his T-shirt. The guy was ripped. He looked as if he'd just come from the gym.

Would it be easier to dismiss him if he had a potbelly, scruffy beard, and beady eyes?

Her training kicked in. For nearly forty years she'd plastered a smile on her face for strangers from all walks of life. Regardless of what they looked like or how they were dressed, regardless of where they came from or where they were going — her job was to make each passenger feel as comfortable and safe as possible.

She offered a friendly smile. "Good morning. I haven't been inside this place in decades. Probably since high school."

"Since high school? Come on." Cocking his head, he rubbed his chin and flashed the most adorable grin. "You look like you just graduated."

"Ha," she laughed, flipping her hair back and feeling flushed. *Now if she was twenty years younger...* She might've been a "Pardon Cougar" in high school, but she wasn't the "other kind" of cougar, the kind who pounced on younger men. She'd noticed the silver Celtic cross ring on his right hand. "Thanks for making this old lady's day." She glanced around the bank. "Not much has changed except the carpet. I remember a bunch of us coming here for prom photos." She gestured toward the spiral staircase. "Back in those days, we thought this was the most glamorous place in town."

The guy glanced at the stairs then back at Trudy. "So you're from around here then? I don't mean to sound forward, ma'am, but you look like an actress I've seen on TV or in the movies."

Her mouth twitched and she suddenly felt shy. She'd heard

that line before, but this young man seemed sincere. "I'm a lousy actress. I was in a school play once, but it didn't require a speaking part."

The man threw his head back and laughed. His upper cheeks turned crimson, and he shoved his hands in the pockets of his gym shorts. "Sorry to have bothered you. Lots of film crews come through this area and I thought maybe, well, you have that look about you, and I was hoping to get your autograph for my daughter."

Daughter. The word tugged at her heart.

She looked around. Momma was still chatting with the teller. Gripping her purse strap, her gaze drifted back to the stranger and the words emblazoned on his hat. "I'm flattered," she said, refraining from asking him the one question throbbing through her mind: *Why are you voting for that guy?*

Reeling her thoughts in before she made a fool of herself, she realized it wasn't her job to grill this young man on his beliefs. Who the heck was she to tell others how to vote? There were years when she didn't even vote. This used to annoy the hell out of her ex-husband, Preston. "Come on, Trudy. Don't be an airhead." It took the last few elections for Trudy to realize she'd been taking her citizenship for granted. It's not something she was proud of, especially being a military brat.

Looking around, the man began to wiggle his toes in his flip-flops, like he was bored and needed to shove off. That's when she noticed his left calf was more defined than his right, crisscrossed with scars. "Well, ma'am, you have yourself a great weekend. And I still say you look like an actress."

Her lips slid back into a goofy grin (she could feel it), and she gave him her best thumbs-up, just like Daddy had taught her.

The man shuffled off, gimping as he called to someone across the way, "Hey Gus, how 'bout them Pardon Cougars?"

Clutching her purse strap, Trudy's heart sprinted as she watched the two men from a distance. She gathered they were discussing the Cougars win against the Hobbs Eagles at last night's football game.

A few minutes later, as she and Jewel exited the building, the man in the red cap hoisted himself into a small SUV parked in the designated Purple Heart slot in front of the bank.

The air rushed out of her lungs. "He's a veteran," Trudy stammered, feeling a twinge of guilt. "A wounded warrior with a daughter. How can he think a man who brags about grabbing women's crotches is going to make this country great again?"

Jewel looked on puzzled. "Your daddy earned a Purple Heart, but he never came home and got a chance to park *his* car in that *purple* parking spot." Grabbing a handle, she lowered herself into the car. "Maybe that young fella can't stand the other candidate. Like I said earlier, I'm not a fan of either one of them."

Trudy went to shut the door. "I think Aunt Star's right. This election is making *me* cranky."

Jewel glanced up at her and then slapped the dashboard. "Come on, girlie. Fire up this baby and let's take her for a spin."

After Trudy backed out of the parking slot, she gunned the engine and they peeled out.

CHAPTER 4

Graffiti and Graves

THE SPEEDOMETER hovered right at fifty as they headed east out of town on Curry Avenue toward the New Mexico/Texas line. A freight train with boxcars covered in colorful graffiti chugged alongside them on the tracks that ran parallel to the divided four-lane highway. This was the same set of railroad tracks that ran behind Jewel's place on the opposite end of town.

"Who could've guessed the sides of boxcars would become a traveling art show," Jewel observed, gazing out the passenger window.

Taking her eyes off the road momentarily, Trudy watched the images flash by before she refocused on the highway in front of her. "It's like tattoos for trains."

"Let's race it," Jewel said, her eyes crinkling in a grin.

Trudy stepped on the gas and the Camaro shot forward, its engine roaring as they caught up with the two locomotives pulling the train. "Hang on, Momma." Trudy hit the power button and the passenger window slid down. Cool air blasted inside, along with the smell of diesel.

Laughing, Jewel stuck her hand out the window and waved to the engineers. The train blew its horn as they sped past.

"How fast are we going?" Jewel hollered as she fumbled for the button to roll the window up.

"About seventy." Trudy zipped around an eighteen-wheeler before she eased up on the gas pedal. She glanced in her rearview mirror, checking for flashing lights. "Are you having fun, Momma?"

Jewel laughed and readjusted her shoulder strap. "Yes, but I think the speed limit is fifty-five. Let's take a back road. Less chance of getting caught speeding."

At the New Mexico state line, Trudy hooked a left and they headed down a paved farm-to-market road a couple of miles before they turned left on Airport Road and headed back toward town. She remembered one summer between her junior and senior year when she and her best friend, Cheri, hopped on bikes and pedaled all the way to the Texas line and back on this remote stretch of road. Five miles each way, no water bottles or cellphones, no weapons of any kind to protect them should a car approach and slow down. All they had in those days were strong tanned legs pumping hard as they kept their tennis shoes from slipping off the pedals.

The road was as narrow as she remembered, no shoulder on either side. The bar ditches were full of ironweed and Russian thistles that would dry up and become tumbleweeds by winter. Off to her left, a plume of dust rose in the air from a combine harvesting a field of sorghum. Was the farmer happy working in his field? What if the farmer was a woman? Trudy had never given it much thought until now. A brown field barren of nothing but dirt and weeds flashed by on their right, a field allowed to go fallow.

There were no other cars in sight. A quick scan at her gauges, then Trudy bore down on the gas pedal and the Camaro accelerated. Her mother slid the passenger window down again and whooped and hollered like a teenager.

Trudy couldn't remember the last time her mother looked so happy.

"Faster, Shep, faster!" Jewel yodeled over the blast of cold air that gushed through the open window. Her eyes brimmed with happy tears.

"How fast do you want to go?" Focusing on the ribbon of blacktop in front of them, Trudy floored it. Who was she to correct her mother in that fleeting moment when Jewel had slipped through a time warp?

"Supersonic!" Jewel yelled back, the mirth in her voice causing Trudy's heart to swell.

Zooming by a field of fat pumpkins ready for harvest, Trudy took her gaze off the road long enough to see rivulets of emotion running along the ridges of Jewel's cheekbones, like raindrops on the hood of a car. The decades fell behind them, and Trudy had become Daddy in the driver's seat and Jewel was fifty years younger as they raced along in Shep's '69 Chevy Camaro. Jewel squealed with glee.

They zipped past fields of corn and cotton and winter wheat. A blue commuter plane rolled down the runway and lifted off as they passed by the municipal airport. The plane passed right overhead, and Jewel waved as if the pilots and passengers could see them below.

"We're the *Flying Cutterbucks*," Trudy yelled over the sound of the wind whipping her hair around. Jewel's hair stayed in place under her knit cap.

Her mother turned, her mouth opened in a big O. "You remember."

Of course, Trudy thought. *Some things you never forget.*

On family outings when she was young, they'd pile into Momma's station wagon, Daddy behind the wheel, Momma riding shotgun. He'd say, "This is your captain speaking. Ready for takeoff?" And Trudy and Georgia would hang halfway out the windows and flap their arms like jet wings. Bogey would climb on one of the girl's laps and stick a pudgy hand out the window and bellow in his little boy voice, "Ready, set, *go!*"

"We're the *Flying Cutterbucks*," Daddy announced into the shiny cigarette lighter he'd pull from the dashboard, pretending it was a microphone. "Sit back and enjoy the ride."

For a few blessed seconds, Trudy's nuclear family was intact.

"Can you believe we didn't wear seatbelts back then?" Jewel hit the power button and the window rolled up and some of the magic faded.

Trudy eased up on the gas as the image of a station wagon full of people singing "Ninety-nine Bottles of Beer on the Wall" disappeared into the past.

"Darling, can you take me home before we visit the cemetery? I need to pee and take a nap." Jewel leaned back against the headrest and closed her eyes.

Visions of tackling years of accumulation ran through Trudy's mind. She was itching to get started. "Sure thing, Momma. While you get some rest, I'll start sorting through stuff."

"Have at it," Jewel said and nodded off.

It was nearly dusk by the time they left the house and drove back across town.

At the cemetery entrance, Trudy slowed the Camaro to a crawl. The tires crunched on chalky gravel as they wound through the front section and turned right past the flagpole.

Jewel pointed to a blue marble headstone a few feet off the caliche road.

The patron saint of clutter strikes again, Trudy thought with a mixture of amusement and sadness as she pulled up behind a half-wall of fieldstone built by the CCC. She shoved the gearshift into park and went to help her mother out of the car. Even from a few feet away, Trudy could see an assortment of items her mother had placed around the upright marker that stood out against the flaxen lawn and flat tombstones.

"How do you like what I've done?" Jewel asked as they approached Bogey's grave. Digging through her purse, she pulled out a small rocket and handed it to Trudy. "Here, place this with the others."

A toy fighter jet and a rocket flanked each end at the stone's base. A squad of small action figures propped against the front of the stone stood guard day and night. Scanning the marker, Trudy breathed in the words engraved in the sky blue marble she and Georgia helped picked out so long ago:

Shepard "Bogey" Cutterbuck
Flying among the stars
1963 – 1974

Stooping, Trudy placed the rocket next to the other trinkets. "You must have to replace these often. They don't look weathered or rusty."

Hugging her purse in front of her, Jewel sighed. "Depends on how much rain we get. Some years are drier than others. I get them cheap at Dollar General. If the wind blows them away, I replace them."

Trudy brushed her fingers over her brother's name. "Momma, tell me the story again how Bogey got his nickname."

Jewel paused to gather her thoughts. "When I was pregnant with your brother, your daddy used to tease me and say, 'Jewel, is our little bogey a girl or a boy?' As you probably know, bogey is a pilot term for an unknown aircraft or blip on radar. Back then, we didn't know the sex of a baby until birth. After your brother was born, Shep kept calling him Bogey."

Trudy smiled. "Daddy and Bogey were the best of buds."

Jewel stared at the grave. "Your Aunt Star says there were two funerals that day. Bogey all decked out in one of your daddy's flight suits. The people at the mortuary were so good to make it fit. And your Daddy's photo tucked in Bogey's hands."

Trudy pictured her baby brother deep in the earth, laid out in his casket like a boy fighter pilot...his lifeless face gray against the olive-drab cloth. "Didn't you stick one of Daddy's nametags on his chest pocket?"

Still clutching her purse as if she didn't know what to do with her arms, Jewel nodded. "Yes, along with a pair of your daddy's wings."

Sniffling, Trudy dabbed her finger at the corner of each eye. Earlier that afternoon while Jewel napped, Trudy wandered into the living room and found her old diary stuck behind a stack of *National Geographics*. It wasn't a formal diary with a lock and key, but a spiral notebook with *Trudy's Tomes* scribbled in big loopy cursive on the cover. Chuckling at her lofty title, she made herself a cup of hot cocoa with a dash of chili powder, Aunt Star's secret ingredient, and curled up in the old recliner to read her youthful musings. While flipping through the pages, she found a letter she'd drafted to her father more than a year after his plane went missing. She read it several times, committing it to memory.

Gazing at her brother's tombstone, Trudy recalled the letter:

April 5, 1974

Ground Control to Major Dad,

Can you hear me? It's Trudy.

We still watch Walter Cronkite every night on CBS News. Once in a while something comes up about Vietnam, and Momma will scoot to the edge of the sofa and hug a small pillow. I watch her from the corner of my eye. She always has the same look on her face, like any second she expects to see you come walking out of a jungle, dragging your parachute.

Last year while all of America was celebrating the return of the POWs, Momma gathered us around the television and told us to look at every face, every man getting off those planes. You know, in case the Air Force was wrong. Bogey stood too close to the television, his small arms crossed in that stubborn way of his. After the last man stepped off the plane, Bogey turned to Momma and rolled his eyes. "I told you he wasn't coming home."

Sometimes it's like your jet took off one day and *poof*, you vanished in thin air. There's this song by David Bowie that reminds me of you. He sings about an astronaut who gets lost in space and doesn't make it back. Every time that song comes on the radio, Momma cranks up the volume.

Bogey still wants to be an astronaut. It's all he talks about when he's not walking into things or complaining his head hurts. He and Momma have been spending a lot of time at the base hospital. Aunt Star says Bogey has an inoperable brain tumor. I guess that means he's got a grenade in his head about to explode. Georgia and I try to act all brave around Momma. Lately, she walks around all stiff like a broom and bristles when you ask her a question. Sometimes I think if I touch her, she'll crack like an eggshell.

Tonight, I caught her pacing up and down the hallway, holding herself like she's fixing to be sick. Then she went and stood in front of the long dresser y'all share. She picked up the framed photo of you standing by your trainer jet at pilot school at Reese.

When I came up behind her and touched her on the shoulder, she wheeled around like she was fixing to hit me with your photo. I'm not sure if I scared her, or if I wasn't supposed to see her crying.

Ground control to Major Dad…
Can you hear me?
Love, Trudy

A breeze picked up and her mother shivered next to her. "I'm heading back to the car. It'll be getting dark soon."

The evening sky had turned to gray with a line of dark clouds rolling in. Here in the southwest, the smell of rain wasn't so much a promise but a tease.

Trudy lingered, gazing at Bogey's grave. "I'll be along in a second." She wished she'd grabbed a warmer jacket. No sooner had she tucked her fingers inside the sleeves of her sweater, using them like hand muffs, than the hair on the nape of her neck prickled.

"Check six!" Daddy's voice boomed in her head. A command Trudy couldn't ignore.

Breathing hard, she pivoted and hyper-focused on her surroundings and what was behind her. She scanned the area looking for *bandits*, Daddy's pilot speak for bad guys. He'd trained his children to stay alert. He called it *situational awareness*, and he hammered it into their heads.

Trudy half-expected to see someone behind her, but it was only a prairie dog munching on grass.

"Some bandit you are," she sighed as the rodent scampered away. When she looked up, a champagne-colored Lexus entered the cemetery from a second entrance and maneuvered along the lane across the section from Bogey's grave. The sedan was sleek and new and shiny. It came to rest about fifty yards away, next to a line of fir trees. Trudy's mind flashed to another funeral she and Georgia had attended with Aunt Star a few months after Bogey's. It was mid-October when they'd ridden with Aunt Star in her Plymouth Valiant, snaking along a few cars behind the hearse and two limousines that had parked about where the Lexus sat now.

They'd begged Aunt Star not to make them go. "Button your lips and stay close to me. People will question our absence if we're not there." Afterwards, they'd gone to Great-Uncle Manifred's mansion in the garden district where a maid met them at the door. Aunt Star instructed them to give the old man a hug. "Tell him you're sorry, nosh on some finger food, and if anyone asks, your momma's in the hospital getting some much needed rest."

"She had a nervous breakdown." Georgia rolled her eyes before they went inside.

"I'm having one right now." Trudy nudged her sister in the back.

But nobody inquired about Jewel Cutterbuck that day. They were too busy gossiping about the tragedy when Uncle Manifred was out of earshot.

"Gladys spoiled him rotten after little Rene died, poor thing, wasn't but three."

"There's rumors he smothered her...but who knows."

"That boy was never quite right and from such a good home."

"Ne'er–do–well. Couldn't hold down a job. Gave his daddy so much grief."

"Stumbling onto the tracks at night. What was he thinking?"

"He wasn't. The louse was probably liquored up and out of his mind."

"God, I hope he didn't know what hit him."

The memory caused Trudy to shudder. She glanced back at the half-wall where the Camaro was hidden from view. She assumed Momma was getting situated and warming up inside the car. Trudy focused her attention back on the Lexus. You didn't see many foreign models in Pardon. Out here, folks tended to drive American-made cars and trucks. From her vantage point, she could see a tall woman in a dark coat and headscarf get out of the Lexus and come around to the passenger side where an elderly woman sat hunched in the front seat. The two women appeared to talk briefly.

Then the woman in the headscarf made her way toward a row of tombstones not too far off the road. In low-heeled pumps, she walked with her head down, stopping every few seconds to look this way or that. She walked with purpose, perhaps a business-woman overdressed for a Saturday.

An old woman's voice trilled, the tone impatient, like she was barking orders or directing the tall woman to go back the other way. The woman in the scarf turned, and headed toward another row of tombstones. Seconds later she stopped abruptly in front of a large tombstone. Her shoulders drooped momentarily before she wheeled around toward the Lexus and hollered, "I found it."

With Momma hidden behind the half-wall, Trudy ducked behind a large statue of Jesus missing a hand. She felt foolish peeking out behind his stiff robe, but she didn't want the woman to see her spying. Since the day Aunt Star forced them to attend the funeral, Trudy avoided that side of the cemetery.

The woman pulled an aerosol can out of her coat pocket. Shaking the can, she bent over and sprayed something up and down the length of the grave. After a moment, she stood, stuck the can back in her pocket, and pulled out a cellphone. Backing up a couple of feet, she held the phone up and appeared to snap photos. She hollered something to the old woman in the car, but the wind shifted and Trudy couldn't hear what she said. The woman in the scarf lingered at the grave as if in deep thought, then she rushed back to the car.

After the Lexus drove away, a hawk keened overhead, dive-bombing at something on the ground.

"What was she doing?" Trudy jumped at the sound of her mother's voice. Jewel was standing at the half-wall, her elbows propped on the ledge. "Aunt Gladys is buried over there somewhere, along with her little daughter and —" Suddenly Jewel stopped as if she couldn't be troubled to finish.

Trudy's stomach twisted inside out. "I'll go check. You get back in the car and warm up."

Dreading the trek to the other side, she maneuvered through the cemetery, careful not to walk on people's graves or to twist her ankle in a prairie dog hole. Seeing the prairie dog earlier reminded her that the varmints were known to build whole towns in cemeteries out west. As Trudy drew closer, her gaze zoomed in on the word spray-painted in big red letters over the brittle grass.

She covered her mouth as the word *rapist* screamed back at her from the grave.

Gulping air, she felt like she'd been sucker punched. Her

heart pumped faster as she looked up at the name on the head-stone:

Manifred "Dub" Hurn II

Our only son

1935 – 1974

Her chest hurt and she stumbled back, her throat parched as awful visions howled through her mind. A severed head and dis-membered legs, the mutilated torso pushed down the tracks by a locomotive pulling freight. The engineer said later he thought it was a stray cow. Would the images ever go away? Her whole body trembled as she backed away as if he was still a threat.

She tore out across the cemetery, grateful she'd worn her rid-ing boots with sturdy soles. Keeping her head down, she counted to ten then backward as her hair swung in her face and she willed herself to calm down. She couldn't risk Momma asking too many questions.

By the time Trudy got back to the car, her whole body was shaking.

Her teeth chattered as she went to start the car and turn on the heater. "I'm freezing, Momma, how about you?"

Jewel reached for her seatbelt. "I'm fine, darling, but I hope you're not getting sick. You're as white as a cotton boll and your face is covered in sweat."

Licking her lips, Trudy lied. "Must be the altitude. It's a mile high here. I need to get acclimated."

Jewel leaned over and touched Trudy's forehead. "You feel cool to me." She studied her daughter. "Did the altitude ever bother you at thirty thousand feet?"

"The cabins are pressurized, Momma. You know that." Trudy shoved the gearshift into drive and the headlights came on. Tires crunched against gravel as they drove away from Bogey's grave, protected by a squadron of tiny super heroes.

"What was that woman spraying?" Jewel asked as they ap-proached the end of the lane where they could either go left or right.

Trudy kept her voice even. "Ant killer. You should have seen the size of those mounds."

Jewel twisted in her seat and Trudy could feel her mother's eyes bore into her. "This time of year?"

"Yup, the seasons are out of whack. This morning felt like Indian summer. We might see frost by tomorrow."

Jewel leaned against her seat and clasped her hands over one knee. "And they say there's no such thing as global warming. Try convincing those ants."

When they got to the end of the lane, Trudy hooked a left instead of going right to avoid driving past Dub's grave even though the graffiti was shrouded in darkness by now.

After they stopped by the store for a few groceries and headed west on Seven Mile Road, Momma dozed off. Halfway home, she woke with a start. "So if that woman was killing ants, why were you hiding behind Jesus?"

Hiding behind Jesus? Trudy scrambled for an answer.

"Uh, I was looking for his missing hand," she offered weakly, praying the gates of Heaven hadn't clamped shut on her forever.

Jewel Cutterbuck let out a quiet laugh. "And what would you do with it if you found it?"

"That's easy, Momma. I'd place it on Bogey's grave."

After a light supper of soup and salad, Jewel retired to her bedroom to read. Trudy rummaged through the cupboard until she found a set of wine goblets with silver etching that read: *Pardon Air Force Base Officers Club.* Sometime after Daddy's plane went missing, one of Momma's friends, a pilot's wife named Shirley, stopped by the house after happy hour with a couple of glasses she'd pilfered from the club. When Jewel tried to refuse, saying, "But that's government property," Shirley shoved the glasses in Momma's hands and remarked, "Honey, after what you've been through, the Air Force at least owes you some commemorative stemware." That night, with Trudy and Georgia and Bogey peeking from the hallway, Jewel and Shirley polished off a bottle of wine courtesy of the O'Club's bartender.

Rinsing off a layer of film, Trudy poured a splash of wine and took a healthy sip. Leaning against the counter, she studied the east wall of the kitchen above the messy table. Fifty-year-old macaroni art mingled with childhood drawings taped to the wall and a giant fork and spoon from an overseas assignment. A red and yellow God's eye made out of yarn and chopsticks captured her attention. One of Bogey's art projects from the base chapel after they moved back to New Mexico. She racked her brain for the Spanish name. Oh, yes, *Ojo de Dios*, Eye of God.

"You are supposed to bring protection and healing," she muttered, eyeing the diamond-shaped weaving over the rim of her glass.

Setting her wine down, she went to grab her cardigan before going outside. Heading toward the spare bedroom, she did an about-face at the hall closet and threw open the door. A Conga line of car coats and parkas danced from hangers as she rifled through them. She stopped when she came to the sage green nylon jacket with bright orange lining: Daddy's flight jacket.

Shrugging into the puffy sleeves, she zipped herself in, inserted her earpiece, and stepped outside to call Georgia. Except for the lamppost out front, all the outside lights were in working order. The backyard spotlight illuminated the vintage travel trailer where she and Georgia used to hang out as teenagers, listening to music on their transistor radios. If she strained her eyes hard enough, she could see the railroad tracks running along the top of the embankment at the end of Jewel's property line. A shiver shimmied up her back.

While she waited for her sister to pick up, two questions clawed at Trudy's brain: Who was the woman at Dub's grave? And what was her connection to him?

CHAPTER 5

Dub

October 1974

THE BATON slams into the middle of Dub's broad back. The blow barely fazes him. If anything, it riles him up. With Georgia pinned in his left arm, sobbing hysterically, Dub swings his upper body around and swipes the baton from Trudy's grip with the power of a gorilla.

For a second, she stares at her empty palm, shocked by his brute strength. Her hand stings from the force. Still in her maxi coat, she tries to tackle him from behind, but she is no match for his body. Slamming into him is like hitting a thick tree. He doesn't budge.

His eyes graze over her when her coat flaps open. "Whew-wee, show me your titties." His voice is the growl of a predator. It sickens her. She has looked the word up in the dictionary after reading a story in the newspaper about a man who preys on people.

Georgia's hair is a tangled mop of spun gold and copper in the crook of Dub's left arm. Trudy can barely make out her sister's face, hidden from view. But what she sees is enough. Georgia is petrified, utter panic in those hazel eyes normally brimming with life. Her long legs, the legs of a dancer, are supposed to be leaping about, kicking the high step and not kicking at an attacker. Georgia's feet, clad in her sparkly dance shoes, scramble for escape.

Shocked by her own building rage, Trudy yells at Dub, "Shut up, you creep." She has never talked to an adult this way. She has

34

been raised to respect her elders.

Aunt Star comes at Dub from the other side, pushing her heft into him. "Let her go, Dub. You got away with it before. Not this time."

He yanks Georgia around like a rag doll and snarls at Aunt Star. "Get away from me, heifer. You're not worth a poke anymore."

Aunt Star's complexion is still smooth at nearly forty, her soft smile and pleasant features always a comfort to those she encounters. But Dub's words twist her face into someone Trudy doesn't recognize. A face full of scorn, shock, and complete hatred for a man she is related to by blood. "You pervert. You make me sick."

Georgia is pleading for "Mommy," her mournful sobs reminding Trudy of the sounds her sister made when Daddy's plane went missing, and even worse, the night their brother died.

"Mommy's at the *funny farm*," Dub spews out, his cruel laughter sending revulsion through Trudy's bones. The whiskey he had consumed earlier seems to fuel his nastiness. He is a crazed animal torn loose in their home. A home he is not allowed to set foot in, and yet he got in.

"It should've been you that died instead of your sister!" Aunt Star hisses, her face as red as the terra-cotta tiles. "You're a waste of protoplasm."

Dub scowls at Star then jams the baton against Georgia's throat. "You'll pay for that, cuz."

Georgia makes a choking sound that hacks at Trudy's heart. She glances around for another weapon. No time to wait.

The soles of Aunt Star's thick shoes squeak as she bustles toward the turquoise phone on the wall, the long cord dangling in a twisted mess from the girls wrapping it around the corner into the hallway. Even from here, Trudy can see the muscles in Aunt Star's thick calves flex beneath her white support hose as she reaches for the receiver and dials.

"You better not call the po-leece," Dub warns. He hurls the baton through the air, hitting Aunt Star in the rump. "Hang up that phone! Or I'll wring her scrawny neck."

Aunt Star drops the receiver, sending it crashing to the tile floor.

Georgia's pleas are more of a whimper. She is struggling to breathe.

"You're crushing her windpipe," Trudy screams, ramming into his side again, trying to throw him off balance. "If my daddy were here, he'd beat the daylights out of you."

Her words seem to stoke his anger. "Where's your flyboy daddy?" His cruel taunts mock at her core. "Got himself shot down."

From somewhere inside comes Daddy's voice. Calm. Reassuring. He is telling her to think clearly, to ignore Dub's insults. They are the insults of a coward, a failure jealous of another's success.

"Three o'clock," Daddy coaxes her in pilot speak. Trudy imagines the number three on the face of a clock. Her head swivels to the right, her eyes fix on the heavy cast-iron skillet on top of the stove, its handle turned outward. The skillet is empty, the stove off. For Aunt Star hasn't had time to change out of her uniform and start supper.

Aunt Star is a blur of white coming toward her. Trudy swallows.

They both reach for the handle at the same time.

CHAPTER 6

Georgia

October 2016

"LUPI SAID to tell you hello." Trudy fiddled with her earpiece and shoved her hands in the pockets of her daddy's flight jacket.

Georgia sounded out of breath, like she was scurrying about performing some task. "I try an' keep up with her on Facebook. Can you believe she gave up a lucrative marketing career to come back to run her grandmother's diner?"

Maybe she wanted to come home, Trudy thought, thinking of herself and reflecting on how she'd flown all over the country, from sea to shining sea, looking for a paradise that never existed and always seemed out of reach, beyond the horizon. From city to city, pushing the drink cart up and down the narrow aisle inside a metal tube crammed with people, she'd felt a tugging, a longing like a voice on the wind, calling for her to come home. She'd wanted to ask Lupi if she'd heard it, too, or if she was back strictly out of obligation.

Under the glow of the carport light, Trudy paced, doing circle eights between Momma's Chevy minivan and the Camaro. "I think she's trying to keep the overhead down. Momma said one of Lupi's cousins comes in to help her out from time to time."

"Yeah, she mentioned something about it on Facebook," Georgia replied in a faraway voice as if she'd been half listening without trying to appear rude.

The clicking of high heels echoed in Trudy's ear. Ever since they were little girls playing dress up, Georgia loved to traipse around in high heels. She'd even worn them with jeans back when that style was so popular. But with age, she'd switched from pointed stilettos to round- or square-toed pumps, and as they chatted, Trudy pictured her sister prancing around in a pair of fashionable Mary Janes.

The storm clouds from earlier ushered in a cold front but no rain or snow. Trudy blew imaginary smoke rings into the frigid air like she'd done as a kid, back when she thought it would be so cool to smoke. "She looks good, feisty as ever," Trudy picked up where she left off. "I can still see you two strutting around the school like it was one big discotheque."

Georgia laughed, her voice growing huskier with age. "I remember stopping in front of the principal's office one time to do the hustle. I think it was Lupi's idea."

"What did Mr. Scanlon say?"

"He poked his head out and said, 'Ladies, save it for the pep rally.'"

"He was such a pushover. Hey, did I catch you at a bad time? Sounds like you're busy." Trudy could hear rustling in the background, her sister whispering to someone in the room.

"My hands are giving me fits today. Gil's here helping me with my zipper. We're going to a play at his new theater. Tonight's the grand opening."

A year ago after Trudy had landed at LAX and was stepping into the crew van, Georgia had called, breathless and giddy with news. "Sis, I just met Gilbert Miguel Vargas. He was on my tour at the Castaneda. He wants to meet for lunch at Charlie's."

Packed shoulder to shoulder in a van full of flight attendants and pilots, Trudy had blurted into her phone, "You mean that old guy with the craggy face who plays all those *bad hombres* on TV? What's he doing in Las Vegas, New Mexico?"

"He lives here," Georgia had gushed, explaining how the actor had returned to his roots and built a hobby ranch on a piece of land outside of town. A ten-minute drive to the community theater he planned to open on Bridge Street, right off the plaza.

On weekdays, Trudy's sister taught dance at Luna Community

College. On weekends, she worked as a Harvey Girl reenactor, donning the crisp black and white uniform of the legendary waitresses who served meals to hungry passengers on the Atchison, Topeka, and the Santa Fe Railway.

"What are you wearing to the play?"

"A slinky dress with lots of sequins. Only cost me ten bucks at a new thrift store in town. I'm overdressed, but..."

Trudy imagined her sister all glammed up in a shimmering gown clinging to her svelte figure. At five seven and well into her mid-fifties, Georgia had worked hard the last decade to restore her dancer's body after years of neglect. Except for arthritis in her hands, she appeared as limber as when they were kids.

"Gil used to hang out with starlets so I have to look the part," Georgia purred with a laugh.

"Darlin', there's a reason I moved back to New Mexico," Trudy heard Gil murmur, his deep sexy drawl oozing with flirtatious undertones.

No wonder the ladies loved his films. His bad boy image and voice drove women crazy.

Listening with greedy ears, Trudy pictured the aging actor with bronze fingers adorned in turquoise and silver rings, coaxing the tongue of the zipper from her sister's tailbone up the hollow of her back to that spot between her shoulder blades where he'd linger to fasten the eyehook. Then Georgia would wriggle her hips in gratitude and reach for her evening bag.

"You wearing your hair up or down?" Both sisters had turned to the help of a hairdresser to keep their locks the luster of new pennies.

"Up-do. French twist. In case we go dancing afterwards."

"You and Gil could start your own version of *Dancing with the Stars*."

Georgia giggled, and Trudy envied her sister's ease at dancing with a partner. Except when it came to fast dancing or her twirling stint in marching band, Trudy had two left feet. Even in grade school, she could flub up a do-si-do in square dance during PE. "Your problem," Preston told her years later before they divorced, "is you want to lead and not follow."

"Everything okay there? You sound funny," Georgia remarked, as if she'd picked up on something in Trudy's voice.

Sighing, Trudy paced up and down the driveway, concentrating on the sound of the gravel crunching beneath her boots, the hum of an occasional car or truck whizzing past on Seven Mile Road. She'd forgotten how black it could get out here on the fringes of town. "I'd give anything for a cigarette right now," she said as another set of headlights pierced the darkness and kept going.

"You haven't smoked in years."

"Since I was thirty-five." *Since I quit cold turkey and tried my damnedest to get pregnant.* "Once in a while I still crave one. Usually when I'm stressed."

"Is Mom's house getting to you? It's like walking into a time capsule."

"It definitely has that seventies feel. It's like she's stuck there."

Neither sister said anything for a moment.

Finally, Trudy pushed ahead. She'd been skirting the issue long enough. "Listen, Georgia, I'm sorry I caught you on your way out." Inhaling a drag from her make-believe cigarette, Trudy held the cold air in her lungs, before she let out a long cleansing breath and started back toward the carport. "When's the last time you talked to Mom?"

"A couple of days ago. Right before you got there."

"Okay. When's the last time you spoke to Aunt Star?"

"I stopped by her place Wednesday. She made me a hot toddy 'cuz my throat was sore. Why, is something wrong?"

Hot toddies, Aunt Star's secret cure for what ails you. Even administering her bourbon-laced brew to two underage nieces on an awful night when she needed them to calm down.

Trudy took a deep breath and forged ahead. "She's fine as far as I know. So you haven't talked to her since Wednesday?"

Irritation crept into Georgia's voice. "What is this, the Spanish Inquisition?"

That was their mother's private joke every time one of their dad's relatives used to call from Kentucky and pepper Jewel with too many personal questions: Was she dating again? Was she ever going to remarry? Did Shep have other life insurance outside of his government benefits?

"Sorry, sis," Trudy laughed, "I was wondering when you last spoke with her, that's all." Trudy stared at the brown tips of her boots, noticing a scuff on the right toe. Bending over to buff it out with her finger, she winced at the crick in her lower back. All that lugging, lifting, straining, and cramming passenger suitcases into overhead bins had taken a toll on her body. "Are you on speaker?" She clenched her teeth and slowly straightened back up.

"No..." Georgia sounded more guarded this time.

"Aunt Star called Momma last night. She was appalled by the leaked tape on that tabloid TV show...oh, I forget the name."

"I rarely watch TV unless Gil's on some rerun or there's breaking news."

"Lately it feels more like breaking wind," Trudy shot back, "especially with this election heating up."

"No kidding," Georgia chuckled dryly. "The media's havin' a field day."

Trudy cleared her throat. "The *perv* came up in Mom and Aunt Star's conversation."

"The *per*...? Oh my God," Georgia gasped. "Who brought him up? Surely not..."

"No, it was Mom."

"*Mom!* But she doesn't know..."

Quickly, Trudy relayed last night's phone conversation between their mother and aunt. And their mother's probing question to Trudy after Star hung up.

Then Georgia said in hushed tones to Gil, "Babe, I need to talk to my sister in private. I'll only be a second."

"Sure, darlin'," came the crusty voice that conjured up images of desperadoes in dozens of films. "I'll wait in the truck."

After a door clicked in the background, Georgia lowered her voice. "Look, sis, I can't talk long."

"I know, I'm sorry." Trudy felt an invisible wall go up. She'd been expecting it, but she also felt bad for having to broach the subject in the first place. "It can wait, uh, we can talk —"

"Tell me now." Georgia's tone shifted from cautious to irritable.

"But Gil's waiting and…"

"Trudy, just say it."

Trudy closed her eyes, dreading her sister's reaction. "Do you and Aunt Star ever talk about that night?" Trudy paused at the side door and held her breath.

"No! Never." Georgia's curt response was meant to shut Trudy down.

Rubbing her temples, she plunged ahead. "Something happened today when Mom and I were at the cemetery." Trudy told her sister about the woman in the Lexus and the graffiti on Dub's grave.

Georgia didn't say anything for what felt like an eternity. Trudy could hear her sister fiddling with her smartphone, like she was multitasking while they were talking. She heard Georgia's labored breathing, pictured her sister huffing and puffing and fanning herself as she walked circles about her bedroom, trying to keep the shock from messing up her makeup. Georgia's voice was hoarse when she came back on. "Sis, I checked the calendar on my phone. You know what today is…?"

Dizzy, Trudy leaned against the side of Jewel's minivan. Since she'd retired, she quit relying on calendars to run her life. Her heart plunged like an elevator dropping too quickly as she mentally tried to grasp the day of the month. She squinted at the screen on her own phone: October 8, 2016. Surely she'd known this on some level.

Trudy knew what was coming next…

"Today's the anniversary of the *perv's* death." Georgia's announcement came out flat, devoid of all emotion.

Trudy searched her short-term memory. Dub's gravestone didn't list the day he died, only the year, 1974. In her mind, all she could see was the word *rapist*.

The outside light flickered by the carport door. "Crap, it's Mom." Trudy pushed up from the minivan. "She's flicking the light on and off. Like when we were teenagers."

"She probably thinks you're out there sneaking a smoke," Georgia snickered, sounding relieved to have something to laugh about.

"Or making out with a boy," Trudy jibed, trying to lighten the mood.

"Look, I gotta go." Before Georgia clicked off, her parting words sent chills zipping up Trudy's spine. "That woman you saw at the cemetery... I wonder who she is? And if there are others?"

Stuffing her phone into her pocket, Trudy looked up as Jewel opened the door and peeked out.

Her mother shrank back as if caught off guard, her mouth hinged open and her hand clutching her chest. "It's one thing to see that old flight jacket on a hanger, but..." Her voice dropped off.

Trudy glanced down then back at her mother. "Oh, Momma, I didn't mean to... I hope you don't mind."

Jewel held the door open wide. "It must be the cold," she said, sniffing the air around Trudy as she stepped inside.

Gliding across the kitchen, Trudy retrieved her wine glass and took a long sip, letting the alcohol seep into her system. Twirling the stem, she gazed at her mother. "I wasn't outside sneaking a smoke if that's what you're implying?"

With eyes glistening, Jewel padded toward her. "Who said anything about smoking?" She reached out and brushed her fingers over the puffy sleeves. "After all these years, I can still smell him."

Unzipping the jacket, Trudy bent her head and breathed deeply into the lining. "You mean that musty smell?"

Jewel leaned closer. "Yup, smells like a fighter pilot to me."

Trudy remembered climbing onto her father's lap when she was young. She thought all daddies smelled like airplane hangars and jet fuel and sweat.

Jewel went to the cupboard and pulled out the other wine glass from the O'Club. Lifting it to the light, she examined the military emblem. "I don't drink much these days, but think I'll join you if you don't mind."

Setting her glass down, Trudy cleaned the other goblet and poured wine and handed it back to her mother.

Jewel lifted her glass in a toast. "To the Flying Cutterbucks," she warbled, her eyes dancing with memories.

They clinked glasses as the sound of thunder rumbled in the distance.

CHAPTER 7

Hit the Bricks

Monday Afternoon

A DISTINGUISHED-LOOKING man about her age smirked back at her from the porch.

Sweet Lord, his dimples were showing! He looked better in person than the photo she'd seen of him on Facebook, not that she'd been trolling.

"Hello, Gertrude." His blues eyes twinkled in amusement as if he enjoyed watching her jaw drop. "I heard you were in town."

Trudy stumbled to find the words. Only one person outside the family knew her given name — her high school boyfriend. To Trudy, her first name always felt clunky, like she'd been born with thick calves and orthopedic shoes.

"Clay Cordova! You ought to be arrested." She held the storm door open, catching herself gazing up and down at him. The edges of his square face appeared rounder, his thick neck framed by the open collar of a Western-style dress shirt. His light denim Wranglers filled out in all the right places. Damn, but he looked good.

Her face grew hot as she realized he was checking her out, too. Her hand flew to her throat. "I've aged." She hoped he wouldn't notice her neck, the lines on her chest from too much sunbathing poolside at too many hotels to count.

"We all have, Trudy. But time has been good to you."

Try telling that to my ex, she almost snorted before she banished Preston from her thoughts.

Clay gestured toward the driveway where his late model Tahoe was parked behind her car. "I saw the Camaro with Texas tags. I figured it was you." He glanced around and ran a hand through a head of silver bristles. "Your old man drove a '69 silver Camaro. You used to worship that car."

Chuckling self-consciously, she eyed his left hand. No trace of a wedding band. "Guess I still do. You have a good memory."

He laughed, his dimples deepening. She could've sworn he blushed. He kicked at something on the porch with the toe of his black Ropers. "Remember how we used to sneak around back? Y'all kept his car stored in that old barn about to fall down."

She scratched her temple and nodded. Of course she remembered. That's where they went to make out. She tried to cover her embarrassment. "Momma Jewel sold Daddy's car to another pilot a couple years after we graduated. I think she kept holding out that Daddy would come traipsing through the door after work one day and say, 'Who wants to go for a spin?'"

Clay pressed his lips together and he gave a slight nod. "I'm sorry about your dad." He peeked over his shoulder at the POW/MIA flag flapping in the wind. "I never met him, but I felt like I knew him through the stories you shared and the photos your mom hung all over the house."

Trudy propped the storm door open with her hip, thankful she'd applied lip gloss and mascara and had slipped into her best white jeans, the ones that showed off her long shapely legs. "Nothing's changed much. If anything, Momma's only added to the clutter, er, I mean collection." She pressed her fingers to her lips as if this could erase her slip-up. "I'm trying to convince her to get rid of stuff."

"Good luck with that. Been there, done that, before my mother died."

"I'm sorry, Clay. Your mom was always polite to me."

Clay hooked his thumbs in his belt loops. "You know she wanted me to become a priest, like her brother. Like that was going to happen."

She studied him. "I bet she was proud of you. I heard you went to college. Became a cop. That's what you always wanted to do."

He rocked back on his heels. "Yeah, I'm the oldest detective on the force. They can't get rid of me. Say, I was in Dallas last summer to attend the fallen officers' memorial. I thought about looking you up. But I wasn't sure..."

"I was probably flying. It's terrible what happened. Five cops... shot dead. For what?" She paused, giving him time to answer. But he said nothing so she rushed on. "I sold my condo near Love Field a few weeks ago. Traded my old TrailBlazer for the new Camaro. Momma's letting me crash here for a while. Until I figure out what I wanna be when I grow up."

He cocked his head and stared at her. "I heard you retired from the airlines. I didn't believe it at first."

"Wow, word sure gets around."

"Come on, Trudy. You know you can't keep secrets in this town."

She felt lightheaded.

"Okay, I confess. Lupi told me. Man, I remember when you couldn't wait to get out of this place."

She twirled a section of hair. "I decided I didn't want to wake up dead in a hotel. And I finally realized I hate airports."

Clay chuckled softly. "Hey, you wanna go get a Coke?"

She bit her bottom lip. "You mean, like when we were kids?"

His face broke into a dazzling grin. "Yeah, then we'll hit the bricks. When's the last time you dragged Main?"

A shot of adrenalin rushed through her. "Oh, in forever. Let me grab my purse and leave Momma a note. Today's Pink Lady day at the hospital."

Clay backed the Tahoe out of the driveway and they headed east into town on Seven Mile Road. Trying to appear at ease, Trudy glanced out the window as the scenery flashed by. One thought skated through her mind: *What do you say to an old boyfriend you haven't seen in forty years?*

Clay glanced at her. "You comfortable? You can adjust the seat if you like."

When was the last time a man, or anyone for that matter, asked her if she was comfortable? "I'm good, Clay. Thanks." Her teeth chattered when she spoke. *Why did that always happen when she was nervous?*

"If you're cold, you can crank up the heat."

The inside of the Tahoe was nice and toasty.

"I'm okay, really." She tucked her hands under her legs and willed herself to stop shaking.

With his left hand on the steering wheel, Clay twisted around and lifted something from the backseat. "Here, drape this over your shoulders."

He handed her a man's all-weather jacket with the words *Pardon Police Department* stitched on the back. "Thanks." She shifted in her seat and snuggled into the warmth, breathing in a scent that could only be Clay's. For a split second, her mind drifted to a time when she wore his letter jacket and chunky ID bracelet.

"Sorry about the dog hair," he said. "Hope you don't mind."

She glanced at the jacket then at him. "I lost my dog Skylar two months ago. She was my golden girl for fifteen years, but boy, was she a lousy retriever." Trudy joked to cover the crack in her voice.

Clay eyed her. "I'm sorry, Trudy. Dogs are family."

For the past fifteen years, Skylar was her *only family* in Texas. Trudy glanced down at her lap then over at Clay. "So...what's your dog's name?"

Clay lowered his voice and puckered his lips. "Hercules."

"Hercules, huh? He must be a big dog with a name like that."

Clay smiled. "Oh, he's big all right, about the size of a football. My daughter gave him to me a few years ago. She thought I needed a *companion.*"

So Clay had a daughter. When he didn't elaborate, Trudy decided not to push it. If she pushed too far, he might start asking her too many questions. The last thing she wanted was for Clay to snoop into her business. Him being a detective and all.

Something ahead caught her attention. "Is that an airplane propeller hanging over the door of that old junkyard?" She pointed to a tired-looking structure where a faded sign read, Drake's Salvage Yard. "I've never noticed that."

"Been there as long as I can remember." Clay wrinkled his brow. "Old Man Drake was a bomber pilot in World War Two. His son runs the place now."

Trudy blinked. "How do you know all this?"

He shrugged. "It's my job. To know things."

She flinched, looking away, hoping he hadn't noticed.

Finally, she mustered, "I think I went there with my dad one time. My memory's fuzzy. You'd think I'd remember a propeller, though. Surely my dad pointed it out to me."

They passed by the ruins of an old drive-in theater. Clay gestured with his chin. "That place has been closed for years."

"Now that's one place I *do* remember. We went there right after we moved back here, before my dad went to Vietnam. We loaded up in the station wagon and Dad and Momma took us to see some western. Momma popped our own popcorn and we three kids crawled on top of the luggage rack, wrapped up in quilts, and we watched the whole movie under the stars."

They fell into a comfortable silence.

The closer they got to Pardon proper, the occasional pawnshop and diner gave way to ranch-style houses and flat-top stuccos with driveways crammed full of pickup trucks, late model sedans, and pop-up campers under aluminum carports. They passed small bungalows consisting of wood siding and a few porches occupied by sagging couches. A couple of trailer parks seemed to slide from semi-respectable into disrepair year after year. A few sprawling two-story brick homes with large circular driveways and attached RV garages boasted that not everything was going to seed in Pardon.

"Momma said y'all got some gully washers this past year."

"Yeah, flooded parts of Pardon. A car washed away over on the northwest part of town...down by the ditch. Driver got out though."

"That's a far cry from a few years ago when y'all had those sand storms. I remember coming home one time and seeing sand piled up along the side of the road."

Clay nodded. "Yeah, for a while there I thought we were headed into another dustbowl."

Trudy listened to the hum of the engine and the tires on the road. Clay cleared his throat a couple of times.

Finally, she laughed and slapped her knee.

Clay looked over. "What's so funny?"

She shook her head and rolled her eyes skyward. "You know we are officially old, right?"

"Oh, yeah. How's that?"

"Because we're talking about the weather." But even as she said it, her gaze kept roaming over his broad chest and shoulders. She couldn't help herself. She giggled and punched him in the arm. He feigned hurt and their laughter broke the ice.

"How come you never came to any of the reunions? Rumor had it you were too good for us once you became a stewardess then married that fancy doctor guy. But I know that's not true."

Her vision blurred and she searched through her purse for a tissue. She would leave Preston out of this. "Wearing hot pants and getting hit on by drunk passengers isn't as glamorous as it seems." Her voice cracked again and she dabbed a tissue at the corners of her eyes and tried to make light of it.

Clay tapped the steering wheel with his fingers. "I've always sensed you had other reasons for staying away."

She sniffed a couple of times, her throat tight. "After a while it was easier to send Momma a pass and let her fly to Dallas. She'd drive to Lubbock or Amarillo and catch a flight into Love Field. When I did sneak into town, I never called anyone. But I did ask a few classmates on Facebook about you from time to time."

She saw his Adam's apple move like he was trying to swallow a hard piece of candy. He shifted in his seat but he stared straight ahead. "Can I tell you something? Promise not to get mad at me?"

She leaned against the passenger door, sitting more sideways than straight.

"One time back in the early eighties, I was at Seven-Eleven buying gas... I passed by the news rack where they keep the gentleman's magazines. And there was this headline on the cover of Playboy: Stewardesses of the Southwest." He scratched at something on his chin. "Man, let me tell you. I was half hoping to see you in that issue and yet dreading it."

Leaning her head against the window, she gazed at his profile. "I almost posed for that piece. They offered me a nice sum of money but I turned it down."

He jerked his head around. "Why?"

"Honestly? It might sound crass..."

"Try me."

She fiddled with a loose thread on her jeans. "I couldn't stomach the idea of millions of men getting their jollies drooling over my birthday suit."

Clay almost choked.

"Nowadays they'd pay me to keep my clothes on," she joked. But her comment was meant to throw him off, to make light of the truth. Her figure might be intact, even in the most flattering jeans, but when she stood nude in front of a mirror, no amount of makeup or miracle cream could resurrect the toned supple skin of her youth. The flaws Preston pressured her to fix.

Clay gave her a mock frown. "I doubt that. From my vantage point, I'd say you've taken good care of yourself."

How she yearned to tell him the same thing. That he was looking mighty fine. That she'd thought about him many times over the years. But the last thing she wanted to do was give the wrong impression. What if Clay only stopped by to say hello and catch up like a couple of old friends?

As they drew closer to town, some of her apprehension faded away. She relaxed and took in the scenery, aware of an invisible current moving between them. Their shoulders were a few feet apart...they hadn't even touched. But there was something there, and she knew he felt it, too. Who was she kidding? She felt it the second she opened her momma's front door and saw him standing on the porch with a mischievous glint in his eyes.

They stole glances at each other. Clay drove and she fidgeted with the strap of her purse and they passed the old Burger Chef that now sold tractors instead of hamburgers. Everywhere she looked, even in certain parts of town, there was no doubt Pardon was a ranching and farming community.

Clay wheeled into the Sonic and they placed their order.

While they waited for their drinks, Trudy said, "Remember that time we called in a large order from the payphone down the street? Said we were a church bus, full of kids passing through town. We ordered like twenty-five hamburgers and fries."

Clay gave her the look. "Yeah, and those poor carhops came skating out with two trays piled high and no church bus."

"I feel kinda bad."

Clay leaned his head against his headrest and gave her a lazy grin. "You laughed so hard you peed your pants."

Their eyes met and she looked away first. "We were such juvenile delinquents back then." Heat rose to her face as she felt his gaze linger.

After a second, he reached into his back pocket for his wallet. "Speak for yourself. If my memory serves me correctly, that prank was *your* idea."

His smartphone buzzed and he glanced at the display. "Sorry, I need to take this."

She fidgeted with the contents of her purse and acted like she wasn't eavesdropping.

"Lieutenant Cordova speaking."

Lieutenant Cordova!

She smiled to herself, taking in the sound of his Tex-Mex accent, not quite Texas, not quite Mexican. He sounded polite but self-assured. Gone was the boy with the dark hair barely touching his paisley collar, the Puka shell choker matching his pearly white grin, the hip hugging bell-bottoms and platform shoes paid for by working afterschool jobs. The popular boy accepted by all the groups from jocks to goat ropers to freaks to the guys in chess club and band. Clay Cordova, homecoming king...the only boy she ever let feel her up before she left town.

Clay continued to make small talk and nodded and glanced at his watch. "Seven tonight? You got it. See you then."

He placed his phone back on the console.

"Do you need to go?" She suddenly realized he had a life and his job wasn't to drive her around town for old time's sake.

"Naw. We're good. I took the afternoon off, but I have a meeting tonight."

The carhop delivered their drinks. Trudy tried to pay but Clay waved her off. "Your treat next time."

Next time. Two little words lingered between them as Clay

exchanged a few bills for two drinks.

After the carhop left, Clay removed the lid of his drink and took a healthy swig. Trudy sipped from a straw, enjoying the sweet syrupy burn of carbonation hitting her pallet. She didn't drink sodas much these days, but when she did, she enjoyed the real thing. No diet drinks for her.

As she sipped away, guarding herself against some God-awful Coke burp, she thought about Clay's explanation that he took the afternoon off. And then it hit her...he took the afternoon off to come see her. A detective with an important job, a detective sipping his drink the same way he did when they were kids. Peel the lid off, take a polite slurp, and then crunch the soft flakey ice.

"I try to reach out to some of our local youth," Clay offered, setting his drink down and starting the engine, "especially kids who might be susceptible to joining a gang one day. I try to show them there's a better way."

"Is this part of your job as a detective?" She stole glances at him, trying to act nonchalant as Clay backed out of the parking slot.

He shrugged and turned right onto Seven Mile Road and headed toward Main Street. "It's volunteer."

This is not what she came back to Pardon for. To hook up with an old flame and all because he looked hot in his jeans and had a soft spot for kids.

Sitting inches away, with the console between them, she realized Pardon didn't look quite as drabby as before. When she drove around town with Momma Jewel, everything looked brown and baked. But not with Clay.

"Okay, boss lady. Let's hit the bricks." At the corner of Main and Seven Mile Road, at the intersection that boasted the straw-colored Quivera County Courthouse on one side and the Greek Revival Methodist Church on the other, Clay took a right and they rolled south toward Hotel Pardon and the red-tiled buildings of the old Santa Fe Train depot. The western sun crept lower on the horizon and long shadows from nearby rooftops slanted across the wide four-lane brick road where Trudy and Clay and their friends had once dragged Main. This was Trudy's favorite part of town, where historic turn-of-the-century buildings mingled with art deco and terra-cotta rooflines, as if mimicking the more cultured parts of The Land of Enchantment.

Passengers over the years occasionally asked Trudy where she was from. When she responded, "Ever heard of Pardon, New Mexico?" their faces always lit up. But then they'd proclaim (as if they hadn't heard the first part) how much they loved visiting Santa Fe, Taos, Albuquerque, Los Alamos, and Gallup, totally leaving out the east side. And Trudy would nod politely and say, "Yes, but where I'm from, there's no mountains or red mesas. It's just flat."

To Trudy, it seemed as if someone in every other car waved to Clay. When she mentioned it, he shrugged and said, "When you're a cop, people either go out of their way to be nice to you or they get out of your way."

They both laughed, caught up in the moment. There was both the unknown and the all-too-familiar between them.

Clay fiddled with the radio dial until he found a station that played seventies and eighties rock. Peter Frampton's "Show Me the Way" came on and she sipped her Coke and slipped into the past while being in the present.

Clay grooved to the music, tapping his fingers and swaying his head and shoulders while she patted her hands against her thighs, one beat off as usual.

Aerosmith blasted out "Big Ten Inch" and she felt as if he could read her mind. How was it they could listen to such suggestive tunes years ago and only flirt on the edges of sex? For they'd never gone all the way. But now in their late fifties with years of experience and God knows how many partners between them...

But wait...she was getting ahead of herself.

"Clay, I feel like I'm sixteen again."

He smiled. "I know, lady-girl, me, too."

Lady-girl!

She paused and glanced at his profile. The decades had been good to him. "Why did you call me that?"

He took a deep breath and looked straight ahead, keeping both hands on the steering wheel. "Because when I look at you, I see the teenage girl I fell in love with and the woman you are now."

She swallowed and played with her straw and glanced out the passenger window. After a moment she said, "Clay, I don't want to rush into anything, okay? Can we just take this slow?"

He glanced sideways at her and winked. "Yes, ma'am. For now, let's enjoy the ride."

She reached across the console and patted his thigh. "Thanks, Clay. I knew you would understand."

He laughed and flashed his boyish grin. "You better remove your hand, Miss Gertrude. Despite my old-timer appearance, I'm still a teenage boy at heart."

Two hours later, they headed back toward Jewel's place. The western sun blazed hot pink and psychedelic orange as it sank on the horizon. Leaning forward in her seat, she gazed out the windshield.

"There's nothing like a New Mexico sunset out here on the high plains. No skyscrapers or mountains or trees to encumber the view."

Clay didn't say anything as he pulled the Tahoe into the long driveway and parked, letting the engine idle. He turned the volume down on the radio just enough where music played softly in the background.

She went to shrug out of his jacket when she felt his hand brush against the side of her face. "Trudy?"

She turned, their eyes meeting. "Yeah?" Her heart thudded wildly and something deep and electrifying stirred within her.

"It's been a great afternoon." He started to say something else but stopped.

Gulping, she reached up and pressed his hand against her cheek. "I have to go back to Texas in a couple of weeks. There's some things I need to do."

He removed his hand, but not before nudging her nose with his thumb. "Last time you told me you were going to Texas, I didn't see you for forty years."

She reached for the handle to let herself out. "I won't be gone long. I promise."

He pulled out his wallet and handed her a business card. "Give me a call when you get back in town. I'm trying to wrap up a case anyway so I'll be pretty busy the next couple of weeks."

After running her finger over his name, she tucked the card in her palm. "Don't forget, my treat next time."

He chuckled softly. "I'll take a ride in your fancy Camaro."

After she closed the door and waved, she watched him back down the driveway. Right before he headed east into town, the passenger window slid down and Clay called out, "Hey Trud, guess what just came on the radio?"

Hugging herself in the late afternoon air, she moved toward him as if pulled by an invisible force. Clay had the volume cranked up high.

Lynyrd Skynyrd's "Free Bird" blasted from the speakers of the Tahoe.

Before he took off, he hollered through the open window, "Fly back to me, lady-girl."

Lady-girl. She could get used to that.

CHAPTER 8

The Blue Door

THE NEXT morning, Trudy stood at the end of the driveway and breathed in the cool dry air of autumn on the high plains. A scent she associated with hayrides, fall festivals, and pumpkins ripening on the vine. For now, there was no hint of the stockyards south of town or the dairy farms that dotted the land around Pardon, but if the breeze shifted, the sweet smell could turn foul in an instant. For once, the whistle of an approaching freight train sounded more like a welcome than a warning.

With the morning paper clutched under her arm, she belted her robe against the chill and ambled toward the house. Momma's blue front door caught her attention behind the solid glass storm door. This was Jewel's attempt for her "casa" to resemble the blue doors seen on dwellings in other regions of New Mexico. Legend says blue paint on doors and windowsills is meant to ward off evil spirits. *Too bad the carport door leading into the kitchen wasn't painted blue back in 1974.*

Fingering a broken wind chime dangling from a small tree where a giant sycamore once reigned over the place, Trudy thought about Clay and her shock at seeing him on her mother's porch. Last night as she prepared for bed, she thought of him again when she slipped into her satiny pajamas and how his name reminded her of the earth itself and his eyes mirrored the sky. In the middle of the night, she rolled over and hugged the pillow next to her and wondered what it would be like to reach over and touch him, to whisper his name in the dark and hear him whisper back.

She moved toward the long covered porch supported by thick pine posts with corbels and beams. The house she'd once dismissed as *primitive* after she first moved to Dallas and left behind her New Mexico ways. This morning the house's simple lines and earth tones called to her, forgiving her youthful snub. A creaking noise caught her attention, and she followed the source to the black wrought-iron sign that swung from the eaves. A sign made as a joke shortly after her parents' wedding announcement ran in the *Pardon Gazette* with their last name misspelled. A sign her momma refused to part with and proved a source of embarrassment to Trudy when she was younger.

Welcome to the CLUTTERBUCKS, it said.

Looking around the property, it seemed to Trudy that her mother had spent the last forty-some years trying to live up to a typo in the newspaper.

Pulling open the front door, Trudy recalled a time when the house bulged with the busy lives of a young family instead of relics from the past. She shuffled inside, pushing against that claustrophobic sensation whenever she first walked into Momma's house. Once inside, she didn't notice it as much. A body had a way of adjusting and adapting, and Trudy tried to go with the flow. But she was also prepared to do battle with her mother when it came time to start pitching stuff.

The aroma of freshly brewed coffee wafted through the house. Jewel stood at the avocado-green stove scrambling eggs in an old cast-iron skillet. Trudy froze. "It's just a tool to cook with," Aunt Star had chirped that night years ago in an odd voice that sounded too upbeat for the occasion.

Jewel motioned for Trudy to set out plates. "I thought we'd have something besides granola and fruit. I already poured you a glass of orange juice. Why don't you pop some English muffins into the toaster?" She pushed back a loose strand of silver hair that had slipped out of one of Aunt Star's knit caps. "They're whole grain. I know how you like to eat healthy."

Trudy kept her voice even. "Momma, is that the same cast-iron skillet you had when we were kids?"

"Yep, old faithful. It didn't take me long to season it either. My nonstick finally bit the dust."

Trudy reached into the cupboard and pulled out two Fiesta Rose dinner plates from Grandma Lily's pottery collection and set them on the counter. She tried to conceal the disgust she felt at seeing the skillet after all these years. They should've gotten rid of it a long time ago. "That thing's ancient. Why don't you let me buy you a nonstick frying pan?" She opened the breadbox and found two English muffins. She checked for mold and plopped them into the toaster.

Natural light spilled into the kitchen from the narrow archway on the east wall that led into the sunroom, the spacious addition her father had built with help from a fellow pilot right after they moved in. While Trudy waited on the muffins, she admired the Mexican tile countertop. Why had she ever thought the vibrant colors and mosaic patterns of the Talavera tiles were too busy? A couple of tiles were chipped and scratched in places, but overall they'd held up. A bit of elbow grease and grout cleaner and Trudy could have them restored in no time. A few years ago she'd tried to talk her mother into ripping them out and getting granite. In a rather shrill tone that put Trudy in her place, Jewel had fired away, "Your daddy special ordered these from Mexico and installed them himself. You rip 'em out, you might as well rip my heart out while you're at it."

Jewel grabbed a potholder and slid the black skillet off the heat. "I'll give you some money. You might check Dollar General."

Trudy went to the fridge to get margarine. "How 'bout we go tomorrow? We can stop by Lupi's for breakfast and then check the new kitchen store across from State Theater? I spotted it when Clay and I were dragging Main."

Reaching for a spatula, Jewel spooned scrambled eggs onto each plate and waited for Trudy to butter the muffins. "Sounds like a plan. How is that handsome devil? I swear, that boy gets finer every year."

Trudy set the plates on the table and pulled out a chair for Jewel. "That *boy* is my age, Momma."

Before Trudy had gone outside to get the paper moments earlier, she'd weaved her way through the darkened sunroom and rolled up every shade on every window that had been shutting out light for years. Then she'd cleared off the kitchen table so people could sit there to eat. Her mother had resorted to eating off TV trays.

Jewel untied her apron and hung it over the back of the pantry door and took her seat. "Wait till you get to be my age. Y'all are youngsters." She eyed Trudy over her black spectacles.

"Now, tell me all about your date."

Trudy ignored her and went to pour their coffee. "I'm going back to Texas in a couple of weeks. I left town without taking care of some stuff."

Her momma looked stricken. "What stuff? You just got here."

"Early voting opens on the twenty-fourth. I wanna get it out of the way, and..." Something caught in her throat. "I need to check on Sarah Jewel's grave. I left town without stopping by there."

Jewel's expression softened. She took a bite of food and chewed thoughtfully. "You could bring her here. There might be a spot next to your brother."

Trudy tore off a section of English muffin and popped it in her mouth. A painful knot lodged in her throat when she tried to swallow.

Jewel looked down at her plate. "I'm sorry, honey. Maybe that was a bad idea on my part."

Trudy reached over and patted her mother on the arm, alarmed at how frail her forearms appeared. "It's okay, Momma. It's not like she ever lived."

For a moment, the only sound in the room was their cutlery scraping against their plates.

Always the lady, Jewel picked up a paper napkin and dabbed the corners of her mouth. "So...tell me about Clay."

Trudy dangled her fork in the air before taking a stab at the eggs. "He's still with the PD, and he volunteers his time with at-risk youth."

Jewel picked up her mug. "I hear he went through a painful divorce. Never remarried to my knowledge."

Sounds like me, Trudy thought. "Do you know how long he's been divorced?"

Between sips of coffee, Jewel said with a lighthearted sigh, "Oh, it's been a few years I guess."

Trudy leaned back in her chair. "Momma, all you have to do is pick up the phone and the gossips in town will give you the scoop."

Jewel raised an eyebrow. "Then the next thing I know they'll be talking about me. That's one of the reasons I like living on the outskirts."

Trudy pushed her plate aside. "Georgia and I've been talking. Maybe it's time you start thinking about selling this place...you know, after we get it all cleaned up...and move into town."

Jewel rose from the table and started clearing the dishes. "What, so you girls can pack me off to the nursing home? No way, José! I'm not giving up my independence *or* this house. Besides," she paused at the kitchen sink and stared out the window that faced south in the direction of the old airfield.

Trudy came up behind her and placed a hand on her bony shoulder. "Momma, no one said anything about a nursing home. Georgia and I were thinking more like a nice retirement community where they have all kinds of activities. But I get it. I think a part of you is still holding out that Daddy will come swooping in over the house and wag his wings before landing."

A funny sound erupted from Jewel's throat. "Well, someone needs to keep the home fires burning until I know for a fact Shep is dead."

Over the years, Trudy had tried to imagine him being held against his will in a country where the war had been over for decades. If he had lived, he'd be an old man now, whittled down to nothing but skin and bones in a pair of prisoner pajamas. But the truth was, he probably died when his jet got shot down. And so he remained forever young in her mind.

Jewel turned to Trudy. "Call me loco, honey, but I thought I heard your daddy's voice last night."

I've been hearing his voice for years, Trudy wanted to tell her. *Does that make me loco, too? Or does it mean I can't let him go?*

Jewel gestured with her chin toward the archway on the east wall. "It sounded like it came from in there...from the room Shep built."

All the hairs on Trudy's neck and arms stood on end. The shaft of sunlight beaming in from the sunroom caused the gold in the Talavera tile to glow. "What did he say?"

"Bogey. I heard him calling for Bogey," Jewel's voice trembled.

CHAPTER 9

Skillet Shopping

"HAVE YOU girls seen this morning's paper?" Lupi placed two tall glasses of orange juice in front of Trudy and Jewel and then handed them menus.

"What now?" Jewel picked up her juice and took a sip. "If it's about the Russians..."

Trudy yawned and savored her first cup of coffee. "Who knows what's real and what's fake news these days?" Instead of scooting into one of four padded booths in the small diner, they opted once again to sit at the counter. For customers who knew Lupi, part of the fun was chatting with her while she prepared their meals and dished out local gossip.

Lupi ducked behind the counter and pulled out the *Pardon Gazette* dated Wednesday, October 12, 2016. "No, I'm talking about local news." She thumbed through the paper and flattened it against the countertop and pointed to a black and white photograph. "A groundskeeper stumbled across this yesterday at the cemetery." Lupi tapped her finger on the newsprint. "The caption doesn't say much, except that the cemetery removed the offensive word, whatever it was. It must be bad if the paper didn't show the full photograph."

The ex-mayor sat in his usual spot at the far end of the counter. For a few seconds, the only sound in the small diner was the clink of his coffee cup as he placed it in his saucer and cleared his throat. "I saw that earlier. Probably kids. At least they didn't knock over any gravestones this time. That happened on my watch a few years back. Perps were never caught."

Trudy's stomach flip-flopped at the sight of the photo. She and Jewel had left the house earlier without reading the paper. She hoped her eyes weren't bulging from their sockets as she stared at the image and tried to hide her reaction. *At least most of the headstone and word had been cropped out of the photo.* The only legible letter was a giant R.

Jewel put on her reading glasses and leaned closer to scan the page. "What an awful prank."

"Yeah, and it's not even Halloween yet," Lupi said, picking up the coffeepot to go refill Mayor Trujillo's cup. Propping her left hand on her slim hip, she poured his coffee.

"That was my thought as well," Mayor Trujillo smiled up at Lupi and tipped his head in thanks for the refill.

Jewel looked up from the paper. She was about to say something but then stopped, as if she'd changed her mind. She folded the paper and pushed it off to the side. Trudy refocused on the menu as if breakfast took precedence over anything in the news.

Lupi sashayed back toward Trudy and Jewel. "You girls ready to order?"

Gulping a swig of orange juice, Trudy held it in her mouth a moment as if she'd forgotten how to swallow. "Uh, I'd like your Spanish omelet. But go easy on the ham. Can I have whole wheat toast with that?"

"Yes, ma'am," Lupi smiled, taking the menu from Trudy. "I can switch the ham for Canadian bacon if you'd like. Less fat."

"Perfect." Trudy gave a thumbs-up and took another swallow of orange juice.

Lupi turned to Jewel. "How 'bout you, *Miss Pardon, New Mexico*? What'll you have?"

Jewel removed her spectacles. "I'll have the same thing Trudy's having, except go heavy on the ham. At my age, I think I can afford to go whole hog." She handed Lupi the menu and spread a napkin on her lap. "Not that I'm bragging, but I was also crowned *Miss Eastern New Mexico* before I left to attend Texas Tech."

"Brag away, Miss Jewel. Seriously, next time you come in, bring one of your old beauty pageant photos. I'll hang it up here in the diner."

Jewel swiveled on her stool and whispered out the side of her mouth, "Trudy, help me remember to do that when we start going through the photos."

"Absolutely, Mom." She patted her shoulder and picked up her coffee cup.

Lupi stashed the menus in a slot next to the counter, removed the paper, turned and cracked eggs, then whisked them in a bowl. "You should've been here an hour ago. I was running around like Chicken Little."

Trudy set her cup down and propped her elbows on the counter, relieved at the change of subject. "I haven't thought of that nursery rhyme in years. Sounds like you were busy."

Facing away from them, Lupi chatted over her shoulder while she prepared the food. "Benny saved the day though —" She flicked her head in the direction of the ex-mayor.

So it's Benny now. Trudy caught herself smiling.

"A bunch of bikers pulled up, what, Benny, about a dozen?" Lupi glanced over her shoulder again. "They were gunning their engines like boys flexing their muscles. I thought the roof was going to cave in."

"Oh, I'd say it was more like a half dozen." Benny Trujillo pushed his plate back and crossed his arms.

Lupi flashed him a look. "Well, it felt like a dozen by the time they staggered in. But those dudes, they turned out to be so polite. Left me a hundred-dollar tip."

"Were they a biker gang?" Jewel asked, tapping her nails against her mug. "I see them sometimes riding two abreast. I always wonder where they're headed."

Benny Trujillo rubbed the side of his face. "They were a bunch of veterans. Said they were headed to Angel Fire to visit the Vietnam Veterans Memorial."

Jewel reached her hand toward Trudy and patted her leg. "We should go there sometime. I think your sister's been there."

The ex-mayor rose and carried his plate and coffee cup around the counter and loaded them in the dishwasher. "Ring me up when you're ready." He walked back over to retrieve his hat and jacket.

Lupi winked at Trudy and Jewel. "Benny would make a good busboy, don't you ladies agree?"

"Hey, I don't know about that, but I *have* offered to keep your books," he chuckled in a voice that went from tenor to soprano in an instant.

Jewel turned to Trudy. "Mayor Trujillo is a retired accountant."

He gave a mock bow. "But I would come out of retirement if my services were needed," he added with a mischievous grin aimed at Lupi.

Good thing Trudy had sat her cup back down or she would've slurped coffee up her nose again.

Lupi turned the heat up on a burner and set an omelet pan on top. "I'll be right with you, Benny."

After Benny paid for his breakfast and left the diner, Lupi set their plates in front of them. "Okay, ladies, be honest. Do you think he's too old for me?"

Jewel picked up her fork. "As long as his noggin's still working, what's age got to do with it?"

Lupi and Trudy peeled with laughter.

"Miss Jewel, I'm hoping more than his *noggin* is still working."

The bell dinged and two middle-aged cowboys strolled in along with an older woman who looked like she'd worked on a ranch her whole life. "Be right with you, folks," Lupi called. "Pick wherever you'd like to sit."

Both men removed their cowboy hats and hung them on a rack by the door. The taller of the two men ushered the woman to a booth near the back. "Watch your step, Mother," Trudy heard him say.

Trying not to appear conspicuous, Trudy peeked at them over her shoulder. The shorter cowboy with a receding hairline scooted into the booth across from the woman while the other man who was completely bald helped his mother into the booth. After he set her purse down, he scooted in next to the other cowboy and they held hands under the table.

Pardon has come a long way, Trudy thought, realizing they weren't brothers. *It's about time, too.* In the old days, the men would have had to play along as if they were just friends.

The woman looked tough as saddle leather. She clasped her hands on the table and pursed her lips. Trudy overheard her say, "So how you boys been gettin' along?"

An elbow jabbed in her side drew Trudy's attention, and she twisted around to find her mother mouthing, "Quit gawking."

Picking up her fork, Trudy speared a chunk of omelet. "Sorry. I'm not used to seeing things out in the open in Pardon. It's nice to see the town making progress." Trudy took a bite of food and savored the flavors of cilantro, Canadian bacon, and onions.

Later, after Lupi rang up their order, Trudy handed her a credit card.

"Where you ladies off to?" Lupi asked, swiping the card and handing it back to Trudy.

"Skillet shopping," Jewel piped up. "Trudy doesn't like my old cast-iron skillet."

"You can't beat it for making cornbread," Lupi added. "Heat a bit of oil in the bottom of the pan before you add the batter and bake it. Stop in for lunch sometime. I make the best corn bread this side of the Pecos River."

On their way out the door, Lupi called as she was going to wait on the two cowboys and the woman, "By the way, Miss Jewel, if you have a spare photo of Major Cutterbuck in uniform, I'd love to hang it on the wall. I've been wanting to come up with a way to honor our local heroes."

"Will do," Jewel turned and waved.

"Oh, and Trudy," Lupi's voice rang out again right before the door closed behind them, "you'll have to tell me how it went with Clay."

At the new kitchen store across from State Theater, Jewel chatted up a clerk about skillet options. Trudy walked a few aisles over, lowered her voice, and called Georgia. When the call went straight to voicemail, she left a message: "You're probably in class. When you get a chance, go online, and pull up today's *Pardon Gazette*. There's a photo I think you'll find interesting. You'll know it when you see it."

As Trudy approached the front of the store to pay for her mother's new skillet, along with two new spatulas, she thought about the two women in the Lexus. Had they'd seen today's newspaper and who were they?

After Trudy and her mom left the kitchen store, they climbed back into the Camaro and ran a few more errands around town. Before they headed west on Seven Mile Road, Trudy kept her eyes open for a champagne-colored Lexus and an unmarked cop car, the kind a detective might drive. Her heart pumped faster at the thought of bumping into Clay unexpectedly. Several times she'd started to call his number, but she changed her mind. Why hadn't he asked for her number instead of handing her his business card? Then again, all he had to do was pick up the phone and call her mom's house phone. There was a time when he had her number memorized. They'd been apart for forty years. What was two weeks?

Jewel twisted in her seat, her face crinkled in worry. "I hope no one ever vandalizes Bogey's grave."

Glancing sideways, Trudy tried to reassure her mother. "They don't stand a chance against those guards you've posted twenty-four hours a day."

Jewel covered her mouth with both hands. "Do you think I'm crazy for posting little toy soldiers on your brother's grave?"

Trudy swallowed, caught off guard by the unexpected lump in her throat. "Nope, absolutely not. Some people might see them as inanimate objects, but I'd like to believe they have super powers."

Crossing her ankles, Jewel turned and looked out her window. "Me, too. Like that statue of Jesus missing a hand. To some, he's just a figure made out of cement. But to others, he might stand for the real thing."

They drove in silence all the way home.

As Trudy pulled the Camaro into the driveway and parked behind the minivan, Jewel twisted in her seat. "And another thing..."

Trudy cut the engine and extracted the keys from the ignition. "Did we forget something in town?"

Jewel's voice scraped with irritation. "That woman at the

cemetery...I didn't get a good look at her. She was too far away. But she wasn't spraying ant killer, was she?"

Before Trudy could respond, her phone pinged with a text from Georgia: Pulled up newspaper. At least it didn't identify grave. Told Aunt Star about photo and lady at cemetery. She hyperventilated. Said to drop it now! It'll only stir up trouble.

Staring at her phone screen, Trudy jumped when she heard her mother unbuckle her seatbelt and hoist her thin frame out of the car. "Hang on, Momma, let me help you."

Clutching her purse and the shopping bag, Jewel closed the door with her hip and shuffled on unsteady feet toward the side door. "Was that your sister? What are you two gossiping about?"

Trudy caught up with her and gripped her by the elbow to steady her. "Georgia was checking in. Here, let's get you inside and I'll make us some tea."

Jewel's hands shook as she tried to push Trudy away and insert the key. "I am not an invalid." Gently, Trudy took the keys and unlocked the door.

Once inside, Jewel gripped the edge of the countertop and eased herself into a kitchen chair. Her blue eyes blazed as she looked around the room then up at Trudy. "Maybe your Aunt Star's right. Maybe we should torch this place. Light it up with me in it. That would make a hell of a bonfire."

Trudy shuddered and went to heat up water for tea. Her mother hadn't talked this way in years. Not since right after Bogey died.

Jewel tore off her knit cap and ran a hand through her thinning hair. "That was Dub's grave wasn't it?" She spit the words out as if she'd bitten into poison. "And I bet it didn't say *rest* in peace. More like *rot* in hell."

Breathing deeply, Trudy filled a Pyrex pitcher with tap water and placed it in the microwave and hit the *start* button. Averting her eyes from her mother, Trudy let out a heavy sigh and stared at the pitcher of water spinning in the microwave. Her stomach began to churn while she waited for the water to boil. She reached into the cupboard for two mugs and the box of orange spice tea.

"Dub died while I was away," Jewel said, pounding her fist on the table. "Every time I visit Uncle Manifred at the nursing home, he brings it up. He asks me if I think Dub committed suicide because he got fired for the umpteenth time or if he fell down drunk and got run over by a train. Like I'm supposed to know what happened. I wasn't even here."

Turning to face her mother, Trudy's dull voice vibrated in her chest when she spoke. "You heard Aunt Star. Karma caught up with him."

Jewel pushed up from the chair, her fist raised in the air like she was ready to punch someone. "Your daddy never did like Dub and said he'd kill him if he ever laid a hand on one of you girls. He hated that Dub lived within walking distance of us."

Trudy closed her eyes and pinched the bridge of her nose. How could she tell her mother she'd felt her daddy's presence that day long ago? Heard his voice guiding her what to do next.

The microwave dinged and Trudy opened her eyes.

Jewel moved to the kitchen window and stared out at the railroad tracks as a freight train blasted past. The dishes in the cupboard rattled. "Uncle Manifred's mortgage company held the deed to this house until I was able to pay off the balance years later once my business took off. When I got out of the hospital months after Bogey died, Uncle Manifred cosigned on the loan that helped me start my business. He'll be a hundred in December. He may be confined to a wheelchair, but all his faculties are working. He mustn't know about the vandalism at the cemetery."

Steam from the scalding water burned Trudy's face as she filled each mug and waited for the tea bags to steep. Aunt Star's warning from long ago clanged in her head: "You must never tell what happened here. Your mother could lose the house and I would go to jail."

CHAPTER 10

face Mask and latex Gloves

"WHY THE face mask and latex gloves?" Jewel raised an eyebrow and frowned at Trudy. "This isn't a leper colony."

Breathing through her mask, Trudy hoisted another trash bag over her shoulder and tromped past her mother who stood wiping her hands on a dishtowel. "To protect myself against dust mites and not having to stop and wash my hands every five minutes," she replied, her voice muffled behind the mask.

Jewel followed her. "My employees never wore masks or latex gloves."

"Mom, don't take it personally. I'm allergic to dust mites, that's all."

"Since when? I never knew that."

Since I came home to clean your house, Trudy thought.

Ignoring her mother's question, Trudy navigated through the narrow archway that led from the sunroom into the kitchen. Hunched over from the weight of the bag, she plodded past the sink and stovetop on her left and through the carport door. Already winded, she vowed she needed to start speed-walking again as she went to the back of the minivan and tossed the bag on top of several others destined for the city dump. That last bag was full of dead plants and other sordid items that had accumulated like layers in an archeological dig.

Over time, the sunroom had become another repository for the things Jewel didn't want to deal with. The house had once been a showplace for squadron parties, and the sunroom, with its floor-to-ceiling windows and slanted beam ceiling, served as a favorite gathering spot when guests weren't mingling on the back patio where Shep would fire up the grill and "burn meat."

As she reentered the house, Trudy reflected on her own habit of tossing stuff on a regular basis. Was it because she'd lived out of a suitcase for so long, or had she become a minimalist to counterbalance her mother's tendency to hoard? Tramping back through the kitchen, she ran her hand over the Mexican tile countertop before she passed through the archway. Her father's hands had touched each tile, and once again she admired the fiesta of gold, red, orange, blue, and green that swirled through each square. *What was he thinking as he laid the tile? Was he thinking he might have to go to war?* They'd only been in the house two years when he got orders to Vietnam.

Back in the sunroom, she tied up another bag that bulged with yellowed newspapers and magazines she planned to drop off at the city's community recycling center. Lifting her mask, she said to her mother, "Remind me why Pardon doesn't offer a citywide recycling program as part of the weekly garbage pickup?"

"Beats the heck out of me" — Jewel stepped out of her way — "but you're welcome to take it up at the next city council meeting. Maybe you can help bring Pardon out of the Stone Age."

Sometimes Trudy couldn't tell if her mother was being serious or snarky. Earlier that morning over bowls of steel-cut oatmeal and blueberries, Trudy had informed Jewel, "We'll start at the back of the house and work our way forward."

Jewel had twirled her spoon in the air and peeked up at the ceiling before she eyeballed her daughter. "Soooo... do the cleaning crews on an airplane always start at the back of the cabin and work their way forward?"

Clearly, Trudy's instructions had irked her mother, longtime owner of Jewel's Cleaning Service, Commercial & Residential. "I've seen them start at both ends," Trudy informed her, letting her mother's snippy comment slide.

That conversation had taken place three hours earlier, and Trudy had been working nonstop since then.

Easing into an upholstered rocker that had belonged to

Grandma Lily, Jewel looked around as if shocked to see the sun-room's terra-cotta floor for the first time in years. "This used to be my favorite room in the house. I loved to sit here and read and watch the airplanes fly over on their final approach into base. But then..." Her voice cracked and broke off.

The telegram came and it was never the same, her mother's unspoken words hung in the air like dust particles caught in the sunlight streaming in from the windows facing east.

Wiping sweat from her brow, Trudy blew hair out of her face and tied up another bag. "And that's why we're going to return this room to its former glory. Then we'll start on the kitchen." She walked over and unlocked two screened windows and raised them several inches to let in fresh air. Birdsong came in on a cool breeze, and Trudy gazed out at the brick patio skirted by a low plastered wall with two built-in *bancos*, benches. The patio furniture could use a pressure wash, and she made a mental note to pick up a power washer at the hardware store along with window cleaning supplies.

"I feel bad you're doing all the heavy lifting." Jewel swayed to and fro in the rocker that only moments ago had been covered in stuff.

Turning away from the wall of windows, Trudy said, "Nonsense, Mom. That's what I'm here for."

"I know, but what can I do to help?"

"How 'bout you make me a pot of your homemade vegetable soup with extra bell pepper? I'll grab the ingredients on my way back from the dump."

"Don't you want me to ride with you? You never know what unsavory characters might be hanging around that place."

"I'm a big girl, Mom. It's city property. I'm sure I'll be fine."

A few minutes later, Trudy unearthed a pile of dead bugs, mostly dried up roly-polies and spiders in the northeast corner of the sunroom. "Momma, can you plug in the vacuum? We've got a pile of dead bugs over here."

Jewel pitched forward and pushed out of the rocker. She grabbed the end of the power cord to the new upright vacuum that Trudy had purchased the day before, along with cleaning supplies, and plugged it into a socket. With a glint in her eyes, she eased back into the rocking chair and launched into a story about a game fighter pilots used to play at the O'Club on Friday nights. "After some fighter pilot would yell 'dead bug,' all the other pilots would drop to the floor and roll over on their backs and stick their legs in the air. The last pilot standing had to buy the next round."

Trudy inserted an attachment on the end of the vacuum's hose and remarked, "I bet Dad was the ringleader, the pilot making the call."

"Are you kidding me?" Jewel slapped the air and made a face. "He was too busy flying with his hands and swapping war stories with other pilots to notice. He had to buy the bar a few times, I recall."

Flicking the power switch, Trudy pulled the mask over her mouth and nose and aimed the suction wand at layers of cobwebs encrusted with carcasses and shells. The roar of the vacuum filled the room as her mind wondered: Did her daddy feel the impact when his jet hit the ground? Did he splatter or did his body roll into a twisted mound of flesh and metal? Like a giant roly-poly? Or was he reduced to nothing more than *burned meat*? Without a body, they would never know. Maybe that's why she tried so hard to remember him whole.

Once she finished cleaning the corner, she shut off the vacuum and leaned backward to stretch. Bracing her hands on her lower back, she scanned the room, thinking about what section to tackle next. Her gaze drifted to the wall of windows facing south with the rustic French doors that opened onto the patio. How many times had they held those doors open for Daddy when his hands were full of tongs and platters of tangy barbeque? "Chow time," he'd holler as he marched from the sunroom through the archway into the kitchen as if he'd just returned from a hunt.

Oh, Daddy, she had the urge to cry out, *you took such pride in providing for your family. Did we ever thank you?*

Glancing past her mother, Trudy gaped at the three-cushioned rustic Naugahyde couch she once referred to as the *chuck wagon,* due to its lumbering construction and wagon wheel armrests.

She removed the mask and turned toward her mother. "Remember how Daddy would come home from flying, suck down a cold glass of sun tea, and then stretch his rangy frame out on the couch?" She pushed the vacuum aside and plopped down on one end.

Her mother stopped rocking and glanced at Trudy as if she were looking right through her. "I thought I saw him there late one night not long after his plane went missing. You kids were already in bed. I heard a noise and came into the kitchen to investigate. When I peeked in here —" her eyes darted wildly about— "the room was completely bathed in moonlight. I'd forgotten to lower the shades. And there he was, stretched out on the couch in his flight suit and boots, his big ol' feet propped on the armrest. Of course when I turned on a light, the couch was empty."

Trudy's scalp tingled. She hugged herself and admired the room her father built with the same hands that flew fighter jets and tossed his young children in the air and caught them before they hit the ground. The loving hands that caressed his wife when he thought no one was looking.

Except for the hum of traffic on Seven Mile Road, a hush fell over the room. Burrowed into the couch, Trudy broke the silence. "Georgia thought she saw Bogey one time a few years after he passed. She was performing at a basketball game during halftime when she looked across the gym and saw him standing under one of the hoops." At the time, Trudy dismissed it as her sister's way of working through her grief. Trudy wasn't so sure.

Jewel tapped her fingers on the arms of the rocker and tilted her head as if she was contemplating what Trudy said. A large ceiling fan whirred above them. Jewel pulled off her knit cap and clasped her hands behind her head. "Your sister shared that with me last time she was home. I asked her if Bogey looked happy or sad. She said he looked at peace. I take comfort in that."

Trudy leaned her head back and stared at the ceiling fan. "Momma, what was harder? Losing Bogey or Dad?" The words slipped out before she could catch them.

Jewel picked at a loose yarn in her knit cap. "With your brother, I at least had some closure. But Shep, well…" She glanced at her wrist. "Mercy, look at the time. It's already ten o'clock. I better go take my pills." With a sigh, she pushed herself out of the rocker. "Can I get you anything?"

"I'm good, Mom. Think I'll take a break and make a run to the dump."

After Jewel left, Trudy waited a second before she rose from the couch and padded across the room in her sneakers to a basket of paperwork sitting next to the rocker. Bending over, she rifled through a stack of papers until she found the folder of newspaper clippings she'd discovered earlier. In case her mother returned, Trudy quickly scanned through the folder, past the stories of her dad missing in action and at least five copies of Bogey's brief obit that barely took up three inches of space in the newspaper. When she came to the headline, "Son of Wealthy Businessman Dies in Freak Train Mishap," she fingered the yellowed clipping and remembered how the story had given her nightmares for years.

Her heart and stomach collided as she began to read:

(Editor's note: reader discretion advised due to graphic nature.)

At approximately eleven p.m. on Tuesday evening, October 8, a Santa Fe train engineer headed eastbound reported a strike as the freight train approached the station a few miles away. Due to blizzard-type conditions and poor visibility, the engineer at first thought they'd hit a stray cow or possibly a hobo crouched down waiting to jump the train. After the engineer released the brakes and the train came to a stop, the conductor got out to investigate.

Human body parts were found splattered on the front of the engine and strewn down the tracks where the strike occurred. A man's wallet was found among bloody clothing and an empty whiskey bottle was found intact near the impact site. Police were called to the scene, and the county coroner identified the dead man as Manifred "Dub" Hurn, Jr., (39) of Pardon, NM. He was killed by blunt force trauma. He was the son of wealthy businessman, Manifred Hurn, Sr., also of Pardon.

Residents living in the area are asked to call the Pardon Police Department if they witnessed anything out of the ordinary on

Tuesday evening. Funeral services are pending.

Trudy heard her mother rooting around in the kitchen. She stuffed the clipping back in the folder and stuck it back into the stack to look at later. Crossing her arms, she stood in front of the wall of windows and looked out at the backyard.

Beyond the patio wall, the rambling lawn her father had planted and watered had long ago surrendered back to patches of sandy brown dirt, prairie grass, and weeds. At least her mother kept it cut back. The small grove of fruit trees that lined the back section of the property had disappeared, along with the old barn. But the chain link fence that ran up and down the east and west sides of the backyard and along the south end, had withstood the test of time. On the west side, a double-swing gate wide enough to drive a car through had been padlocked for years after Jewel sold the Camaro and had the barn torn down. A single gate at the southeast corner of the yard stayed unlocked.

How many times had their dad lectured them not to go through that gate? "That's for the gas man to come in to read the meter. If I ever catch any of you kids outside that gate or near those train tracks, I'll tan your hides from here to kingdom come."

Trudy glared at the gate as if danger still lurked there on the other side. She shivered, visualizing the *perv* sneaking along the tracks from his casita up the road and slipping through the gate before he made his way across the backyard and knocked on the side door under the carport. Somewhere in the back of her mind, Trudy had some vague recollection of Dub hitting the floor, his head bent at a slight angle, the side of his face exposed all slack-jawed and slobbery, while Aunt Star knelt over him checking his vitals. But mostly Trudy's memory was fuzzy.

While she was out running errands, Trudy would call Georgia one more time and ask her to help her remember. Calling Aunt Star and peppering her with questions would get her nowhere. Trudy had learned this the hard way years ago on a layover when she called Aunt Star after drinking a couple of margaritas. "I guess the fool got run over by a train," Aunt Star huffed, catching her breath several times before she quickly changed the subject.

In the kitchen, Trudy grabbed a bottle of water from the fridge and handed her mom the keys to the Camaro. "Feel free to take it for a spin while I'm gone."

"Not on your life, darling. There are too many bells and whistles."

At the city dump south of town, Trudy slowed the minivan to a crawl as she approached a shack where a grizzled fellow in a gray uniform met her at the gate. As she rolled down her window, the man's gaze traveled to the faded blue military sticker on the van's windshield. Without warning, he snapped to attention and gave her a crisp salute. "Good morning, ma'am." His hands and face were covered in grime.

His actions were so unexpected. It took her a second to respond while she processed that he'd spent time in the service. She eyed the stitching on his nametag: *Tiny*. Surely that was his nickname. "Hello there. What branch were you in?"

"Air Force, ma'am, military police." He grinned awkwardly, revealing a mouthful of broken teeth.

She tried to picture him in his younger days, a one or two striper in a clean uniform, his service revolver strapped to his hip, as he waved cars with military stickers through the front gate of an American base somewhere around the world. "So you were a sky cop then." She smiled, and for a moment, memories washed over her of uniformed airmen saluting her father and him saluting back.

"We don't get many officers out this way," Tiny said, glancing around as if part of him was back in the military and not working the gate at a smelly dump. Blue stickers on a windshield used to signify the vehicle belonged to a commissioned officer while a red sticker implied the car belonged to an NCO (noncommissioned officer).

"Oh, I'm just an aging brat." She needed to clear that up, not mislead him into thinking she was worthy of his salute. "My father's the one who served, not me."

He relaxed his stance. "Doesn't matter, ma'am. I was saluting the rank."

"Oh, okay, well...do you want me to pull up a bit?" She felt a pang of sadness for him, for the life he'd once led. But she could sense a man like Tiny wouldn't want her pity. "The bags marked with an R stay. I'm dropping those off at the recycle place in town."

Tiny directed her to pull up a few feet. "I'll grab those bags and you'll be on your way." Behind his helpful smile, she detected a beaten-down look in his eyes.

Pulling forward, she tried not to make a face as she breathed in the foul air. After he unloaded the bags, he pointed to where she could turn around. Before she left she tipped him twenty bucks.

He gaped at the money, his bottom lip quivering. "You're a good person, ma'am."

"I don't know about that, but I do know life can be brutal at times."

A part of her wanted to tell him how her dad was missing in action, that his body and jet had never been found. But why unload her baggage on this tired old vet who looked like he was barely scraping by. "Hey, Tiny...?" She started to thank him for his service, but the words always rang hollow the second they left her lips. She'd said them too many times to too many uniformed passengers over the years. After a while she'd sounded like a robot. There had to be another way.

Gripping the steering wheel, she bowed her head a second to think. With the election looming a few weeks away, she wondered if a working-class man like Tiny would fare any better no matter who was president? *Or were men and women like Tiny so far down the food chain they would always be at the bottom of the pecking order regardless of who was in power?*

When she looked up, tears clouded her vision. "Tiny...?" She called him by name again and peered into his eyes. "You've been a blessing to me today. Thank you." She patted her hand over her heart as if to make a point. "I appreciate you."

He blinked a couple of times and pressed his lips together and nodded. As she drove away, she watched him in her rearview mirror. He stuck his arm up and waved and she tooted the minivan's horn. Veterans Day was coming up in a few weeks, and she wondered how a veteran who'd served his country with pride had ended up working at the city dump. It didn't seem fair.

At the community recycling center, she pulled up and unloaded the two bags in a big bin that reeked of sour beer and sticky soda cans. Before heading to the store, she saw the text her mother had sent five minutes ago, asking if she was okay. Trudy had the urge to text her back and say, "Hey, Mom, your *unsavory* character turned out to be a broken-down vet employed by the city." Instead, she texted she was fine and would be home shortly after stopping by the store. Here she'd traveled all over the country for nearly forty years, encountering thousands of strangers each month on planes, in airport terminals, and hotels, but now that she was back in Pardon, she might as well be sixteen with a swinging ponytail out driving the family station wagon.

Dashing through the supermarket, she grabbed the ingredients for soup, along with a loaf of crusty multigrain bread, and a bottle of cabernet. Back at the minivan, she stashed the groceries in the passenger seat and came around to the driver's side. As she went to open the door, she gazed at the crinkled blue sticker centered at the top of the windshield. The words "Department of Defense" and "Pardon Air Force Base" tugged at her heart. Until Tiny pointed it out, Trudy had barely given the decal any thought.

On closer inspection, she realized her mother had scraped the base access sticker off the old station wagon when she traded it in and taped it to the minivan's windshield at a time when she no longer had base privileges. Long before the base had closed, when Major Cutterbuck's benefits and pay had stopped, Jewel the loyal pilot's wife had acted out of defiance. As if a blue government sticker on her windshield could help keep her husband alive.

Climbing into the van, Trudy unscrewed a chilled bottle of water and emptied it in one long swig. She needed to swallow the lump swelling in her throat.

Before putting the transmission in reverse, Trudy mentally shifted gears. Contemplating the newspaper clipping about the freak train mishap, she inserted her earpiece and punched in her sister's number. While she waited for Georgia to pick up, three words rolled through her mind: blunt force trauma.

CHAPTER 11

Carport Door

"TELL ME what you remember." Trudy pulled out of the parking lot and headed toward the house. The minivan sputtered along, lacking the get-up-and-go of Momma's old nine-passenger station wagon with passing gear.

Georgia sighed on her end as if it took all her energy to talk about it. "He knocked on the carport door. Said he needed the keys to Daddy's Camaro. Said Momma called him from the hospital...that she needed him to fire up the motor so the oil wouldn't turn to sludge. He said it took a *man* to keep a fine car like Daddy's all tuned up and running properly."

"And you believed him," Trudy cut in, her tone flat as the landscape around Pardon. "'Cuz he mentioned Daddy's car."

Georgia's voice thickened. "I didn't see the whiskey bottle until I'd unlatched the screen door and he was halfway inside."

"Is that when he grabbed you?" Trudy heard the tremor in her own voice.

"No, he took a swig of booze and asked, 'Where's your big sister?' When I didn't respond, he mumbled, 'Guess you'll do.' I didn't know what he meant at first, but the second I turned my back to get Daddy's keys from the cupboard, I could feel Dub's eyes on me like creepy crawlers. I tried to act brave as I went to hand him the keys. He stood there leering at me, wiping his mouth with the back of his hand before he set the bottle down. I remember his hands; they were huge, with fingers thick as clubs."

At the next intersection, Trudy hooked a right and headed

west on Seven Mile Road. Her heart spun as she dreaded the next part, and yet she needed to hear it in order to piece together what happened that night.

Georgia paused to catch her breath. "I told him to take the keys and leave. That I had a lot of homework and Aunt Star would be home any second. He could leave the keys outside by the carport door when he was done."

"So that's when he grabbed you," Trudy finished.

"Yeah. I tried to run into the sunroom and escape through the back door, but the fucker was quick. He blocked the archway and shoved me against the kitchen table. The next thing I knew, Aunt Star was yelling at him. I never heard her come in. I was screaming too hard trying to fight him off. I weighed all of ninety pounds back then."

Misty-eyed, Trudy blinked and noticed several cars zipping past her on the left. She glanced at the speedometer and realized she was going thirty-five in a fifty-five miles-per-hour zone. "And then I walked in." She pressed her foot on the gas and the minivan hiccupped and lurched forward.

"And all hell broke loose," Georgia declared, sounding congested.

Trudy shuddered and breathed through her mouth, her nose stuffy all of a sudden. Neither sister said anything for a moment.

After a long pause, Georgia broke the silence. "One time when Bogey was catching fireflies down by Dub's place, he spied the *perv* peeking through a neighbor lady's window. When Dub saw him, he threatened to feed Bogey to a pack of coyotes if he squealed. That poor kid. He lay awake for several nights listening for their howls."

"Did Bogey tell you this?" Trudy pictured their little brother hiding under the covers in case Dub came looking for him.

"Yeah, he made me pinky swear not to tell anyone, not even you. It happened right after Daddy left for Vietnam. Poor kid thought Dub would snatch him if he told. Plus, Bogey knew better than to go near Dub's place. He thought Momma would ground him."

As Trudy listened, she felt an intense hatred for a man who'd been dead for years.

"Hey, sis, can I put you on hold for a sec? I think one of my students is calling."

While she waited for Georgia to return to the line, Trudy spotted a boarded-up fireworks stand to her left. Flicking on her turn signal, she changed lanes, and veered off the highway onto an unmarked dirt road.

The minivan bumped along the rutted lane past a shaggy grove of cottonwood trees shimmering in spun gold. Before the road came to a dead end, Trudy stopped in front of a cluster of abandoned casitas on her right and shifted to park, letting the engine idle.

Straining forward in her seat, she peered through the windshield toward the tracks and thought about the newspaper clipping she'd read earlier that morning.

One thought whistled through her mind: *Was Dub conscious when the locomotive plowed into him?*

The last time she'd ventured down this road, Clay was driving his mother's Fort LTD with Trudy nestled beside him. It was fall semester, their junior year in high school. They'd been going steady a few weeks when Clay pulled onto the dirt road at dusk and gestured toward the tracks. "This where that dude died a year ago?"

Trudy had acted indifferent. "Yeah, a little farther down the tracks. What a dumbass, huh?"

With the sun flaring on the western horizon, they'd held hands and scaled the berm and walked alongside the tracks. Even at sixteen, Clay played the part of the investigator, asking lots of questions. "How was he related to you? When did you last see him? Why did he live like a pauper if his dad was one of the richest men in town?" Trudy had kept her voice even and told him how days after the mishap, townsfolk would drive out and gawk up and down the tracks like turkey vultures looking for carrion.

"You calling *me* a turkey vulture?" Clay had teased, and soon they were back in his mother's car making out under the cover of darkness. A porch light from one of the casitas winked on and off every time Clay started the engine to run the heater.

Georgia's voice broke the silence. "Sorry 'bout that. Listen, sis,

I've been thinking a lot about that night. My one consolation: At least he didn't rape me."

Something broke inside Trudy. "Jesus, Georgia, he could've killed you. Snapped your neck in half."

"But you put up a fight. You saved my life."

Teeth chattering, Trudy began to shake as she shoved the gearshift into drive, did a K-turn, and headed back to the main road. She was looking forward to a hot shower, pouring a glass of cabernet, and savoring the aroma of Jewel's homemade soup simmering on the stove.

"But somewhere out there is a lady in a Lexus," Trudy reminded her sister. "And she knows something we don't."

Georgia sighed. "I know. Makes you wonder."

Trudy turned left onto the highway and headed toward the house.

"We were both sobbing hysterically that night," Georgia continued. "But I remember how Aunt Star trilled her tongue and clapped her hands to silence us. 'Hush,' she said, 'He's just knocked out. Probably seeing the Fourth of July behind his eyeballs.' Then she placed her palms on her knees and pushed herself up from the chair and said, 'When he comes to, he'll mosey on back to his place and never mess with us again. Some fresh air will do him good. One of you girls run get me a sheet. We're going to roll him on top of it and drag him out the door.'"

Jewel's house came into view. Trudy spotted her mother gazing out the living room's picture frame window. Trudy wondered how long her mother had been standing there waiting for her to return. She pulled off the highway into the long driveway and tooted the minivan's horn. Momma waved then disappeared from the window. She was probably headed to help Trudy unload groceries.

As Trudy parked under the carport and cut the engine, she said to her sister, "I just remembered something. After we hauled him outside and drank hot toddies and ate breakfast for dinner, didn't Aunt Star leave the house bundled up in a parka?"

"I don't remember," Georgia said. "I think I was drunk and passed out by then."

CHAPTER 12

Stranger to the Ground

Near Dallas Love Field

BREAK RIGHT!

His voice snatched her out of her funk. Gripping the steering wheel, Trudy jerked it hard right and slammed on the brakes.

Nine o'clock! came his second command.

Straining against the shoulder strap of her seatbelt, she swiftly glanced left.

A white soccer ball bounced into the street and rolled past the Camaro's front bumper. A tall athletic blonde, with a single braid swatting the air, chased after the ball. She wore pale blue gym shorts and a sweatshirt, her coltish legs pink from the cold. A white sweatband on her forehead accentuated her high cheekbones and Nordic features.

"Jesus!" Trudy yelped, expelling a lungful of air. She'd missed hitting the teen by seconds. Her hand jittery, Trudy fumbled for the power button and slid her window down. "You okay?"

Blushing, the girl picked up the ball and nodded sheepishly in Trudy's direction. Her piercing blue eyes flashed both shock and relief. This time, she looked both ways before she jogged across the narrow lane.

Shaken, Trudy couldn't move. "What in God's name were you thinking?" she wanted to lash out at the girl. She was old enough to know not to chase after a ball in front of an oncoming car. She had that moneyed look, and given the neighborhood Trudy had cut through on her way to the storage unit, she assumed the girl attended Highland Park High, Hockaday, or Ursuline Academy.

From the corner of her eye, Trudy spotted a middle-aged man in an argyle sweater and brown loafers, his hands stuffed in the pockets of his trousers. Standing in front of a Mediterranean Villa with a manicured lawn set back off the winding lane, the man shook his head at the girl, most likely his daughter. An elaborate flowerbed skirted the house and overflowed with a cornucopia of colorful pumpkins and exotic gourds in all shapes and sizes. That's one thing Trudy could always count on when driving through the swanky neighborhoods of Dallas in the autumn, the rich spared no expense at decorating.

The man's gaze shifted toward the Camaro. "I'm sorry," he mouthed, his expression one of a parent who'd been terrified one second and embarrassed the next.

I almost killed your daughter, Trudy had the urge to yell. Instead, she offered a half wave, took a deep breath, and rolled up her window.

Straightening the wheel, she settled back against her body-hugging seat and checked her instruments. It was eight o'clock on a Monday morning, October twenty-fourth. Fifteen minutes earlier, she'd checked out of the hotel and was headed to the storage unit near the airport when she took a detour at the last second.

She'd been in a trance ever since.

After she'd veered off Lemmon Avenue to Lovers Lane, she hooked a left at Inwood Road and cruised along until she passed the big contemporary house she'd once shared with Preston. Behind the gated iron fence, a red Lamborghini sat in the circular driveway. At the top of a short flight of stone steps, art deco doors of stained glass led into a gray structure that felt more like an art gallery than a home. Wasn't that just like the good doctor to park his flashy sports car out front for show? His version of yard art, along with the large metal sculpture that resembled a scalpel pointing skyward from the garden next to the entrance. A ten-foot-tall Frankenstein decked out in black and purple stood erect next to the doors.

"Halloween in the *hood?*" Trudy had chided when he bragged

about the huge sum of money he'd paid an artist to create the monster. "Where I come from, most people carve pumpkins and make scarecrows out of rags and straw."

"You're from Podunk, New Mexico," he'd responded in a tone that sliced through her heart like the blade of his scalpel.

Dry mouthed, Trudy had sped past the mansion and whipped a U-turn and slowed down as she glanced over one last time. A round window on the upper level — right above the entry — beckoned her to look up: *the designer nursery that never got used*. Something inside of her clenched as her eyes drifted back to the steps, those *artistically* uneven steps. Her gaze shifted to a two-story jungle gym with a winding tube slide peeking from the side yard that led around back to a Roman pool where Preston tried to *train* her to "swim nude like a seal."

Before Trudy had looked away, she spotted two dark-haired little girls running around the yard, both dressed in matching pink coats. A young woman with long jet-black hair stood nearby, her almond-shaped eyes trained on the girls.

Was the young woman their mother or nanny? Trudy had heard rumors that Preston had remarried a model and they had twin girls.

"She's not getting any younger you know. She'll be forty-one this fall," Trudy had overheard Preston confide to a male visitor who'd dropped by the house the same day she'd come home from the hospital, empty-handed, her heart aching with a new kind of grief. A grief her mother knew all too well after losing a child. "Nine months and nothing to show for it but bags under her eyes, a loose belly, and about sixty extra pounds. Maybe she'll give up this mommy notion and pursue a real career."

A real career... Preston had been hounding her for years to quit flying and go to college so she could get a *real* job.

Still in her robe and slippers, Trudy had shuffled into Preston's study and glared in his direction. Seven years her senior, the plastic surgeon with a shaved head and celebrity grin plastered on billboards all over Dallas, sat in his leather chair, sipping a cocktail. He refused to look at her. Here they'd lost a child together, but all he seemed to care about were *appearances*.

At least the visiting art dealer had the decency to rise from his chair and offer his condolences. "I'm truly sorry for your loss."

After Trudy thanked him, she leaned against a tall bookcase and pressed one hand to her belly. Gazing out the window that overlooked a late summer garden, she caught her breath at another wave of postpartum contractions and gritted her teeth. "I see you're in top form, *Dr. Vanderwell*. Isn't it encouraging knowing when you're not cutting on people, you're entertaining them?"

The art dealer stared at his polished shoes, twiddling his thumbs. Before Preston buzzed the housekeeper to help Trudy back to bed, he sipped his drink and blinked at his guest. "Don't mind my wife. It's the painkillers talking."

Like a sucker punch to her womb, that long-ago conversation shot out of nowhere. Her right hand slipped from the steering wheel to massage her belly. A belly she'd worked hard to tone and showed no signs she'd ever given birth; a belly that occasionally cramped for no reason except to remind her of afterpains...

Seeing the property and the woman hadn't hurt as much as seeing the young children living in the spaces Trudy once occupied. The spaces meant for her and her daughter. Had Trudy remained, she'd be trapped inside a menagerie of art and Preston's ego. Or most likely he'd have cast her aside by now like an artwork he no longer admired.

Why had she stayed married to him after he turned on her? His behavior toward her only grew worse after she lost the baby. To this day, she couldn't be sure if Preston was a callous cad or if his cruelty served as a defense mechanism. Even at the graveside service attended by a few of her colleagues and a chaplain assigned to the mortuary, Preston stood off to the side, drawing in measured breaths. Trudy couldn't tell if he was bored, or trying to hold back guilt by practicing breathing exercises like the ones she'd learned in childbirth classes.

That's the question she was asking herself when she broke out in a cold sweat and veered off Inwood and cut through a quiet residential street to head back toward the storage unit. The answer rested deep in her being, along with other dark secrets she'd been afraid to examine until now.

If she hadn't heard her father's command across the airwaves of time, that beautiful blonde girl in her rearview mirror would be road kill by now. Instead, the soccer player kicked the ball toward the man in the argyle sweater and scampered across the leaf-strewn lawn to live another day.

The look in the girl's eyes haunted Trudy all the way to the storage unit.

Had Sarah Jewel lived, she would be eighteen. Probably the same age as the girl Trudy almost ran over.

A slow mist began to fall as Trudy pulled in front of the storage unit and parked. Before getting out, she scanned the area for *bandits*. Even though the site was secured with controlled access and surveillance cameras mounted at various locations, a woman could never be too careful. After driving by her former home moments ago, she let it sink in that some bandits were easier to spot than others.

Key fob in hand, she went to unlock the garage-style door. The roar of a Southwest 737 taking off from Love Field echoed off the soupy clouds. Out of habit, she looked up, but the jet had disappeared into the gray.

Grabbing the wet handle, she slid the metal door up, flicked on the overhead light, and stepped out of the cold damp air. Dust hadn't even settled in the space she'd rented weeks ago after she sold her condo, a renovated loft in an old building that flirted on the edges of Dallas's toniest neighborhoods.

Crossing her arms, she looked around. Forty years after moving to Dallas, her household belongings now fit in a space half the size of a single car garage. By the time the movers had come to collect her things from the condo, all that was left were her clothes and airline uniforms, her king-sized sleigh bed and custom-designed bookcase and desk, her favorite reading chair and lamp, boxes of treasured books, and a few pieces of art and sculpture she'd collected after the divorce, mostly flea market finds Preston would find appalling. Most of her furniture went to needy families, her high-end washer and dryer to a nearby women's shelter, her refrigerator to a community center in Oak Cliff.

"I'm learning to travel light again," she explained when one of the movers commented that a lady of her means usually had acquired more by now. "Oh, I've had plenty," she assured him. "But I'm letting go of a few things."

"I think she's one of those *million dollar babies* I heard about in the news," he whispered to his helper as they hauled her bookcase out the door.

"Say again?" the other guy shot back.

"You know, those workers at Southwest who've been with the company forever...story goes they didn't get paid much back in the day, but they did get company stock. Now it's worth a lot."

Trudy had followed both men out the door, playing dumb to their gossip. After they'd deposited her items at the storage unit, she gave them generous tips and asked about their families. She never forgot her early years with the airline when she lived paycheck to paycheck, struggling to make ends meet. Between her own investments and a generous settlement from Preston — she considered it *hush money* — she could go anywhere and do anything. While money could keep the bill collectors at bay, she learned a long time ago that it couldn't buy happiness.

The head mover asked if she had grown children or grandchildren and she caught her breath, tongue-tied at his question. It took her a moment to answer. "Nope, just me." Looking around at her things that day, he scratched his head and asked where she was headed.

"West," she grinned, offering no other explanation.

Another plane took off and thundered overhead. She moved toward the firebox where she kept her important papers. The sound of the jet filled her mind with visions of the house on Seven Mile Road. As the temperature dropped and the mist grew thicker, cherished voices from the past swirled around her.

"How come they call it Seven Mile Road?" Bogey asked the first time they pulled off the highway onto the narrow lane leading up to the house with the giant "For Sale" sign that read

"Hacienda with Acreage and Barn."

"'Cuz it's seven miles from town to the base," Daddy explained, glancing over his shoulders before they clambered out of the station wagon and raced toward the house. Momma said, "Looks just like the 'Palace of the Governors' in Santa Fe...if you chopped it in half."

Georgia beat a path to the front door where she commenced to tap dancing up and down the length of the long covered porch. Bogey skipped over to a large plant and poked his finger on the spiked tips of the bladelike leaves shooting out in all directions. "This is a yucca," he yelled. "The state flower of New Mexico. I looked it up in the encyclopedia."

"If your momma swoons over the rest of this place, we'll be living smack dab in the middle of paradise," Daddy winked as he waited patiently for Trudy to stop dragging her heels and get out of the car. "We'll have the best of both worlds."

"I liked that brick house in town next to the country club," she'd pouted up at him.

"Country Club?" Daddy thumbed her on the nose. "You kids get to swim at the Officers Club pool. That's a privilege and don't you forget it."

"Only one problem," her mother said a few minutes later as they walked out back where Daddy was already making plans for a sunroom and patio extension. "This *hacienda* is too darn close to the tracks."

"Nothing a chain link fence won't fix," he countered in that way of his that always won Momma over.

Two days after they moved in, Aunt Star showed up with a pan of red chile enchiladas and disturbing news that the family menace had moved into a vacant casita half a mile away.

Crouching in front of the firebox, Trudy inserted the key and lifted the lid. While she rifled through the folders searching for her voter ID, another memory punched through the fog: Aunt Star plopped down in a kitchen chair and mopped her brow with a dishtowel. Her arms were thick as any man's from lifting patients in and out of hospital beds, her knees in white support hose, exposed and splayed apart. Dub lay face down on the terra-cotta tile, a huge lump swelling on the crown of his head.

"Can we call the police?" Georgia sniffled as she ran into Aunt Star's arms.

Aunt Star swallowed and shook her head. "Certain menfolk in town won't appreciate our dilemma. They'll try to blame it on us. They always do. It's a man's world, loveys," she sighed, breathing hard as if she'd had the wind knocked out of her. "Sometimes we womenfolk have to take matters into our own hands."

Paralyzed with shock, Trudy had stood rigid, unable to move, the weight of the skillet still in her hands. "It's done," came Daddy's voice from somewhere in her head as the wind picked up outside and snow flurries began to fly. Then something inside of her cracked and she thought her chest would cave in when she couldn't stop crying.

Later that night as she and Georgia curled up with Aunt Star on the crushed velvet sofa sipping hot toddies to calm their jittery nerves, she instructed them: "You tuck it away deep inside of you, so deep that your body will absorb it...and you go on with your lives."

Trudy had tried to follow her aunt's directions...her unwritten rules of engagement. But some memories were always lurking below the surface while others played hide and seek and refused to reveal themselves no matter how much Trudy racked her brain for recall. Because the harder she tried to forget, the more she wanted to remember.

Trudy lifted a manila envelope, peeked inside, and pulled out her voter ID card.

The wail of a siren pierced the air outside the storage unit, probably a fire truck and an ambulance blasting down Lemmon Avenue on their way to a call. Trudy closed the lid and locked the firebox. Struggling to her feet, she stashed the card in her slouchy handbag and looked around to see if there was anything else she needed before she headed to the polls then one last stop by the cemetery.

Her gaze steadied on a small cedar box sitting on top of a carton labeled "Sacred Books."

Skylar!

Choking back a knot of sorrow trapped in her throat, Trudy walked over and picked up the box and held it against her chest. "Hello, Miss Bossy Pants," she whispered, missing the feel and scent of warm fur brushing against her cheek, the sudden draft of cool air as Skylar's bushy tail swished back and forth, her happy meter.

For fifteen years, Skylar stayed by her side, loyal to the end, unlike Preston with a pecker full of wander*lust*. After Trudy walked out of the mansion fifteen years ago, she found the sunlit loft the same day she found herself standing in the middle of an animal shelter, lost and looking for pure love. The golden-haired puppy with the eager eyes yapped to get her attention, and when Trudy bent to pick her up, the puppy jumped into her arms and they found a home in each other's hearts.

They aged together, the four-legged lass and her two-legged mistress. And when aching joints and blindness threatened to end Skylar's walks through the neighborhood and local parks, Trudy loaded her up in the TrailBlazer and they went for long drives so Skylar could sniff the air and feel the wind in her face.

When Skylar died the day before Trudy had to leave on a three-day trip, she paid the pet sitter a month's wages as a thank-you for all the years the sitter had loved on Skylar while Trudy was flying. Then Trudy took Skylar for one last ride on the way to the vet to be cremated. Her death had made Trudy's decision to leave easy. No more ties to Texas.

"Come on, old girl, you're coming with me. Time to set you free." Trudy placed the container by her purse and opened the carton filled with her most cherished books. As she gazed at the covers and spines, she breathed in the aroma that always reminded her of walking into a library or bakery housed in a basement. She found the smell of old books intoxicating.

Three titles caught her attention and she scanned trying to decide which book to pick up first.

The image of a white dove and a black bird nose to nose drew her to pick up the dog-eared paperback of *Death Be Not Proud*, the slim nonfiction she read for a high school English class. The author had written about his teenage son's battle with a brain tumor. Holding the book in her hands, Trudy recalled feeling a sense of empowerment as she rose from her desk that day and approached the podium. She paused to make eye contact before she opened her oral book report with a dedication to the memory of her little brother who had died a couple of months before of the same illness that killed the boy in the book. Her teacher commented later how poised Trudy appeared as she stood before the class discussing such a heavy subject. "You didn't look nervous or scared at all," the teacher said. Trudy had shrugged and said, "After my father went missing and my brother got sick, what's left to be scared of?"

Lots, she would find out a couple of months later.

Setting the book down, she picked up a trade paperback of Margaret Atwood's *The Handmaid's Tale*. A birthday present from Georgia sometime in the nineties, Trudy opened the book and read the following inscription:

> Sis, this novel is set in a dystopian society ruled by a bunch of fundamentalist white dudes who've overthrown the American government. They kidnap women of child-bearing age and force them into servitude where their sole purpose is to bear children for the ruling white men whose wives are barren. How twisted is that? Of course it could never happen here, but the story makes you think. Hope it resonates.
> Happy Birthday,
> Georgia

Trudy shivered and closed the book, recalling how the narrator had been stripped of her identity and forced to wear a long red cloak and white bonnet with wings that covered most of her face. Images of women in black burkas competed with handmaids in red.

One thought niggled through her mind: *What if it could happen here?*

She pictured herself in the story, too old to bear children. Would she be forced to work as a *Martha*, cooking and cleaning for the commander and his bitchy wife? Or sent to the colonies to clean up toxic waste? No way could she be an *Aunt*, dispensing pain and misery on the handmaids. But what if she was younger and cloaked in red, giving birth to dead babies one right after the other? Oh, she'd be salvaged for sure, strung up in a public hanging, and left to dangle at *the wall*.

After driving by her former home moments ago, she realized Preston had a lot in common with the fictional commander in the story. Preston had tried to rule over all aspects of her life, but in the end he had lost when she took her power back and left. Unlike the narrator in the tale, Trudy had the freedom to walk out.

Freedom...a word tossed around like penny candy at a parade. Something she'd taken for granted for too long...but not today. Today, she was exercising her right to vote.

A whiff of jet fuel caused her to look up. She set the book down and breathed in the smell mixed with cold air coming in from the open door of the storage unit. As quickly as it came it left. She glanced down again at the box of books.

Blinking back at her like a beacon of light from the control tower of some remote air base, the one book she pilfered from her mother's house and forgot to return: A first edition of *Stranger to the Ground* by Richard Bach. A gift her father had given her mother before he left for war. Trudy took it without permission on a visit home years ago and forgot to return it. Most of the story was lost on her...but not the feeling of being in flight...inside the cockpit of a fighter jet...as if the reader was the pilot at the controls.

She thumbed through the pages. A yellowed letter fell out.

There was that scent again, a mixture that always reminded her of military uniforms and airplane hangars. Or perhaps it was merely the exhaust from a city bus passing by, and yet it wasn't the same. She began to read the letter dated 25 December 1971:

My Dearest Jewel:

After being around an "arrogant fighter pilot" for years, I think you'll understand the things Bach says in this book. He even uses the term "arrogant fighter pilot." I've underlined the things he captured or described in a special way I've never been able to.

From the moment we met when I was in pilot school at Reese, you wanted to know what it felt like to be at the controls of a jet. Richard Bach lets the reader see the world and life through the eyes of a fighter pilot. In some ways it looks no different than when we're zooming down the highway in the car. In other ways, it's very different.

So, my lady, I hope by reading this book, you'll get to know the other side of me you once said you wished you could meet, the one who straps on a G-suit and helmet and climbs a ladder to his "office."

Merry Christmas, my love,
Always and forever,
Shep

Trudy's eyes welled up as she folded the letter with care and inserted it back in the book. At that moment, she knew she wasn't alone. Another jet took off from Love Field, the sound of the engines roaring in her ears. She couldn't see the plane from her vantage point inside the cold storage unit...yet she knew it was there somewhere overhead.

Just like she couldn't see her dad, but she felt his presence.

She placed the book with the letter in her handbag, turned out the lights, and left.

At the cemetery after she voted, Trudy unlocked her trunk, retrieved a flathead screwdriver she kept in her toolbox, and removed the tiny brass plaque on the box containing Skylar's ashes. After she put the screwdriver away and shut the trunk, she walked toward the children's section. Stone cherubs and lambs greeted her as she approached the grave and set the box on the wet grass turning yellow. The mist from earlier had stopped, and Trudy wondered if the ground would be covered by a blanket of frost the next morning.

Kneeling over the tiny flat headstone, she ran her right hand over the inscription:

Sarah Jewel
Stranger to the ground
August 13, 1998

"My precious babe, I would have given you my last breath just to see you take your first. You came and left so quickly it didn't seem right to burden you with a last name."

She glanced from the tombstone to the brass plaque in her left hand:

Skylar
My sweetest girl
2001- 2016

"We rescued each other. You watched over me for fifteen years. Now I need you to watch over my daughter."

With reverence, Trudy placed the plaque next to Sarah Jewel's name and stood back a moment.

"Sarah Jewel, had you lived, you would be eighteen and old enough to vote. We could have walked into the polls together, exercising our rights that so many women fought for. To quote your Great Aunt Star, 'It's a man's world, loveys. Sometimes we womenfolk have to take matters into our own hands.' So, lovey, today, in your memory, I voted against powerful men like your father who view women as sex objects." Trudy's mind flashed to another grave back in New Mexico, the one stained with graffiti. She took a deep breath. "Today, I voted against men like the *perv*."

She turned her attention to the plaque.

"Skylar, you've been here before. All those times you sat on your haunches and listened to me tell you about the baby with copper hair and blue eyes, a tiny red mouth opened like a baby bird...only no sound came out. You were such a good listener, offering me your paw for comfort. Sometimes resting your chin on my shoulder."

Bending down, Trudy tore a tiny opening in one corner of the plastic bag and sprinkled Skylar's ashes around the perimeter of the small grave, creating a barrier of protection. With the last remaining ashes left in the bag, she fashioned a crude pair of wings in the center of the grave.

Rising, she stood back to examine her handiwork.

In many ways, Sarah Jewel remained a stranger, a tiny being

who existed for a short time within her. And yet Skylar's heart and soul was as familiar to Trudy as most of her family members, maybe even more so.

Before she left, she dropped the cedar box and plastic bag in a nearby trash receptacle and rinsed her hands with a bottle of water she had stashed in her purse.

A sense of release washed over her, as if a weight had been lifted. Reaching for her phone, she sent her mother a text. Seconds later, Jewel texted back: Supper ready when you get here. Baked acorn squash and chicken rice casserole. Drive safe.

Trudy started to tell her mother about the book she'd taken from her years ago, but something told her to wait. Better to ask for forgiveness than permission.

She punched in her coordinates in the Camaro's navigation system, took a deep breath, and eased out of the cemetery. Moments later, she cruised down ribbons of concrete as she headed west, the Dallas skyline in her rearview mirror.

She called Clay's number.

He picked up on the second ring. "Lieutenant Cordova speaking."

For a second she couldn't find her voice. She began to shake. Finally, she stammered, "Clay? It's me. I'm coming home."

Clay hesitated. "Is this the one and only Gertrude Cutterbuck? Best lookin' twirler in the band?"

Trudy giggled. Nothing Clay said or did felt lecherous. "I couldn't twirl for shit, Clay, but glad you think I looked good in my uniform."

He let out an exuberant laugh. The kind that could help her forget she'd ever known heartache. A laugh that could send her flying straight back to Pardon...a place that held so much promise.

With the silver Camaro practically on autopilot, Trudy headed toward the little house of shrines on the edge of town, roughly seven hours away.

She could feel her whole face break into a grin.

CHAPTER 13

Our Lady of Assumptions

A FEW days before Halloween, a yapping Hercules greeted Trudy at Clay's front door. The Chihuahua reeled back on its hind legs and bared its teeth.

"You're a feisty little fella," Trudy laughed, leaning down to the dog's level. He pawed at her against the storm door's glass surface, his nails clicking away. "Guess you're not here to say hi but to defend your territory. Trust me, dude, I get it."

When she straightened, Clay's dimpled grin welcomed her as he went to unlatch the door. He scooped the dog up in one arm and held the door open. "Don't worry. Only one of us bites."

She tossed her hair back and smiled at his humor, at his attempt to put her at ease. Dragging Main and riding around like they were kids was one thing. But today he'd invited her to his house, a mid-century ranch with a pitched metal roof and a wide driveway that curved up to a two-car garage. Located on the corner of Coronado and Cibola in Northwest Pardon, Clay's neighborhood was across town from the wood-frame bungalow where he grew up near Our Lady of Assumption, a mission-style Catholic church with its own grade school.

Adjusting her purse strap, she crossed the threshold and breathed in a pleasant aroma. "Smells good in here." She glanced around, surprised by the open floor plan. Interior walls had been knocked down to eliminate boxy rooms. Dark hardwood floors contrasted against hand-troweled Navajo white walls. Splashes of color from a few Southwestern paintings appealed to her senses, along with the familiar aroma.

Clay gestured to a large candle burning in the center of a massive coffee table with spiral legs. "Sandalwood. Remember? Every time we'd walk into the old TG&Y, you'd head straight for the candle aisle. You'd sniff every votive until you found the bin marked 'Sandalwood.'"

"Ah, and then I'd inhale. My drug of choice." Closing her eyes, she breathed deeply, letting the fragrance carry her back. Even before her eyes fluttered open, she could feel two pairs of eyes studying her. "You have a good memory, Clay."

Hercules expressed his displeasure with a grumpy grrr. Clay stroked the spot between his pointy ears. "Settle down, Little Man. She's our friend."

Clay's voice calmed the dog and sent ripples of pleasure throughout Trudy's body.

She swallowed, hoping Clay hadn't noticed. "How long have you lived here? This house has good bones." The second she said it her face grew hot. She was thinking the same thing about Clay.

"A couple of years. I bought it as a foreclosure. Saw its potential."

Without asking, she headed straight for the kitchen area. "This is lovely." She ran her hands over the white quartz countertops and marveled at a thick supporting pillar wrapped in stainless steel to match the appliances. "Are the cabinets bamboo? I love the effect of the frosted glass doors."

"Yup, very affordable. My cousin Hector flips houses. He bought them ready-made and added some extra touches to give them a custom look. I helped out on weekends and holidays when my schedule allowed it."

"You guys did a marvelous job."

"Thanks. We gutted it down to the studs. It's not a mansion, but it suits me."

Suits me, too, and mansions don't always make for happy homes. She knew that firsthand. Her eyes roamed over everything, including Clay when he wasn't looking.

Craning her neck, she gazed at the white cathedral ceiling. A dark beam ran the length of the ceiling from the entry to the back of the house. Wedge-shaped transoms at each end of the house let in lots of natural light and added to the overall design. Twin sliding glass doors overlooked a covered patio and a bricked-in backyard featuring desert landscape.

She turned and gazed at the rest of the open room. Instead of a man cave jammed with dark furniture and the mandatory recliner, she found a chalky low-slung leather sofa and matching chair gathered near the corner fireplace. Approaching the empty firebox, she imagined herself tangled up with Clay in front of a blazing fire, his bronze skin warming her up on a cold night.

Clay's shoulder brushed against her, and she caught her breath. "Next time you come over, I'll build you a fire. It'll give me a good excuse to get more firewood."

Sweet Lord, she was about to burst. He aroused feelings in her she'd sent into hibernation.

At the sliding glass doors, she peered out past the covered patio with its stone pavers to the flowerbeds filled with white gravel and the occasional rosebush and pear cactus that lined the back wall. A lone oak clinging to its last leaves stood guard in the middle of a neat square of yellow Bermuda grass. For a long time, she'd felt like that lone tree, clinging to something she needed to let go of. But the fear of exposure kept her from completely dropping her guard.

"I thought about putting in a pool, but —"

"Having a pool isn't everything," she cut in, hoping he wasn't trying to apologize for the view. No shimmering water feature to impress her. Clay's yard appeared sparse by Preston's standards, but how could she tell Clay at that moment, as he stood next to her stroking the top of Hercules's innocent head, that she was trying to block the image of Preston coaxing her to strip bare. To dive into the blue so he could sit on the top step and *get off* while she glided up and down the pool, pretending not to notice.

"But then I thought about the upkeep. The sandstorms we get," Clay finished after a moment, his voice nudging her back.

Breathing in the scent of sandalwood and Clay beside her, she wanted to reach out and touch him. Instead, she blathered on nervously about how she'd pulled into a motel on Highway 84 outside of Lubbock the other day and asked the proprietor why the swimming pool had been filled in. "You can't miss it," she rushed on, "the kidney-shaped lawn in front of the entrance. The blue rim with black numbers painted every few feet. It's a dead giveaway."

Clay nodded, studying her. "Yeah, I know the one. It's right off the highway."

"The lady behind the counter was real nice. She told me the maintenance got to be too much. Blamed it on sandstorms — just like you said — and nothing to stop the wind."

Clay shook his head, pressing his lips together in a boyish pout. "I'd be pissed if I was a kid staying there. So you're standing on the rim at the eight-foot mark, imagining yourself diving in, but all you can see is a plot of grass and an urn with flowers in the spot where the diving board had been. Damn, I'd feel cheated."

Trudy turned, catching a glint in Clay's blue eyes. How they shimmered with mirth sometimes when he looked at her.

Averting her eyes, she bit her lip and stared out at the backyard. "Okay, maybe I was wrong. Having your own pool *is* nice at times, but..." — her voice was a quivering mess — "I guess it boils down to who you choose to go swimming with." She left it at that.

He blinked at few times as if trying to comprehend. Finally, he said, "I see."

But of course he didn't. How could he? Clay had no idea what weird crap she had put up with over the years. The pool incident was just one of many.

A long silence passed between them.

After a moment, she gestured at Hercules. "Why don't you and your guard dog show me the rest of the place?"

Hercules growled.

Trudy reeled back, heeding his warning. She'd dealt with her share of passengers and fussy lapdogs over the years. Hercules needed to gain her trust. "Do you have any treats?"

"Aw, so you're going to bribe him. C'mon, follow me."

At the kitchen island that also functioned as a room divider, Clay reached under a bin and pulled out a small container and peeled off the lid. "Here you go. Make him work for it."

"I'll have him eating out of my hand, Clay Cordova. You watch."

Clay leaned against the counter, looking amused.

Selecting a few heart-shaped treats, she leaned toward the dog cradled in Clay's arms and kept her voice even. "Okay, Mister Hercules. Don't take a finger." The dog followed her every move, his eyes bulging from his tiny head. When he snapped at the treat, she pulled back. "Okay, let's try again." Using the same soothing voice that calmed nervous fliers, she held the treat toward him. This time Hercules nibbled politely and waited eagerly for the next round. After a few more tries, he allowed her to pet the top of his head.

"Good boy," she cooed.

Clay let out an exaggerated sigh. "That's a relief. I'd hate to have to choose between you and the dog."

Tossing her hair back, she caught the slight smirk twitching at the corners of his lips. His dimples pulled her toward him like a magnet. Sweet Jesus, he could flirt.

So she flirted right back. "Well, I know my place. And I know who's the boss around here."

Another devilish grin caused her heart to sputter. The same closed-mouth grin that captured her attention in civics class their junior year. Clay stashed the bag of treats and shifted the dog in his arms. "C'mon, let's go see the rest of the house."

The three of them paused in front of a white oak bookcase built into the west wall. Besides books, the shelves were devoted to photos of a dark-haired beauty with Clay's dimples but lighter complexion. The girl in the photos went from a gapped-tooth first-grader to a middle school spelling bee winner to an older version of the girl in a variety of caps and gowns and honor society cords.

Trudy's heart clutched. Her voice throbbed in her ears when she spoke. "Your daughter?"

Clay picked up a photo. "This is Cinda. Short for Lucinda."

Trudy put on her brave face. "She's named after your mother." To Trudy's knowledge, Clay had no idea she'd lost a child. Mentioning her would dampen the mood, taking the joy from Clay's face as he stared at his daughter's photo.

Shifting Hercules again, Clay picked up another photo and passed it to Trudy. In the picture, Cinda's dark bobbed hair and fringed bangs framed a confident grin. A handsome blonde woman several years older leaned against her.

Trudy's gaze shifted between the two women then up at Clay. "Cinda's mother?" A twinge of jealousy ripped through her core.

Clay shook his head. "That's Roxy, my daughter-in-law. They waited until it was legal in all fifty states." He beamed like any proud father.

"Oh, wow," she exclaimed, feeling stupid. After working with people of all persuasions, Trudy should've known better than to make assumptions. Of course the attractive blonde was Cinda's wife, not her mother. "Do they live around here?" She passed the photo to Clay and scanned the rest of the bookshelf. No sign of his ex anywhere.

"Seattle. Cinda's an attorney. Makes more money than her old man. And Roxy's a child psychologist." He placed the photo back on the shelf. "Let's go see the rest of the house. Then we can grab a bite to eat."

As he led her through a wide opening into a short hallway, she felt a sense of relief at Clay's acceptance of his daughter. Trudy didn't want to spend time with a man intolerant of others. They peeked into a guest room/combination study to the left, a generous hall bath in the center encased in tones of cream and brown granite and tiles on the countertop and floor.

"Nice bathroom. I like how you kept the shower and tub separate. Pretty snazzy."

"The original floor plan had three bedrooms. I wanted to create the illusion of space so we sacrificed the third bedroom for a bigger guest bath and master suite."

Stepping back, he let her pass into a generous room filled with natural light and a king-sized bed with a mission-style headboard carved out of white oak. The headboard matched the nightstands and the coffee table in the living room.

Wiping her brow, she hoped he hadn't noticed the slight tremor in her hands or the quiver in her voice as she commented on the space. She gazed up at the transom windows on the north wall. "This room has good energy. Your whole house does."

He strode across a Navajo rug at the foot of the bed and

pressed a switch on the north wall. "Check this out." Automatic blinds built into a large windowpane opened and closed. "It's for lazy people." He laughed and walked back toward her.

She lingered at the foot of the bed, and glanced at the brown and teal throw pillows lined against the headboard.

"Do you always make your bed so neatly?" she joked, feeling her face and neck turn crimson.

"Only when Hercules and I are expecting company, right, boy?" He ruffled the dog's ears.

Back in the big room, Trudy waited while Clay took Hercules out to potty. As the dog trotted off, Clay shrugged into a black jacket and rubbed his hands together. The temperature must be dropping.

Glancing back at the bookshelf, she recognized a small photo stashed up high atop a stack of green and silver books lying on their sides. Yearbooks! Approaching the stack, she felt her throat tighten as she stood on her tippy toes and gaped at the young couple grinning back. *Senior prom!* Clay looked so tall and handsome in a tuxedo with a green bowtie and platform shoes, but the sunburned girl in a flowered formal with enough ruffles to trim a pair of kitchen curtains? What had she been thinking back then? Not to mention the mop of ringlets that spiraled downward in tight coils from a hot curling iron. Trudy covered her mouth and giggled.

How long had he been displaying their photo? Maybe he'd stuck it up high at the last second when she rang the doorbell earlier.

The sliding glass door slid back and she turned quickly from the bookcase. Hercules scampered toward her like they were best friends.

Bending, she rubbed him behind his ears. "Oh, so now you like me do you? Just 'cuz you think I'm the treat lady."

Clay blew out the candle and tossed a doggy toy up on the couch. "Go to your place, Little Man." Hercules jumped on the couch and settled his chin on a pillow, his large eyes trained on his master. "If a burglar tries to break in, you know the drill." Hercules lifted his head and snarled through bared teeth.

Trudy laughed at the dog's antics.

As they went to leave, Clay's hand grazed the small of her back. "Didn't you bring a warmer jacket? It's getting cold out."

"I'll be fine." Before she'd left her mother's place, she'd tried on three outfits. At the last minute she went with her old standby: warm leggings and riding boots and her favorite long cardigan, a thick wooly number with deep pockets and a hood she could throw over her head.

Near the front door, she recognized a piece of Mexican folk art that hung on the wall. Pausing, she reached out and brushed her fingers over the colorful figure of a woman in a long blue robe with rays of sunshine forming a halo behind her. "This hung in your mother's house. I know it's *Our Lady*, but I forget what it's called."

"A Retablo. Or altarpiece for you *gringos*," he teased.

Admiring the sacred figure, she recalled the time she and Georgia attended Saturday night mass with Clay. Before he picked them up in his mother's Ford LTD, Momma Jewel had instructed them that they weren't allowed to take communion at Clay's church because they weren't Catholic. When their mother was out of earshot, Aunt Star took them aside and said, "You girls waltz up that aisle like everyone else, stick your tongues out at the priest, and let him dole out his wafers and wine 'cuz God won't know the difference."

Trudy chuckled at the memory. "Remember that time Georgia and I took communion at your church? Your mother about fainted."

"Yeah, it was pretty funny. Poor Mom, she thought Father Griego was going to excommunicate her."

Halfway out the door, she handed Clay the keys. "You drive."

He threw his head back and laughed. "You trust me?"

"I better," she kidded, "you're a cop."

But his question lingered. She'd known him since high school. Yet there were all those lost years. Part of her was afraid of divulging certain secrets. And the other part was afraid Clay might become disenchanted once they got intimate. She wasn't perfect anymore — Preston had assured her of that — and she sure wasn't sixteen.

Watching Clay aim the key fob to unlock the car, she realized something. He'd carted Hercules all over the house, never once stopping to set him down, not even after Trudy gained the little dog's trust. Had Clay been hiding behind the dog the whole time, using him as a buffer until he took him outside? What if Clay was just as nervous as Trudy?

She bit her bottom lip and grinned.

After she slid into the passenger seat and buckled in, she glanced sideways at Clay. While she instructed him on how to adjust the seat, she breathed in the scent of sandalwood that followed him from the house to the car. Watching him fiddle with the knobs, she began to associate the intoxicating scent with Clay.

Backing out of the driveway, they headed east, zipping through neighborhoods that went from flattop stuccos to sprawling brick ranches with circular driveways. He pointed out new parts of Pardon she'd never seen. He stopped in front of a gated community and let the engine idle.

"This one's only been here a couple of years. You like it?"

She gawked at the pueblo-style neighborhood of elaborate homes with golden tan walls and palm trees shooting skyward. "Sandstone Oasis, huh? One thing's for sure, those palm trees aren't natives." She glanced at Clay. "You know anyone who lives here?"

"Sure," he shrugged, tapping the steering wheel. "Doctors, lawyers, a judge. I can sweet-talk the guard and see if he'll let us in?"

Was he trying to impress her? She didn't want to hurt his feelings, but she'd seen her fill of gated communities back in Dallas. Seems like everywhere she went these days, walls were going up where people had money. "Clay, I have another place in mind. A place you weren't allowed to go as a kid. Not until you met me. 'Cuz you didn't have the right ID."

He frowned for a second and then his face broke into a wry grin. "Let's do it. We'll take the back roads."

Gunning the engine, they sped out of the affluent side of town and headed west.

CHAPTER 14

Ghost Town

THE CAMARO cruised across the overpass and descended toward the entrance of the front gate. Clay tapped the brake as they approached the guardhouse. No armed airman stepped out to greet them or asked to see their IDs. No black and yellow barrier arm went up to let them pass or stayed down while a guard interrogated them on their need to come on base. All military insignia had been stripped from the building, the windows boarded up.

Clay glanced at Trudy. "I remember the first time I came on base with you. You were driving your mom's station wagon. Georgia was with us."

Trudy leaned against the headrest and sighed. "I was so nervous that day. I'd never driven on base before."

Clay slowed the Camaro to a crawl as they passed by the former guardhouse, its gray paint chipping away from neglect. "The young airman working the gate that day got an eyeful."

She twisted in her seat. "Whaddya you mean? All I remember is feeling like a fraud. My hands were clammy as I gripped the wheel and tried not to brake too hard. And then Georgia had to go and poke her head out the window and inform the guard I'd just gotten my driver's license."

Clay made a face. "Yep, and then she asked the guard if he thought she still looked pretty, even with a mouthful of braces."

"That poor airman," Trudy snickered. "He probably thought we were a bunch of spoiled brats."

Clay wiped his brow in an exaggerated fashion and laughed.

"I'm sure he enjoyed every second you sisters graced his presence. When you rolled down the window and flashed your dependent ID, his eyes bugged out. The dude was probably expecting a mom and a carload of kids. Not some hot-looking babe in a tangerine halter-top and cutoffs."

Her mouth fell open. "How can you remember what I was wearing? That was decades ago."

He waggled his brows. "Trust me, I remember." His voice rose an octave, like a teenage boy whose voice is caught somewhere between adolescence and adulthood.

They stayed on the main road that snaked around the golf course, now gone to seed. Even the airpark was gone. Trudy rolled down her window and gazed at the empty space where a display of fighter jets once rested on poles next to bronze plaques that told their history. "I wonder what happened to the jets?"

"Maybe they went to a museum?" Clay offered, sounding hopeful.

"Or the scrapyard," Trudy countered, a tone of pessimism creeping into her voice.

Clay drove her by the hospital where she'd been born, where Bogey spent his final days before being flown to Lubbock for some last minute miracle that didn't come.

They motored by the base theater, commissary, and BX. Not a car or person in sight, only pigeons and sparrows roosting on rooftops, parking lots, and telephone wires. Trudy gawked up at the red and white checkerboard water tower that rose like a lonely sentry over the place. She read the faded words "Pardon Air Force Base" out loud. "At least they didn't try to cover up the name."

Later, as they meandered through base housing, Trudy rolled down her window again. "All these quarters sitting empty." She glanced sideways. "It's a shame these houses are going to waste. Couldn't the city or state offer them as affordable housing?"

"I've been saying the same thing," Clay nodded.

He stopped the car in front of a sprawling one-story home with a huge orange brick chimney and a big circular driveway. "This where the head honcho lived?"

Trudy gazed at the house, the largest one in the cul-de-sac.

"Yeah, the wing commander lived here. Daddy called him 'The Big Enchilada.' Guess that wasn't politically correct back then."

Clay let out a quiet chuckle. "How come you guys didn't live on base?"

She shrugged. "My dad was a bit of a rebel. He liked having his own space." She fiddled with a button on her cardigan. "You know he built the sunroom at our house. He wanted to buy more land when he got back, open up a go-cart place, but then..." She gazed out the window, then over at Clay. "Let's go down by the flight line."

They headed across base, careening past the base chapel, the rec center, rows and rows of empty barracks, the headquarters building vacant along with the tall flagpole. "This place looks like a ghost town," Trudy said. "The footprint of the military is still visible, but nothing's being done to preserve it. Once it lost its mission, its purpose, the Air Force just let it go."

Clay didn't say anything, just nodded.

After a while, Trudy said, "I've felt like that at times, Clay, that I lost my mission. My purpose, especially after I lost —"

Oh, God, not now. I'm sorry, baby girl.

"After I lost my desire to keep flying," she recovered quickly, hoping he hadn't noticed her change in tone, the sadness that overtook her at times.

He took his gaze off the road long enough to acknowledge her, and she could tell he'd been listening with his whole self, even while driving.

"Over there." She pointed to a plain-looking structure sitting not far off the road. "Pull in there. That's my dad's old squadron."

They parked and got out. Trudy craned her neck and gazed skyward. "If you listen, you can almost hear the jets."

Their hands stuffed into their respective pockets, they walked side by side toward the building. High overhead, a metal clamp clanged against an empty flagpole where her Dad's squadron flag once flew.

She peeked through a grimy window. "Anybody home?" Her forehead rested against the cold glass, her breath fogging the window.

"I bet if you listen closely, someone will whisper back." Clay's voice caressed her in all the right places.

She glanced over her shoulder, breathing in his boyish grin so warm and tender, his dimples tempting her to come closer. He looked so sexy standing there in his jeans and cowboy boots, his hands stuffed into the pockets of his jacket. Stepping away from the window, she fought the urge to reach out and poke him. To tag him and run, make him chase her, like a couple of kids on a playground.

I'll show you mine if you show me yours...

She blushed, feeling both impish and wild.

God! Where did *that* come from? He did that to her, brought out another side of her she'd almost forgotten. "Come on, let's skinny through that open gate."

A red and white "restricted area" sign dangled from a chain-link fence that separated the old squadron building from the ramp and taxiway. Another sign said: "No Unauthorized Personnel Beyond this Point."

Clay hesitated, always the cop following rules.

"So who's gonna stop us? You see any sky cops around?" she teased.

He glanced around as if he needed to check, just in case. "You're right." Then he held out his hand, and they slipped past the old warning sign and through the opening in the chain link fence and walked out onto the ramp.

"Over there." She pointed. "That's the direction he took off from."

Clay's hand felt warm and reassuring as they strolled farther out onto the tarmac. Weeds sprouted through seams and cracks in taxiways, the high plains reclaiming its own.

"The day he left, I had the urge to run after him, to catch him one last time, to give him one last hug. But he was too far out; he'd already crossed those lines where only jet mechanics and other pilots were allowed to go."

Brushing hair out of her eyes, she saw something move out beyond the edge of the runway. She stared hard, trying to make out the grayish-yellow shape. Was it a coyote loping along or a tumbleweed? Whatever it was moved again and then disappeared.

The wind howled around her like an invitation, and she took off running down the center of the runway, her arms outstretched like wings. "Come on," she hollered over her shoulder. "This is the last place I saw him alive."

She ran until she was out of breath, until her lungs burned, until the sound of jet engines spooled down in her memory. The runway stretched on before her with no end in sight, and she turned to see Clay's dark silhouette framed against the azure sky. Even from this distance, she could see his arms stretching outward as if he were waiting to catch her.

Like all those times Shep Cutterbuck threw his young children in the air...

Gulping, she brushed the heel of her hand over the dampness wetting her cheeks.

Fixing her eyes on Clay, she whispered into the wind, "Is he the one?"

Daddy's robust voice reverberated back to her like a sonic boom. *Bird Strike!*

That was not the response she'd wanted to hear from the only man she'd ever trusted, besides Clay. A wave of disappointment slapped against her as she watched a large sandhill crane approaching. The bird soared gracefully overhead, almost at eye-level, and landed on the other side of the runway. So this was Daddy's sign for her to keep moving, to keep searching. Sandhill cranes were notorious for getting sucked into jet engines and could ruin a pilot's day. During squadron parties at their house on Seven Mile Road, Trudy had listened hungrily to her dad and the other pilots as they talked with their hands about flying.

And yet, as she glanced back and forth between the crane and Clay, she remembered something else, and her heart quickened with hope.

There was another time Daddy used the term *Bird Strike*, and the memory flew back to her at the speed of light. She could smell the base bowling alley; see Daddy in his Bermuda shorts, the ones that showed off his bowlegged calves. He picked up a sky-blue bowling ball and turned to wink at Trudy and her siblings. Clad in rented bowling shoes, he glided to the spot where he released the ball and sent it rolling down the center of the lane until it *smacked* against the pins, knocking them all down. "Bird strike!" he yelped, throwing his arms up in victory.

"Bird strike!" she yelled and took off running down the center of the runway, her focus on the man whose eyes mirrored the sky.

                        ∾

Barely five feet away from him, she blinked in confusion as Clay snatched his cellphone from his jacket pocket and glanced at the screen. "Hey, baby," he said, waving Trudy over.

A woman's voice, strong and self-assured, a hint of Latino in her accent, resounded into the cold air. "Hey, Papa. How's your Saturday going?"

"I'm standing in the middle of a runway at the old air base and gazing at the most beautiful woman." He wrapped his free arm around Trudy's waist and pulled her close. Their first embrace since they were kids, and she breathed in his scent, brushed her cheek against the side of his face.

Shaking, she grinned stupidly at Clay's phone, at his beautiful lips forming words. Flipping her cardigan's hood over her head, she listened with her whole self.

"You're at the old base? What are you doing th..." His daughter paused and then she squealed, "Oh my God! You're with the *stewardess*."

Clay's eyes shined as he nodded at Trudy. "Yes, ma'am." His voice burbled with happiness.

"Just be careful, Papa," she warned. "You've had your heart broken before..."

Clay closed his eyes and turned away. He'd failed to tell his daughter he had her on speaker.

Glancing at the asphalt, Trudy hid her face beneath her knitted hood. She had no idea how many women had broken Clay's heart. At their age, no telling how many hearts they'd broken between them. And yet...

The sandhill crane flapped its wings, made a bugle call, and took off. Breathing deeply, Trudy watched it until it disappeared. She hoped the rest of the flock was out there somewhere on the horizon, waiting for the straggler to join up.

Clay was still talking to Cinda. "Yes, honey, that time of year. I'll make sure Hercules wears his sweater from now on."

Trudy froze in place, measuring every breath. Something moved again near the edge of the runway. She squinted into the late autumn sun high in the sky, welcoming the warmth. Whatever was out there blended in with the ocher-hued grasses of the plains. It moved again. By now she was sure it was a coyote, keeping a close watch on its territory.

CHAPTER 15

The Conquistador!

November 2, 2016

AUNT STAR'S voice jangled from the cellphone where Jewel had placed it on the kitchen counter with the speaker on high. "Sister, just because a man's coming to dinner...I don't see what all the fuss is about."

"It's not just any man," Jewel shouted from across the room where she rummaged around inside the avocado green refrigerator. "It's Trudy's high school boyfriend!"

"*High school* boyfriend?" Aunt Star shrieked. "Isn't that like buying back your own hand-me-downs years later?"

"It's Clay *Cor-do-va*. The kids went steady their junior and senior years."

"Oh...the dashing boy whose mother made the best tamales."

"Clay's a detective," Jewel bragged, shutting the refrigerator door and setting a tossed salad in a vintage stoneware bowl and a bottle of vinaigrette dressing on the counter.

"A *detective?*" Aunt Star's shrill tone could've cleared the room. "In Pardon?"

"He's the oldest one on the force." Jewel smiled knowingly like she thought she had the upper hand. "He graduated from New Mexico State and ended up back here."

Trudy sat a few feet away, listening to their conversation as she lounged in a Spanish-style leather armchair, flexing her legs after being on her feet all day. Up since dawn every day this week, she'd been sorting and cleaning and moving furniture around. Once she'd plopped down in the chair minutes ago, she didn't want to budge. Every joint, every muscle, every bone rebelled.

"A detective," Aunt Star repeated as if she needed to try on this new information. Any unease got covered up with a joke. "Sister, you got any weed stashed in the house? First place he'll check is the freezer."

Jewel winked at Trudy. "Nope, Trudy and I smoked it last night."

Aunt Star chuckled. "Ask that girl when she's coming to see me. Now that she's *retired*, she's run out of excuses."

"Ask her yourself. She's sitting right here on the throne."

"The *throne*? I thought you said you were in the kitchen."

Laughing, Trudy curled her hands around the scrolled ends of the walnut armrest, letting her fingers slide into the grooves where the ends resembled human fists. "Hey, Aunt Star. I've been on my feet all day. I'm relaxing in the *conquistador* chair. I moved it into the kitchen where the table used to sit."

"Oh, I always loved that chair, but it was buried under a pile of *crap* in the back bedroom. So where's the table?"

"In the sunroom," Jewel cut in, ignoring the jab. "I'm enjoying that space again, thanks to Trudy. And you should see how she cleaned up the east wall here in the kitchen and rearranged some of the artwork. She even hung one of my old pageant photos."

Yesterday, after Trudy lugged the heavy masculine chair into the kitchen and polished the wood, Jewel cupped the side of her face and declared, "It looks so different in here. Funny how you can look at something so long, you don't see it anymore."

Early this morning, Trudy walked into the kitchen and caught her mother sitting in the armchair, gazing at an old black and white photo taken moments after nineteen-year-old Jewel Hurn had been crowned Miss Eastern New Mexico. "I wasn't exactly a pinup girl," her mother said, flicking her wrist in the air and passing the photo to Trudy. "Star got all the curves, but I carried myself well, I had a winning smile, and I could twirl a mean baton. Remind me to take that other photo to Lupi next time we head into town. The one of me being crowned Miss Pardon New Mexico.

Along with one of your dad in uniform."

Star sighed. "Well, Miss Beauty Queen, it's about time you start enjoying that house again. Look at all the work Shep put into it. While you're at it, why don't you upgrade your appliances? I hate to break it to you, Sister, but avocado green's been out of style for years."

Jewel frowned at the refrigerator humming by the side door. "My appliances are like me, old but functioning."

Despite the ravages of time, Trudy saw her mother at all ages, from the beautiful young woman she worshiped as a child to the dignified woman before her who never apologized for her wrinkles. She might joke about her age, but she never apologized.

Grabbing two hot pads, Jewel turned toward the stove. The oven door squeaked when she propped it open. The savory aroma of roasted meat, potatoes, onions, and bell pepper permeated the air.

"Smells good, Momma." Pushing herself out of the chair, Trudy reached over and turned on a table lamp sitting atop a small red desk she'd carted out of Bogey's bedroom. She checked her cellphone, no new messages from Clay, but he should be arriving any minute. It had been Jewel's idea to invite him to dinner.

After checking the roast, Jewel let the oven door shut with a bang, her editorial comment to her sister.

While Aunt Star jabbered away about politics, Jewel tossed the hot pads on the counter, grabbed the cellphone, and padded toward Trudy. "How do I look?" she mouthed, twirling this way and that in sequined slippers, a pair of tailored slacks, and a silk blouse that matched the velveteen beret sitting at a jaunty angle atop her silver spiked hair.

Trudy lowered her voice and placed her hands on her mother's frail shoulders. "Like a gal ready for a night on the town." This was the first time in weeks that Trudy had seen her mother in something besides velour warm-ups, pajamas, and knit caps.

Jewel set the phone on the desk and adjusted the beret. "It'll keep my head warm at least." She ran an elegant hand over the top of the desk and picked up the phone. "Star...you remember the little gray desk in Bogey's room?"

Aunt Star stopped yapping mid-sentence and switched gears. "Of course I remember. I can still see him sittin' there doing his homework without being prodded. Unlike two girls I know..." Her words drifted off, tinged with a mixture of joy and sorrow.

Bending her head toward the phone, Trudy pictured her elderly aunt seated in her leather recliner, knitting caps for patients at the state hospital where she used to work once she left Pardon. "You kept us in line," Trudy said, avoiding any mention of that awful night that hung between them, even though the burden of silence weighed heavier each year.

Eyes glistening, Jewel spoke up. "Trudy gave that little desk new life. She painted it a bright red and set it against the east wall here in the kitchen."

"You can't miss it," Trudy joked, trying to keep the conversation lighthearted.

"It's *poppy red*," Jewel informed her sister. "That's what it said on the paint can."

"*Poppy red?* Well, you know what they say about poppies, don't you?" Aunt Star cleared her throat, and Trudy knew what was coming, a case of one-upmanship between the sisters.

Jewel tapped one foot impatiently and horned in, "I should know. I've lived it. They're the color of sacrifice and remembrance."

Being a know-it-all, Aunt Star couldn't resist. "You're right, Sister, but did you know the American Legion hands out little paper poppies each year in exchange for donations to support veterans?"

"Have you forgotten that I've given talks at the American Legion, the VFW, and the local Air Force Association Chapter?" Jewel barked back.

After an icy pause, Aunt Star said, "Mercy, I need to run. You girls make sure you get out and vote. It's high time we get a woman president running this country."

"I voted early," Trudy volunteered.

"Reckon I'll cast my vote for the lesser of two evils," Jewel groused. "I can't imagine a man who brags about his sexual conquests getting elected, especially by women."

"Women make excuses for men all the time," Star stated. "Even smart ones."

Trudy winced. She'd made excuses for Preston for too damn long. By the time she fled, he'd slashed a piece of her soul, whittled away at her self-confidence. Part of her was still healing, even after fifteen years.

After Star hung up, Jewel grabbed a stack of dinner plates and silverware and headed into the sunroom. Alone in the kitchen, Trudy inspected the floor, pleased how the terra-cotta tiles shined after she'd mopped that afternoon. How many plates and glasses had been dropped over the years, the shard remains brushed into a dustbin and thrown in the trash. She'd recalled the time a cantaloupe rolled off the counter, how easily the melon bruised without splitting wide open.

Walking over to the side door, she jiggled the handle out of habit. Ever since her talk with Georgia last week, Trudy imagined the door in a constant state of unlock. Flicking on the outside lights, she checked it one more time to be sure.

A beam of headlights illuminated the driveway. Must be Clay. As she scurried around and bent to check her reflection in the side of the old toaster, her phone dinged with a new text message. Pulling her cell from her pocket, she peered at the display: Thank you for helping your momma get her house in order. Give my best to Clay. Stay strong. XO A.S.

Heading toward the front door, Trudy breathed through her nose. What Aunt Star meant was *stay silent.*

CHAPTER 16

All Souls' Day

"YOUR KNIGHT in shining armor couldn't make it, so he sent me."
Clay leaned against a porch post, his sheepish grin reeling her in
one dimple at a time. He held two floral bouquets in one hand
and a bottle of red wine in the other.

Laughing, Trudy gazed at his tweed sport coat, open collar
shirt, and pressed jeans. "You look nice. You must be freezing."
She opened the storm door wider for him to pass, the rush of cold
air from outside a welcome relief from the heat that fired through
her body the second she'd read Aunt Star's text.

"Forecast calls for snow." He stepped inside and handed her
the wine. "I like your ponytail." He tilted his head, studying her.
"You wore it like that in high school."

Biting her lip, she smiled at the expensive wine label and the
compliment he'd so freely given. She'd read somewhere that an
elegant ponytail on some women can act as a facelift. At the last
minute, she'd gathered her hair in a satiny band right above the
nape of her neck.

Clay glanced around, getting his bearings as if he needed to
shake off the last forty years since he'd been in the house. "I remember this room. The books, the kiva fireplace in the corner,
your mom's rock collection in the window, but that big screen TV
is definitely new."

Trudy leaned in. "I'm trying to convince her to spring for a
new living room set." She gestured toward the gold sofa, the
crushed velvet cushions sagging in the middle. "Money's not the

issue. It's letting go of things she associates with...you know...my dad and brother."

His head swiveled this way and that before he strode across the room, the heels of his black cowboy boots tapping softly on the tile. He stared at the enlarged photo of her dad standing by a jet. "I lit a candle for him tonight at Mass, your brother, too. I stopped by the church when I got off work." He glanced over his shoulder and shrugged. "You know, being it's All Souls' Day."

He'd gravitated toward her dad's photo before, back when they were teenagers. That didn't surprise her. But for him to light a candle in honor of her dad and brother, two people Clay had never met? Her throated tightened. She envied his ease at announcing a good deed, a deed with no strings attached.

Gripping the wine bottle, her mouth twitched as the confession welled up and escaped through her windpipe. "I haven't been to church in years."

Sometimes, like now, words flew out of her mouth and circled around her. Maybe that's why Aunt Star didn't quite trust her with their secret. *You tuck it away deep inside of you, so deep your body will absorb it...*

But her body didn't absorb it. It grew like a tumor deep within her, threatening to rupture at the slightest reminder.

Still holding the flowers, Clay strode toward her. He touched her forearm. "Sorry I had to go out of town on your birthday."

Blinking, she noticed how her hand strangled the neck of the wine bottle.

He chuckled dryly. "You squeeze that bottle any tighter, you'll pop the cork."

His comment made her laugh. How she'd missed his sense of humor. She loosened her grip. "Thanks for your text."

On Monday, he'd sent her a message from Las Cruces: Happy 58th Birthday, Bewitched. Save me some treats! LOL!

She'd blushed at the promise of more things to come...

"Those flowers sure smell good." She glanced at the twin bouquets, and then into his sky-blue eyes. She could float there forever, riding his thermals.

He winked and handed her a bouquet. "One's for your mom. I need to stay on her good side."

As Trudy went to usher him through the living room into the kitchen, he leaned closer and gave her a peck on the lips. They hadn't seen each other since Saturday after they left the base and grabbed dinner in town. Afterwords, they lingered over small talk in his driveway, Trudy in the driver's seat and Clay riding shotgun. They talked about classmates who'd died right after graduation and more recently. They discussed how it was getting harder to stay in shape at their age. Clay said he worked out at the gym when time permitted. Trudy confessed she'd stopped walking after Skylar's death, explaining how she felt off-balance without Skylar by her side, like she'd lost a limb. When Clay inquired about Trudy getting another dog, she shrugged and said, "I'm not ready." He paused briefly then said, "Give it time. Skylar will let you know."

Before he got out of the car that night, he reached over and brushed his lips against hers — a tender but tentative kiss. "I have to drive to Las Cruces tomorrow on business. Sorry I'll miss your birthday." She'd smiled, surprised he remembered after four decades. "You're a *Halloween* baby," he'd teased. After she'd backed out of the driveway, she glanced in the rearview mirror as Clay unlocked the door and scooped Hercules up in his arms. He stood at the door watching her drive away.

All the way back to her mom's, she couldn't shake Cinda's warning: "Just be careful, Papa. You've had your heart broken before."

As she prepared for bed that night, Trudy phoned her sister. "We barely kissed," she told her. "We were together all day." Georgia yawned and observed sleepily, "Lupi told me Clay's ex-wife hurt him bad. Said it had something to do with their daughter. Clay's probably testin' the water before he dives in." Sometime during the night, Trudy dreamed she and Clay were running down the runway, hand in hand, and when they reached the end where the asphalt stopped, their feet left the ground and they flew among a flock of large graceful birds, each calling to the others in flight. Long after she awoke, she'd slumbered in bed feeling weightless, unencumbered by the pull of gravity. In her mind, her long supple limbs wrapped around him, yearning to go to a place they'd never been.

"Well, hello, handsome."

Jewel's sudden appearance in the kitchen startled Trudy. She pulled away from Clay like they'd been caught necking. His kiss from a moment ago lingered on her lips.

He knuckled her playfully on the nose and turned to address her mother. "You're looking beautiful as ever, Miss Jewel."

"Liar." She reached up on her tippy toes and gave him a hug. Then she held him at arm's length. "Last time I saw you, you pulled me over for speeding. Back when you were a beat cop."

He threw his head back and laughed. "That was years ago. Hopefully I just gave you a warning."

"Yep, you let the old lady off easy. Trudy tells me you're quite the remodeler."

Clay scratched the side of his face. "That would be my cousin Hector. I was merely his apprentice."

Jewel patted Clay's arm. "I'm sure you were more than that. Come, I want your expert opinion on something."

Was it Trudy's imagination, or did her mother stand taller, smile brighter, as she looped her arm through Clay's and led him down the hallway? Trudy followed, curious what her mother was up to.

Although her mother had dated off and on since Trudy's dad disappeared from the radar, nothing much came of it but a chance for dinner and a movie or play or a concert at the community college. Everyone understood Jewel Cutterbuck's heart belonged to a tall lanky fighter pilot forever young and handsome, an American hero and the father of her three children.

But that didn't keep her from enjoying herself in the presence of a handsome man.

At the entrance to Bogey's bedroom, Jewel flipped on the light switch and gestured to a bare window overlooking the sunroom. "I want that window knocked out along with most of the wall. Maybe install French doors or carve out a wide archway." She blinked up at Clay, deferring to him. Then she led him across the small room.

Flabbergasted, Trudy's jaw dropped as she leaned against the doorframe. This was the first she'd heard about her mother wanting to knock down a wall. She and Georgia had spent years discussing ways to remodel and update the *hacienda with acreage*. Trudy had even offered to bankroll the whole thing. But always, Jewel shot down their ideas.

As Trudy visualized the project, she mentally rearranged the furniture in the sunroom. "Momma, it seems natural to join the two rooms together. Let in more light. But you'll have to move the chuck wagon."

Clay's head swiveled. A look of amusement spread over his face as their eyes met across the room. His expression conveyed two things to Trudy: he remembered her nickname for the Western-style couch, plus all those late nights when they snuggled under a blanket on the Naugahyde cushions after her mother had gone to bed.

"And what may I ask is the *chuck wagon*?" her mother said, peering back at Trudy over the rim of her spectacles.

"The couch, Momma," Trudy giggled, avoiding eye contact. "It butts up against the wall on the other side of this room."

"Your daddy handpicked that couch at the old Lawson's Mercantile on South Main right after we moved back," her mother said. "It might weigh a ton, but it'll outlast us all." She lifted her chin up at Clay, letting her hand slide up and down his arm. "Well, Detective, what's the verdict? Can we tear down this wall?"

"Absolutely, Miss Jewel." Clay stepped closer to the window and examined the area. He knocked up and down the wall in a few places. "You'll have to put up with construction dust though."

"I figured as much." Jewel opened the window and poked her head into the other room. "You can take a break from cleaning for a while, girl...all that extra dust might set off your *allergies*."

Trudy studied the wine bottle in her hand, feeling tipsy although she hadn't had a drop to drink. Her eyes drifted back and forth between Clay's broad shoulders and her mother's head bobbing around in her sporty beret. "Don't you worry about me,

Momma. I'll strap on a face mask and be good to go."

Her mother ignored the barb and shut the window. "After Shep built the sunroom, I was worried Bogey would feel cut off because his window no longer looked outside. That this room would feel like a cave. But he claimed he liked living in the dark. Said it was good training for when he traveled to outer space." Her mother glanced up at Clay, keeping her voice even. "My son got his wish. It came earlier than I expected. He's up there flying among the stars. That's what it says on his tombstone."

Clay wrapped a protective arm around Jewel, letting her lean into him.

Trudy's eyes misted up. *Maybe the interior window made Bogey feel safer, too. After all, it could keep out a pack of hungry coyotes...or a peeping Dub.*

A hush fell over the room — an impromptu pause for a moment of silence to honor a boy taken too soon.

Except for her mother's computer desk and a poster of Neil Armstrong taking his "one small step for man," Trudy had stripped the room bare of her brother's belongings. It was the first room she had tackled the morning after she returned from her overnight trip to Texas. Before her mother left to volunteer at the hospital's information desk, she told Trudy: "I trust your judgment. Just don't throw anything away he made with his hands. Put everything in that new keeper box we bought at Walmart."

After a day of pitching stuff, Trudy had dropped off several large bags of outdated but wearable clothing at the Salvation Army. Her brother's collection of books on space and aviation went to Pardon Library. The plastic container she'd shoved into the closet held his prize-winning Pinewood Derby car, a few drawings and papers, selected sport trophies and team jerseys, and a Bible he received from the base chapel in third grade.

When Jewel had returned later that day, she stuck her head in the door and gasped. Not at the bare walls, but at a fabric growth chart Trudy had discovered taped to the back of Bogey's closet door. "I completely forgot about that," her mother said as she ran her slender fingers along the canvas that resembled a giant measuring tape. "While you girls' heights shot up, Bogey's stopped at four foot ten inches in 1974."

Trudy straightened her shoulders. "Time for wine," she caroled, breaking the moment of silence and to lighten the mood. "Clay came for dinner. Not a memorial service." She started to leave the room.

"I'll second that," her mother chimed in, turning to Clay. "Now, how do I get hold of your cousin? Let's get this demolition started."

Clay pulled out his wallet and handed Jewel a business card. "Here's Hector's number. Tell him I said to give you a military discount. He served time in the Marines."

Her mother took the card and leaned her head on Clay's shoulder. "I've been wanting to make some changes for years," she sighed, "but it took our girl coming home to get me motivated."

Our girl. Trudy had a hunch her mother was already incorporating Clay into the family.

Alone in the kitchen, Trudy stood at the sink sipping a glass of tap water. Her mother and Clay were still in the bedroom discussing *the wall* project. As Trudy gazed past her reflection in the window, she couldn't shake the feeling that something was out there watching her.

And because it came from the direction of the old base and not the edge of the railroad tracks, she wasn't afraid.

Setting her glass in the sink, she filled a crystal vase with water and arranged the flowers and took them into the sunroom and placed them in the center of the round pedestal table that had been in the family for years. Moving the heavy piece the other day without help took some doing. Instead of waiting on the yardman, like her mother insisted, Trudy had used what Aunt Star referred to as *good ol' female ingenuity.*

Once Trudy separated the pedestal from the top, she turned the top on its side and rolled it into the sunroom and propped it against Grandma Lily's rocker. Jewel leaned against the rocker to keep it from swaying. After Trudy maneuvered the solid oak pedestal onto an old quilt and dragged it into the sunroom, she hoisted it in place in the right corner near the wall of windows. With the rocker supporting the bulk of the top, Trudy lifted one side and used her torso to push and slide the top in place on the pedestal. Then she tightened the hardware, brought in the chairs, and popped two Tylenol for her aching joints and muscles.

Stepping back, she admired the floral centerpiece and the three large speckled brown and turquoise dinner plates from her mother's Red Wing Bob White stoneware collection. Each plate featured a mother quail and two chicks. When she and Georgia were little, they called them the *blue birdie plates*. After Bogey was born and Trudy was old enough to count on her fingers, she informed her mother the plates were missing a chick.

Through the archway, she heard her mother order Clay, "Sit there."

Bustling into the kitchen, Trudy found Clay making himself at home in the conquistador. Stretching his legs, he crossed his feet at the ankles and offered a contented smile. Her mother stood nearby, holding court. "It was Trudy's idea to *rearrange* the furniture."

Clay twisted in the chair and gestured at the turquoise phone hanging above the poppy-red desk. "I can't believe you still have that."

Jewel fiddled with her beret. "That old touchtone works just fine, not to worry. I do keep a newfangled version with all the bells and whistles back by my bedside, but these days I mostly use my cellphone." She reached over and twirled her finger through the coils of cord plugged into the base and receiver. "I recall how a certain girl in this room tied up this phone line for hours on end. And her sister did, too."

Trudy made a face and went to open the wine. "Clay, you must be starving by now. You're going to think Momma and I are terrible hostesses." She stole a glance his way then uncorked the wine and filled three goblets. "Momma, you go first."

Her mother took a healthy sip, smacked her ruby lips with pleasure, and announced, "This is the good stuff." Setting her wine on the counter, she went to lift the roast from the oven.

Turning, Trudy sashayed toward Clay with a goblet in each hand. Once again, she'd ignored the seasonal rule about not wearing white after Labor Day. She'd slipped into her best white jeans — the ones that gave the illusion of long and lean — and a formfitting teal-colored V-neck sweater.

Right before she passed Clay his wine, Preston's voice snarled through her mind. "You fat cow. You used to be sexy once. What happened to you?" *After all these years, his cruelty still picked at an old scab of self-doubt.*

Clay rose from the chair. His expression told Trudy he approved of the view — a jiggle and wiggle appealed to him. They clinked glasses and offered to help Jewel with the food preparation, but she shooed them away.

Wine in hand, Clay walked into the sunroom. His whole face lit up as he gazed at everything. He pointed to the far side of the room. "Over there's where we played Twister." He brushed up against her, tugging her ponytail.

Heat rose to her face as she recalled the white floor mat with red, yellow, green, and blue dots. While Georgia spun the spinner and played referee, Clay and Trudy were human game pieces, their youthful bodies entangled around each other on the mat.

After Jewel brought the food in and they took their seats, she tapped her spoon against the side of her water glass. "I'd like to propose a toast."

All three raised their wine glasses. "To the renewal of old friendships," she said, a slight tremor in her voice.

They ate, sipped wine, and caught up on local gossip. Clay regaled them with stories of attending Catholic grade school and getting in trouble with the nuns.

Jewel twirled her fork in the air. "My goodness, Clay. I can't see you ever getting into mischief."

He chuckled, charming them with his boyish grin. "Of course I shaped up by the time I met your daughter." He winked at Trudy before he stabbed his fork into a hunk of meat and began chewing.

Batting her lashes, Trudy kept a straight face and kicked him under the table. "Except for the prank you pulled at Sonic," she muttered out the side of her mouth.

Halfway through dinner, Jewel set her fork down and placed her hands palms down on each side of her plate. Her eyes glistened and her voice trembled. "Everyone I've ever loved has sat around this table."

Having just taken the last savory bite of potatoes and carrots, Trudy stopped chewing and stared at her mother. *Oh Lord, you've had too much to drink...now you're going to get all melancholy again.*

Jewel picked up her wine glass, drew it to her lips, and took a healthy swig. Then she peered over at Trudy. "Except for Sarah Jewel."

Trudy froze. Her eyes burned as she stared at the mother quail visible to one side of her plate. Fingering the cloth napkin on her lap, she twisted the edges of fabric, rolling it between her fingers as her heart collided with the back of her throat.

Her mother kept yapping. "Even though I never met her, I love her just the same."

Stop, Momma! Trudy took a deep breath, held it there a moment. Her throat swelled like she'd swallowed an olive pit.

By now, Clay had set his fork down and stopped chewing. His eyes darted back and forth between Trudy and her mother. "I'm sorry, I don't mean to pry. But who is Sarah Jewel?"

When Trudy didn't answer, her mother squirmed in her chair before she hunched forward, her lips parted in an O. Her eyes pleaded with Trudy: *You mean you haven't told him yet?*

Leaning back, Trudy smoothed a hand over the top of her head and took a deep breath. She clasped her hands in front of her plate and addressed Clay. "She was a sweet soul who passed through my life briefly on her way to someplace else." She set her napkin down and pushed away from the table. "Will you excuse me for a moment?"

In the kitchen, she tore off a paper towel and dabbed at the dampness on the back of her neck and forehead. She should've told Clay sooner. It wasn't her mother's fault. *Buck it up, Cutterbuck.*

Circling the kitchen, she composed herself and grabbed the wine bottle. Halfway through the archway, she heard her mother say, "I realize you deal with real crimes like rape and murder, but has there been any more vandalism at the cemetery since that graffiti artist struck?"

Trudy halted midstride. Her heart thumped wildly as she waited for Clay's response.

"Not that I know of," he said.

Her mother took a delicate nip of wine and set the glass down, wrapping her elegant fingers around the stem. "I'm sure Trudy's mentioned it before, but Bogey's buried out there and I'd hate for anything to happen to his grave."

Clay cleared his throat. "It was probably an isolated incident, Miss Jewel. I don't think you have anything to worry about."

Trudy breezed into the room. She gave her mother the evil eye behind Clay's back and swiped her finger across her throat, a signal for her to *can* it. "Who wants more wine?" she asked, her tone too chipper. "Clay, how 'bout you?"

He waved her off. "None for me. I have to drive home."

"Momma?" Trudy gave her a tight smile and eyed the empty glass her mother held out.

"Just a tad, dear. I've about reached my limit." *I'll say*, Trudy thought, pouring enough to fill the bottom of the glass.

Plopping down in her chair, Trudy freshened her own glass and set the bottle on the table.

Clay glanced sideways, concern in his eyes. "You okay?"

She pressed her lips together and nodded. "Um-huh."

They resumed eating.

A few minutes later, Jewel let out a series of yawns and announced groggily, "I'm turning into a pumpkin." She started to stand up but wobbled back down.

Clay bolted out of his chair and went to steady her. "You all right, Miss Jewel?"

She gave him a loopy grin. "I'm fine, Clay. Guess I can't hold my liquor like I used to."

You can say that again, Trudy thought as she helped her mother stand up.

"I'm sorry I left you with a mess, but Cinderella is going to bed." As her mother latched onto Trudy's elbow, she tore off her beret and plopped it on Trudy's head. "You kids have fun."

"I'll be right back," Trudy whispered to Clay. "Make yourself at home."

In the master bedroom, Trudy helped her mother undress and put on flannel pajamas. As she tucked her into the king-sized bed her parents bought when they moved back to Pardon, she thought how tiny and feeble her mother appeared among the pillows and comforter. As she bent to kiss her goodnight, her mother curled into a fetal position and sighed. "Clay's a good man. Just like your daddy."

"I know, Momma, get some sleep. You threw a wonderful dinner party."

On her way out, Trudy took off the beret and placed it on her mother's long dresser next to her parents' wedding photo. As she turned out the light, her mother whispered in the dark, "Don't worry, Tru-*dee*. I didn't tell Clay about the woman at the cemetery."

Trudy paused in the doorway, rubbing her forehead. Her voice vibrated in her chest and eardrums when she finally spoke. "Thank you, Momma. That's our secret, okay? Get some rest."

She'd almost blurted: *You tuck it away, deep inside of you...*

Ducking into the hall bath, she checked her makeup and popped two more Tylenol. All that cleaning and moving furniture had caught up with her. One thing was for certain, after her mother's remodeling project was done, Trudy would hire professional cleaners to scour the entire house and wash the windows. Then she'd figure out her next move: would she get a part-time job or go back to school? Settle down and build a house in Pardon or somewhere else in New Mexico? All of that depended on one thing: where she stood with Clay.

When she returned to the kitchen, he'd already loaded the dishwasher and put the leftovers away. She felt like ringing up Aunt Star and bragging, "See, not all men are scoundrels." She found him in the sunroom with the lights dimmed, gazing out the windows. She sidled up next to him, elbowing him in the side. "Thanks for cleaning the kitchen."

He jutted his chin at something out the window. "Remember that time you and I walked along the tracks? It was fall, we'd just started dating."

She leaned forward to peer out the window. "Like yesterday."

She hoped that's all he remembered: scrambling up the berm, making out in his mother's car afterwards.

He touched the back of her neck and began massaging out the kinks. His fingers remembered all the right places to help her relax. Her head lolled and she found herself floating away with him.

"When I was young, I used to lie in bed at night and listen to the trains and planes and dream of all the places I would go when I grew up," he said. "After you left town and I headed to college, I told my mom I wasn't coming back except to visit. But after I graduated and got married, I realized I was all she had left, not counting distant family. By the time Cinda came along..." The muscles in his jaw flexed. He stopped talking as if he'd been traveling down a dark road of thought and came to a dead end.

"How long have you been divorced?" she finally asked.

He began to stroke her ponytail. "About thirteen years. But we separated long before that. When Cinda came out at eighteen, my ex told our daughter she wished she'd been diagnosed with cancer or got killed in a car wreck."

Trudy recoiled at the thought of a woman saying something so vile to her own flesh and blood. *So that's what Lupi meant when she told Georgia, Clay's ex hurt him bad.*

"Jesus, Clay, your poor daughter. I'm so sorry. What woman says that to her child?"

He shrugged and looked away. "Part of it was her upbringing, I guess. She grew up in a strict religious family. They all disowned Cinda and me once I made it clear I wasn't sending her to some crazyass intervention camp where they try to convert people. As you can imagine, my daughter has nothing to do with her mother."

"God, of course not." Trudy felt a deep revulsion for a woman she'd never met...a woman who threw away her daughter for being gay.

Clay continued to run his fingers through her hair. "So, you wanna tell me about Sarah Jewel?"

Trudy swallowed. "I was forty. She was the most beautiful creature I'd ever seen, but she was stillborn. They let me hold her so I could say hello and goodbye all in the same breath."

Clay shook his head. "I'm so sorry for your loss, Trudy. I had no idea."

She stared straight ahead, her pulse thrumming in her ears. "She was buried in a tiny white coffin. I took care of all the arrangements. Preston wanted nothing to do with it."

"I'm so sorry," Clay whispered again and again as if he didn't know what else to say.

Her voice cracked as she struggled to finish. "He told me I turned him off...he couldn't deal with the fact I'd given birth to something dead."

"That doctor dude, he didn't deserve you. I'm sorry you had to go through all that alone. If I'd known..." Clay's voice rustled around her, soothing her like a grownup lullaby.

The floodlights illuminated the patio and parts of the back-yard beyond the plastered bench walls. Breathing in his scent, she listened for the rumble of a locomotive, the clickety-clack of box-cars rolling along the tracks up on the berm. But there was noth-ing but darkness and an eerie quiet out past the fence line. Until Aunt Star told her the truth about what happened, Trudy would always look out beyond the back gate, see a ghost train rolling by, each phantom car a reminder that fast-moving machines are un-forgiving on the human body.

As Clay reached for her hand, it began to snow like that night long ago, when a blanket of white covered everything, including any evidence Dub had pulled himself up from the cold concrete floor of the carport and stumbled into the night.

CHAPTER 17

Demolition Day: Dust Will Fly

November 9, 2016

THE HOUSE sat nestled inside a cloud. The fog had rolled in some-time in the middle of the night, veiling the morning in an eerie gray mist.

At the base of the flagpole, Trudy straightened after replacing the light bulb on the spotlight that illuminated the flags from dusk to dawn. Gazing up, she could barely make out the flags as they drooped in the soupy air: the black and white POW/MIA flag with a silhouette of a man and a watchtower and the New Mexico state flag, with its ancient Zia sun symbol — a geometric red circle with groups of rays pointing in four directions against a yellow back-ground.

Their limp posture matched her mood: a feeling of defeat as if every hope and dream had been crushed overnight. She wasn't alone. Her mind drifted to Aunt Star's group text at sunrise. It had jarred Trudy awake: I hung my American flag upside down on the front porch in a sign of distress. Make no mistake, girls. Our civil rights are at stake. The election was rigged! How else can you ex-plain how the Orange Cheese Puff pulled this off!

As Trudy huddled in bed, she pictured her aunt's small pink adobe on a busy street and people gawking at the inverted flag draped across the porch. Her act of protest was sure to start tongues wagging in her small scenic town.

Within seconds, a string of text messages volleyed back and

forth between the women in the family. First Jewel: Be careful, Star. I don't want some nutjob coming after you. Georgia chimed in: I'm depressed. How am I going to face my students? Aunt Star to Georgia: Chin up, gal. Put one foot in front of the other and breathe. Drop by after work if you get a chance. Misery loves company.

And finally, it was Trudy's turn. She drew in a deep breath, held it a moment before she exhaled, and tapped the keyboard on her phone: This feels like DOOMSDAY.

The moment she sent the text, she recognized a seismic shift within her: *She didn't know she would care so much...about the outcome of an election.*

Her mother poked her head in the door a few minutes later. "I'm going to make coffee. Unless the world ends this morning, Hector should be here at nine."

Trudy set her phone on the nightstand and tried to go back to sleep. She punched her pillow a few times before giving up. After sliding into her robe, she limped into the kitchen, fumbled for her coffee cup, and joined her mother at the table in the sunroom.

But there was no sunshine warming the room on this chilly November day. The patio and everything beyond had been swallowed up in an opaque mass that hovered over the land.

Jewel's hand shook as she pushed aside a plate of half-eaten toast and picked up her coffee mug, gripping it in both hands. "Even Mother Nature is protecting herself. Why else would she cover up in a shroud of fog on the morning after?"

Trudy sat in a stupor, rubbing sleep from her eyes after sitting up half the night watching the election results. Glancing out the window at the ghostly gray, she lifted the mug to her face and savored the aroma of dark roasted coffee. After a couple of sips, she regarded her mother. "You've hardly touched your toast."

"I'm not hungry this morning. I ate enough to take my pills." Her mother released the death grip on her mug and pushed the plate of toast toward Trudy. "Here, you take the other half."

Trudy licked her finger and dabbed at the crumbs before she nibbled a wedge of toast. "Momma, would Daddy have voted for a woman if he were here? It's been bugging me since I went to bed."

Jewel let out a heavy sigh and stared out the window. "Funny you should ask. I was thinking the same thing yesterday as I drove to the polls. Knowing Shep, there's no way he would vote for a draft-dodging braggart who disrespects Gold Star families..." She paused to take a breath and turned to look Trudy in the eye. "And then have the *audacity* to claim he'd always wanted a Purple Heart."

Trudy swallowed a bite of toast. "I keep thinking about that young man we saw at the bank. I can't get over his friendly face or the web of scars on his right calf."

Her mother nodded and picked up her mug. "Unlike that young man you encountered, the Orange Dude doesn't know the first thing about service and sacrifice."

They fell into a comfortable silence.

While Jewel sipped her coffee, Trudy polished off the last piece of toast then glanced at her watch. "I better get dressed. Looks like zero visibility out there, but I don't want to get caught in my bathrobe in case Hector shows up on time."

Jewel directed her gaze toward the chuck wagon that sat at an attractive angle facing the southwest toward the old base. "He might have to wait for the fog to lift. Leave that plate. I'll get it."

Rising from the table, Trudy stopped and placed a hand on her mother's shoulder. "Enjoy these last vestiges of peace and quiet for a while, Momma. Things are about to get crazy."

Her mother reached up and patted Trudy's hand. "Are you referring to the wall project or the state of the union?"

"Maybe both."

At the archway to the kitchen, Trudy paused and said, "I'll bring in the paper, but first I need to change the light bulb on the spotlight out front. It blew out in the middle of the night."

Her mother swiveled in her chair. "The one beneath the flags?"

"Yeah, I noticed it when I came to bed around three."

Hoisting herself out of the chair, Jewel wriggled her fingers at Trudy and uttered a spooky "woo-OOO-ooo" before she began clearing the table. "Maybe it's a sign there are other forces at work."

Breathing in the vaporous air, Trudy reflected on her mother's last comment as she turned away from the flagpole and gaped out at the thick haze. The giant yucca appeared in the middle of the yard like a creature from another world. "Daddy," she yelled into the murk, "was that you passing by when the light bulb blew? Do you fear for our country...and the very ideals you lost your life defending?"

The rumble of an engine out on Seven Mile Road drowned out her voice. The motor grew louder as the sound of tires crunched in the gravel driveway.

Must be Hector. How on earth did he drive in this weather?

She brushed a loose strand of hair from her face and moved toward the driveway.

His candy-apple red pickup emerged through the cloud and came to a stop. She was close enough to see chrome on the front bumper and a sticker that read, "Where the bumf**k is Pardon, New Mexico?"

She laughed out loud. She'd missed seeing that the day he came out to give them a bid.

"Imagine that," her mother called from the front door. "A contractor who's on time."

A wiry man about five foot eight inches walked toward them out of the fog. His brown eyes glittered in a friendly greeting. "Good morning, ladies. Are we ready to tear down a wall?" Despite flecks of gray in his day-old beard and deep grooves around his eyes and mouth, he had the weathered face that grew more handsome with age.

She didn't remember him in high school. He was a few years younger than Clay.

"How on earth did you drive in this fog?" Trudy reached out and shook his hand. The hand of a working-class man, strong and firm, rough like sandpaper.

"There were a few patches of fog in town, but nothing like out this way. It seemed to get a lot thicker about a mile back. About the time I passed Drake's Salvage Yard."

*Old Man Drake was a bomber pilot in World War Two...*Clay's voice rolled through her mind as she pictured a giant cloud swooping down and covering everything that lay in the junkyard, located to the east of her mother's property, even including the airplane propeller guarding its entrance.

Maybe Momma wasn't joking about *other forces at work.*

Hector wore a pair of loose jeans, work boots, and a T-shirt with a Marine logo. He didn't wear a jacket even though it was cold.

Before Hector headed down the hall to get to work, Jewel led him into the kitchen. "My sister and two daughters think my kitchen is outdated. Maybe they're right." She crossed her arms and lifted her chin in defiance. "I don't care what you come up with, but my Mexican tile countertop stays."

Trudy took a seat in the conquistador. Once again, Momma was full of surprises. "Hector, my dad ordered the tile special and installed it himself right after we moved in. He did more than fly jets. He liked to build things."

Hector glanced over his shoulder at Trudy, acknowledging her with a thoughtful blink. He had a slight overbite that appeared more prominent when he was concentrating, the way his tongue curled over his bottom lip.

He listened respectfully then turned and swaggered over and ran his fingers along the tiles. "The major was an excellent craftsman. I can tell he took pride in his work."

Jewel glanced over her shoulder, her eyes dancing with satisfaction at Hector's praise of her husband's work. "See, Trudy, what did I tell you?"

Hector scanned the room from one end to the other. "The tiles are gorgeous and add character." He inspected the cabinets, the sink, the range and matching fridge, and dishwasher. "These are easy fixes. A new sink and faucet, new doors on the cupboards, a fresh coat of paint, stainless steel appliances..." He spun and walked back and stood next to Jewel in the center of the room. "Mrs. Cutterbuck, have you ever thought about installing a free-standing island?" He glanced down and stamped his feet as if marching in place. "Right here. It would give you extra countertop and make the room appear bigger."

Trudy's jaw dropped. She and Georgia had been saying the same thing for years.

Jewel clasped both hands on top of her head, nesting them on her knit cap. "Why, Hector, I think it's a marvelous idea. Work me into your schedule after that wall comes tumbling down."

The fog lifted by noon. After Hector left for lunch, Trudy drove into town to grab a few items at the grocery store. As she pulled into a parking spot, her phone pinged with a text from Clay: Babe, how're things going with Hector? Have you had on any local news? Someone painted swastikas all over the front and side of Gold's Department Store at the corner of Main and Fourth. I'll call you later.

Two things struck Trudy as she bent over her phone to text him back. Clay hadn't called her *babe* since high school. And sadly, Pardon wasn't immune to the hatred and intolerance spreading across the nation.

Inside the store, Trudy grabbed a cart and wheeled up and down each aisle, loading up on fresh fruit and veggies, multigrain bread, fish and chicken, orange juice, skim milk, wine, laundry detergent, and paper products.

At the checkout, a stone-faced male cashier in his twenties greeted her with a robotic voice. "How's your day going?" His expression lacked all emotion as he rang up each item.

She pushed her cart forward and studied him a second as she went to insert her card in the scanner. Glancing left and right, she muttered, "Honestly, it kinda sucks." She tried to gauge his reaction.

He blinked and kept a straight face. "The election?"

Nodding, she scribbled her signature on the display and removed her card. "Yeah."

He handed her a receipt as a young woman started bagging her groceries in plastic bags. "A lady came through my line about an hour ago all jubilant and stuff," he volunteered, keeping his voice low. "She bought meat trays from the deli, a bunch of helium balloons, a bag of paper horns, wine, beer, margarita mix; you name it, even a donkey piñata."

Trudy flinched. "That poor piñata. It'll take a beating for sure."

The hint of a chuckle escaped his lips. "I wonder what she'll fill it with?"

"No telling," Trudy laughed as they exchanged glances and the void in his eyes lifted.

"You take care," he told her as she tipped the female bagger, grabbed the plastic bags by their handles, and headed for the exit.

Aunt Star was right: *misery loves company.*

As the electronic doors swooshed open, she came upon a young Latina mother pushing a shopping cart with one hand and struggling with a bouncing toddler in the other. A baby carrier with a squalling infant was strapped to the front of the cart. The toddler broke free of his mother's grip and scampered away, giggling in his escape. In that instant, the frantic mother let go of the shopping cart and started screaming hysterically in Spanish to the young boy who laughed and kept running, darting in and out of parked cars in a game of hide and seek. The shopping cart with the baby began to roll sideways into the parking lot.

With bags swinging from both hands, Trudy dashed forward, hollering, "I've got your baby." Seconds before the cart careened into an oncoming car pulling into a slot, Trudy yanked hold of the handle and wheeled it around. Gasping for breath, she peeked into the carrier. A pair of big brown eyes with cow lashes gaped back at her, a tiny purple bow clipped to a headful of black hair. The baby had stopped crying, but her tiny fist batted the air. "Hello, little one," Trudy cooed, her eyes blurry as she stared at the helpless infant.

By the time the young mother grabbed her toddler and rushed back, her tan face was streaked with tears. "Gracias," she said, keeping her eyes downcast as she propped the toddler on one hip and grabbed the cart with her free hand and pushed it toward an older model sedan.

"Would you like me to help you to your car?" Trudy called after her, but the woman kept moving and never looked back.

As Trudy headed to her own car, she found herself haunted by the look in the young woman's eyes: a look of utter fear and distrust. The woman never spoke one word of English, and she kept her head down the whole time. Given the outcome of the election, Trudy couldn't blame her.

Before she fired up the engine, she scrolled through Facebook. A post from Lupi popped up in her newsfeed. "I feel violated. How could anyone vote for this asshat?" Someone named Cassandra from Los Angeles replied, "This whole thing feels orchestrated. Like a collective rape." Trudy's heart plunged when she read Georgia's comment in the thread: "This is an affront to anyone who's ever had to fight off a monster."

Resting her forehead on the steering wheel, Trudy breathed deeply, then sat up, checked to make sure she was strapped in, and backed out of the parking slot.

Five minutes later, she motored down Santa Fe Way before she headed south at the bend in the road where it converged with North Main. American flags lined both sides of Main Street for Veterans Day coming up. A few blocks later, she slowed down as she approached the intersection of Main and Fourth Street. While she waited at a red light, her gut twisted as she glared over the steering wheel at the side of Gold's Department Store, a two-story tan structure which sat directly to her right on the opposite side of the crosswalk. Ugly black swastikas covered the side of the building.

When the light turned green, she crept forward and caught another glimpse of the storefront smeared in more black swastikas. Two Pardon Police SUVs were parked out front and crime tape warned people to stay back. She looked for Clay but didn't see him. He'd probably been there and left. A KOB TV news van from Albuquerque had parked by the curb where a TV reporter was interviewing someone on camera. The department store had been in business for decades and was considered high end. When Trudy was in high school, she remembered meeting the store's founder, a Holocaust survivor, and one of the biggest philanthropists in Pardon. The store's owner had never forgotten one of his liberators was a soldier from Pardon.

At the next intersection, she cut right and drove past the old two-story post office with its light brown and orange tile roof and wide marble steps leading up to a series of tall archways. The building was magnificent for a town the size of Pardon, and she acknowledged its grandeur while she grappled with the fact that someone had defaced another building in town with symbols of terror and intimidation.

Two blocks later, she took a right at La Casita Street and slowed down as she passed by Our Lady of Assumption Church, tapping her brake to admire its thick tan walls and twin bell towers, each topped by a cross. Her gaze drifted to the third cross, stationed directly over the main entrance. Each time Clay went to Mass, he entered through those imposing wooden doors. It was so natural for him to believe, to cling to the faith of his childhood.

Easing her foot on the gas, she approached the schoolyard and rolled down the window to listen to the chatter of children at play. Girls and boys, mostly Hispanic, were bundled in winter wraps even though the November sun blazed high overhead. A little boy running a stick along the chain link fence stopped and looked in her direction. Fifty years ago, that might've been Clay, stopping to stare at a flashy sports car cruising by.

She waved at the boy but he didn't wave back. Could she blame him? She left before he alerted the nuns or whoever ran the school that some strange lady was sitting in her car, maybe waiting to shoot up the school. When Trudy was his age, her biggest fear at school was pooping her pants or getting sent to the principal's office. But as she drove away, she realized the boy looked sad or even worried. Maybe his dog died. Maybe his family life was in shambles. But what if it was something else, something dark and ominous brought on due to the election? What if his mother had come from Mexico looking for a better life? She could be a student, a professor, a doctor, an accountant, a plumber — she could be anybody — and now her biggest fear was getting sent back. What would happen to the boy?

For the first time in her life, Trudy felt bewildered and betrayed by her own countrymen. Is this how many of the Vietnam veterans felt after returning from war to an ungrateful nation? And yet, she'd read in the news where many of those same veterans, along with other hardworking people, voted for a man who treats women as sex objects and who only seems to care about himself. How could so many good people place their trust in such a man?

The whole thing scared her, and her mind drifted back to the swastikas painted on Gold's Department Store. As she zigzagged down a few more streets, passing a variety of bungalows, some with big porches and others with simple stoops, she imagined Nazi storm troopers decked out in WWII style helmets and uniforms parading up and down the streets of Pardon and the rest of America, ripping people from their homes and tossing them like trash into the back of military cargo trucks.

Back on Seven Mile Road, she passed a corpulent young woman walking along the shoulder against traffic, pushing a bicycle with a wire basket mounted on the handlebars. The road was flat, but the woman plodded along like she was pushing the bike uphill. She couldn't be more than eighteen to twenty, pasty with long stringy hair, a red tank top and black tights, and so grotesquely disproportioned, Trudy's throat swelled with compassion. The woman's small head and narrow shoulders sat on top a body with globs of flesh that hung from her upper arms and skirted her hips like a puffy tutu. The woman grew smaller in her rearview mirror before she disappeared from sight.

If Nazis ruled the world today, Trudy thought with a shudder, they'd destroy a gal like that. They'd shoot her on the spot, confiscate her bike, and kick her into the weeds for vultures to feed on.

Passing the grain elevators to her left, Trudy jumped when her phone rang, the ringer amplified through the Camaro's audio system. Georgia's name lit up on the dashboard display. As Trudy pressed the control button on her steering wheel, Georgia's comment on Lupi's Facebook post earlier burned in her mind. "Hey, sis, what's up?"

"Can you talk a sec? I'm on my lunchbreak." Georgia sounded down.

"Sure. I'm just out running errands." Trudy flicked on her blinker and moved into the left lane to avoid hitting a tractor that had pulled onto the highway.

Her sister's voice gushed out of the speakers like a hot blast of wind. "First, how's the remodeling project going?"

"Good. Hector taped everything off with sheets of plastic before he gave Momma a sledgehammer and let her take the first strike. She barely made a dent, but she had fun and told him she was taking her frustrations out on the wall. Then Hector picked up an ax and dust started flying. Those plastic sheets are for show. Dust is like water: it finds its way in, through every crack and crevice."

"I can't wait to see it," Georgia said. "Mom should've done this years ago. Maybe Hector can sweet-talk her into updating the kitchen and baths."

"He's already on it," Trudy replied. "For some reason, hearing it from a man carries more weight than from one of us. So what's up?"

Georgia sighed. "I need to vent. I was scrolling through the news earlier and saw where a fight broke out at an elementary school outside of Atlanta. A group of white kids started taunting a group of Hispanics during recess, telling them to go back to Mexico and or some bullshit. Then some black kids stepped in to defend the Mexicans and all hell broke loose — bloody noses and black eyes. Girls yanking hair out."

"Jeez, even the kids are turning on each other," Trudy said, glancing in her side mirror before moving back into the right lane.

"The principal, who happens to be black, gathered the kids up in the auditorium. They had a come-to-Jesus talk. He said it's the first time his students have ever seen him cry."

"That's so sad, sis. Stuff's happening here in Pardon, too. Someone spray-painted swastikas all over the front and side of Gold's Department Store. I drove by there a few minutes ago."

"That's disgusting," Georgia snapped. "What's happening to our country? Daddy would be heartbroken."

"Or pissed!" Trudy said.

Keeping her eyes on the road, she imagined a map of the United States, similar to ones she'd seen in social studies textbooks in grade school. But instead of symbols depicting farms and cities dotting the land, she saw something else, something so disturbing she interrupted Georgia to tell her about it. After she explained about the map, she added, "Instead of smokestacks depicting factories and industries in various states, I see little chimneys cropping up around the country."

"Chimneys?" her sister said.

Trudy shifted in her seat. She took her left hand off the steering wheel to rub the back of her neck. "Yes, Georgia, crematoriums. Like the ones used in Nazi Germany."

"Oh my God, sis. Now I'm gettin' paranoid. Maybe all that dust is playing havoc with your head."

As the Camaro rolled past Drake's Salvage Yard on her left, Trudy glanced over in time to see the sun glint off the old propeller on the front of the building.

CHAPTER 18

News from the Turquoise Phone

HECTOR WASN'T back from lunch when Trudy pulled the Camaro beside the minivan under the carport and cut the engine. It was nice to park in that spot again after she'd tossed old bicycles with flat tires and boxes of junk that had sat there for years, some of it left over from her mother's cleaning business. Slinging her purse over her shoulder, she unfolded herself from the car, grabbed the bags from the trunk, and hurried toward the side door. She was anxious to tell her mother about the swastikas at Gold's Department Store.

Inserting the key, she nudged the door with one foot and pushed it open with her hip. As she went to lug in the groceries, she called out, "Momma, you won't believe…" Halfway through the door, she froze. White dust had settled on every surface she'd spent weeks cleaning.

Her mother leaned against the wall next to the red desk, the elongated telephone cord wrapped around her frail form like a cocoon, as if she'd stood in place after answering the house phone and turned herself around and around like a jewelry box ballerina. Her head bent at an odd angle, she held the receiver against her right ear and nodded to someone on the other end as if the caller could see her. Her purple knit cap puddled at her feet where she'd flung it off at some point.

Jewel's eyes were wild and huge as she signaled for Trudy to come closer. Trudy shoved the bags onto the counter and dropped her purse and rushed over. Bending to retrieve her mother's knit cap, she shook the dust off and noticed *Stranger to the Ground* splayed open face down on the desk, now layered in a chalky film.

"Who is it?" she mouthed, fidgeting with the cap.

Jewel's mouth opened and closed like a fish out of water. She closed her eyes a couple of times but said nothing.

Swallowing hard, Trudy held her breath, expecting bad news. Had something happened to Aunt Star? Maybe she'd suffered a stroke, her disappointment in the election too much to bear? Surely Georgia was okay; Trudy had talked to her not five minutes ago. Maybe Uncle Manifred had finally croaked, not quite making it to his hundredth birthday in a few weeks.

At last Jewel uttered, "I'll be here. You can also reach me on my cellphone, day or night." After she rattled off the number, she said into the phone, "Thank you for the news. Bye now." As she went to hang up, she noticed how she'd wrapped herself in the cord. She stared at the receiver in her hand then up at the base.

"Momma, is everything okay?" Setting the knit cap on the desk, Trudy took the receiver from her mother's hand and began to unravel the coils from around her torso and over her head.

Nodding, her mother blinked a couple of times but didn't make a peep while Trudy freed her from the cord. As Trudy placed the receiver back on the base, her mother gripped the edge of the desk for support. "I'd just turned off the TV and was on my way to the sunroom to read when the phone rang." With stiff jerky movements, Jewel reached for the conquistador and plopped down.

Trudy glanced around, her throat parched. The room felt still and she thought she might choke on sheetrock dust. "Who was that on the phone?" she coughed, hovering over her mother.

Jewel tapped her fingers on the scrolled ends of the armrests. She took a deep breath and sighed. "A casualty officer from the Missing Persons Branch at the Air Force Personnel Center in San Antonio." She paused as her eyes darted about the room.

Casualty officer thrummed in Trudy's ears. "What did he say?"

Jewel's lips quivered, along with her hands. "It was a woman. Colonel Washington, I didn't catch her first name." Jewel tapped the balls of her feet up and down on the terra-cotta floor, her gold-sequined slippers tamping the dust into caked powder. "It's been years since I've heard from them. *Years!*"

"And what did she say, this lady colonel?" Trudy leaned closer, pulling her hair to one side, then the other. Her heart hurt.

"Some Vietnamese farmer led a team of investigators to a remote crash site..." Jewel halted midsentence and bent over in the chair, crossing both arms over the back of her head, reminding Trudy of an airline passenger bracing for impact. After a few seconds, Jewel straightened, took a deep breath, her words choppy as she continued. "On the side of a hill in the middle of the jungle...near the place where they think your dad's plane went missing." She blinked up at Trudy in disbelief. "They found a few bone fragments along with some pieces of metal..." her voice trailed off.

Trudy's throat closed up. She couldn't breathe. Scrambling to the sink, she opened the window, poured a glass of tap water, and drank. Cool air rushed in from outside along with a memory...

One night while polishing his black flight boots, Daddy looked up when Trudy ambled into the master bedroom. He motioned for her to come closer. "I'm gonna tell you something I haven't told the others." He dipped the end of an old T-shirt wrapped around his finger and swirled it around in a tin of black paste. Applying the cloth to the toe of one boot, he worked in a circular motion. "I have orders to Vietnam. Since you're the oldest, I'm counting on you to help your mother and look after your brother and sister while I'm gone." *Vietnam*, that's all it took. Trudy had squeezed her eyes shut as if she could expel the word that had slipped through her ears. "No, Daddy, not Vietnam," her voice cracked before she turned and bolted straight for his open closet...to hide her face from him.

Her mother cleared her throat, drawing Trudy back to the present. "They'll run a DNA test and see if it matches the samples they collected from us years ago."

Trudy stared out the window, her vision blurry. "What about Daddy's backseater, Lieutenant Miller? Did the colonel say anything about him?"

"No, and I didn't ask. I wasn't thinking too clearly."

"Didn't you used to correspond with his mother? He was so young, I recall."

"For years," Jewel sighed. "Until she died of cancer...that poor woman left this world never knowing what happened to her son. Just like your Grandma Cutterbuck."

As Trudy went to set her glass in the sink, a sound from the other room caused her to jerk her head around — a sound of something soft crashing to the floor.

Her mother twisted in the big armchair. She'd heard it, too. "What was that?"

Particles of white powder swirled ghostlike through the narrow archway leading from the sunroom into the kitchen. Had a chunk of drywall detached itself from a board where Hector had been working, or was it something else?

Her mother bolted out of the chair, her fingers steepled under her chin. "Shep?" Her voice trilled in the silence that followed.

Teeth chattering, Trudy began to shiver, her gaze drawn to the red and yellow weaving she'd left hanging on the east wall a few weeks ago. Bogey's God's eye stared back at her, daring her to believe.

After a moment, her mother walked toward the archway. "Wouldn't that be just like your daddy, trying to send us a signal from the other side."

A knock at the side door sent Trudy's heart skittering. She whirled, half expecting to see a tall lanky fighter pilot jiggling his car keys in the air and grinning — wishful thinking — or a nightmare...Cousin Dub standing there, his face glistening and accusatory.

But it was Hector... back from lunch.

By late afternoon, everyone in the family, along with close friends, had been notified of the news. In a text to Georgia right after lunch, Trudy wrote: Now we wait.

Georgia replied: Sis, we've been waiting for 44 years. I'm not holding my breath. Mom sounded good when she called. A little hyped up though.

Aunt Star texted Trudy moments after Jewel's phone call with the news: For the sake of your momma, I hope the DNA matches. Jewel needs closure. Glad you're with her. Make sure she eats and gets some rest. Keep an eye on her blood pressure. Her cuff should be in the back bathroom or in her nightstand.

After Trudy took her mother's blood pressure, she reported the reading to her aunt: Momma's BP is 120/70. She's taking a nap. Hector brought her a pair of earplugs when he came back from lunch. He felt bad about all the noise.

No sooner had Trudy made a cup of hot tea and burrowed into the worn recliner when Aunt Star fired back: Glad her BP is normal. Mine's sky-high. I just saw on KOB News about some varmints painting swastikas at Gold's Department Store in Pardon. It's only going to get worse. I could use a set of earplugs myself every time the Orange Cheese Puff opens his trap.

Trudy sipped hot tea and typed to the roar and grind of power tools reverberating throughout the house: Anybody give you any lip over your upside-down flag?

Her aunt's quick comeback made Trudy chuckle: Nah, my fake shrunken heads are still on the porch rail from Halloween. Those bad boys should scare off any troublemakers.

A sweet message from Lupi followed: Trudy, your sister sent me a note on Facebook about the call your mom got. I'm thinking of y'all. Tell your mom the next time she stops by the diner, her meal is on the house. BTW, your parents' photos are hanging on my new Honor Wall. They add a little class to the joint. LOL.

You are so thoughtful, Trudy wrote back. I'll let Momma know. BTW, I saw your post on Facebook earlier but didn't comment. Georgia calls me a lurker. ;) I feel violated, too, on many levels. I keep thinking about my dad. What he would say about all this. I think he'd be one pissed-off fighter pilot.

A few minutes passed before Lupi responded: Thanks. And if the Russians are involved, well...Benny said it's time to organize like they did in the sixties. Later, got customers to feed.

And if the Russians are involved...

Trudy swayed to and fro in the rocker, recalling a phrase she hadn't thought about in years. *The Russians are Coming* used to put fear in her heart as a kid growing up during the Cold War. *Damn,* she thought, scanning over Lupi's text as she took another sip of tea. *What if they were already here!*

A text from Clay appeared on her mobile screen as she set down her cup. Hearing from him helped ease the anxiety roiling in her chest: Babe, I'll stop by when I get off work. Hope you don't mind, but I told Cinda about your mom's phone call. She said to tell you she's thinking of you.

Oh my, so Clay told his daughter. Trudy got the feeling Cinda had grown up hearing all about the pilot's daughter whose dad disappeared over the skies of Vietnam.

Pocketing her cellphone, she set her cup in the sink and moseyed down the hall to check on Hector. The tap-tap-tapping of an old-fashioned hammer echoed up the hall, a welcome relief from the racket of power tools.

"Sorry about all the dust," Hector said, glancing over his shoulder when she entered the room. Perched halfway up a ladder, he wielded a hammer and drove another nail into a small section of new drywall that formed the wide archway.

Clasping her hands under her chin, her eyes watered as she gazed around her brother's former bedroom. The walls and terracotta floor were bathed in a golden light that flooded in from the sunroom through the new archway. "It's heavenly," she told Hector.

"Glad you like it, but I can't take credit for the light. That's the sun doing its trick." His eyes swept over the space. "It reminds me of an interior courtyard. Just needs a few plants." He picked up a nail and hammered away.

With her hands still clasped in front of her, she breathed in the smell of new sheetrock and approached the archway. A seam in the floor still divided the original foundation from the one her dad poured for the sunroom. If Hector couldn't find matching tile, he said he would get creative. The light filled her with a sense of wonder, the way it shone from one space into another, even spilling behind her into the hallway.

A sense of peace enveloped her as she flung her arms wide and crossed from one room into the other. She took a few steps forward then twirled around and gaped through the new opening. "Daddy and Bogey," she whispered, her voice thick with emotion. "I'd like to think that somewhere out there beyond the horizon, you two guys have joined up."

Hector watched her from his stance on the ladder. His brown eyes softened as he lowered his hammer. "May I ask you a question about your dad?"

She walked back toward him. "Sure."

"Is his name on The Wall in D.C.? Even though...you know..." He glanced at the section he was working on then picked up another nail.

Stuffing her hands in her pockets, she regarded him. "Yeah, it's there all right, along with fifty-eight thousand others, give or take a few."

He started to lift his hammer. "So his status, then. He's no longer listed as MIA?"

"Um" — she paused and pursed her lips from side to side — "Officially? The Air Force declared him dead years ago. But since his body was never found, he remains missing in action in our family. That could all change though after today. We'll have to wait and see once they run the forensics."

Hector gave her a thoughtful nod and drove another nail into place.

She walked under the arch and crossed the room. At the doorway, she hesitated and glanced back at Hector. "I know this is just a job for you. But what you've done here today, joining these two rooms together..." She choked up. It took her a moment to regain her composure. "It means a lot to my mother. It's symbolic, you know." She offered a slight smile.

Shifting the hammer to his other hand, Hector sniffed and rubbed the tip of his nose with his thumb. "It's an honor to do this for your family. I'll be back tomorrow to texture the new section and repaint the walls."

She gulped back a lump in her throat and nodded. "Be careful, Hector, Momma may try to adopt you after today." He laughed and she turned and headed down the hall to peek in on her mother.

By six that evening, Hector had the whole archway framed and all the debris from the demolition cleaned up and carried off.

As Trudy went to show Hector out, Jewel rushed up and gave him a hug.

"I had a dream this afternoon while I was taking a nap," she volunteered, her voice croaky as she held him at arm's length. "Shep taxied his jet up to the back of the house, opened the cockpit canopy, and gave a big thumbs-up." Before Hector could respond, Jewel turned to Trudy. "Darling" — her blue eyes sparkled — "Bogey was sittin' in the backseat, grinning from ear to ear."

Trudy's vision was still cloudy long after Hector backed his big red truck out of the driveway and headed into town. After Jewel went to make dinner, Trudy meandered down the hallway to put some clean towels away in her mother's bathroom. Passing her dad's closet, she set the laundry basket down, and pulled open the door.

A whiff that was part musky, part musty greeted her. A row of forest green Nomex flight suits hung limp on hangers where they'd spent the last forty-plus years in limbo. After the Air Force returned her dad's personal effects, her mother slipped each flight suit onto a hanger with the belief that sooner or later Shep would return. Some of the flight suits still had salt stains under the armpits.

One flight suit stood out near the back: a red short-sleeved nonregulation number covered in colorful embroidery and un-official irreverent patches. The hangers skidded on the metal rod as Trudy quickly pushed the heavy uniforms out of the way to get to it. Daddy's party suit! All the combat pilots had one for special occasions. They were made out of lightweight material and pro-moted an *esprit de corps* among the pilots in a squadron. She reached for it and smiled as she read the nametag out loud on the chest pocket: *Clusterfuck*. Major Shep Cutterbuck's call sign amongst fellow fighter pilots when they were horsing around. She fingered the nametag before letting go of the party suit and plung-ing her arms deep inside the long sleeves of one of the regulation flight suits her dad wore on a regular basis.

"Major Dad to Ground Control," she called, flinging her head back and thinking of her mother's dream. "Can you hear me? It's Trudy."

The sound of loose change jingling in a pocket filled the air. There was no mistaking that sound: loose change jingling in a leg-pocket of a flight suit.

"Daddy?" She spun around.

Clay stood in the doorway in a charcoal gray suit, a blue dress shirt opened at the collar. His hands were stuffed in the pockets of his dress slacks, the source of that familiar jingle of coins she'd mistook for her dad's. "You okay?" He looked around. "I could've sworn I heard you talking to someone?"

She blinked at him a second, trying to clear her head. "I never heard the doorbell," she managed hoarsely.

Clay looked so handsome, but she stood frozen in place, mute, up to her elbows in green sleeves.

Clay glanced over his shoulder toward the hall then back at her. "I knocked in case your mom was resting. She let me in. She asked me to come back here and check on you." His eyes honed in on her forearms buried in the sleeves. He removed his hands from his pockets, letting his arms dangle at his sides.

Embarrassed, she bowed her head, unable to speak and released her arms and let the flight suit fall back in formation with the others.

"Trudy?" Clay's voice rustled around her, a gentle caress in her ears whenever he said her name.

Lifting her gaze, she watched him open his arms.

"Let me hold you," he said. She turned away from the closet and they walked toward each other.

As he encircled her in his arms, she hid her face in his chest. All her fears fell away as Clay rocked her in his arms and let her weep for her lost father, her baby brother, a daughter she only knew in her dreams, and for the four decades she'd spent running away from home. From everything that was sacred.

Then slowly, she lifted her chin to him and they bridged a forty-year gap with a kiss that sealed them together beyond anything physical.

CHAPTER 19
Eject! Eject! Eject!

MUFFLED VOICES and the clatter of cutlery faded into the background when Clay glanced up at the photo hanging above their booth at Lupi's. "Do you think your dad would've approved of me?"

Trudy held her mug halfway to her lips. Her focus shifted from Clay's handsome face to the photo of her dad, a smaller version of the one that hung in her mother's living room. It was Saturday morning, around ten-thirty, the day after Veterans Day. Clay had the day off, and they'd just finished brunch and were lingering over coffee. "Of course he would've approved of you. You two would've hit it off. Why do you even ask?"

Clay studied his hands before looking at her. "Don't get mad at me, okay?"

She set her mug down. "Uh-oh, here it comes." She scrunched her face in mock pain.

"That fancy doctor guy, your ex? Would your dad have liked him? I hear surgeons make a lot of money. A lot more than cops."

Not fair! She wilted under Clay's gaze. Her shoulders drooped as she stared across the booth at him. Her mind scrambled for a response. "My dad was never impressed with status. He would've seen right through him." She kneaded that spot between her eyes. "He doesn't matter anymore. He's ancient history."

Clay shrugged and took a sip of water, crunching the soft ice. "Is he? 'Cuz sometimes I get the feeling..." His voice went flat, but his question hung between them.

Was it that obvious? She'd been divorced fifteen years. Fifteen years trying to recover from an abusive relationship. Gulping, she refused to look at Clay and picked up her water glass and sipped from her straw and watched Lupi chatting with a tableful of customers.

He nudged her with his voice, keeping it low. "Trudy, it's me, your old friend, Clay. What did that guy do to you?"

His question shattered her confidence, the confidence she'd worked so hard to rebuild over the years. She felt exposed; unable to speak of the pain and humiliation she'd endured. Instead, she averted her eyes and breathed in the aroma of warm sopapillas, puffy fried pastries being delivered to a table a few feet away. A little boy in a booster seat clapped his chubby hands in anticipation as his mother filled the sweet treat with honey and passed it to him. The boy took his first bite and giggled as honey dribbled down his chin.

"Did he hurt you...physically, verbally, what?" Clay's question drew her back, and she glanced at him, unable to dodge the probing look in his eyes as he waited for her to reply.

"He screwed with my head," she blurted in a raspy whisper that gushed out of her like a cleansing wind. There, she'd finally admitted it. She'd never told anyone, not even her lawyer or the judge who presided over her divorce. Mostly she hid the truth from herself, because it was too painful to admit, especially since she'd stayed way past her expiration date.

But Clay didn't even budge. He'd probably heard everything in his job.

Biting the side of her mouth, she cupped her chin in one hand and sighed. "In the early days of our marriage, he treated me like a princess. But then, as time passed..." She stopped and reached across the table and gripped Clay's arm. "Please don't tell anyone, especially Momma. I don't want her to know."

His eyes narrowed on her. "It wasn't your fault. The way he treated you."

"I know, it's just that...well, I don't want to hear anyone tell me, 'I told you so.'" She let go of his arm and took another sip of water.

Clay shifted in his seat. He picked up his spoon, twirled it between his fingers. Then he set the spoon down and pushed his plate aside and glanced across the booth at her. "He the reason you lost the baby?"

Oh God! A furnace blasted through her system. Picking up her napkin, she dabbed her forehead. Finally, she looked at him. "I'll never know for sure. I don't like talkin' about it. All I know is I should've left him then. But I stayed on three more years, like an *idiot.*"

Clay chewed the inside of his mouth. His chest rose and fell as he regarded her across the table. "Sounds to me like you might have suffered from Stockholm syndrome. You ever heard of it?" There was no judgment in his voice.

Slowly, she nodded. "Yeah. Isn't that when a victim feels empathy for her captor?"

Clay lifted his glass and crunched the last flakes of ice. "Yes. I'm glad you got out in time before he did more damage."

The boulder sitting on top of her chest rolled away. She breathed easier. "Can I tell you something? I don't want you to think I'm weird."

"Babe, you can tell me anything you want." He gave her that lazy grin, the one she'd fallen for in high school.

She propped her elbows on the table. "One time right after nine/eleven when the world felt upside down, sorta like it does now, I'd just come home from a trip. As I went to pull in the garage, I heard my dad yelling, 'Eject! Eject! Eject!' I rushed inside and started packing. I only took what would fit in my car. Before I fled, I found an old prescription pad and left the doctor a note that said, 'Take two painkillers, and call your lawyer in the morning.'"

Clay scratched his temple then rubbed his chin. "So you're saying your dad came to warn you to get out?"

Trudy nodded and tilted her head and gazed up at her dad's photo. "I believe in my heart that he did. And another thing," she said, glancing back at Clay, "my ex hated it when I talked about my dad. He was jealous of his combat medals."

Clay frowned and shook his head and cracked his knuckles.

"That says it all right there. Any man who's jealous of a genuine war hero is no man at all. He's a coward."

Lupi bustled up with a coffeepot in her hand. "Who needs a refill?" Her eyes darted back and forth between them.

"None for me." Trudy smiled and held her palm out. "But you can bring me the check whenever you're ready."

"No way," Clay objected, wagging his finger.

Lupi propped her hand on one hip. "Listen, Detective. This is an equal opportunity zone. If the lady wants to pay for your meal, let her pay."

Clay laughed and threw his hands up in surrender. "Okay, okay. You're the boss around here. Nobody messes with you, Lupi."

"Damn straight," she nodded and grinned at Trudy. "You like the Honor Wall?" Setting the coffeepot down, she gestured to a collage of photos grouped under a banner that read, "Pardon's Best and Brightest."

Trudy scooted to the end of the booth to get a better look. Glancing sideways, she scanned past the photo of her dad by his jet and one of her mother being crowned Miss Pardon New Mexico. Directly beneath the banner, the formal portrait of the diner's founder, Guadalupe Belen, hung front and center. Her dark hair coiled in a beehive from the sixties, she could've been Lupi's twin, not her grandmother. Trudy's gaze swept past other local dignitaries, including Mayor Benny Trujillo standing behind a podium, some judge cloaked in a black robe, gavel in hand. A framed yellowed newspaper clipping captured the moment Mr. Milton Gold cut the ribbon at the grand opening of his department store. She paused at the photo of a soldier with serious dark eyes, his green Army uniform contrasted against the red, white, and blue of an American flag. "Who's that on the end?"

Lupi's eyes softened. "Aw, my cousin's son, Ruben Sandoval. He was killed in Iraq right after the invasion. He was only nineteen."

"I'm sorry," Trudy offered, sad for a young man she never met.

Lupi picked up the coffeepot and turned to leave. "I'll be right back with your check. You two behave while I'm gone."

Trudy called after her, "How come your photo's not on the wall? Didn't you graduate magna cum laude from Harvard?"

"Yale," Lupi answered and kept moving across the diner, a woman on a mission with a business to run, a woman who for all her tough talk put others first.

A teenaged girl clad in an apron snaked around the tables and began clearing the booth next to them. Crockery and silverware clanged together as the busgirl dumped everything into a gray tub. Clay excused himself to visit the men's room while Trudy rooted through her purse for breath mints and her credit card.

When Lupi returned with the check, she whispered to Trudy, "How's it going with Clay?"

Trudy bit her bottom lip and smiled. "So far so good. Taking things slow. We're definitely not in high school anymore."

Lupi looked around. "You should've seen his face light up the day I told him you were back in town."

Beaming, Trudy went to pass Lupi her credit card when Clay walked up and stood with one hand crossed over the other right below his belt buckle. Being in his presence made her feel euphoric. The plan was for them to head back to his place and check on Hercules, maybe watch a movie, and hopefully pick up where they left off the other night.

Lupi took the credit card and turned to Clay. "Any more on the culprits who vandalized Gold's Department Store?"

He pressed his lips and shook his head. "Nah, but we'll find 'em. Someone will get to braggin' and someone else will squeal."

"Any chance it's linked to the recent vandalism at the cemetery?" Lupi turned to Trudy. "Remember when that photo ran in the paper? You and your mom were here that day. We talked about it."

Rattled, Trudy's heart yo-yoed, but she kept her voice even. "Didn't Mayor Trujillo think it was kids?" Even as she planted the diversion, she pictured the lady from the Lexus spray-painting *rapist* on Dub's grave. Sometimes, like now — when she was with Clay — she wished she'd never witnessed it. One more burden to carry...another burden to cover up.

Fingering his upper lip, Clay cut in. "Benny's probably right.

What happened at Gold's Department Store...well, given the history of the place and the founder, it feels more sinister than some bored teenaged punks looking for trouble. Rumor is it's some hate group out of West Texas. Possibly the same one that hung effigies after President Obama was elected."

After Lupi rang up their order and returned Trudy's credit card, she said, "We all need to stay vigilant."

On their way out the door, Trudy observed the diverse clientele — a mixed race couple with two little kids, two young people with tattoos and piercings, an older gentleman in overalls cleaning his fingernails with a toothpick...probably an old railroader.

This is a safe zone, she thought, waving goodbye as Lupi stopped to chat with an attractive young woman in a hijab who'd slipped in unnoticed and seated herself at the far corner of the counter.

Out on the sidewalk, Trudy stopped to fasten her cardigan and read the hand-painted sign that had been on the front of the small stucco building as long as she could remember: *Eat At Lupi's Diner: Authentic Mexican Food*. The temperature hovered in the low forties. The snow that fell last week had melted the second it hit the ground. Rain was in the forecast along with the first hard freeze.

"Burr, it's getting cold out." Clay zipped up his jacket and they held hands and strolled toward the Tahoe parked in the gravel lot next door to the diner. Lupi owned that lot, too. As Clay went to grab the door handle, Trudy's phone buzzed.

She reached into her purse and glanced at the screen. "It's Momma." She looked up. "I can let it go to voicemail...?"

He glanced around and held the door open. "She's either checking on you or something's wrong. Better answer."

Trudy pressed the phone to her ear. "Hey, Momma, everything okay? Clay and I are just leaving Lupi's."

Her mother sounded out of breath. "Sorry to bother you, darling, but there's a wild animal bedded down at the base of the flagpole. It's been there all morning since you and Clay left to go to breakfast."

"Hang on. Let me put you on speaker." She pressed the display and held out the phone. "Describe the animal, Momma." Trudy glanced at Clay who stood patiently waiting, a toothpick lodged between his teeth.

"It looks like a coyote. I'm wonderin' if it's injured. I don't see any blood, but it's been curled up at the base of the flagpole and hasn't moved. Right in the spot where my jonquils come up every spring."

Clay took the phone and motioned for Trudy to climb in. "Miss Jewel, are you inside the house?"

"I'm standing at the living room window. I was looking at my rock collection."

Trudy clicked her seatbelt and pictured her mother doddering in front of the windowsill, picking up each rock and reminiscing about all the places she'd visited in her lifetime.

"Stay put. We're on our way." Clay passed the phone back to Trudy.

"What about Hercules?" Trudy asked as Clay fired up the Tahoe and pulled out of the gravel parking lot and headed west on Seven Mile Road.

"Little Man will be fine. You can slip him some extra treats when you see him." He laughed and shot her a wink and gnawed on the toothpick.

Leaning against the headrest, she gazed at him, wishing she could tell him everything: everything dating back to the night in the kitchen when she saved her sister's life.

CHAPTER 20

Coyote Yellow

THE MUD-COLORED house with the long front porch came into view. Clay flicked the left turn signal and tapped his foot on the brake. Gravel crunched beneath the Tahoe's tires as they pulled into the driveway and came to a halt behind the minivan and Camaro parked under the carport.

Trudy's heart sputtered at the look of worry etched on her mother's face as she peered out the picture window, her fingers pressed to her lips. "She's probably been standing there all morning."

How many times had her mother stood in that same position, waiting for her and Georgia to come home from a school event or date? Or the times as a young pilot's wife when she waited for her hero, Shep, to fly over the house and rock his wings before touching down on the runway southwest of their home?

"I'll say one thing about Momma," Trudy observed as her mother disappeared from the window. "She never stops worrying or waiting!"

Clay shoved the gearshift into park and cut the engine. "That's some coyote all right." He chuckled and grabbed the keys. "The only thing that dog has in common with a coyote is his ancestry."

"And his coloring," she countered. "It's coyote yellow." She whipped out her phone and sent her mother a text: It's a dog, not a wild animal.

Two pointy ears twitched when her mother cracked opened the blue door and poked her head out, tugging at her knit cap.

The creature was curled near the base of the flagpole, a couple of feet from the spotlight.

Clay stashed his sunglasses on the dashboard and got out. "Approach with caution. We don't know if it's injured."

On the drive out, he'd entertained Trudy with stories from his early days as a street cop when he occasionally got stuck with animal control duties. On one call to the rich part of town, a resident complained a skunk was floating in her swimming pool. When the woman answered her door, her face slathered in cold cream, she found a police officer in uniform staring back. Keeping a straight face, Clay held up his badge and announced grimly, "Skunk Patrol. Where's the suspect?"

Laughing, Trudy had gazed at Clay all the way to the house, mesmerized by his aura. If bucket seats and a console didn't keep them apart, she'd have slid over and put her head on his shoulder like old times.

Now, not taking her focus off the dog, she unfastened her seatbelt and climbed out and followed Clay. They crept forward, hoping the stray wouldn't get spooked and run off. A pair of amber eyes locked in on her, following her every move. She'd read somewhere to never make eye contact with a strange dog, but the look in this dog's eyes wasn't caution or a warning to stay back. The look was utter exhaustion. A look that conveyed: I'm worn out from traveling. I need a safe place to rest and someone to love me.

"Be careful," Jewel's shrill tone pierced the cold air from the porch where she had barricaded herself behind the storm door.

This wasn't the first time a stray dog had appeared in their lives...

Trudy bit back the bitter memory of the skinny brown dog that had wandered into their yard a few weeks after Bogey died. Panting, the dog with pitiful eyes appeared out of nowhere, its patchy fur barely covering its ribcage. Trudy and Georgia begged Momma to let them keep it, but Momma started cursing and carrying on, calling the dog *a flea-bitten rabid mongrel*. When Trudy smarted back, "You're the one foaming at the mouth, maybe *you've* got rabies," Momma backhanded her and picked up a broom and chased the dog out of the yard and up onto the highway and smack-dab into the grille of an oncoming semi. That little brown dog went flying, broken and bloody, and Momma crying for God to take her, too. The next day, Aunt Star called in sick and took Momma to the doctor. That's the last time Trudy and Georgia saw her until she came home from the hospital months later, weeks after Dub's funeral.

"Don't go crazy on us this time, Momma," Trudy mumbled loud enough for Clay to hear. He knew about the tragedy involving the brown dog. It's one of the first things Trudy confessed to him when they started dating in high school. Back then, Trudy told him everything, everything but the night in the kitchen when she took Dub down with a single whack to the head.

"We'll split off and give it a wide berth." Clay gestured with his right hand, dropping it to his side. "Don't go at it head on."

"Lieutenant Cordova, the doggy whisperer," she teased, letting Clay be the expert. *Men, they think they know everything,* Trudy could hear Aunt Star snap.

As they drew closer, the dog lifted its head, panting in Trudy's direction. "It's okay, we're here to help you." She talked to the dog in the same soothing voice she used on nervous passengers. The dog began to whimper and whine, sounding like Skylar when she'd wanted Trudy's attention.

With a knot in her throat, Trudy took another step and continued to talk in soft tones. The dog rolled over on its left side, acting submissive, exposing its pale underbelly. Trudy caught her breath at the sight of an old scar where the right foreleg had been amputated at the elbow. "She's missing a limb, poor baby."

Clay moved in for a closer inspection, brushing up against Trudy. "Looks like it hasn't slowed her down though. She got this far on three legs." He pointed to a spot on her lower abdomen. "And she's spayed, too. This tells me she had a good home at some point in her life."

Against her mother's pleas to be careful — "it might have fleas or rabies" — Trudy dropped to her knees and began to stroke the dog's head, then her chest and belly. "Is anyone looking for you or worried sick 'cuz you're missing?"

Clay knelt beside Trudy. "I can check with dispatch to see if they've had any calls. We can also call the shelter."

Jewel let the storm door click behind her as she stepped to the edge of the porch. "My guess is someone passing through dumped her on the side of the road and kept going. Maybe they loved her once then considered her a liability. She's probably thirsty. You want me to fetch some water?"

Trudy glanced up. "That'd be great, Momma. I found our old plastic cereal bowls still in the cupboard. One of those should work."

"Don't fill it all the way," Clay said over his shoulder. "We don't know the last time she ate or drank. Best to introduce water slowly, then food. We don't want to shock her system."

Jewel pulled the storm door open to step inside. "Good point, Clay. That's what they did when the POWs came home. They put 'em on a limited diet before they served them a feast. A feast Shep Cutterbuck never got to enjoy." The storm door banged behind her.

Trudy and Clay exchanged glances and turned their attention back to the dog. She was filthy, the pads of her paws rough and worn. "Looks like you've been travelin', haven't you, girl?" At the sound of Trudy's voice, the dog let out a weary sigh.

Jewel returned with a faded plastic bowl and set it on the ground next to the dog. Slowly, the dog scrambled to its feet and lapped some water then circled and bedded back down and rested its head on Trudy's foot.

Stroking the dog's fur, Trudy gazed up at the flags swirling in the breeze. The red Zia sun symbol in the center of the yellow cloth captured her attention. In the back of her mind, she remembered Bogey looking up from his encyclopedia where he'd been reading about the New Mexico state flag, explaining how the rays on the sun motif represented the four directions: north, south, east, and west.

"Which direction did you come from?" Trudy said, shifting her eyes from the flag to the dog.

Clay's voice whistled around her. "Maybe she's a gift from the plains."

The dog blinked, and Trudy turned to Clay and her mother.

"She needs a name, even if her time here with us is brief." Relaying Bogey's findings about the flag, Trudy said, "How 'bout Zia, since she's yellow like the sun in the sky and we don't know which direction she came from?"

"She's probably starving for affection." Clay massaged the back of Trudy's neck. "She'll most likely respond to anything."

For a second, Trudy couldn't help but think of her mother. All those years Jewel had gone on alone, without her beloved Shep by her side to share life's joys and sorrows.

Both flags snapped in the breeze, and Trudy's gaze traveled up the pole to the POW/MIA flag. "Zia. Zia Mia." The dog's head snapped up and she looked straight at Trudy and stuck out her lone front paw.

"Well how 'bout that?" Clay elbowed Trudy in the side. "Looks like you're the doggy whisperer now."

Trudy turned to catch the flirtatious glint in his eyes. She felt her bottom lip curl in response.

Jewel craned her neck skyward. "It's supposed to rain later this afternoon. Could turn to sleet. I know she's filthy, but I can't stand the thought of her freezing to death."

Trudy stared at her mom. *Are you the same woman who chased a stray into oncoming traffic?* "How 'bout the carport?" she suggested. "We can make her a shelter and she can bed down there."

Jewel flicked her wrist, dismissing the idea. "We might as well bring her into the house. I'll grab some old quilts and make a pallet in the kitchen. What's a little dog hair and dirt when we've been living with construction dust?" She stepped inside and closed the blue door.

Leaning down, Trudy patted the top of Zia's head. "Well, wonders never cease around here. Come on, girl. You heard the woman. Let's go inside." Straightening, Trudy turned and stretched. She took a few steps and waited.

Zia trotted along, stopping once to squat and pee. Clay brought up the rear, following Trudy and Zia around the corner, under the carport, and through the side door.

Jewel dropped a stack of quilts in Clay's arms. "Here, you do the honors." She turned to Trudy. "There's some leftover chicken and rice from last night. It's not spicy. That should work until you take her to the vet or shelter or whatever you two kids are scheming up."

Zia sat on her haunches, licked her lips, and let out a yelp.

"Don't look at *me*," Jewel stuck her hands on her hips, trying to act tough. "I'm not the sucker here. *She* is." Jewel jutted her chin at her daughter, and Zia slowly turned her head and stared at Trudy.

Trudy chuckled. "Maybe so, Momma. But who's the one barking orders?"

Jewel crossed her arms and eyed the dog. "Let's hope you're housebroken."

"She's not a puppy, Momma."

Clay bent and spread the quilts next to the refrigerator. Trudy poked him in the side and whispered, "Sorry she's being so bossy. I think it's a defense mechanism."

Retrieving the leftovers, Trudy cut a small chicken breast into chunks and spooned it over white rice. She zapped it in the microwave a few seconds to take the chill off.

When she turned to set the bowl down, she realized she and Clay were the only ones in the kitchen. "Where'd they go?"

Clay grinned and gestured toward the sunroom. "Your mom's giving her the grand tour."

Trudy's jaw dropped. "Zia followed her? Momma never acted this way around Skylar. She always kept her distance."

"Maybe she's trying to make up for what happened to that other dog." Clay brushed a strand of hair from her eyes and kissed the top of her head.

Moments later, Jewel and Zia emerged from the hallway. "I was showing her around. She had to stop and sniff every baseboard."

While Clay coaxed Zia onto the pallet, Trudy let Zia nibble a few pieces of chicken from her fingers. Zia smacked her lips and whimpered for more.

Jewel clasped her hands under her chin. "Gracious me, she's a polite eater. I'd be woofing it down. She's probably been living on ranch scraps and chicken feed."

Trudy set the bowl on the floor and Zia dived in, gobbling each morsel until the bowl was empty. She continued to lick the bowl, pushing it around the kitchen floor.

Tossing her arms in the air, Jewel chuckled, "Guess I spoke too soon."

"We'll let this settle on her tummy before we give her anymore." Trudy picked up the bowl and set it in the sink. While her mother made goo-goo eyes at the dog, doting on it and patting its head, Trudy whipped out her phone and snapped a photo and sent it to Georgia and Aunt Star before her mother could object.

Within seconds, Trudy's phone pinged with a text from Aunt Star: Merciful Lord! Did a bolt of lightning strike Sister on the head? Joking aside, we know what happened last time a stray wandered onto her property.

You mean that innocent brown dog or the perv? Trudy refrained from texting back.

Her phone pinged again, this time with a text from Georgia: Is Mom going to let you keep it? LOL! Seriously, I still think about that poor dog we named Brownie.

Leaning against the counter, Trudy thumbed the keys on her screen as the memory played in her mind: Remember how we buried him in that unmarked grave at the edge of our property?

Georgia replied: Yeah, that trucker was so nice. After he hit Brownie he stopped to help.

Trudy wrote back: He held onto Momma and kept her from running onto the highway and becoming the next casualty. You ran in the house and called Aunt Star at work.

After a couple more texts back and forth, Trudy pocketed her phone and went to join Clay and Zia on the floor.

Jewel's cellphone rang where she'd left it sitting on the red desk. She ambled over, took one look at her screen, and sighed into the phone, "Yes, Star. There's a big yellow dog in my house. Looks like *somebody* spilled the beans." She narrowed her eyes at Trudy and disappeared through the archway, her phone pressed to her ear instead of on speaker.

"Your mom okay?" Clay twisted his head around after Jewel was out of earshot.

Trudy shrugged and stroked the dog. "She's probably pissed 'cuz I told her sister."

"Why would she be pissed?"

"'Cuz that's one more thing Aunt Star can needle her about."

They stopped talking when Jewel reentered the room and set her phone down. Gripping the edge of the counter with both hands, she stood at the sink and looked out the window. "I told your Aunt Star, apparently Zia's a survivor like the rest of us."

"Don't be mad at me, Momma."

Her mother let out a weary sigh but didn't turn around. "Oh, honey. I'm not mad at you. I'm mad at *myself.*"

Trudy pushed her hair back and studied the way her mother stood rigid as if she was working up the courage to say something else.

Abruptly, her mother swiveled and faced her. "I'm sorry about what happened to that brown dog." She scratched her eyebrow and pursed her lips. "Those were rough times back then."

"It's okay, Momma," Trudy said, pretending it didn't hurt. Pretending the cushion of time healed all wounds. Gripping Clay's shoulder, she struggled stiffly to her feet and went to hug her mother. "I'm glad that trucker stopped to help. He was a nice man."

Her mother's eyes watered. "He sent me a Christmas card one year with a photo of a POW/MIA bumper sticker on the back of his rig. I wrote him back and thanked him for saving my life, from keeping me from doing something selfish and stupid."

Trudy gulped, seeing the pain in her mother's expression. This was the first time her mother had opened up and talked about her nervous breakdown, and right in front of Clay. No code words this time like *go away*, no talking around it or covering it up. It's like it took that phone call from the Air Force to give her permission to let go...a little bit at a time.

Clay stood and zipped up his jacket. "Ladies, I'm fixin' to run into town to check on Hercules. You want me to stop by the pet store and grab a small bag of dog food? A little something to tide her over for now?"

Trudy plopped down on the edge of the pallet and rubbed the

dog behind her ears. "Do you mind picking up a red collar and..." She stopped herself, realizing she was rushing things.

Clay sucked his teeth a second. "You want me to get a nametag? Have her name engraved? Just in case?"

Trudy started to get up. "Let me give you some money."

"You can pay me back later." He waggled his brows and she blushed to her bones, picking up on his insinuation. If her mother hadn't called about the dog, interrupting their date, they'd probably be back at Clay's snuggling in front of a warm fire. And yet, Trudy felt a sense of relief. Except for a few tender kisses and cuddling since she'd been home, they hadn't been intimate since high school. He'd never seen her fully nude, without a stitch of anything on except jewelry and makeup. She'd been with other men since her divorce, but like she'd admitted to Clay at breakfast, her ex let her know she wasn't young anymore.

Early that morning, she'd agonized over whether to pack an overnight bag. Instead, she stashed a travel-sized bag of toiletries into her purse along with lip gloss, mascara, and clean underwear. After that first visit with Clay, she'd started to apply her weekly doses of estrogen cream again, because like her female gynecologist once said, "Sometimes girls our age need help in the lubrication department."

"Miss Jewel," Clay addressed her mother. "How would you like to ride into town with me? It's a good excuse for you to see more of Hector's handiwork. And as an added bonus, you can meet Hercules." He squeezed Trudy's shoulder. "Okay with you, boss?"

Trudy reached for his hand, squeezing him back. How did he know she needed time alone with the dog? Time to get to know Zia, time to admit it was okay to move on. To love another dog as much as she'd loved Skylar, even if it was only for a couple of days. "Momma, I think it's a marvelous idea. I'll stay here with Zia and keep her company."

Hesitating, Jewel pulled her cap off and raked her elegant fingers through her tufts of hair. She glanced at the turquoise phone. "I don't know, I..."

Her look conveyed to Trudy: what if the Air Force calls with news while I'm out?

"Momma, you gave them your cellphone number, remember? And I checked your answering machine in the bedroom. It's working fine, so..."

Jewel looked at her cap, then at Clay. "I suppose Trudy's right. It was only four days ago...oh, why not? First let me run and slap on some lipstick. I'll be right back."

After she left the room, Clay went to the sink to wash his hands. As Trudy lounged next to Zia on the floor, she looked up in time to catch Clay standing in front of the framed photograph of her mother being crowned Miss Eastern New Mexico. The image was imprinted on Trudy's brain, along with her mother's maiden name, *Jewel Hurn*, splashed in bold script at the bottom of the photo. Drying his hands on a paper towel, Clay lingered there in deep thought. She thought she heard him utter a faint "Huh?" before he turned to toss the crumpled paper towel in the trash.

With a spring in her step and her ruby beret perched at a jaunty angle, Jewel breezed into the kitchen and grabbed her purse off the red desk. "Well, Detective. Shall we?"

Clay extended his arm. "You're lookin' spiffy, Jewel *Hurn*." He winked at Trudy. "Don't worry, Gertrude. I'll keep *Miss Eastern New Mexico* out of trouble and bring her back before curfew."

Jewel patted Clay on the arm and they headed out the carport door. It was the first time she'd left the house in days.

After Trudy heard the door close, she let out a huge sigh. Her heart pumped wildly as she wondered if Clay had seen a photograph of Dub's vandalized grave *before* the editors cropped it for public viewing in the *Pardon Gazette*? For surely the police report contained an image of the entire tombstone showing the deceased person's full name: Manifred "Dub" Hurn II.

First Momma prodding Clay for information the other night at dinner and now Lupi this morning at breakfast. Was Clay putting two and two together? God, she hoped not.

As she snuggled up next to Zia, she said a silent prayer: Please, Clay. For once, don't ask too many questions.

Late that night, long after Clay had gone home and Trudy had taken Zia out back to potty, she locked up the house, checked on her mom, then got Zia settled on her pallet in the kitchen. The storm blew in right before midnight, moments after Trudy had crawled into bed and texted Clay goodnight. Before she turned out her bedside lamp, she scrolled through her phone, looking at photos of missing dogs sent in by their owners and posted on area shelter websites.

Several yellow dogs were listed, but none were missing a limb.

Outside Trudy's window, the wind howled as rain pelted the glass. It sounded like boards and nails groaning, being pulled apart from the ruins of an old tree house in the Cottonwood next to the house. Or were those small animals caught in nature's wrath? As the storm raged on, Trudy heard a whimper coming from the hallway. Looking up from her phone, she watched Zia barrel through the bedroom door, jump onto Trudy's bed, and burrow her face under the blankets.

Trudy couldn't help but laugh. She set her phone on the nightstand and turned off the light. Despite the fact Zia hadn't had a bath, and Trudy barely knew her, she opened her heart to this stranger and couldn't kick her out.

Rolling on her side, Trudy tried to reassure her. She peeled back the covers and was greeted by hot doggy breath. "So you think you can just nose your way in here and hunker down without permission? You don't care what any of us look like, how young or old we are, rich or poor, what titles come before or after our names...you want to be loved. I get it, girl. Goodnight."

Zia yawned and let out a contented sigh.

Trudy nuzzled her face in Zia's fur. She smelled of brittle tumbleweeds and rain.

As the two of them began to nod off, Clay's voice brushed through Trudy's thoughts: *Maybe she's a gift from the plains.*

CHAPTER 21

Secret Agent

SPORTING A new red collar and a set of tags, Zia loped along the fence line in the backyard, stopping occasionally to paw at the earth with her left front foot. The rain had finally stopped late Monday afternoon, and by Tuesday morning, water still stood in places. Rivulets ran through silty patches of yellow prairie grass, all that was left of Shep Cutterbuck's oasis.

Huddled in her nubby cardigan, Trudy perched on a plastered bench and inhaled the cold air and watched Zia play. Yesterday, she and Momma loaded Zia in the minivan and drove through the rain to see Dr. Chung, the same vet Clay entrusted Hercules to. Dr. Chung had examined Zia nose to tail, inspected her for heartworm and other ailments, and remarked she was in pretty good shape for a stray with three legs. While a young vet tech ran a scanner over Zia's body and determined she didn't have an embedded microchip, another tech called around to other local vets and shelters in the area to see if anyone had reported a missing dog fitting Zia's description. After an extensive search by telephone and internet, the tech popped her head back in the exam room while Dr. Chung was giving Zia a round of vaccinations, and announced, "Looks like she's all yours. No one's reported her missing."

"You okay with that, Momma?" Trudy asked with a half smile.

Jutting her chin at the dog, Jewel said, "First stop's the beauty shop. Not me, *her*. Guess we'll use that groomer Clay told us about. This one's on me."

Nose to the ground, Zia sniffed her way toward the vintage travel trailer, its flat tires melted into rims that formed puddles of rubber in the ground now turned to muck. The summer before Daddy went to war, he bought the 1965 white Shasta camper from another pilot in the squadron. With Daddy playing airline pilot, he hitched the camper to the back of Momma's station wagon and the family headed west. Crossing deserts and mountains, they gawked at giant redwoods and ran screaming into the Pacific Ocean before it slapped them back to shore, leaving them breathless and running back for more. When they returned, Daddy parked it behind the carport and it rarely left except for a few times when Aunt Star and a friend borrowed it to go camping, but mostly it stayed put, serving as a glorified clubhouse on wheels.

As Zia explored the ground around the camper, Trudy rose from the bench to stretch. Bending over, she touched her toes then slowly flattened her palms against the patio and held it for twenty seconds. Georgia's advice from a chat long ago chimed in Trudy's head: "If we can touch our toes, Sis, we can stave off old age a little longer."

"I'm touching my piggy toes," Trudy groaned, counting to twenty before she pulled up from the stretch and looked around for Zia.

The dream that woke her at sunrise returned. As she walked to the edge of the patio to keep an eye on the dog, the dream reeled through her mind like an old memory. Wanting to capture it in writing, to help her make sense of it, she pulled out her smartphone, opened the notes app, and began thumbing the keys on her screen:

Alone on the shoulder of a steep mountain road, I stood in the bend of a hairpin curve and searched the deep canyon below. All I could see for miles were large boulders dotted with prickly pear cactus and the occasional glint of metal from some long ago wreck.

Then from somewhere behind me, the sound of children singing, "Ninety-nine Bottles of Beer on the Wall" echoed through the mountain pass. Whipping my head around, I watched Momma's station wagon careen around the curve in the road and sail over the side of the mountain. But instead of crashing into the canyon below, the station wagon sprouted wings and rode the thermals across a tranquil sky.

As the sound of children's voices faded and I longed to join them, a passenger door flung open and Bogey tumbled out. From my spot on the road, I thrust giant arms skyward, for I was the big sister, and it was my job to catch him. But no matter how far I stretched, I couldn't reach him, for my arms weren't long enough. When I woke up, my eyes leaked with tears, and Zia stared at me from her spot on the bed where she rested her chin on my belly.

After pressing *done*, Trudy looked up from her notes and blurted into the cold air, "It's not my fault, Daddy. I followed your orders. I tried to protect him, but that ugly little tumor was bigger than all of us. Even the 'gods' in white coats couldn't save him."

Stunned by the words that tumbled from her mouth, she breathed deeply and tried to jettison the guilt.

Zia's sharp yelp pierced the cold morning air. Stuffing her phone in her pocket, Trudy dashed off the patio. "What is it, girl? What's got you so riled up?" Sidestepping mud holes, Trudy picked her way to the back of the camper where Zia pawed frantically at something near the left rear tire.

"Hope that's not a prairie dog town you're bothering." Trudy bent this way and that, trying to get a closer look.

Using her front paw and snout, Zia dug at something in the ground. A few seconds later, she swung her head around, proudly showing off a mud-caked object clenched in her teeth. Before Zia could dart off with her prize, Trudy tried to pry it from her jaws. "Drop it, girl. Let me have it, please." Her tone was firm, but polite.

Zia shook her head as if to say, "No. It's mine. I found it."

"Drop it," Trudy commanded again, and this time the dog unclamped her jaws and the object fell into Trudy's right hand. Using her thumb, she brushed away some of the grime. A sense of foreboding stirred in her chest, and suddenly it hurt to breathe. "What were these doing under the camper?" She stared at a pair of men's eyeglasses, or what was left of them.

Zia whimpered and pranced about as if she half expected her mistress to return the treasure.

Mud sucked at the soles of Trudy's sneakers as she squished

her way back across the yard. "Daddy's galoshes would've come in handy about now," Trudy said as Zia trotted beside her. "Kinda wish I would've kept 'em."

Tracking mud across the patio, Trudy plunked down on a plastered bench and turned the glasses over in her hand. "Daddy had perfect vision. He wore aviator-style sunglasses, and these aren't sunglasses."

Zia stood in front of her, slowly wagging her tail. Her left hand free of grime, Trudy caressed the dog's face and cooed, "Since you're my secret agent, be a good girl and tell me who these belonged to."

Swiping her tongue across her lips, Zia sat back on her haunches and dangled her front paw in front of Trudy.

"Oh, you wanna shake on it first, huh?" Trudy stuck out her left hand and shook Zia's paw. Then Zia yawned and rested her paw on Trudy's knee and stared up at her with an expectant look in her eyes, reminding Trudy of Skylar.

The sound of metal clanging against metal echoed from the front of the house. Even out back, Trudy could hear the flags snap in the breeze. As she brushed dirt from Zia's nose, Trudy asked her, "Where did you come from, girl?" But all Zia did was blink.

Twisting around on the bench, Trudy stood and peered out beyond the railroad tracks to the southwest. She couldn't see the old runway from her mother's backyard, but it was out there less than two miles away. Out beyond a concertina wire fence that separated government property from civilian land, a fence that might have a hole big enough for a stray dog or coyote to pass through. As Trudy reached for the top of Zia's fuzzy head, she looked down and said, "Was that *you* stalking me on the edge of the runway a few weeks ago?"

Zia whimpered and let out a heavy sigh that sounded more like a snort.

"I'll take that as a yes. Come on, girl. I'm glad you found me. Let's go inside."

As they approached the sunroom's French doors, Trudy looked back one more time toward the old base before she kicked off her sneakers and told Zia, "Stay put. I'll be right back."

On stocking feet, Trudy padded through the sunroom into the kitchen and grabbed a hand towel. Setting the mud-caked eyeglasses in the sink, she went to wipe Zia's feet.

Back in the kitchen a few minutes later, Zia lapped water then Trudy gave her a treat. At the sink, she turned on the tap and gently washed the mud from the gold metal frames. One lens was missing, the other cracked, but the frames were intact, although a bit corroded.

Placing the frames on a paper towel, she pulled out her phone, snapped a photo, then trudged over and sat down in the armchair and stared at the eyeglasses drying on her lap. Water dripped from Zia's chin as she swung her head around and made a beeline across the room. Placing her chin on Trudy's knee, she closed her eyes and let out a wheezy sigh, her interest in the eyeglasses forgotten.

Picking up the frames, a sense of foreboding returned. Then a primal fear charged through her so fast, she hit the back of the chair like she'd been electrocuted. Dropping the glasses in her lap as if they posed a physical threat, she gripped the chair's sturdy arms as the air whooshed out of her lungs. Zia whined and backed up a few steps, tilting her head this way and that. Swallowing hard, Trudy glared at the eyeglasses and remembered bits and pieces, part of her memory as fractured as the cracked lens.

Dub's gold spectacles fly through the air as he crumples to the floor with a thud. His legs writhe a few seconds then stop. Hours pass. Woozy from Aunt Star's magic drink, Trudy stumbles up the hallway from the bedroom she shares with her sister. Georgia is conked out. At the entrance to the kitchen, Trudy stops when she sees Aunt Star all red-faced and gasping for breath. Bending over, her aunt picks something up off the floor and stashes it in a pocket of her uniform, now ripped at the seam under her right armpit. As she bundles up in a parka, she sees Trudy swaying there by a kitchen chair. Her finger to her lips, Aunt Star whispers hoarsely, "Go back to bed, Lovey. You have school tomorrow." As Trudy turns and walks sideways down the hall, she hears her aunt open the side door to go out. Cold air gushes in, and the smell of snow follows Trudy as she staggers back to bed.

Zia nudged Trudy on the knee. She blinked, stunned by the memory. Pulling out her phone, she sent her sister a text: Was the p wearing his glasses when we dragged him out the door?

Within seconds Georgia replied: I don't remember. I think I squeezed my eyes shut and tried not to look.

Trudy sent her the photo she'd taken moments ago, with the caption: Look what my secret agent dug up under the camper.

Your secret agent? Oh, you mean Zia? Holy crap, sis! You think those were his? What were they doing under the camper?

That's what I'd like to know. Trudy's thumbs flew over the screen: Maybe Aunt Star found them later and went outside to give them back, but he'd already left so — *she buried them under the camper to hide evidence he'd been here. But the thought was too horrifying to voice to her sister.*

OMG, what if the perv was blind as a bat without glasses? Maybe that's why he stumbled onto the tracks.

Combined with a concussion and no telling how much booze was in his system. FYI, I'm sending the photo to Aunt Star.

She may get defensive. Don't say I didn't warn you. Must run. I'm teaching three classes this afternoon.

Trudy glanced at Zia. "Well, here goes." After clicking the photo, she added: Look what Zia found buried under the camper. You know anything about this? As soon as she sent the text, she deleted the photo from her camera.

A rap at the side door startled her. *Would she ever stop jumping every time someone knocked at the door that led to the carport?* Her hackles up, Zia growled and raced to the door and barked at the silhouette that loomed on the other side of the sheer fabric panel covering the door's upper window.

Scrambling to her feet, Trudy skidded across the kitchen in her socks and peeked out. Hector stood a couple of feet back, waving a measuring tape in his right hand. Seeing his friendly face quelled some of the anxiety roiling within her since discovering the eyeglasses.

She shushed Zia. "Calm down, girlfriend. It's Hector. He's our friend." Hooking one finger through Zia's collar, Trudy opened the door. "Hope you like dogs."

Hector grinned. "Clay told me about her." He bent to scratch Zia behind her ears. "I'm a dog lover myself. Got three big rescues at home." He glanced over his shoulder at the empty spot where the minivan usually sat. "Guess your mom's not around by any chance? I was out this way on another job. Figured I'd drop by and get some measurements for the kitchen redo."

Trudy tried to ignore the slogan emblazoned on his red T-shirt that stretched across his compact chest: Make America Great Again. *Good grief, Hector, too?* "Um, she drove into town to take a friend to the doctor. She should be home soon. You're welcome to come in."

Trudy stepped aside to let him pass.

Hector gave a polite nod and entered the house. "It won't take long."

"Take all the time you need. Zia and I are hanging out. By the way, Clay took Momma by his house the other day. She was impressed with your work. She couldn't get over the photos y'all took of the house before you gutted it."

Hector looked around, sizing up the kitchen. "Glad she approved. I'm surprised Hercules behaved. Last time I stopped by there, he tried to block me from entering. He thinks he's ferocious. I almost stepped on him, trying to get in the door."

Trudy laughed. "The secret, Hector, is to ply him with treats."

Hector stood with his hands on his hips, gazing from corner to corner. "I'll remember that next time." He pointed at the ceiling. "Your mom okay with me installing new lighting? I'm thinking two or three pendant lights over the new island." He turned to look at her.

"Hector, I'm pretty sure Momma will love whatever you do." His overbite was adorable, his workmanship topnotch. He'd served his country as a Marine and rescued dogs, and yet she couldn't get past the words on his T-shirt.

Until this election, she'd never dreamed of talking politics. But the outcome had suddenly emboldened her. And she came right out and asked him, "Hector, why do you support him?" She gestured at the slogan.

Patting his chest, Hector glanced down as if he'd forgotten what shirt he'd slipped over his head that morning before work. "Look, I'm not a big fan of everything that comes out of his mouth, but..."

Incredulous, she interrupted him. "Hector, I don't mean to sound rude, but I don't understand. You're a Latino, and yet you voted for a guy who calls Mexicans rapists and drug traffickers!"

Hector froze. His overbite disappeared behind pursed lips. He gazed at the measuring tape in his hands. "I voted for him because he is a businessman and not a politician. He says he's going to fix Washington and bring back jobs." Hector pivoted and began measuring the cabinets, jotting down numbers with a stubby pencil in a mini spiral notebook.

Trudy pulled open the refrigerator and grabbed a bottle of water. "My mom says she hasn't seen this kind of division since the Civil Rights Movement." She set the bottle of water on the counter and called to Zia. "C'mon, girl. We better leave Hector alone before he kicks us out."

As she and Zia meandered into the sunroom, Trudy gazed at the brilliant light that spilled through the new archway into the other room. Jewel had taken Hector's advice and adorned the space with clay pots overflowing with leafy plants. Trudy's gaze shifted to a slim row of Mexican tiles with bright swirls and geometric patterns inlaid in the seam created where the wall came down.

Curling up at the end of the Naugahyde couch, she called out, "Hector, you're a *genius. You* should run for president." Zia jumped up beside her and plopped her head on Trudy's lap. Now that Zia had been to the groomers, Momma said she was allowed on the furniture.

Hector appeared in the narrow archway, the measuring tape clenched in his right fist, his ankles crossed and his shoulder braced against the wall. Crisscrossing his arms, he hooked his hands under each armpit, leaving his thumbs exposed. "That'd mean I'd have to wear a suit and tie to work." He gestured to the mosaic design on the floor beneath the new arch. "You like it? I tried to match the new tiles to the ones your dad installed on the kitchen counters. They're not an exact match, but I liked the idea of continuing the theme into other areas of your mom's house."

Hector's attention to detail and his thoughtfulness touched her deeply. Her heart overflowed with respect and a deep admiration for this hardworking man who acknowledged and honored her father by keeping his memory alive in tile. Yet she still couldn't fathom how a man like Hector — a military veteran who served his country in an age when there wasn't a draft — could support a man who dodged the draft five times and hid out during the Vietnam War...the war that took her father's life. But she also had to acknowledge that a person's values couldn't always be measured by a few words silkscreened on a T-shirt, no matter how offensive she or anyone else might find it.

Her voice quivered when she spoke. "Hector...my dad would be so honored by your work. He loved this house. He poured his soul into it."

Nodding thoughtfully, Hector uncrossed his arms and feet and turned. "My cousin, he carried a torch for you for years." He cocked his brow and pointed with the measuring tape. "But you did not hear that from me."

She smiled, her face growing hot. "What was his ex-wife like? Cinda's mom?"

Hector blew out a puff of air, his lips flapping together like a horse. "A gringo like you. Pretty, but a real prude. And she didn't like me one iota."

"How so?"

"'Cuz I rode Harleys and drank beer and told her to piss up a rope."

Trudy chuckled. "Why did you tell her that?"

"'Cuz I defended my cousin when his daughter came out and said she was a lesbian."

CHAPTER 22

Dancing with a Three-legged Dog

HOURS AFTER Zia uncovered the spectacles, Aunt Star still hadn't replied to Trudy's text. Alarmed by her aunt's silence, Trudy knelt in front of her parents' vintage console stereo and tried to stay busy. A sofa pillow cushioned her knees from the unforgiving tile. "Does this thing still work?" she asked, trying to keep irritation from creeping into her voice. Moments earlier, she'd removed a Navajo blanket of bright geometric designs draped across the low-slung cabinet, exposing the top for the first time in years.

Nearby, Jewel rifled through a box of photographs propped on the coffee table. She eyed Trudy over the rim of her reading glasses. "The needle broke years ago, and I think one of the speakers is busted." She picked up a photo, studied it, and then tossed it aside.

"Crud. I was hoping we could listen to some old tunes while we work. I remember how you and Daddy always cranked up the stereo anytime you had friends over."

Jewel tilted her head thoughtfully. "Sometimes we danced, too. Long into the night after you kids were in bed and all the guests had left."

The longing in her mother's voice tugged at Trudy. "Momma, you want me to find a repairman in town who might be able to fix it?"

Her mother stared at something in the distance then shook her head. "You and your sister can fight over it after I'm gone. Sell it to a collector or one of those pickers like you see on TV."

Lifting the lid, Trudy inhaled the fumes of old wood and neglected electronic equipment. Her nose dripped and she reached into her pocket for a tissue. Pinching it to her nose, she stared at the needle on the record player docked in the armrest. A vinyl record covered in a fine layer of dust sat motionless on the center spindle. "Momma, there's a record left on here."

Jewel blinked in Trudy's direction. "Really? What is it?"

Gently, Trudy lifted the record from the spindle and held it up to read: "It's 'Whipped Cream and Other Delights' by Herb Alpert and the Tijuana Brass." After all these years, she could still picture the sexy girl on the avocado green cover: the doe-eyed brunette with a dollop of whipped cream atop her head, licking the tip of her finger. Her bare shoulders and the swell of cleavage partially smeared in white cream gave the illusion of nudity without revealing too much.

The weariness in Jewel's eyes faded. Clasping her hands, she walked over to see for herself. "Shep and I practically wore that album out."

Sorting through old photos had left Jewel on edge. Maybe seeing the iconic album cover would lift her mother's spirits and take Trudy's mind off Zia's disturbing find buried under the camper. "Here, hold this a sec." Trudy passed her the record.

As Jewel balanced the disc in her fingers like it was made of gold, Trudy slid a cabinet door open in the console and flipped through dozens of LPs in their original jackets. Her fingers filed past The Mamas & The Papas, The Beatles, The Doors, Joan Baez, Billie Holiday...

And suddenly there she was, the girl covered in whipped cream. Trudy pulled the jacket from the rack. Using the console for support, she pushed herself up from the floor. "Makes you wonder what fans enjoyed more: listening to the music or eyeing the cover."

"It was scandalous when it first came out," Jewel hooted, looking on. "I imagine lots of good Christians hid it when the preacher made house calls."

Trudy chuckled and slipped the record inside the jacket. Flipping it over, she scanned down the list of songs. "I remember most of these. Georgia and I used to listen to them over and over. We'd bop around, pretending we were on American Bandstand."

They took turns reading some of the titles out loud:

"'Taste of Honey.'"

"'Tangerine.'"

"'Whipped Cream.'"

When Trudy got to "Love Potion No. 9," she shimmied her shoulders and did a mock striptease.

Her mother laughed, cupping the side of her face in one hand. "His music's so upbeat and happy. I could use a dose of that right now." She turned her attention back to the box of photos.

Trudy set the album on the coffee table and reached for her smartphone. Searching the internet, she found the familiar list, made sure the volume was on high. Right before she hit *play*, she grinned coyly at her mother. "Hey, Momma, here's 'A Taste of Honey.'"

As the sound of Latin guitars and smooth brassy trumpets and trombones filled the room, Zia peeked around the corner.

"Come here, girl," Trudy called, dancing clumsily in place to the saucy south-of-the-border music that wouldn't let her sit still. Jewel sat on the edge of the sofa, tapping her feet and swaying her shoulders.

Zia trotted into the room, her tail wagging like a metronome. Without hesitation, she reared up on her hind legs, resting her lone front paw on Trudy's chest.

"Look, Momma, she wants to dance." As Trudy reached for Zia's front paw, her two *left feet* and Zia's rear legs synchronized in a herky-jerky slow dance.

"Can you grab my phone and take a picture so I can send it to Georgia?"

Jewel hoisted herself off the sofa, fumbled with Trudy's phone, and snapped a couple of photos. "Tell her we've got a three-legged dancer in the family," Jewel said, setting down the phone.

After dancing with Zia, Trudy eased the dog's front paw back onto the floor. Picking up her phone, she texted her sister a photo, checked for any new messages from Aunt Star — there were none — and then searched for another Herb Alpert tune.

At the first brassy notes of "The Lonely Bull," Trudy bowed ceremoniously and pretended to be a matador dressed in a fancy costume before a cheering crowd — anything to take her mind off those spectacles hidden out back.

Clapping, Jewel said, "Play another one," when the song ended.

"Sure thing, Momma." Trudy scanned the list. "Oh, I think I remember this one from *The Dating Game*."

The flirty jazzy melody of "Whipped Cream" prompted Trudy and her mother to strut. They paraded around the living room between the coffee table and sofa. Jewel twirled an imaginary baton and Trudy marched behind her playing air trumpet. Zia nosed her way between them, tail wagging, wanting to join in.

When the music stopped, Jewel plopped onto the couch, winded. "That was fun. I should do that more often. Keep the sludge moving through my veins."

As Trudy began to search the playlist for a slower song, her mother held up a photo for Trudy's inspection. "Looky here, it's you and Preston."

Preston! Trudy stiffened at the sound of his name. *How could two syllables represent so much disgust?*

She set her phone down and glared at the statuesque bride in the photo, a young woman of thirty in bare shoulders and lace, posed next to a tuxedoed groom a few years her senior but reeking of the spoils of success.

"Who's that *ridiculous* couple?" She made a face and crossed her two index fingers in front of her as if she could block the image. "They scare me."

Jewel gazed at the photo. "I'll say one thing. Preston threw a helluva party. He wouldn't let me spend a dime, and there I was the mother of the bride."

Trudy cocked her head and rolled her eyes. "Momma, the reason he paid for everything was so he could show me off to all his highfalutin' friends."

Jewel pursed her lips. "Well, could you blame him?" She glanced at the photo, and then stuck her tongue out. "Your daddy and I made pretty babies."

"Momma, I hardly recognize that stupid girl. I squandered my identity when I married him, and it took me years to dig out of that rut. I'd like to think I'm a lot smarter now."

Jewel tapped her finger on the photo. "You weren't stupid, just *impressionable*."

Trudy bowed her head, hiding a half smile. "I burned my wedding photos years ago. You should pitch it."

"Or I could snip *him* out of the picture," Jewel suggested. She scissored two fingers over Preston's profile and snapped them together when she got to his crotch. "Ouch. Guess Lupi's rubbing off on me."

Trudy chuckled at her mother's warped sense of humor.

"I read in some magazine recently where he's been operating on wounded warriors," Jewel continued. "Doing facial reconstructions."

Breathing through her nose, Trudy gazed out the picture window. "Yeah, it's challenging to hate him when you read stuff like that. At least he has *some* redeeming qualities."

Jewel sniffed. "He never liked coming here. He always inspected his fork and knife before eating."

"Don't take it personally, Momma. The man had a few idiosyncrasies."

"Your Aunt Star never liked him. She called him *persnickety*. We all tried to warn you, but you kept telling us how he made you feel like a millions bucks."

"He did at first. And I ignored every...red...flag."

Jewel was silent a moment. "He tried to isolate you from us, you know that, right?"

Trudy scratched her nose. "I'm sorry I put y'all through that hell."

"Did he ever lay a hand on you?"

Heat surged through her body. She snatched up the album cover off the coffee table and fanned herself. *Oh, Momma! There are so many different ways to get manhandled.*

While Trudy searched for a way to explain, Zia let out a loud yawn and scrambled to her feet and left the room. Trudy's gaze followed her until she disappeared around a corner.

It would be easier to follow Zia into the other room and not have to face her mother's probing questions.

How could she explain to her mother — or anyone for that matter — how Preston began to *operate* on her when she reached her mid-thirties? It started so subtly, those sweet nothings in her ear. She'd be standing in front of a mirror getting dressed or stepping out of the pool when he'd come up behind her and run his hands along the contours of her body. He'd start with her eyes and work his way down. At first she found his behavior arousing. But over time his whispers turned into "a little nip here, a little tuck there. That's all it'll take to keep you fresh and looking like a ten."

And that's when she realized he'd been *sculpting her* with his hands.

Finally, she gestured at the bride and groom in the photo. "Preston wanted me to go under the knife. He had all these plans to keep me looking as young as that *impressionable* girl in the photo."

Jewel shuddered. "Knowing him, he wanted to use you as his *practice* dummy."

Trudy flinched. She didn't know whether to laugh or be insulted by her mother's comment. "The more I resisted his scalpel, the more resentful he became. It's like he couldn't quite forgive me for aging."

"But Trudy, you're dodging my question. Did he ever hit you?"

The more her mother pushed, the faster Trudy fanned herself with the album. Clay's question rolled through her mind: *What did that guy do to you?* It was one thing to admit it to Clay, but for some reason, she felt a need to protect her mother from the truth.

"Momma, for the record, mostly I put up with mental and verbal abuse. Let's say sometimes it takes longer for those scars to heal. He put down my job, my friends. Every time I came home from a trip, he questioned my every move. He said the only reason I kept flying was to screw all the crewmembers.

"When my biological clock started ticking, I told Preston I wanted a baby. Every time I brought up the subject, he tried to convince me that a child would interfere with our lifestyle. He even joked, 'I'm raising you. What do I need with a baby?' So when I turned thirty-five, I'd had enough. But instead of divorcing him like I should have, I stopped taking my birth control pills and quit smoking. The day I told him I was pregnant that last time, he pleaded with me to get an abortion."

"He was probably hoping you'd miscarry — like the other times," Jewel said quietly.

Something inside of her broke free. "Momma, the night I went into labor, he was pissed that I'd interrupted his cocktail and paperwork. I'll never forget how he clenched his jaw when he looked up at me as I stood in the doorway of his study, doubled over in pain. I was in the middle of a contraction and needed to get to the hospital."

Jewel rubbed the side of her neck. "Did he drink every night?"

Trudy shook her head, irritated at the interruption. Still fanning herself, she began to pace the length of the living room. "Only when he wasn't on call or scheduled for surgery the next day. He was extremely regimented."

She pinched the bridge of her nose as that awful night tumbled through her mind. "Preston stared straight through me like he had two glass eyes. When he finally rose and came around his desk, he walked right past me like he was in a daze. Out in the entryway, he picked up my overnight bag — you'd think it weighed a ton — and headed for the garage. Before he disappeared around the corner, he said, 'Meet me out front.'"

"Out front?" Jewel growled. "You mean he left you standing there...?"

Trudy swallowed the knot at the back of her throat. "It was already dark and the security lights were on by the time I got to the front door. I was halfway down the steps when he pulled the Hummer around and rushed to help. It's like it finally dawned on him that I was going to have a baby. As I went to navigate the second to last step, my knees buckled and my legs went out from under me."

She closed her eyes, trying to shield herself from the horror registering in her mother's soft blue eyes. She could hear her mother swallow as if her throat was constricted.

In a voice thick with pain, Jewel asked, "Darling, are you saying you fell? Or did Preston trip you?"

Trudy's eyes fluttered open. Her chest squeezed as she gazed at her mother and shrugged. "I'll never know for sure, Momma. He claims he tried to catch me." She paused and blew out a lungful of air. "But he said I was too *cumbersome*."

"Cum-ber-some?" Her mother scowled and repeated the word like she'd bitten into something sour.

"I gained *seventy* pounds," Trudy explained. She didn't mention all the times he called her *a fat cow* or the time he changed all the locks while she was on a trip.

"And you lost every ounce of it and more," her mother countered, sitting up straighter.

Biting the side of her mouth, Trudy continued, "After he helped me into the Hummer, he cursed all the way to the hospital. By the time we pulled into the ER, he was calm, cool, and collected. The celebrated *Dr. Vanderwell* once again. They wheeled me right into delivery...but the baby was already in distress..." She broke off, continuing to fan her face.

Her mother gazed at her. "And all this time I thought the complications stemmed from you giving birth later in life."

Trudy clutched the record album against her chest. "There was nothing wrong with the baby until I went down."

Her mother sat in stunned silence. After a long pause, Trudy mentioned seeing the two girls in pink coats playing in front of the mansion a few weeks ago.

Jewel's whole body went rigid. Her eyes watered as she began to crumple the wedding photo back and forth in both hands like she was forming a meatball. The sound of crinkled paper filled the room. Her voice trembled when she spoke. "My darling girl" — she shook her fist in the air and tossed the balled-up photo across the room — "if I ever see Preston Vanderwell again, I'll knock his teeth out."

Trudy retrieved the photo and tossed it in the trash. "Then he'll be the one needing cosmetic surgery."

~

Stepping out onto the front porch a short time later, Trudy beat the Navajo blanket against the side of the house. She held her breath as decades of dust flew through the cold air, along with Aunt Star's silence and thoughts of Preston. Back in the house, she stashed the Herb Alpert album with the other LPs and closed the lid to the stereo. As she smoothed the Indian blanket in place over the console, she heard Zia lapping water from her dish.

"That's a *happy* sound," her mother remarked, gesturing toward the kitchen. "When you get a chance, can you play us another Herb Alpert tune? Something snappy."

"Something *snappy*, huh?" Scanning her smartphone, Trudy grinned when she came to a title she hadn't thought about in years. "Hey, Momma, remember this jingle from the TV commercial?"

Trudy hit the *play* button.

"The Teaberry Shuffle," Jewel chortled as she did a jig about the room as if she were eight and not approaching eighty. "What I'd give for a stick of that gum about now."

Zia trotted into the room, water dribbling from her chin. Once again, she leapt upward, her front paw reaching for Trudy.

"You're my secret agent, aren't you, girl?" Trudy whispered as she and Zia began to shuffle this way and that. When Trudy glanced into Zia's face, she was greeted by hot doggy breath and a mouthful of teeth. "Look, Momma. Zia's smilin'."

Jewel leaned against the recliner, catching her breath. "That's my *granddogger*." Her eyes twinkled and her smile concealed any disappointment that her two daughters had failed to give her grandchildren to spoil. "Darling, don't take this the wrong way," she shouted over the din of music, "but after talking about *you know who* earlier, I'm so glad you took your maiden name back. *Trudy Vanderwell* always sounded a bit pretentious to me — sometimes you flitted around like a girl puttin' on airs."

Trudy's jaw dropped. "So, you're saying I acted like a fake?"

Her mother gave her an exaggerated nod and rubbed at something on the back of the chair. "Sorta like the time you got your first training bra and stuffed it with dime store falsies. Remember?"

Trudy flung her head back and snorted. "Of course I remember, Momma. You told half the family."

Her mother chuckled and pushed away from the recliner. "Only your Aunt Star. Okay, well, maybe your Grandma Lily, too, but she was pretty much deaf by then."

Shaking her head, Trudy rolled her eyes and regarded Zia's canine grin, how her mouth sprung open exposing a wedge of pink tongue and teeth. "Oh, so you think it's funny, too, huh, girl?"

Jewel made a beeline for the hallway. "I better run to the potty before I pee my pants." She turned and glanced over her shoulder at the last second. "Oh, honey, you were so afraid you wouldn't grow boobies."

Boobies! The word hung in the air long after her mother left the room. Her mind whirling, she gazed into Zia's trusting eyes and remembered. She'd been so naïve back then, so impatient for puberty. Once it hit, she'd learned that a trim but curvy figure could take a young woman far in life, but it could also bring unwanted advances.

Her first lesson had been that fateful night in nineteen seventy-four: *Whew-wee, show me your titties...*

It continued when she began flying. When Trudy was a new hire, one tipsy male passenger thought it was his God-given right to slap her behind every time she passed by his aisle seat. He'd wink and whisper, "Nice buns and melons, hon." Unlike Aunt Star, who'd been too afraid to report Dub's assault, Trudy worked up the courage to notify the captain. When the plane landed, a ramp supervisor and a security guard met them at the gate and Trudy identified the passenger. As the guy was hauled off in handcuffs, he snarled at Trudy, "Bitch! You're asking for it in that skimpy uniform."

Aunt Star was right about one thing, Trudy thought, *they'll try to blame it on us. They always do.*

Swaying to the beat of the music, Trudy banished the sting of the man's insult from her memory. She concentrated on the feel of Zia's left paw resting in her right hand. "I bet you had to fend off your share of doggy dicks, huh, girl?"

Zia smacked her lips and snapped her jaws together as if she were speaking.

"I'll take that as a *yes*, girl. It's exhausting, isn't it?"

When the song ended, Zia collapsed on the floor, panting. Trudy's phone pinged with a new text. She snatched it up, not knowing if it was from Aunt Star or her sister: Looks like Miss Zia won the dance contest! ;) A girl after my own heart. Give her a kiss from her Aunt Georgia. I can't wait to meet her. On other matters, I sent Aunt Star a text and told her to contact you. Said it was urgent. Ref a certain pair of men's eyeglasses.

Later, after Trudy took Zia out back to potty, Aunt Star finally returned her text. As Trudy scanned over the message, she stumbled toward the low plaster wall and plunked down on one of the *bancos*. Bending over her phone, she tried to slow her breathing, but with each word, her heart pumped faster in her chest: Come to Las Vegas this weekend. We're long overdue for some girl talk. As much as I'd love to see that handsome boyfriend of yours again after all these years, best to come alone. You've heard the old saying: What happens in Las Vegas stays in Las Vegas. That applies here. ;) You know I'd do anything for you and your sister. I've always tried to watch over you girls. Please dispose of the eyeglasses pronto! No need to worry your momma about this while she's waiting to hear back from the Air Force.

Trudy closed her eyes, Dub's eyeglasses tucked safely in the pocket of her cardigan. Instead of throwing them away, she would ignore her aunt's request. Sometimes the victors of a battle kept war trophies.

CHAPTER 23

The Dating Game

BEFORE SHE left the house the next evening to drive into town, Trudy bent down and cupped Zia's face in her hands. "I'm going to spend time with Clay, the nice man who helped rescue you."

Zia blinked, thumping her tail wildly.

Trudy giggled. "I'm glad you approve, now listen. I need you to help me be brave. It's been a long time since I've been on *this* kind of date with a man. You know, we might get *nakey*."

The dog tilted her head and gave Trudy a thoughtful look. Then she licked her lips, sat on her haunches, and stuck out her front paw.

Trudy flattened her palm against Zia's rough pads; her claws still nubs from her homeless days roaming the plains. "Your travelin' days are over, aren't they, girl?" Glancing at the gash where Zia's right leg had been, Trudy reached down and gently inspected the area. "Despite missing a limb, you've sure learned to compensate. Be a good girl and keep Momma company. I'll be back in the morning."

Kissing the top of Zia's head, she turned to leave when Jewel entered the kitchen and cleared her throat. "Darling, I take it you're spending the night?"

Trudy bit her lip. "I'll be back in time to take Zia out for her morning ritual and feed her breakfast."

Her mother reached for the edge of the counter and picked up a copper watering can. "No need to rush. I'm quite capable of taking care of her. After all, I raised three children, much of that time on my own while your father was away on Air Force business." Turning on the tap, she filled the can with water and called to Zia, "Come on, girl. Let's go water plants. Trudy has a hot date."

Right before Jewel disappeared through the archway, she turned. "Don't forget I'm meeting Hector this weekend to pick out appliances. You're welcome to join us."

Trudy twisted the doorknob and glanced over her shoulder. "Momma, about that. I'm going to see Aunt Star and Georgia this weekend. I know it's last minute, but..."

Jewel's mouth sprung open. "Oh." Trudy could tell her mother was trying to hide her disappointment that she hadn't been invited. She scratched at something in her ear and looked down at the dog. "Are you taking Zia?"

"I was hoping you would watch her. If it's not too much trouble."

Holding the watering can by the handle, Jewel balanced it in her other palm and turned to leave. "Trouble? Are you kidding me? I love having Zia here. She's like having another person to talk to."

Trudy called to Zia, "Come here, girl." She knelt down and gave her one last hug and whispered in her ear, "Don't go digging up any more buried treasures while I'm gone."

Alone in Clay's master bath, Trudy gazed at herself in the mirror. Her hair tumbled luxuriously past her bare shoulders, thanks to conditioner for mature hair and a blow dryer on low heat. Turning this way and that way, she decided she was in good shape for a woman her age. She had all four limbs, her own set of teeth, and good health.

Smiling coyly, she picked up her cellphone, scrolled quickly through her playlist, and pressed Herb Alpert's "Lollipops and Roses," the saucy tune that played on *The Dating Game* at the end of the show when the bachelor and bachelorette finally met face to face.

Heat fired through her loins as she strutted out of the bathroom and saw Clay waiting for her on the bed, the sheets pulled back exposing his brown chest and arms. Trudy recognized he was no longer her high school sweetheart, but a full-grown man. Earlier, she'd found a vile of Viagra left out on the countertop, possibly Clay's subtle message that he was no longer as young as he used to be. A bottle of personal lubricant sat on the nightstand. He'd thought of everything.

"That's some birthday suit you're wearing." He tossed his head back and grinned at her playfulness, at the instant recognition of a popular tune they'd grown up with.

Trudy had never felt so sexy, so free in her own skin.

Sashaying across the room, adorned in nothing but light makeup and coral nail polish, she tossed her phone onto the bed and stood before him, biting the tip of her finger like the girl on the cover of *Whipped Cream*. Clay's eyes filled with wonder as he held out his arm for her to join him. She twirled and fell laughing into his arms as the song ended.

They took their time, no longer rushed, two lovers no longer worried about being caught. Finding pleasure in each other's arms, they joined together as one.

Later, as they snuggled and talked, Trudy felt content in his arms, the rhythm of his heartbeat reassuring as she played with the silvery hairs on his chest.

Clay shifted on his side, propping up on one elbow. "Got a question for you."

Spent from lovemaking, she didn't even flinch. "What's that, Detective?" She yawned, feeling lazy and satiated.

"Wanna go steady?" He looped his fingers through hers. "Like when we were kids?" His question was so endearing, his expression tender.

Her head on the pillow, she gazed up at him. "You better clear it with Hercules first. Doesn't he have a say in the matter?" She gestured toward the living room where they'd left Hercules propped on his pillow, keeping guard.

Clay chuckled. "Little Man approves, trust me." He waggled his brows. "Why don't we get the dogs together this weekend? Make sure they get along."

She hadn't told him yet that she was going out of town.

"Clay" — she hesitated — "I'm going to visit Aunt Star and Georgia. Momma said she'd watch Zia for me."

Clay didn't say anything for a second. "Do you want me to come with you? I can get my neighbor to look after Hercules."

She searched his face, seeing his goodness. He was everything she'd hungered for. Handsome, sexy, steady...and yet, if she let her guard down too soon...

"It's a girls' weekend," she purred, "but I promise to be back Sunday night. Maybe I can stop by here first before I head to Momma's. If it's not too late."

He rolled on his back and pulled her on top of him. "Little Man and I'll be waiting."

They left the house the next morning before dawn, the temperature hovering in the low thirties. Hercules curled up on Trudy's lap as the Tahoe sped east on Curry Avenue. At the New Mexico state line, Clay pulled over and went inside a convenience store and returned with two coffees, bananas, and granola bars. "Figured you'd wanna eat healthy."

She smiled at his thoughtfulness, at the way he tried to please her without going overboard. He was easy to be with, said he liked seeing her without makeup, her hair pulled in a high ponytail.

Hercules yapped and scrambled out of her lap and jumped into the backseat. He circled a few times to get comfortable. Clay swung the Tahoe left instead of driving through a wide railroad crossing. They motored north a short distance and pulled over at a picnic table under a large sycamore tree. Clay put the Tahoe in park and let the engine idle so the heater could run. They sipped coffee, munched breakfast, and watched the sun come up over the horizon.

"I used to come here sometimes to reflect, especially after I got divorced." Clay gestured with his chin toward the east, across vast fields of winter wheat and other crops still hidden under the cover of darkness. "Sometimes I'd end up going running. Not much traffic out on these farm-to-market roads."

"But why this particular spot?" Trudy took a bite of granola, savoring the chocolate chips and oats. "Look around, all you see is Texas."

"Yup, as far as the eye can see."

The Chihuahua snored softly from the backseat.

Hector's words drifted through her mind. *My cousin, he carried a torch for you for years.*

An airliner headed west, its lights blinking high above the earth. Trudy leaned forward, pointing it out to Clay. "Have you ever seen Eastern New Mexico from thirty thousand feet? It looks like a patchwork quilt of circles and squares."

Clay smiled. "You get circles when farmers use center pivot irrigation."

"Aw, so that's how those are formed. And here I thought it was because farmers drove around in circles when they plowed their fields." They both laughed and she continued, "I finally taught Momma how to track my flights on the internet. I'd give her my flight number and she could follow the little jet icon on her computer screen. About the time my plane flew over the state line, she'd run outside and look. I'd call her after I landed and half the time she'd say, "Darling, did you see me wave my dishtowel?""

Clay chuckled and took a sip of coffee and leaned his head against the back of the seat. "I used to think of you every time an airliner flew over. One time when Cinda was about eight, she said to me, 'Papa, how come you always look to the sky?' I told her, 'Somewhere up there is a girl I once knew.' She got all serious and asked, 'Did she die?' And I said, 'No, baby, she's a stewardess.'"

Trudy stopped chewing and tried to swallow the last bite of her granola bar. Tears welled up and she looked away, not wanting Clay to see her cry.

"And then Cinda said, 'Is she the girl in the prom picture you keep in the shoebox in your closet?' And I said, 'Yes, she was my first girlfriend.' And Cinda said, 'Papa, Mom's jealous of her.' And I laughed and said, 'Are you?' Cinda rolled her eyes and said, 'No, Papa. I want to meet her.'"

Trudy laughed through her tears but it came out a snort. "Cinda sounds like an old soul. I hope I get to meet her one day."

"Me, too," Clay added softly, his fingers tapping the steering wheel.

Trudy gazed at his profile a moment. She wanted to tell him that every time she flew over Pardon, she tried to get to a window and look for certain landmarks like Main Street and Seven Mile Road. If she had time, she'd follow the highway leading west past Momma's house to the air base and the runways running north and south and east and west before being called back to check on her passengers. But after hearing Clay's story, she wanted to sit there quietly with him, and drink in the sunrise.

"I'm thinking about retiring next year." His voice broke the silence. He stared out the windshield, sipping his coffee.

She picked up the other banana and peeled back the top. "What will you do? Police work has been your life." She took a nibble, but her heart quickened.

The sun rose higher on the horizon, the fields bathed in gold and pinks. A flock of Canadian geese honked overhead and landed in the field in front of them.

"Well, that depends." He continued to sip his coffee. "On where things stand with us."

A sharp yip came from the backseat. Hercules jumped onto the console between them, his big round eyes staring straight ahead as if he wanted to watch the sunrise, too.

Trudy twisted in her seat. "I'd say it's looking good so far." Her gaze drifted past two pointy ears to Clay's dreamy eyes, twinkling back at her with a mixture of love and mirth.

Maybe once he retired, she would tell him everything. But until she met with Aunt Star, all she had to go on were a few hunches, a fuzzy memory, and a pair of eyeglasses hidden in the back of her trunk.

Clay reached for his phone. "I'm not a big fan of selfies, but I promised Cinda I'd get a photo of us together. You okay with that?"

Trudy objected: "But, Clay, I don't have any makeup on and..."

"Neither do I," he teased.

She leaned into him, the sides of their heads touching as Clay held the phone at arm's length and said, "Cheese."

Right when Clay went to snap the photo, Hercules popped his head up and posed.

CHAPTER 24

An Old Activist

Las Vegas, New Mexico
Friday, November 18, 2016

THE PINK adobe with the American flag hanging upside down from the front porch eaves filled Trudy with a mixture of pride and dread. For Aunt Star to flip the flag in front of her charming bungalow in a gentrified neighborhood of Victorian mansions, storybook cottages, and small Italian villas meant one thing: she was furious at the outcome of the election.

If Aunt Star gave a hoot what her neighbors thought about the inverted flag, she didn't act like it. In a pair of knit slacks and thick-soled shoes, she stood at the top of the porch steps and waved her cane in the air like an extension of her arm while she waited for Trudy to get out of the car. A row of fake shrunken heads left over from Halloween grinned ghoulishly from the top of the porch rails. Mr. Grumples, Aunt Star's fat tabby tomcat, perched on one end of the rail, swishing his fluffy tail as if he ruled the neighborhood.

Taking a deep breath, Trudy exhaled, pushed opened the door, and climbed out. Flashing her brightest smile, she slung her purse over her shoulder and greeted her mother's only sibling. "Afternoon, Aunt Star. I see you sent the welcoming committee." She gestured toward the porch. "You plan on leaving them out through Christmas?"

Aunt Star shrugged, her once strong shoulders rounded with

age under her thick sweater. "You mean the heads? Shoot, why not? Their eyes glow red and green when you plug them in." Her soft features broke into an impish grin. Although Star was two years older than Jewel, her plump cheeks and neck appeared less wrinkled than her younger sister's.

Trudy laughed and mounted the steps. Where her mother was slender, Aunt Star was big boned. As Trudy hugged her, she found her aunt's extra layers of padding reassuring, such a contrast to her mother's bony frame. "Those heads are pretty ghastly," Trudy said, stepping back. "Do they scare off trick-or-treaters?"

"Nah, I still ran out of candy this year."

"Knowing you, that's 'cuz you dole out the good stuff."

Aunt Star gripped the foam handle of her cane in both hands. "Personally, I find those fake heads a lot more attractive than the bumbling bully we're subjected to every time you turn on the TV. Come inside. Mr. Grumples and I will show you around. It's been eons since you were here."

The cat hopped off the rail and brushed against Trudy's ankle. She bent down and rubbed his soft head and furry neck. He greeted her with a loud purr.

"Mr. Grumples can't stand him either," Aunt Star said, raising her chin toward the flag and tapping her cane against the porch floor for emphasis. "He took great offense when he heard that fool bragging on TV about grabbing women's lady parts. Mr. Grumples is a feminist, you know."

At that, Aunt Star opened the door and the cat darted inside.

As Trudy glanced back at the flag, Aunt Star said, "That's some fancy sports car you've got there. Let's take it when we go meet your sister for our private tour of the Castaneda."

They both turned to gaze at the silver Camaro sitting in the narrow driveway, the front grille splattered with bugs from Trudy's three-hour road trip. "It's fun to drive. It has a lot of get-up-and-go."

"Shep would approve, no doubt about it." Aunt Star's words lingered in the air as yellow leaves fluttered about, dancing onto the porch from a mature American elm standing guard over the tidy lawn.

A trio of pumpkin candles flickered from the white mantel, the votive holders glowing deep orange and filling the small living room with a spicy scent. Native American pottery of every size and shape lined the shelves on one wall, leaving space for framed photos and books. Aunt Star had been visiting reservations and pueblos for years and her collection of native artwork had grown. She had a flare for decorating, and each pot, each kachina or storyteller, had its place. Trudy called it organized chaos, but instead of feeling hemmed in by all that art — like her days with Preston — she found Aunt Star's home warm and vibrant.

The walls were plastered Navajo white, the perfect palette for Southwest art. Various hues of pinks and raspberries mingled with turquoise and creams around the room, from the large area rug bursting with geometric designs of corals and greens to pillows tossed across the sand-colored couch and a flamingo pink throw over the back of Aunt Star's tan leather recliner. Splayed open next to her chair sat her magenta paisley knitting bag with various shades of yarn peeking out. There was no doubt about it: pink was Aunt Star's favorite color, right down to the exterior of her home and the frosty pink lipstick she still wore at eighty-one.

"I had the whole place renovated since last time you were here. Come on, let's go see the kitchen."

Trudy set her purse on the coffee table, her attention drawn to a framed poster of Georgia O'Keeffe's famous painting "Chama River, Ghost Ranch" hanging next to the television. As she ambled toward it, she felt pulled by the blue waters snaking through an arroyo of red and tan bluffs dotted with green scruffy brush. "I've seen this image dozens of times over the years, but I never get tired of looking at it." She turned to gaze at Aunt Star. "You ever wish you could step into a painting and stay there? Like this one?"

"Shoot, yeah. Sometimes I turn off the TV and stare at it. I imagine myself floating down that river without a care in the world. Then my smartphone snarls at me with one news update after another, and I'm reminded that a con artist with an overinflated ego will be moving into the White House come January. What an insult."

"You can turn those notifications off if you get tired of them."

"Nah, and miss the world crashing around us? I have a hunch that everything we've worked for the past fifty years will be rolled back. I hope I'm wrong."

"Have you been following any of the women's movement pages on Facebook? Georgia's friend, Lupi, told me about a group of women who are trying to organize some national protest. Maybe around the inauguration."

Aunt Star let out a weary sigh. "I'm too old to still be protesting this shit. Can you see me creaking along in some march?" She raised her cane and pointed it toward the front door as if shaking a stick in warning. "But protest I will. Heck, I started the day after the election."

"How long you gonna keep the flag upside down?" Trudy glanced in that direction.

"As long as it takes. Or until they wrestle me into a box and shut me up for good." Aunt Star put her cane down and hobbled toward the kitchen. "Are you hungry? I can set out some cheese and crackers. We can sip some spirits before we go meet your sister."

"Sounds good to me." Trudy followed dutifully behind, hoping Aunt Star would serve something besides hot toddies.

Mr. Grumples looked up from his dish when they entered the U-shaped kitchen with butcher-block countertops and sparkling white appliances. "My contractor tried to talk me into granite and stainless steel but you know me, I have to be different."

"I like all the white. It reminds me of you in your old nursing uniforms," Trudy teased. "I still picture you like that sometimes. All starched up from head to toe."

Aunt Star leaned on her cane. "I was so glad when we switched to scrubs. A lot more comfortable."

A baker's rack stood next to the wall by the entry, a bevy of small plastic bags containing various sizes of knit caps took up one shelf. Trudy picked up a forest-green cap, the only one not in a bag. "You do beautiful work, Aunt Star. I've been meaning to tell you." She set the cap down. "Think of all the people who are wearing your caps right now."

"They keep your head warm, that's for sure. I need to sew my special label on the inside of that green one." She picked up a tiny rectangle of cloth and handed it to Trudy.

Turning the label over in her hands, Trudy admired the lettering stitched in hot pink: *Handcrafted by Star Hurn.* In the top right corner, she fingered a tiny falling star stitched in yellow. "Did you sew your labels inside Momma's caps? I never thought to look."

Aunt Star nodded. "Heck, yeah. That's my trademark," she quipped. "Catch a falling star and put it in your pocket," she crooned in a wobbly voice. "Perry Como. It was a big hit before your time."

Trudy placed the label in her aunt's hand. "Georgia and I made wishes on falling stars when we were younger. We thought they'd bring us good luck."

Her aunt set the label on top of the green cap and sighed. "Luck. It must've been in short supply on November eighth. Sorry to grumble, but I'm having a hard time accepting this huge defeat. I hope I live long enough to see a woman president. We owe the suffragettes that much, that's for sure." She moved toward the refrigerator. "Why don't you go bring in your things, and I'll fix us a nice snack."

Outside, Trudy breathed in the pleasant scent of piñon and aimed her key fob at the Camaro. The trunk popped open as a late model car cruised by, the white-haired male driver rubbernecking to get a closer look. She couldn't tell if the driver's pensive eyes were gawking at her or the flag. Laughing, she gave him a two-finger salute — the universal peace sign — and the car sped up and kept going. As she reached into the trunk to retrieve her suitcase, her gaze fixed on the lumpy gym sock she'd stashed in a corner next to her toolbox.

For now, the gym sock would stay hidden in the trunk. Trudy would wait for the right opening, and then show Aunt Star the eyeglasses. No sense getting her visit off to a bad start.

Lugging her suitcase up the steps, she rolled it through the living room into the spare bedroom by the hall bath. She plopped down at the foot of the double bed and gazed around, recalling the last time she'd stayed at Aunt Star's years ago. She'd come for a weekend visit after flying into Albuquerque and renting a car. Georgia had just bought a house a few streets over and was camping out in one corner of the living room while the whole house was undergoing a renovation. Aunt Star had insisted Trudy stay with her, even though Aunt Star's friend, Bernie, short for Bernice, was also visiting that same weekend. At the time, Trudy didn't give it a second thought that Bernie slept in Aunt Star's bedroom.

Old photographs, many from the sixties, covered the wall facing the foot of the bed. One showed a younger Star Hurn barefoot in ratty cutoffs, her voluptuous breasts braless and drooping beneath a T-shirt, her strawberry-blonde hair parted straight down the middle and cinched in a ponytail at each ear, a headband strapped around her forehead. She was at some rally, holding a sign that said, "Women Demand Equality."

Trudy pushed off the bed to get a closer look at another photo that captured her eye. There was Star in her mid-fifties, wearing baggy jeans, her long hair shorn. She was sitting on a campstool outside a tent, the flap open. Beside her stood her friend Bernie, tall and rigid as a board, her thin lips always at the ready with an eager smile, a twinkle in her kind eyes. Bernie was a veterinarian from West Texas. Trudy had always assumed that Bernie and Aunt Star were best friends, but Trudy wondered if there was something more to their relationship. For Aunt Star had never married, and Trudy had assumed her capable, independent aunt was happier living alone, being a nurse, being far away from Pardon. But now she wondered: Were Star and Bernie a couple? And if so, how sad they had to keep their relationship a secret, as if it were something that must be hidden, something to be ashamed of.

Bernie had been dead twenty years. A nephew had taken over her veterinarian practice.

Back in the kitchen, Aunt Star directed Trudy to slice an apple and Swiss cheese and arrange them on a small platter with wheat crackers and a clump of grapes. While Trudy prepared the snack, Aunt Star hooked the crook of her cane over the lip of the counter and set out two pink depression era wine glasses. "A little vino is good for the soul, I always say."

"I'll drink to that," Trudy joked.

Uncorking a bottle of Burgundy, Aunt Star filled their glasses halfway and handed one to Trudy. "In the words of some of our greatest activists, 'We shall overcome.'"

Trudy lifted her glass. "I consider you one of them. You've been fighting for women's rights for decades. I'm sorry I never appreciated it until now."

Aunt Star tilted her head in thought. "Women's rights are human rights, are they not?"

Trudy took a sip of wine, welcoming the dry, full-bodied flavor and any calming agents the wine might dispense. After Aunt Star took her seat and hooked her cane over the back of her chair, Trudy pulled out a chair to join her.

She wanted so badly to talk about the eyeglasses Zia dug up, to discuss the circumstances surrounding the awful night when Aunt Star cajoled her and Georgia into silence. Trudy wanted to ask her all these things, but instead, she sipped her wine, placed slices of cheese and apple on crackers, and munched away. She hadn't eaten since breakfast.

At one point, Mr. Grumples brushed against her ankles, meowed, and jumped onto her lap. He curled into a ball on top of her cloth napkin and began purring. "Well, hello, Mr. Grumples. You're pretty friendly for a curmudgeon."

Aunt Star raised her glass and cocked an eyebrow. "Mr. Grumples is picky about who he chooses to associate with, but he knows a kindred spirit when he sees one." She sampled her wine, smacking her lips with pleasure. After she set her glass down, she gazed at the cat. "Mr. Grumples showed up here one morning a few years ago, all scratched up and bleeding. Guess he'd been in some kind of fight. I'd lost Miss Pearl, my white Persian, and I wasn't exactly in the mood to take in some alley cat looking for a handout."

Trudy ran her hand through his rich fur, enjoying the warmth of his plump body, the vibrations he made every time he purred. "He's a smart cat," she murmured, grinning at her aunt. "Who better to patch him up than a nurse?"

"A sucker you mean," she cackled, but a smile emitted from her eyes as she gazed across the table.

Seconds passed. Satisfied he'd been properly petted, the cat jumped down and darted under the table.

With her hands free, Trudy picked up her wine and admired the contrast of dark Burgundy against the pink stemware. Inhaling the deep earthy aroma, she took a sip and out of nowhere, Clay's voice echoed through her mind as if they were still sitting in the diner back in Pardon having breakfast. *What did that guy do to you?*

Closing her eyes, she set the glass down, feeling flushed. When she opened them again, she plucked up a grape, nibbled it, and then popped another one into her mouth. As she chewed, the ugly assault of words from that horrible night in her mother's kitchen prodded her as if the monster were here in Star's tiny kitchen. *You're not worth a poke anymore.*

Crinkling the cloth napkin between her fingers on her lap, Trudy breathed through her nose then blurted out, "What did Dub do to you? I mean long before he attacked Georgia that night in the kitchen?"

Aunt Star stiffened, her frosty pink lips parted in shock before she clamped them shut. Grabbing her cane, she pushed herself up from the table. With one hand gripping the crook of her cane and the other the back of her chair, she took a deep breath, lifted her shoulders, then dropped them with a loud exhale. "He raped me. When I was thirteen."

Trudy stared at her, seeing the pain etched all over her aunt's soft face, her cheeks as inflamed as the letters spray-painted in red across Dub's grave.

"Come on, Mr. Grumples," her aunt huffed. The cat darted out from under the table and disappeared around the corner.

"Did you tell anyone?" Trudy followed her aunt into the living room where she made a fuss plumping up a pillow with the tip of her cane.

"Didn't have to." Aunt Star straightened, looking around as if she couldn't remember why she walked into the room. "His mother waltzed in and caught him in the act. He had me pinned down in the pool house, dry-humping me from behind like some animal, both hands on my bare breasts. We'd been swimming and

I went into the pool house to use the restroom and..."

Trudy leaned against the doorframe, wincing. Her chest squeezed with pain. She took several deep breaths, hoping to slow her heart rate. "I hope Aunt Gladys beat the crap out of him. I don't guess she called the police?"

Aunt Star shook her head. "Not hardly, but she smacked him good across his bare back with a pool pole. Left a huge welt." With both hands gripping her cane, Aunt Star lifted her quivering chin in defiance. "Some will argue that I wasn't raped, because like Aunt Gladys said, 'At lease he didn't *penetrate* you.' But that's hogwash; I don't need a dictionary to tell me I was *violated*."

Aunt Star took a deep breath and continued, "I'd been swimming at the mansion dozens of times as a kid. But something changed when Dub hit puberty. He became mean, aggressive. And that day as he was assaulting me, he snarled in my ear, 'Keep your mouth shut, slut. If you tell anyone, I'll hurt you good.'"

Trudy pushed away from the doorframe and plopped down on the sofa catawampus from the leather recliner. "What a disgusting pig. I'm sorry, Aunt Star. Me and Georgia and Bogey only knew him as a creep, someone Momma and Daddy ordered us to avoid."

Aunt Star gripped her cane, her chest heaved with each breath. She looked around for Mr. Grumples. He'd curled up in a corner of her recliner.

Aunt Star resumed her story, as if she hadn't heard Trudy's last comment. Once Star began the telling, she couldn't seem to stop. Maybe that would bode well when Trudy got around to pressing her about the eyeglasses. "Of course Dub blamed me. Told his mother I led him on. She told him to shut up, that his father would handle it when he got home from work."

Trudy hesitated, doing the math. "Where was my mom? She would've been eleven then."

Aunt Star leaned on her cane even more. "Jewel was at church camp. Mother had gone along to chaperone. My dad was still at the garage. Aunt Gladys drove me home in her Cadillac. I'll never forget the way she looked down her nose as she approached our working-class neighborhood. As she parked in front of our gray stucco with a giant swamp cooler plugged into the living room window, she told me to stop blubbering. Laid a guilt trip on me. Told me to get over it. Boys will be boys, and if I didn't want that kind of attention, I better stop parading myself in front of her son. The next time I swam at her house, I better cover up. Wear one of my daddy's grimy T-shirts from work. The last thing she said before she drove off was, 'Don't tell anyone what happened, I mean it. If word gets out, who you think people will believe? The son of one of the most respected and wealthiest men in town, or you, the daughter of an auto mechanic?'"

Incredulous, Trudy gnawed at her right thumbnail. "It's a good thing that old hag is dead or I'd be payin' Gladys a visit."

Aunt Star let out a puff of air. "In some odd way, she was both my accuser and my protector. Anytime I was at their home, she made sure I was never alone in the same room with Dub. The same went for Jewel. A few years later, Dub got sent to New Mexico Military Institute in Roswell. God knows why. At some point he got kicked out and returned to Pardon. I shudder to think who else he tormented and terrorized."

Perhaps the lady in the Lexus at the cemetery, Trudy thought, keeping it to herself for now because Star's revelation was a lot to process all at once. And if she pushed too fast, her aunt might shut down before Trudy could bring up the eyeglasses.

With measured breaths, she stared at the blue river snaking through the canyon in the painting. Like Aunt Star, she pictured herself floating down that river, the sun hot on her back, the water cool and cleansing. *But could any amount of healing water truly wash away the pain of abuse? Regardless of the severity, abuse was abuse, whether it was sexual, mental, or verbal.*

Aunt Star's voice drifted as she hobbled toward the small hallway away from the living room. "We better use the facilities before we go see your sister."

With that, Trudy hoisted herself off the couch and went into the kitchen to put the fruit and cheese back in the refrigerator. At the baker's rack, she paused and ran a finger one more time over the tiny yellow star stitched into the upper right-hand corner of the label. And the name Star Hurn stitched in bright pink. Maybe

Aunt Star would open up more once Trudy got her out of the house.

Later, as she went to help Aunt Star into the Camaro, Trudy asked, "Did Grandma Lily know what happened to you?"

"Not that I'm aware of. I was too afraid to tell anyone after Aunt Gladys shamed me into silence. Uncle Manifred wielded a lot of power in that town. Still does. He could've made life difficult for Mother and Daddy."

After Trudy backed out of the driveway and headed south toward Railroad Avenue, she said, "So how did Momma know to be afraid of him if you didn't tell anyone? You said she was at church camp when it happened."

Aunt Star's chest rose and fell as she gazed straight ahead. "Because I started having nightmares, and apparently one night I talked in my sleep and Jewel overheard me screaming for Dub to get off me."

CHAPTER 25

Walking in Her Footsteps

"I STILL say they should rename this street *Harvey Girl Way*. Those gals were more than glorified waitresses...they had gumption. They were risktakers who helped bring a certain civility to the American West." Aunt Star gripped her cane stashed between her legs and gazed out the passenger window at the back side of the historic Castaneda Hotel, a massive two-story mission revival-style building on Railroad Avenue.

All discussion about the assault in the pool house had stopped minutes earlier when Trudy revved the engine and Aunt Star leaned back in her seat and laughed that they were "street racing." A few seconds of going fast and hearing her aunt's laughter reminded Trudy of summer vacations as a kid when they visited Pardon and hung out with their fun-loving aunt before they moved back to Pardon for good and she became the family caretaker.

Trudy parked next to the curb and cut the engine. "Holy moly, with the exception of her hairdo and spiffy new aqua specs, I'd say there stands Lily Knutson's ghost framed in that archway. Her costume looks authentic." She blasted the horn at her sister a couple of times, mimicking the passenger trains of old chugging into the depot next door with carloads of hungry passengers.

Her coppery hair puffed up in a loose bun, Georgia Cutterbuck waved enthusiastically from the walkway of the arcade that wrapped around the horseshoe-shaped building. Clad in a long-sleeved black dress and starched white apron that fell just below her knees, and topped with a black bow tie, she lifted her skirt a few inches and broke into a cancan.

"That's my sister," Trudy chuckled. "She's got a dance move for every occasion. If I tried that, I'd fall and break my hip."

Aunt Star pushed her door open and plopped her cane on the ground. "Dance a few steps for me, Georgia girl. I'm out of breath just watching."

In a pair of black Mary Jane shoes with one-inch heels, Georgia tap-danced down the brick promenade then spun and tapped back toward them. "You girls ready for the tour?" Her husky laughter echoed up and down the arched breezeway.

"Shoot, yeah," Aunt Star shouted, grinning up at her niece. "I wish your grandma could see you in that getup. After listening to her stories when we were kids, Jewel and I always suspected being a Harvey Girl was the highlight of her life."

"Look at you," Trudy hollered, rushing around to help their aunt out of the Camaro. "For a second you looked like Grandma Lily in those old photos of her in uniform."

Georgia laughed, the lenses of her new eyewear accentuating her hazel eyes that crinkled at the corners. "Except I'm twice the age Grandma was when she worked here, and she wore her hair in a bob."

Meandering through the gate in a chain link fence that skirted the perimeter of the building, Aunt Star cleared her throat and proclaimed, "The Castaneda was built by the Santa Fe Railroad in conjunction with the Fred Harvey Company and opened in 1899 as the first flagship trackside hotel on the Santa Fe line." She paused to catch her breath. "This grand ol' dame boasts a tall bell tower seen for miles around and a central courtyard that faces east toward the tracks."

Georgia clasped her hands and squealed like a woman half her age. "So you were listening the whole time I was practicing my spiel?"

"Heck yeah, and if I wasn't so old, I'd be sportin' one of those costumes and helping you give tours." Reaching for the metal rail, Aunt Star gazed up at the gray sky then huffed as she navigated the two steps leading to the veranda. "Sure smells like snow although I didn't see it in the forecast." She walked over to one of the arches and peered at the depot next door. "Aw, the glamorous days of train travel. At least Amtrak still stops through here." She leaned on her cane as if lost in thought.

Before stepping up onto the veranda, Trudy glanced at the sky then noticed the faded white lettering that curved around the top of the arch. The stylized wording *Castaneda Hotel* reminded her of a sign she'd seen over a cantina somewhere on her travels.

With Aunt Star out of earshot, Trudy reached to hug her sister and whispered in her ear, "We need to talk. It's about the *perv*."

Georgia lowered her voice. "Wait till we're upstairs."

After they embraced, they held each other at arm's length, both trying to outdo the other with compliments. "You look happy," Trudy said, nudging her sister on the cheek.

"So do you." Georgia grinned, wiggling her eyebrows. "You'll have to bring Clay next time."

"He wanted to come, but..." Trudy flicked her head in their aunt's direction. "You know..."

Georgia nodded then led them down the walkway to a pair of double doors. "Okay, ladies, you want the official tour or the *family* tour?"

Trudy and Aunt Star exchanged glances and shrugged. "The family tour's fine if it means you get out of here sooner, but I'm still paying the full fee," Trudy assured her.

Georgia adjusted her glasses. "Thanks, girls. I feel funny charging you though. Being family and all."

"Bah." Aunt Star jutted her chin in the air. "Would Lillian Gertrude Knutson have traveled all the way from Kansas to work here for free? Heck no. She answered the call for 'Young women, eighteen to thirty, of good character, attractive, and intelligent.' They were promised good wages, room, and board. This is extra income for you, lovey. No need to apologize."

Georgia curled her fingers over her lips and averted her eyes. "Just trying to pay off my house and student loans. Been a long day. I have to be back here by nine in the morning. The tour director and I and another Harvey Girl are expecting a Rotary Club from Albuquerque and a busload of college students from Las Cruces. So as soon as we're done here, I'll run the key back to the

Plaza Hotel, change out of this uniform, and we can meet at Charlie's for an early supper."

"Will Gil be joining us?" Aunt Star asked as Georgia propped the door open to let her pass.

"Not tonight. He's teaching an acting class to some disadvantaged kids so we'll hook up with him tomorrow afternoon at the Plaza."

As Georgia went to lock the door behind them, Trudy noticed her sister wince. "Your hands bothering you today?"

Her sister made a fist. "My right one. Probably the weather. As long as this arthritis doesn't affect my feet, I'm good."

Inside the large lobby, Trudy gaped at the high pressed-tin ceilings, crown molding everywhere, the long elegant check-in counter to the left and the black and white tile floor leading to the grand L-shaped staircase to the right. The room was stripped bare of furniture except for a painted desk and a straight-backed chair in the corner nook by the stairs. Something tickled the back of her neck and she spun, slapping the air behind her.

Georgia giggled, pulling her hand away in time. "Some say this place is haunted, sis."

Trudy shivered but shrugged it off. "Have you ever experienced anything weird while you're here?"

Her lips crimped in a wry grin, Georgia let her gaze travel up the grand staircase painted white, past the maroon-carpeted risers, to the landing flooded with natural light from a huge skylight above the stairwell. "One time I thought I heard laughter upstairs. Maybe one of Aunt Star's former patients escaped from the state mental hospital."

Shaking her head, Aunt Star frowned then walked over to inspect the stairs, her breathing labored with each step. "Don't suppose they've put an elevator in yet?"

"Not yet," Georgia apologized. "But one's coming with the renovation."

"I figured as much," Aunt Star sighed. "I'll hang out down here when you girls head up."

Rubbing her right hand, Georgia nodded toward the nook by the stairs. "Back in Grandma Lily's day, a newsstand stood over there. They sold everything from postcards to tobacco to trinkets and souvenirs."

"Sounds like an airport," Trudy quipped, walking over to peek through a set of double doors into a huge dining room that appeared as big as a ballroom. Aunt Star sidled up next to her, sounding winded.

Georgia sashayed across the lobby and motioned for them to follow her through the double doors. "The dining hall could seat over a hundred people and the lunchroom half that. Grandma Lily earned about fifty dollars per month, along with room and board. Sadly, only white women were hired back then. Someone like Lupi couldn't have applied to work as a Harvey Girl until around the Second World War."

Trudy shook her head. "Thank goodness times have changed."

Halfway across the dining room, Aunt Star stopped to catch her breath. "Let's hope we don't regress." She glanced around then stared at the floor. "Girls, we are literally walking in Lillian Knutson's footsteps. I never thought I'd live to see this day."

Trudy strode back toward her. "Haven't you been in here before?"

Aunt Star shook her head. "This place was boarded up for years. I've only seen it from the outside. The bar was opened off and on. But nobody I know hung out down here. It'll be nice to see it shine again. Mother and the other girls would be pleased, I'm sure."

They meandered into the kitchen with its high ceilings. Georgia pointed out the original oven that took up an entire brick wall, a huge icebox that resembled a wardrobe, an industrial dishwasher, and a long countertop where mounds of dough over the years had been rolled out for bread and pastries. "Everything was baked fresh on the premises," Georgia explained.

"Criminetly," Aunt Star said, eyeing an old white mixer that came up to her chest. "Mother wasn't exaggerating when she talked about this mixing machine being five feet tall." She glanced over at Trudy. "Get a picture of me and Georgia so I can send it to Sister. She'll never believe me otherwise. She'll accuse me of embellishing the whole thing."

Georgia bustled over to the mixer and Aunt Star and Trudy took turns posing with her. Each time the camera flashed, Georgia flexed her right foot and pointed her toes, her signature pose.

During the picture taking, Aunt Star wobbled as she snapped a photo of the sisters by the mixer, her cane hooked over her left forearm. "You're definitely Shep Cutterbuck's girls, right down to the firm jaw lines and stubborn chins."

Georgia elbowed Trudy. "What's a stubborn chin? I've never figured it out."

Trudy giggled. "Means we're part mule."

"Post it to Facebook and tag me," Georgia said, fiddling with the tie on her apron.

"Yes, ma'am," Trudy said, tapping the keys of her phone as she posted a photo on Facebook. She wrote, "Star Hurn and Georgia Cutterbuck, mixing it up in the old kitchen of the historic Castaneda Hotel in Las Vegas, New Mexico."

Aunt Star gazed out the large windows above the pastry counter. "Look, girls, it's snowing."

Georgia motioned for Trudy to join them at the window. "See that Italian-looking two-story building across the street, the one with the pressed metal façade and the display windows with transoms?"

Trudy held her camera up and snapped a photo. "Lots of beauty hiding behind all that grime and neglect."

"That's the Rawlins Building," Georgia pointed out. "It was built around the same time as the Castaneda. That's where Grandma Lily and the other Harvey Girls lived. It served as the dormitory in those days."

Back in the lobby, Aunt Star made a beeline for the straight-backed chair by the grand staircase. "You girls take all the time you need. I'll play solitaire and people watch."

Halfway up the stairs, Trudy caught the glint in the old woman's eyes.

"Just kidding," her aunt teased, pulling out her cellphone. "But can you imagine what this place was like during its heyday? Must'a been something."

Upstairs, Trudy and Georgia headed down the long hallway

on the south wing. A few seconds into their tour, Trudy heard a noise.

She spun around. "Did you hear that?"

Georgia pursed her lips from side to side and raised her eyebrows. "It's an old building, Sis. Stuff creaks." She walked a few feet. "Did you bring the eyeglasses Zia dug up?"

Nodding, Trudy moved down the hallway. Shafts of sunlight spilled from the open doorways of several rooms as they meandered down the narrow passageway, glancing left and right into rooms with peeling wallpaper and paint, some with ceilings caving in. "They're in the trunk of my car." Poking her head into a generous-sized room, Trudy strolled toward the bay window and gazed down at the depot. She glanced over her shoulder as Georgia entered the room. "Come here, I need to tell you something."

Georgia let out a heavy sigh and walked over and looked out the window. "What's wrong?" She sounded peeved, obviously tired from a long day.

Keeping her voice low even though they were the only ones upstairs, Trudy began: "Dub assaulted Aunt Star when she was thirteen...in the pool house at Uncle Manifred's. Aunt Gladys saw it happen, covered it up, and told Aunt Star to keep her mouth shut."

Georgia drew back in revulsion, her eyes wide with shock over the rim of her aqua frames, as if she didn't believe what Trudy said. As if her mind needed time to grasp it. "How do you know this?" Skepticism soured her voice.

"Because she told me this afternoon over wine and cheese. I flat out asked her what Dub had done to her. Don't you remember how he taunted her that night? He called her a heifer and said she wasn't worth a poke."

Georgia began pacing around the room, fanning herself with both hands. "I don't remember anything but that monster's hand over my mouth. I couldn't breathe. I thought he was going to kill me."

Trudy approached her, barely touching her shoulder. "You okay, sis? I'm sorry, but I thought you needed to know."

"Just give me a second. I need to calm down. Let's go walk to the end of the hall then we better head back. I don't like leaving Aunt Star downstairs by herself."

Shoulder to shoulder, the sisters made their way down the length of the hall, peeking in open doorways and commenting on the various guest rooms, at the beautiful old doorknobs and window configurations. To lighten the mood, Trudy bumped her hip against her sister and they giggled and broke into the monkey walk back toward the stairwell. Even during the saddest times in their life, they'd always found a way to have fun together.

Standing under the huge skylight, they studied each other a minute. Finally, Georgia said, "I'm glad you told me. I don't get it, though. Why would she reveal what Dub did to her as a kid, but she won't talk to us about the night he assaulted me?"

Reaching for the banister, Trudy took a deep breath then slowly exhaled. "Because she's hiding something," she whispered, her knees stiffening up as she descended the stairs.

At the landing, Georgia pressed her finger to her lips as they rounded the corner. The top of Aunt Star's head was visible, a shaft of sunlight from the skylight giving it a halo effect. She was hunched over her cellphone, texting. Swiveling in her chair, she craned her neck in their direction, squinting up at them. "You girls about ready to go see the lunchroom then call it a day?"

"Unlike Grandma Lily, there's nothing wrong with her hearing," Georgia mouthed as she rolled her eyes at Trudy then breezed the rest of the way down and went to help Aunt Star out of her chair. "You meet anyone while we were gone?" Georgia chuckled, catching Trudy's eye as she gripped the banister and took each step, one stiff leg at a time.

"Heck no, but Sister sent a batch of photos showing off her new appliances. She said Hector starts installing next week."

A short time later, they made their way to the former lunchroom at the front of the building on the south wing. Trudy paused as she watched her sister maneuver, pointing out where the large lunch counter used to sit, the double doors where hungry passengers would flood in for a quick lunch. "The staff used all kinds of codes; even down to how coffee cups were placed on saucers, which helped run things more efficiently, especially during rush hour."

Striding across the room, Trudy pushed through the door and stepped out onto the arcade. Skipping down the snow-covered steps, she looked up and down the tracks, imagined a big locomotive still hissing and steaming after it squeaked and squealed to a stop.

Aunt Star's shrill voice pierced the cold air. "Trudy, you and Mother were no different really. You worked as an airhostess serving passengers on planes. Mother worked as a hostess serving passengers coming in off the trains."

Trudy pointed to a row of black and white birds perched on a nearby telephone wire. "What are those birds called? I've been seeing them since I left Santa Rosa and headed north on Highway 84. They're so striking, but they sure make a ruckus." Turning, Trudy mounted the steps where Georgia held the door open.

"They're called the black-billed magpie of Northern New Mexico," Aunt Star offered, waiting by the door. "Mother told us a story about a cantankerous old cook that worked here. Anytime he caught them standing around chatting, he called them a bunch of gossiping magpies and told them to get back to work."

Trudy made a face and stuck her hand on her hip. "Wonder what he called a bunch of fellas standing around smoking and joking?"

"Gents," Georgia cracked with an eye roll.

A floorboard creaked somewhere behind them. Aunt Star frowned then shook her cane in that direction. "Probably that cantankerous old cook, upstaged in the presence of strong women."

They all laughed.

Aunt Star dug through her purse. "You girls go make a wish at the fountain." She handed them each a penny like they were kids, then ambled outside and plopped down on a bench.

Trudy followed Georgia down the steps and halfway across the courtyard to the fountain, nothing more than a sphere of cement, its murky water dappled with fall leaves. Snow dusted the grounds and the rooftop of the building, reminding Trudy of a giant Mexican gingerbread house sprinkled in powdered sugar.

As tiny snowflakes danced through the air, Trudy and Georgia squeezed their eyes shut, each made a wish, and then they tossed their pennies into the fountain.

Georgia glanced sideways at Trudy, her lips pursed in a coy smile. "What did you wish for?"

"That Aunt Star tells us the truth. I'm going to hit her up about it tomorrow before we meet Gil." She glanced around then peeked over at Georgia. "Do you believe in ghosts? I know we've been joking about it since we got here, but seriously, do you think our loved ones can communicate with us from the other side?"

Georgia shrugged. "I don't know. It's not something I sit around thinking about. Look, we better go. Aunt Star's probably tired and I'm freezing." She turned to leave.

Trudy tugged on her sister's sleeve. "Sis, that night in the kitchen when I picked up the skillet? I felt Daddy's strength coming through my hands."

Georgia began to knead her reddened knuckles, and over the rim of her glasses eyed Trudy. "What are you talking about?"

The dark thought that had nagged at Trudy's conscious for decades exploded within her. "What if I killed him?" she hissed sideways, spittle spewing from her lips.

Georgia stiffened, her back straight as the train tracks stretching before them. "Sis, stop it. That's crazy talk."

Trudy leaned in closer. "What if Aunt Star's been lying to us the whole time? What if he was already dead when we dragged him out the door? Look at her arms. She was always as strong as an ox."

Aunt Star pushed herself up from the bench. "You girls about ready? Charlie's closes at six, it's coming up on five now."

Georgia peeked over her shoulder toward the bench where Aunt Star stood waiting. "I don't like where this is going. Look, I need to go take some Tylenol and lock up. I'll meet you at Charlie's as soon as I change and turn in my key." With that, her sister strode off, the skirts of her Harvey Girl costume swishing as she made her way toward the arcade, up the steps, and through the lunchroom doors.

Inhaling the cold air, Trudy stared straight ahead at the railroad tracks that ran north and south. The snow melted the second it hit the rails, but was already sticking to the ground. Tomorrow she would show her aunt the eyeglasses, no matter how upsetting it might be. She had to know the truth. Turning, she watched the old activist shuffle down the walkway and disappear around the corner, the thick soles of her shoes worn at the heels.

Following in her footsteps, Trudy paused as a black-billed magpie flew right past her at eye level, its white wingtips fanned out, reminding Trudy of the black and white spectator pumps Grandma Lily always wore to church before she died.

The bird landed on top of the bell tower and let out a harsh, raspy call, yakking and gossiping about something.

CHAPTER 26

Riddle Talkers

TRUDY FIDDLED with the gym sock hidden deep in the pocket of her nubby cardigan. She was working up the courage to spring the eyeglasses on her aunt, and to demand an answer for why they were buried beneath the camper. But after Aunt Star's revelation yesterday about the attack in the pool house, Trudy wasn't feeling so brave. Or brazen.

Seated next to Aunt Star on a bench by the gazebo at Old Plaza Park, Trudy gazed at the front of the historic Plaza Hotel, a grand three-story Victorian building overlooking the plaza. Georgia had phoned earlier saying she and Gil were both running late, but they were looking forward to meeting up at the hotel for drinks and dinner. Most of the snow from yesterday had melted, and the late afternoon sun warmed things enough that Aunt Star wanted to sit outside and "soak up the rays" while they waited for Georgia and Gil to arrive.

Last night after their tour of the Castaneda, the three women chatted and giggled over chips and salsa and glasses of iced tea. Halfway through dinner, Georgia whispered conspiratorially across the booth to Trudy, "Gil and I are playing house. Aunt Star, close your ears." Georgia went on to explain that a month ago she rented her tiny Italian villa — furniture and all — to a young college professor teaching at Highland University and she was staying at Gil's place, a Southwestern-style hobby ranch with a couple of horses on a patch of land outside of town. No wonder she'd suggested Trudy stay with their aunt and not at her place.

Aunt Star had looked up from her bowl of tortilla soup and chuckled, "You don't need my permission to shack up. As for Gil, if he hasn't figured it out by now...at seventy."

They all laughed, pretending they didn't share a history with the predator buried in the cemetery near Bogey's grave. Aunt Star regaled them with stories growing up with Jewel in Pardon, how they loved to hang out at their daddy's shop, Stanley's Garage, and drink bottles of Coca-Cola and eat Cracker Jack from the vending machine. Or visit the Pardon Zoo with their mother and make faces and throw peanuts at the monkeys, back when the zoo was nothing more than a clump of cages and a clanking miniature train with open-air cars that skirted the perimeter.

After their coffee arrived and they split a decadent slice of chocolate cake, Clay had texted Trudy with the photo he took of them the other morning at sunrise. She'd blushed at his comment that he and Little Man went to get firewood and were wondering what she was doing for Thanksgiving the following week. Cinda and Roxy were flying to her parents in New Hampshire, and he and Hercules would sure love it if Trudy, Jewel, and Zia joined them for an informal dinner. Hector was bringing venison sausage and smoked wild turkey, and said Jewel's kitchen would be out of commission until after the holidays.

As she texted him back, Georgia kicked her under the table and teased, "We know who *you're* talking to, sweetie, and it sure isn't Mom."

Trudy had glanced up from her phone to find her sister smirking knowingly and Aunt Star stirring her coffee ever so slowly as she feigned disinterest. As soon as Trudy lifted her fork to take another bite of cake, Aunt Star cleared her throat and inquired, "Has Detective Cordova heard any more on the vandalism to Gold's Department Store? I hope he nabs the bastards."

"The investigation is still ongoing," Trudy informed her. "Although Clay suspects a hate group out of West Texas."

Someone honked a car horn in front of the hotel, jarring Trudy from her thoughts.

Aunt Star shifted on the park bench next to her. "You know there are over nine hundred buildings in town listed on the National Register of Historic Places?"

Clutching the gym sock, Trudy gazed around the oval plaza at the variety of architecture, from Victorian and Italian, to Moorish, Greek, Tudor, and California Mission Revival influences. People strolled around the park, some staying on the winding paths and others cutting through the yellowing grass where patches of snow lingered in the shade.

"Aunt Star?" Trudy started to pull the sock from her pocket. Her voice thrummed in her ears as she began to grill her aunt about that night. "I've been having flashbacks since Zia dug up that pair of men's eyeglasses under the camper."

Aunt Star looked away. "I hope you disposed of them like I asked."

Trudy gripped her fist tighter around the sock, still buried in her pocket. She could feel the outline of the frames as she rubbed her thumb over one end of the sock. "I saw them fly off his face and land on the floor."

Aunt Star took a few shallow breaths and rubbed her left kneecap. She studied the mottled trees overhead and said nothing.

Trudy babbled on, frustrated by her aunt's silence. "Later, I saw you leave the kitchen all bundled up with something in your hand. I think it was his glasses. Georgia and I have a couple of theories."

The old woman waited, her silence prompting Trudy to keep going.

"One, we think you went outside to give them back and realized he'd already left. And if he was blind as a bat and couldn't see without them, especially in a snowstorm at night, it's possible he stumbled onto the tracks."

Aunt Star breathed deeply, the crook of her cane gripped in both fists. "How he died is immaterial. I'm glad he's no longer a menace to society." She sounded weary.

Trudy licked her lips, her mouth dry as her heart thudded against her chest. She rushed ahead, despite a warning bell clanging in her head. "Our second theory is Dub was already dead when you went outside to check on him. That you waited until we were asleep...then dragged his body through the back gate and placed him on the tracks, knowing a freight train would come along and turn him into mincemeat. Then you found his glasses when you came back into the kitchen and buried them to hide the evidence he'd been at our house."

Slowly, Aunt Star turned her head and narrowed her eyes on Trudy. The look on her aunt's face sent chills up Trudy's spine. Made her question her own sanity. As if her suggestion was the most asinine thing Aunt Star had ever heard in her life. That maybe Trudy was as crazy as some of her aunt's former patients.

Rattled, Trudy's hand went limp in her pocket. She released her grip on the sock and reached for her purse and a stick of gum. What she'd give for a cigarette right now.

"Hello, lovelies. Sorry I'm late." Georgia's deep throaty greeting extinguished Aunt Star's smoldering glare. One end of Georgia's fringed neck scarf fluttered behind her as she strode across the park toward them in black tights that showcased her dancer's legs and a peacock blue cape that swirled around her with each step.

"She moves like a butterfly she's so light on her feet," Aunt Star observed, looking relieved that her other niece had showed up, interrupting Trudy's probing interrogation.

Trudy had long suspected that Georgia was her aunt's favorite. Not because of anything Georgia had done so much as what she didn't do. She never challenged her aunt for the truth, unlike Trudy who'd badgered her occasionally over the years. Plus Georgia lived in the same town and doted on her, whereas Trudy only popped in every few years, fishing for answers.

As Georgia approached, Aunt Star called, "Where's Gil?" She seemed to be looking past Georgia as if any second he would come bringing up the rear.

"He'll be along shortly. He was feeding and brushing the horses last time we talked." Georgia loosened her neck scarf. "Whew, turned out to be a nice day. Sun feels good." She sat down next to Aunt Star and reached behind her back like she was resting her arm on the bench. After yanking a strand of Trudy's hair, she slyly removed her arm and pushed the bridge of her aqua frames up on her nose in a dramatic fashion, her signal to Trudy: *Did you show her the glasses?*

Leaning forward, Trudy barely shook her head and acted as if something was in her right eye. Then she unwrapped a stick of gum and stuck it in her mouth.

Georgia squinted at her sideways, looking puzzled.

Aunt Star let out a loud huff and slammed her cane down. "You girls think I'm stupid. I know what's going on!" She took a deep breath, jutting her chin in defiance. "Now here's the deal. The three of us survived a horrible encounter a long time ago. In the process, some bad stuff happened."

Trudy leaned back on the bench and watched a young couple roll their suitcases up the sidewalk and into the Plaza Hotel. From the corner of her eye, she could see Georgia fling her scarf over her shoulder and sit back all regal like, her nostrils flaring as she breathed through her nose and waited.

Aunt Star took a deep breath and continued, her voice thick with emotion: "Sometimes love crosses all boundaries...sometimes we must do things to protect those we love."

Even if it means the unthinkable, Trudy thought, chewing her gum and playing with the foil wrapper, flattening it with her thumb against her thigh. "Even if it means doing things that could send us to jail?" With each breath, her chest caved in a little more.

Georgia twisted on the bench. "Stop it, sis. We need to let this go." She fanned her face with both hands, her manicured nails painted the same shade as her cape.

"Nobody's going to jail," Aunt Star's voice crackled between them. "Not as long as I'm the matriarch in this family."

"I felt Daddy's presence that night," Trudy blurted. "It's like he was there and helped me lift that heavy skillet."

Aunt Star gasped. Her pink lips trembled and tears leaked from the corners of her eyes. "Shep hated Dub," she spat after a few seconds.

Georgia untangled the scarf at her neck like she couldn't breathe. "Did Dad know Dub attacked you when you were younger?"

Slowly, the old woman nodded her head. "Jewel told Shep although I asked her not to. But who could blame her. It was right after you kids moved into the house on Seven Mile Road. The moving van had barely left when we got wind Dub had rented a casita within walking distance. That's when your dad paid Dub a visit. Shep threatened to kill him if he ever hurt one of you kids."

Trudy rocked back and forth on the bench. A heat welled up within her and she felt like she might explode. "I'm not leaving town until you tell me the truth. Was Dub dead when he hit the floor?"

Aunt Star heaved a sigh and white-knuckled the cane. She stared straight ahead without speaking.

Georgia broke the silence and whimpered into her scarf.

Rigid against the back of the bench, Trudy found her courage. "So if he was dead when he hit the floor, how did he end up on the tracks?"

Aunt Star continued to grip her cane. "What do you do with trash?" she bristled, her voice cold and harsh. "You take it out."

*To the tracks...*Trudy thought, closing her eyes against the image of her aunt dragging Dub's stiff body across the yard all by herself, through the back gate, and up the berm where she laid him across the steel rails while a blizzard howled around her.

Georgia choked out a painful plea: "We must never tell Mom the pervert died in her kitchen."

Aunt Star cleared her throat and gripped the crook of her cane, repeating the words from decades ago. "You tuck it deep inside of you, so deep your body will absorb it."

Trudy and Georgia leaned forward, each grabbing hold of the cane. Without saying a word, the three women renewed their code of silence. A silence to protect themselves along with Jewel and the house she worshipped.

Trudy couldn't help but wonder if the cane they were clinging to was a shepherd's staff or a lightening rod?

Gulping for air, she pushed off from the bench. "I'll be right back." She hiked toward the hotel, passing a tall flagpole displaying three flags: the red, white, and blue of the American flag, the stark black and white of the POW-MIA flag, and the yellow and red of the New Mexico flag.

By the time she reached the hotel lobby, she could breathe again.

After she left the ladies room and lingered by the walnut stair-case where a scene from *No Country for Old Men* had been filmed, she meandered down a wide crooked hallway until she rounded a corner and stepped into an exquisite room with a fourteen-foot tall ceiling. Natural light poured in from two massive bay windows with display cases filled with art. The windows overlooked the plaza and flanked a set of arched glass doors capped by a tall tran-som. A handful of round tables covered in white linen cloths had been set up for some event.

"They call this room the Old Library." A woman in a black shirt and white collar sat on a sofa shoved against the far wall. Warmth radiated from her smile.

"Oh, sorry to disturb you," Trudy apologized. "I didn't see you sitting there."

"You're not disturbing me. I was hanging up with my husband when you walked in." She placed her phone on the armrest. "This room is peaceful. You're welcome to join me."

"Are you a priest?" Trudy fiddled with her purse strap and glanced around. They were the only ones in the room.

"Yes, with the Episcopal Church. My name is Gracie by the way."

"Nice to meet you. I'm Trudy, and I haven't been to church in a *long* time." She bit her lip, feeling shy and awkward. She tried to gauge the woman's age, but it was getting more difficult the older she got. The woman was long and lean with an athletic build, pos-sibly a hiker or bicyclist.

"I hear that a lot. It's okay."

"May I ask a dumb question? I grew up protestant, so I'm not sure what to call you."

"There are no dumb questions," she smiled. "You can call me Gracie. Or Priest Gracie is fine. Whatever makes you feel comfort-able."

Priest Gracie had a no-nonsense cropped haircut, an open smile, the slightest hint of lip and eyeliner. She reminded Trudy of a female captain she'd flown with over the years. Smart. Sensi-ble. Friendly. Approachable.

"I don't want to take up your time, but may I talk to you a moment?"

The priest motioned for her to sit down. "Please, come have a seat. I just got back from conducting a funeral and stopped by here before I go up to my room to change for dinner."

"Guess your white collar attracts people," Trudy said, sitting on the opposite end of the couch.

"Or repels them," the priest chuckled. "What's on your mind?"

Her hands tucked between her legs, Trudy began. "Do you think God punishes us for our sins? I mean...like the *big ones* in the Ten Commandments?"

Priest Gracie uncrossed her legs and folded her hands on her lap. "I believe in a benevolent God. A God who weeps when we weep and rejoices when we rejoice."

Trudy stared at her feet then into the priest's compassionate eyes. "I walked in on something when I was a teenager, and my actions saved my sister's life. It was self-defense, but in the process someone died." Trudy paused, waiting for the priest to say something. Instead, she nodded thoughtfully for her to go on.

Her throat tight, Trudy continued: "When I was forty, I lost a baby girl at full term. She was stillborn. She'd be eighteen by now. I keep thinking God is punishing me. You know, a life for a life."

Priest Gracie turned toward Trudy. "God is love, Trudy. Love has no need to settle scores. I'm sensing you have a broken relationship with God because you blame yourself in some way. Guilt can do that. It can cause us to construct invisible walls to keep God and others out."

Trudy closed her eyes and breathed deeply. She saw herself pick up the skillet...

Her eyes fluttered open and she rose off the sofa and moved toward the bay window, her face damp with perspiration. Aunt Star's comment from earlier drifted past her mind: *How he died is immaterial. I'm just glad he's no longer a menace to society.*

"I believe our creator is in the midst of whatever is troubling you." Priest Gracie followed her and stood next to her.

Gazing out the window, Trudy sniffled and watched Aunt Star walking arm in arm with Georgia as they promenaded around the Plaza. An overwhelming sense of loyalty surged through her, driving out all other thoughts. "See those two women there? That's my aunt and sister. My aunt's a retired nurse. She's spent her life taking care of people and fighting for women's rights. And my sister's a teacher. She teaches dance at the community college."

"I can tell you're proud of them. We women need each other, especially during times of crisis."

Was this female priest hinting at something bigger, something beyond the realm of their previous discussion? Hector had taught Trudy about making assumptions. So she waited, not wanting to offend the woman, in case...in case Trudy was wrong in her assumptions. Finally, she spoke her mind: "We're all upset about the outcome of the election."

"Me, too," Priest Gracie sighed. "Lots of people I know are. Many of my parishioners have been confiding in me. Others, sad to say, are quite happy about the upset."

Relieved, Trudy gestured to the four-foot-tall Talavera pottery statue of a Franciscan priest in a colorful robe propped on a riser in the bay window, a white dove perched in each palm. "There's one problem with the Padre there."

Priest Gracie furrowed her brow. "Oh? I love his vibrant colors." Her gaze lingered on the statue. "He's supposed to represent Saint Francis of Assisi, the patron saint of animals."

Trudy nodded. "Oh, don't get me wrong, he's lovely all right. But I have a hunch if Aunt Star walked in here and met you, she'd look at him and say, 'Where's his female counterpart?'" Trudy gestured toward the other display window filled with large metal animal sculptures. "You're a woman priest. When's the last time you saw a woman of the clergy depicted in art? And I'm not talking about nuns or angels."

Priest Gracie studied the padre figure. "Her time will come. It may look insurmountable, but the day will come when women gain their rightful place in society and stand equal with men. I believe we already do in the eyes of our creator."

The rumble of motorcycles vibrated through the window as two Harleys passed by in tandem in front of the hotel. A man rode a few feet ahead of a woman.

"You know they filmed the movie *Easy Rider* here," Priest Gracie said, as she and Trudy watched the riders circle the plaza before they disappeared back down Bridge Street.

Moments later, a silver Ford Dually pickup pulled up next to the curb across from the hotel. An older guy with a salt and pepper ponytail climbed out of the cab, his trademark craggy features unmistakable as he shut the door and swaggered up the sidewalk in a black T-shirt and jeans toward her aunt and sister. He looked as if he stepped right off the set of some action-packed show where he played the assassin.

"That guy looks so familiar." The priest crossed her arms, one finger tapping her lip as if trying to place him.

"Aw, that's Gil," Trudy smiled. "My sister's boyfriend. He's an actor. Been in lots of films. Usually plays bad guys, but my sister says he's a real sweetheart. I'm fixin' to go meet him." She watched Gil give her sister a kiss on the cheek before he offered Aunt Star his arm inked in tattoos as they crossed the street in front of the hotel. No wonder Aunt Star was always asking about him. He played the adoring gentleman and she loved the attention. Who wouldn't? Before stepping off the curb, Georgia bent over her phone texting before she followed after them.

Trudy's cell pinged and she glanced at her screen: Gil's here. Meet us in the lobby. Hope you're ok.

Stepping away from the window, Trudy turned to leave. "Gracie. Thank you for listening. You've helped shed some light on a complicated situation."

Gracie's eyes glinted with understanding. "Peace to you, my sister."

They walked out of the room together. As Trudy rounded the staircase by the lobby, she glanced over her shoulder to wave goodbye. Priest Gracie had stepped onto the elevator. She lifted her hand and smiled.

The Plaza Hotel bar was a favorite gathering spot for locals and hotel guests. It was almost dark by the time they found a table for four by a window overlooking the park. At night, Plaza Park glittered with thousands of tiny white lights strung in trees. Even the gazebo's canopy and rails were outlined in lights, giving it the look of a stationary merry-go-round. From her vantage point at the round table, Trudy could look out the window to her right and see the park and turn to the left and watch the bartender creating concoctions at the elegant bar capped in granite. The place was packed on this Saturday night, a week before Thanksgiving.

Trudy averted her eyes from the big screen television mounted high on one wall across the room, glad Aunt Star had her back to the television where the president-elect was yammering about something, most likely himself. At least the volume was on mute.

Georgia sat to her left and Gil directly across from her next to Aunt Star. Their server had just delivered drinks, and Georgia asked him to hold off bringing menus until they had a chance to visit for a few minutes. No sooner had the server left when all three women's cellphones pinged with a group text from Jewel. She'd sent a photo showing where Hector had outlined a section of kitchen tile in bold black marker. This is where the new kitchen island will go, Jewel wrote in her text, attaching a photo of Zia plopped on her haunches right in the middle of the rectangle, her left paw dangled in the air as if she were waiting for someone to shake it.

After glancing at the image, Trudy gazed out the window a moment, looking past her reflection. For a split second, her mind replaced the shape of a rectangle with the outline of a body like the ones seen in crime photos. Turning back to the others, she tried to read the expression on Aunt Star's face, then on Georgia's. Were they thinking what she was thinking?

The island would sit directly over the spot where Dub died.

Aunt Star held her phone in one hand, typed away with one finger, then smiled coyly when she hit *send*.

Trudy read the text: Looks good, Sister. Please give my regards to Hector for bringing your kitchen into the 21st century. And tell Miss Zia that Mr. Grumples says meow.

Georgia chuckled then sent her own comment: Can't wait to see the island, Mom. Daddy would love all the home improvements you've made. As Georgia went to put her phone away, she winked at Trudy then tickled Gil in the side. "Sorry, babe. We're not trying to ignore you."

Gilbert Miguel Vargas toyed with the sides of his downward-turned mustache going gray around his generous mouth. He picked up his longneck beer and took a tug, his bronze fingers ringed in silver and turquoise. "I grew up in a household of women. I'm used to chattering hens."

A guy at the next table looked over in recognition when he heard Gil's gravelly voice.

Their server returned with menus and left.

Stashing her phone in her purse, Trudy asked Gil, "Why did you leave Hollywood? Were you tired of the rat race?"

Gil set his beer down and gazed thoughtfully across the table. "After I realized I could earn a decent living at it, I always said I'd leave on a high note when it was time. And I did." He gave Georgia a squeeze. "And then this little gal waltzed into my life and turned my brain upside down." He made a face and they all laughed.

Georgia laid her head on his shoulder. "Aw, that's so sweet, but tell them why you opened Storrie Theater."

He scratched his stubble-free jaw and stretched back in his chair. "I grew up a poor Mexican kid from the west side of Las Vegas, still known as Old Town by some. I was always getting into trouble until I discovered theater in high school. So after I returned home, I opened the theater as a form of outreach. We're between productions, but I'm hoping to get more community involvement. Get kids interested in the arts in general and keep them off the streets."

"Gil," Aunt Star lifted her chin in his direction, her elbows on the table as she clasped both hands, "you might think about hosting a wine and paint night for young mothers who've been cooped up with little ones all day. The lobby's a perfect venue for events unrelated to theater. It could help generate income and draw attention when you're in between plays."

"Good thinking, Ms. Star. Maybe you can teach a knitting class, too."

Trudy raised her glass in agreement. "To Aunt Star, knitter extraordinaire."

Aunt Star eyed Trudy across the table. "Why thank you, lovey."

Georgia put down her menu and batted her lashes at Gil. "Honey, what's the best line you ever delivered in a film?"

Gil toyed with the paper napkin under his longneck. "Let's see, I had lots of good ones over the years, but the line I wished I'd had" — he lifted his beer, took a swig, and flashed a crooked grin — "Some people just need killin'," he growled in that distinct gravelly voice that caused patrons to turn and stare at their table.

Georgia groaned, looking squeamish. She refused to look at Trudy.

Aunt Star gasped, her pink lips parting as she squinted at something over Trudy's shoulder. After a moment she reached for her martini and slurped.

Time slowed. Trudy felt her throat close up as she jumped up from the table and managed a raspy, "I need some air." She rushed for the nearest exit.

Outside on the sidewalk, the cold air slapped her in the face as she looked around and headed toward the gazebo. Fluttering in the crisp cold air, the three flags she passed earlier were lit up under a bright spotlight. The silhouette of a man and barbed wire called to her as she cut across the grass.

At the base of the flagpole, she huddled in her thick cardigan, Dub's glasses still in her pocket. Craning her neck, she called to the man on the flag: "Did you feel that way, too, when you were dropping bombs over a war zone? That some people just need killing?"

The face on the flag rippled in the night.

Fingering the sock in her pocket, she called again, "Daddy, can you hear me?"

Nothing.

Ever since her mother received the phone call from the Air Force, Trudy could no longer hear his voice. He'd gone silent.

With tears clouding her vision, she heard a flap of wings as a black-billed magpie landed on top of the flagpole. It yakked a second then took off, flying across the plaza toward Bridge Street. Choking back tears, she cut across the park in the same direction until she came to the red and blue *Santo* of the Virgin Mary.

At the foot of the sacred statue, a tall wood carving sculpted from a tree trunk, she saw where people had left offerings: prayer candles, stuffed animals, photos of loved ones encased in plastic covers. Through blurry vision, she pulled the sock from her pocket and dropped the mangled pair of glasses into the heap of items left at the Madonna's feet.

"You okay?"

She whirled at the familiar voice. There, wringing her hands like a mirage stood Georgia, her coppery hair tumbling over her shoulders like that night long ago. "Sis, we're getting worried about you. Gil was being funny. He has no idea about the night Dub died."

Reaching for Georgia's hand, Trudy felt her sister's strength as she guided her back up the walkway across the park. As they drew closer and crossed the narrow street in front of the hotel, Trudy spotted Gil next to her aunt. The actor who'd played dozens of killers over the years had one arm around the old woman, patting her attentively on the shoulder.

Georgia tapped the window as they passed by, giving them a thumbs-up.

Aunt Star twisted in her chair and gazed out the window, the concern in her eyes turning to relief as she motioned for Trudy to come in out of the cold.

Right before they went inside, Georgia poked Trudy in the back and whispered, "Sis, just 'cuz you took down a monster didn't turn you into one. You did the right thing."

CHAPTER 27

Woman in the Lexus

December 9, 2016

TRUDY HAD been dreading this visit to the nursing home to see Uncle Manifred since she'd hugged Aunt Star goodbye three weeks ago and returned to Pardon. As Trudy and Jewel dropped off the birthday cake and a bouquet of balloons in the dayroom, they paused in front of the big screen TV. CNN was reporting the death of United States Senator John Glenn of Ohio, at the age of ninety-five. Someone had turned the volume on high.

"Now there was a great *American*," Jewel crowed, adjusting her red beret and talking over the newscaster. "Not only was he the first American astronaut to circle the earth, but he was a genuine war hero, a *fighter pilot*, like your daddy." She glanced sideways at Trudy.

"Bogey worshiped both of them," Trudy reminded her mother as they shifted their attention back to the television.

An elderly woman shuffled by in a yellow housecoat and slippers, eyeing the cake and balloons. "Is everyone invited to the party?" she asked, looking hopeful.

"Yes, indeed," Jewel reassured her. "Stick around. We're going to fetch the birthday boy." She paused again to look up at the television screen. John Glenn's image had been replaced by an ad for easy weight loss. "Ads today are dumb. I sure miss those old Palmolive commercials where Madge dipped a woman's fingertips in green dish soap." She looked back at Trudy. "You remember that ad, honey?"

"Sure do. Georgia and I acted it out, taking turns playing Madge." Trudy nudged her toward the doorway to the hall, smiling at the woman in the yellow housecoat as they filed past. Trudy's chest felt heavy as they headed down the hallway. How was she going to look the old man in the eye after learning how he and Aunt Gladys shamed Aunt Star into silence?

Love has no need to settle scores, Priest Gracie's words darted in front of her as she made her way down the hall. *But what happens when love is used to manipulate others?* Trudy wished she'd asked the priest.

And then there was that *other* matter...the one involving Dub's death.

But today, on Manifred Hurn Senior's one-hundredth birthday, Trudy couldn't weasel her way out of this visit even though she'd been avoiding him for years.

Rounding the corner, she squared her shoulders and put on her best flight attendant face. Jewel belted out, "Happy birthday to you," as they entered his room. She stopped singing when they saw the old man slumped over in his wheelchair, a line of drool hanging from his bottom lip and pooling onto his shirt. His thick wire-rimmed glasses hung halfway down his nose.

"Oh dear, we'll have to wake him. Can't have him sleep through his party." Jewel shed her coat and laid it on the bed, along with her purse.

Trudy walked over and smelled a bouquet of flowers placed by his bedside. "Did you send these?" she asked, glancing over her shoulder. "They're beautiful."

Jewel shook her head and ambled toward the wheelchair. "Most likely from someone he's done business with. Open the envelope and see who they're from."

Trudy pulled out a signed placard and read it out loud: "Happy hundredth birthday. Best wishes, Madeline." She inserted the note back into the envelope. "Oh, wait, she included her business card." Trudy lifted it from the envelope and relayed the information to her mother.

Madeline T.
Million Dollar Broker
Caprock High Plains Realty & Land Co.
Lubbock, Texas

"Nobody I know," Jewel said, motioning Trudy over. "Come feel his skin. Do you think he feels cool? Honestly, I can't tell if he's breathing."

Trudy stuck the business card in the envelope and walked toward the window where her great uncle was parked in his wheelchair. She wrinkled her nose, detecting a foul odor. "Do you smell that?"

Sniffing the air, Jewel scrunched her face. "Oh dear. That can't be good. You know that happens sometimes when a person dies. All their sphincter muscles relax and their bowels cut loose."

Trudy reached down and barely touched the back of his gnarled hand. His fingernails had yellowed with age like the pages of old paperbacks, the skin on his face and forehead mottled like autumn leaves. "He feels cool to the touch." She withdrew her hand, the unpleasant task over. She wasn't put off because he was old, she was repelled by some of the things he represented, like the abuse of power.

She stepped back a few feet and stared at him, at the pajama-clad legs where his bony knees stuck out through the material. She remembered the stocky businessman in dress shirts and suits, the slicked-back hair he was always combing. The polished wingtips he paid a shoeshine boy to buff twice a week. The stocky man with a broad shiny face and apple cheeks that resembled Dub's, only Dub had a sinister sneer where the senior Hurn had a ready smile and easy handshake for wheeling and dealing.

"I better go get a nurse," Jewel said, backing out of the room. "You stay here with him. I can't believe he skipped out before attending his own party."

"I don't think he had a choice," Trudy said dryly, curling one finger under her nose.

After Jewel pattered out of the room, Trudy gazed out the window and tried to ignore the stench permeating the air. From the corner of her eye, she saw a tall woman in a headscarf and dark coat, wearing low-heeled pumps, exit the main entrance of the nursing home. She looked like the woman who had vandalized Dub's grave.

Trudy stepped closer to the window to get a better look. Sure enough, the woman climbed into a champagne-colored Lexus with Texas tags and pulled out of the parking lot, turning left onto Curry Avenue and heading east, toward Texas.

Slowly, Trudy turned to stare at the bouquet of flowers on the bedside table. A second later, she dashed across the room, tore open the envelope, and reread the unusual name on the business card: Madeline T. Leaving her business card equaled leaving her *calling card* as her mother used to refer to those name placards she left in the entryways of colonels and generals when she and Daddy had to put on "face time" and socialize.

Pocketing the card, Trudy whispered, "Madeline T., who are you?" before she shifted her focus back to the once powerful man whose body was cooling off fast. Soon rigor mortis would set in.

Muffled voices in the hallway caused her to look up.

A certified nursing assistant in polka-dotted scrubs breezed into the room, a stethoscope dangling from her neck. The young black woman approached the wheelchair. Trudy stepped aside and glanced at her nametag.

Donita acknowledged her with a polite nod then bent over the old man to check his vitals. "Mister Man, you still with us, baby?" Her voice was soothing as she reached for his bony wrist to feel for his pulse. "Hmm..." She pursed her lips as she inserted the ends of the stethoscope in her ears and placed the bell on his chest to listen. After several seconds, she shook her head and pressed her lips together, wrapping the stethoscope back around her neck.

"Is he gone?" Jewel asked from the doorway.

Donita nodded. "Poor Mister Man, looks like he won't be attending his birthday party after all." She walked to the bed and pressed the call button for a supervisor.

Trudy took a step forward. "He must've died right before we got here."

Donita nodded, looking sad. "Poor thing. I always liked Mister Man. Felt sorry for him when he told me how his son died."

Trudy swallowed and didn't comment, thankful the woman didn't elaborate. Jewel walked back across the room and hugged Trudy from behind. Reaching around, Trudy embraced her mother, realizing at once Jewel's dilemma. Uncle Manifred had helped her out financially years ago, and yet he covered up and protected his son from taking responsibility for a horrible crime he committed. No telling how many either.

A nurse supervisor and a social worker entered the room. After the head nurse checked the old man's vitals, she offered her official condolences. Jewel asked the social worker to contact the mortuary and Uncle Manifred's attorney, whose name and number were on file. As the social worker went to leave, she stuck her head back into the room and said the coroner would be along shortly. "Would you like me to cancel the party?"

"Absolutely not," Jewel said, directing Trudy to go text Aunt Star and Georgia then head straight to the dayroom to start serving cake.

As Trudy strolled down the hallway, her mother stuck her head out the door and hissed, "Be gentle on them. They get upset when another resident dies."

Trudy spun on her heels, walking backward. "I was a flight attendant for forty years, Momma. I know how to talk to people."

Outside the dayroom, Trudy leaned against a wall and typed a group message: Hey, Aunt Star and Georgia, Mom asked me to text y'all and let you know Uncle Manifred died this morning. We found him slumped over in his wheelchair. We thought he was sleeping.

The party will go on without him! About 20 residents are gathered in the dayroom. Headed there to serve cake. I'll send more details soon. Mom's supposed to speak with his attorney this morning. If he left anything for me, it's all yours, sis. So you can pay off your student loans.

Sad news about astronaut John Glenn...Bogey sure worshiped him.

I love you both,
Trudy

For now, she decided not to mention the woman in the Lexus. Until she had more facts, it could simply be a coincidence.

Before she put her phone away, she sent Clay a text about her uncle. He fired right back: I'm sorry for your loss, babe. He the uncle whose son got killed by a train? You girls come hang out with me tonight. Bring Zia so Hercules will have someone to talk to. LOL Tell your mom I'll build her a warm fire. There hasn't been any more vandalism reported at the cemetery so that should put her mind at ease.

Back in the dayroom, Trudy introduced herself and announced matter-of-factly, "Thank you all for coming. Manifred Hurn Senior passed away in his sleep sometime this morning." After a few audible gasps, Trudy added, "On behalf of the Hurn family, please stay and have cake and punch. We appreciate you being here."

As residents and caregivers lined up for cake, an image of the orange man with straw-colored hair flashed on the television screen. His smug lips puckered up, he yelled like a carnival barker, "Lock her up!"

"Somebody shut him up!" Jewel Cutterbuck's shrill voice trumpeted through the air as she walked into the dayroom and glared at the television.

Trudy stood frozen, the cake knife suspended in the air as she stared at her mother in her red beret and matching blouse, her dress slacks flared at her ankles as she twirled around on her ballet flats, searching for someone to help her find the remote.

An elderly gentleman set his paper plate down, rose from his chair, and walked over and picked up the remote. With quivering hands, he aimed it at the television and cut the power. Trudy watched her mother thank the man then wave at a few familiar faces.

An elegant woman with short red hair and emerald earrings clapped as she approached the table. "See, there are still a few good men around." She smiled, thanked Trudy for the cake, and then joined the others already eating. Trudy assumed she was referring to the lovely gentleman who turned off the television.

Jewel mingled for a few minutes before she walked up and whispered to Trudy, "The funeral home is here to pick up his body. Apparently, he wanted to be cremated and didn't want a service."

"For a man of his standing in the community?" Trudy watched a male nursing assistant push a shriveled up woman in a wheelchair into the room. Shrouded in a quilt, the woman pointed her finger impatiently in the air as she directed the young man where to park her wheelchair.

Something about the woman's voice sounded familiar, a high-pitched trill Trudy was certain she'd heard before. The male caregiver locked the wheelchair in place and approached the table. Trudy passed him two plates of cake. "I'm sorry for your loss," he said. "Miss Vivian says thank you for the cake. She would tell you herself but she's rather shy and hard of hearing."

Trudy and Jewel glanced over at the lady in the wheelchair. Miss Vivian was arranging her quilt on her lap and didn't look their way.

"Tell Miss Vivian we're delighted she's here." Jewel smiled and handed him forks and napkins. "Is she a new resident? I've never seen her around. But then it's been a while since my last visit."

"She's been living here about two months." The caregiver smiled politely, balancing the plates in his hands.

"Is she from here?" Jewel absently ran her finger through a frosting rosette.

"I'm not sure, ma'am. But her daughter's some big shot real estate agent in Lubbock. She visits a couple times a week."

Trudy felt the blood rush from her head as he walked off. She glanced sideways at her mother.

Jewel sucked the frosting from her fingertip. "You're not looking so swift, darling." She paused to smack her lips. "Didn't you say the lady realtor who sent those flowers is from Lubbock?"

Trudy nodded and poured two cups of punch and handed one to her mother. "Drink up. Too bad it's not spiked." She hadn't told her mother about seeing the woman in the Lexus leaving the nursing home.

Lifting a cup to her lips, Jewel murmured, "When I spoke with his lawyer by phone moments ago, he told me there might be a few surprises."

"Surprises?" Trudy turned to catch her mother glaring at the lady in the wheelchair, practically smothered in a quilt.

"That old bird, Miss Vivian...she and her daughter better not try to pull a fast one. I warned Uncle Manifred a long time ago that some woman might come along and try to swindle him out of his money."

Reaching into her pocket, Trudy fingered the business card. If Madeline T. turned out to be the woman driving the Lexus, Trudy had a hunch she wasn't after Uncle Manifred's fortune.

She was after something else, something that involved Dub.

By the time they pulled up to the house, it was late afternoon. Trudy and Jewel were both exhausted from dealing with the lawyer for Uncle Manifred's estate. Hector and a helper had left for the day after installing new cabinet doors in the kitchen and bathrooms. Tomorrow they'd return to touch up a few areas and build the island from scratch.

After Trudy got her mother settled for a nap, she made a mug of hot tea, grabbed her laptop and a handful of dark chocolates, and moseyed into the sunroom where she curled up on one end of the chuck wagon with Zia and began to compose an email:

Subject: Meeting with the lawyer

Hello, Aunt Star and Georgia,

Once again Mom asked me to relay what's going on with Uncle Manifred's estate. I decided to put this in an email rather than calling. That way you can refer to it as needed. Fasten your seat-belts, girls. We're in for a bumpy ride.

Today, in a meeting with Uncle Manifred's lawyer, Mom and I learned some shocking news. First, the old man left all of his money and vast land holdings to Madeline T., a real estate broker from Texas. Madeline T. is Manifred Hurn Senior's illegitimate granddaughter, the same woman Mom and I saw at the cemetery vandalizing Dub's grave. Second, she was born sixty-three years ago to a twelve-year-old girl named Vivian who was sexually assaulted in an alleyway on her way to the library by Dub when he was about fifteen.

Vivian was returning a library book when he attacked her. Because Dub threatened to kill her if she told, and because she was so young, she didn't tell anyone about the assault. Her parents were poor, she lived on the wrong side of town, and they accused her of being promiscuous when she turned up pregnant. She didn't know the name of her attacker until three years later when she saw Dub's senior photo in the *Pardon Gazette*. And still, she told no one.

By then, she was fifteen and wanted to forget about the attack. Baby Madeline had been given to Vivian's Aunt Fay who lived in Texas. Vivian's mother and Fay were sisters. Fay had a nice house and yard and drove new cars that never broke down. Fay lived far enough away that the little baby could have a fresh start and because Fay couldn't have children of her own, she was happy for the gift of a baby, regardless of how she came into the world.

On occasional family get-togethers, Vivian kept her distance from the "younger cousin" who grew up to be a successful businesswoman. As Vivian aged, she tried not to dwell on the baby she'd given up. Madeline had a good life, that's what mattered.

Then one day a few months ago, the family charade came crashing down. Vivian got a call from a distraught Madeline. Fay Tea, the lady Madeline had called "Mother" for sixty-three years, spilled the beans on her deathbed that Madeline was her niece, that "Cousin" Vivian who lived in Pardon, New Mexico, was Madeline's birth mother. Can you believe this crap?

Fay Tea's dying request was that Madeline forgive the family for lying, and to reach out to Vivian, her birth mother, and help her get settled into a nursing home in Pardon because she had no family left in the area and she was in bad shape.

Shortly after Madeline got Vivian moved in, Vivian confessed that Madeline was conceived during an act of rape, and the father of the rapist was no other than Manifred Hurn Senior, who happened to live two doors down from Vivian. When Madeline first approached the old man with the news, he accused her of fabricating the whole thing. Once her attorney presented the old man with enough evidence along with DNA testing, he changed his will.

For the record, Madeline never asked for a dime. She's apparently wealthy in her own right. So her motive was never to go after his money, but in the end, I suppose that's all he had left to give her.

Because the one thing he seemed incapable of giving was a verbal *apology*.

Aunt Star, if anyone has a reason to contest the will it's you. But given the delicate circumstances the three of us found ourselves in years ago, I'd rather not tangle with Madeline's lawyer. Not that she would care how her father died...but you never know...

For now, Madeline wants no contact with our family. She told the lawyer this has all been a shock to her system and she needs time to process. Can't say as I blame her. It's certainly been a shock to us. Apparently, the old man croaked shortly after she stopped by his room to deliver flowers. Nothing suspicious, he just checked out.

BTW, while Mom and I were serving cake, Vivian and her caregiver stopped by the dayroom. We didn't speak to her, only to her caregiver. Looking back, it's clear she didn't want to make eye contact with us. Most likely she came to celebrate once she learned of the old man's death. Vivian is probably a few years younger than Mom, but clearly the woman's in bad health and it shows. As for Madeline, I looked up her profile online since I've only seen her from afar. She's tall and slender, regal even. Her professional photo appears a bit dated, but she definitely has Uncle Manifred's ready smile, rosy cheeks, and apparently his business savvy.

I'll close for now and give you a chance to process. For obvious reasons, please don't cc Mom on this thread.

When Mom gets up from her nap, we'll load up and head to Clay's for supper. Zia and Hercules get along great. She bosses that little dog around and he bosses right back. Mom and I are going to help Clay decorate his house for Christmas. It'll keep her mind off things and give her something to do.

Trudy

Re: Meeting with the Lawyer

What a surprise! But then nothing much surprises me these days. How's Sister? Keep an eye on her blood pressure. Jewel had a better relationship with him than I did. He did help her out after Shep got shot down. I wish I could say I'm sad, but mostly I'm relieved. Understandably, my relationship with him grew more complicated over time. He covered up for his son at the expense of others. I suspect he skedaddled out of there so he wouldn't have to face the prospect of being publicly humiliated in case Vivian made a stink at his birthday party. As for Madeline, I hold no ill will toward her. Something tells me she'll put that money to good use. My heart breaks for her mother, though. Vivian probably still has nightmares. We'll talk soon. Thanks for being Sister's secretary. And yes, best to keep some things private.

Still hanging my flag upside down,
Aunt Star

Re: Meeting with Lawyer

Please tell Mom I'm thinking of her. I know without Uncle Manifred's financial help, Mom would've lost the house after Daddy's plane went missing. Aunt Star, I'm sorry he didn't leave you anything. If anyone was owed part of his estate, it's you. I'm stopping by after work. Gil's teaching an acting class tonight. I could sure use one of your hot toddies; my throat's a bit sore from crying after reading about Madeline and Vivian. We'll drink a toast to them and all the fearless women in our family. We're all survivors in our own way.

I love you all,
Georgia

~

December 20, 2016
Group email from Lupi Belen
To: Trudy, Georgia, Jewel, Star Hurn
Hey Chicks,
Game on. Let's make it official and launch the Women's

March on Pardon to be held Saturday, January 21, 2017 to coincide with the Women's March on Washington, D.C. the day after the inauguration. Sister Marches are being planned across the nation and in several other countries. Let's have our voices heard and advocate for women's rights and human rights and honor those courageous sisters who marched and protested for all of us to have the right to vote.

Benny Trujillo says he'll take care of the permit. This is still a conservative town, but being he's a former mayor, he still has some pull. We'll set up headquarters next door in the parking lot. That way I can keep it separate from the diner. 'Cuz not everyone who loves my food loves my politics. Hehe. Since it's off-season, Mary Ortiz has offered to let us borrow her snow cone hut. Having a designated structure makes it real and serves as a place where we can distribute fliers and other items for the march. We can talk about hours of operation later. On the day of the march, we'll gather on the courthouse lawn.

You chicks heard of the Pussyhat Project? It's a social movement sweeping the country to bring awareness to women's rights. It's also a way to keep your head warm and flood this nation with the color *pink* on January 21, 2017 when people all over this country gather to protest the president-elect's derogatory comments about grabbing women's genitalia. Pink is feminine and empowering. Two young women in California came up with the idea.

Ms. Star, Trudy tells me you're a *knitter*! We could use your help. I'm not a knitter, but my understanding is the basic pattern is a rectangle. When worn, each point forms kitty ears. Clever, huh! And for those who want to contribute but can't physically march, knitting a hat for someone else is a great way to be involved and still participate.

There's a simple pattern online. Google pussyhatproject.

Think of it as a grassroots effort, but with pink flooding the streets of our nation and world. Let's show Señor Grab'em not to mess with us. To paraphrase Helen Reddy's famous song about female empowerment: We Are Women, Hear Us Roar.

Who's in?

Lupi

December 20, 2016

Group email from Star Hurn:

Count me in, Lupi! And please call me Aunt Star. I have fond memories of you and Georgia prancing all over the house. I've been knitting caps for years. I'll do anything to help advance the rights of women and all those who feel they don't have a voice. I may be too old to march with my feet, but my fingers and knitting needles can do their own marching as I work the yarn.

December 20, 2016

Group email from Lupi:

May Day, May Day! Mary Ortiz's husband is afraid they'll lose customers come spring. Whatever! We need to find an alternative structure to serve as headquarters. Anybody got any bright ideas?

December 21, 2016

Group email from Trudy:

Lupi, we've got you covered. Remember the old travel trailer that sits out back of Mom's place? Mom says it's time to put it back in service! It needs new tires and the license plate and registration have expired, but I'll take care of it. Clay's got a trailer hitch on the back of his Tahoe. He can haul it into town for us.

Aunt Star, I ordered more pink yarn for you in various shades. Lupi says some women of color prefer darker tints, so let's oblige. The package should arrive tomorrow.

December 22, 2016

Group email from Georgia:

Aunt Star, Gil says you can set up a knitting circle in the theater lobby! He'll advertise on the marquee and issue a PSA for local knitters who want to participate in the Pussyhat Project. I'd knit but my talent is in my feet and not my fingers. Keep flying your flag upside down. Even some of my students have commented. Word is getting around here on campus.

Trudy and Mom, I'll catch up with y'all later. Lupi, can't wait to see you in January. We might have to break out some of our old dance squad routines for the march.

Group email from Lupi:

Thank you, Cutterbuck family and super knitter Aunt Star! Time to get to work. We have a march to plan. Nobody grabs our VJJs without our consent!

Feliz Navidad!

Chapter 28

Women's March on Pardon & Pussycat Hat Headquarters 2017

January, Friday the 13th

A SMALL crowd of protestors had gathered on the sidewalk in front of the travel trailer parked in the lot next to Lupi's Diner. A large banner announcing the women's march hung across the top of the camper. To the right of the camper door, Trudy had draped a POW-MIA flag that morning at her mother's request.

"As a military family, we have to take any opportunity we can to remind people there are still service members missing in action," Jewel had stated on their drive into town.

"Be prepared for some pushback," Trudy told her gently. "That's all I'm sayin'. It's one thing when you fly your flag at home. It's another when you hitch it to another wagon."

"Bring it on. I've been waiting for forty-four years to raise a stink. People have so many misconceptions about the military and military families. They trot us out when it's convenient for their parades and when they need to pat themselves on the back. That flag's a stand-in for your daddy. Because I can tell you right now, if Shep were here, he'd be appalled by the fake patriotism and inappropriate comments coming out of that showboat's mouth."

After Trudy pulled on a pink kitty hat, she tacked the flag to the side of the trailer while Jewel unlocked the door and hauled out lawn chairs and set up camp for another day. With the inauguration one week away, interest in the women's march had increased since they'd set up headquarters two weeks ago. Already, they'd passed out hundreds of fliers and distributed fifty knit caps Georgia had shipped from Aunt Star's knitting circle based at Gil's theater. Two more caps were sent priority to Seattle so Cinda and Roxy could have them in time before they flew to Washington, D.C. next week for the march on the nation's capital.

By now, Trudy and Jewel were used to the occasional hoot, holler, or honk from some car passing by on Seven Mile Road, but today was the first time counter protestors had appeared holding picket signs. A patrol car cruised by and parked on the opposite side of the diner. The uniformed police officer stayed in his unit, but was obviously there to intervene if things got out of hand. Trudy wondered if Clay had sent the officer. Until today, she'd only seen a couple of patrol cars in the area. None of them had ever stopped and parked.

A woman with long frizzy hair and a hawkish face yelled from the sidewalk, "Shame on you for disgracing the POW-MIA flag." She turned and said something to the others. Seconds later they began to chant, "Shame on you, shame on you, shame on you for disgracing that flag."

Jewel sighed. "How can they stand there and say that? Or support the orange braggart who claims Senator John McCain isn't a war hero because he got shot down and captured? Like that coward would know. He didn't go to war. He hid. I can only imagine what he'd say about your daddy."

By now, Trudy could feel her simmering rage began to boil. She didn't know what *Señor Grab'em* would say, but she recalled what another gutless creep growled decades ago: *Where's your fly-boy daddy? Got himself shot down.* As the protestors chanted, Dub's cruel remarks mocked her from the grave.

She had the urge to get up out of her chair and go scream in their faces to shut the hell up, but she stayed put, took a deep breath, and then slowly exhaled. "You hanging in, Momma?"

Jewel brushed at something on her slacks. "Been hanging in for forty-four years. Why stop now?"

"Looks like your flag has drawn some ire from a few citizens in town," Mayor Trujillo chuckled as he walked up and dropped off a new stack of fliers. "Lupi sent me to check on you. You ladies need anything?"

"A different president-elect," Jewel snorted as she stashed the fliers in the box next to her lawn chair. "One who doesn't disrespect war heroes or brag about how *hot* his daughter is," she added with disgust.

Trudy greeted the former mayor. "Thanks for making more fliers and posting them all over town. Looks like your press releases are working, too. We've heard from lots of people who said they heard about the march either on the radio or read about it in the *Pardon Gazette*."

Benny Trujillo tipped his felt cowboy hat and glanced back at the protestors. "They have every right to protest. But remember, so do we. That's the beauty of our constitution." He walked off.

A chubby blonde bundled in a parka paced up and down the sidewalk, carrying a sign with a picture of a black cat and bold red letters that proclaimed, "He can grab my pussy any day." She hollered at Benny, "Hey, you in the cowboy hat, go back to Mexico!"

Trudy stiffened at the woman's crude, inflammatory remark. She waited for Benny to react.

The mayor, a retired accountant, a college graduate born and raised in Pardon, looked over at the woman and tipped his hat. "Good day to you, Señora. Let's hope that black cat of yours doesn't come alive and jump off your sign and cross in front of you while you're out here being an informed citizen. You know what they say about black cats and Friday the thirteenth." He laughed and headed toward the diner.

"He's a class act," Trudy remarked as she watched him open the door and disappear inside.

Jewel crossed her arms and smiled smugly at the round woman who was sticking her tongue out in their direction. "Like our current first lady reminds us, when they go low, we go high."

"Right now I'd like to give that woman a fat lip." Trudy bristled between clenched teeth.

"Go high, darling," Jewel chimed, waving at the protestors like they were best friends.

A few minutes later, the sound of a cowbell clanged in the air. Lupi moved toward them, her dark hair in a topknot, and wearing a light jacket over her apron and dark slacks. She balanced a tray with a thermos and paper cups in one hand while ringing the cowbell in the other. "Benny said you need backup. I made you chicks some Mexican cocoa."

Jewel rubbed her hands together. "Sounds delicious. I bet it's got a kick."

"And then some," Lupi giggled. "The cayenne pepper should warm you up."

While Trudy took the thermos and handed her mother the cups to hold, Lupi stashed the tray under her arm and glanced at the side of the trailer. "Ladies, I've been praying every day that the military makes a positive ID. I may have a mouth on me, but that doesn't mean I don't pray."

Lupi placed a hand on Trudy's shoulder and squeezed. Trudy reached up and felt her friend's slender wrist. She squeezed back. "Thank you, Lupi. I kinda struggle in that department."

Jewel held out both cups and waited for Trudy to pour the rich concoction. "Smells heavenly."

After Trudy poured the cocoa, she screwed the lid on the thermos and set it down on a three-legged camping stool between the two lawn chairs. Savoring the rich hot liquid, she murmured between sips, "Hits the spot, Lupi. You know any of the protestors?"

Lupi made a show of squinting in their direction. "The chick with frizzy hair. She was a goat roper in high school. From what I remember, she thought she was hot shit. The little fat one waving her pussy in the air, she used to call me a spic on a regular basis. I wanted to kick her ass, but I knew if I did, I'd get kicked off the dance squad."

The woman with frizzy hair began to lead another chant: "Shame on you, shame on you, shame on you for disgracing the flag."

A few seconds later the chubby blonde began to heckle, "You and your silly pink hats. You're a joke. So are you, Lupi Belen! Your food sucks."

Lupi clanged her cowbell high in the air, adding to the cacophony. She yelled something in Spanish before she turned and said to Trudy and Jewel, "I need to get back to the diner. Come inside if you need to escape. Just lock everything up first."

"I'll come in if I need to potty." Jewel burrowed into her lawn chair. "The party's just getting started."

"Thanks, Lupi," Trudy said. "We'll stick it out till noon. Then I need to get home to let Zia out and Mom can take her nap. I'll be back for the afternoon shift though."

As Lupi passed in front of the protestors, she clanged the cowbell one more time. "If you chickas get hungry, come break bread in my diner, 'cuz for all our differences, we still need to eat. And some of us have a history, dating back to high school."

After Lupi left, Trudy noticed her mother was unusually quiet, her face drawn and tight beneath her pink knit hat. "You okay, Momma? Forget about those protestors. You knew we'd catch some blowback."

Jewel set rigid in her lawn chair and faced the sidewalk, staring down the woman with the hawkish face. After a few minutes, the woman retreated, scolding them over her shoulder, "Shame on you. You're a bunch of traitors."

"Traitors, traitors," the rest of the group chanted before they broke up and headed in different directions.

Trudy felt like giving them the finger. Instead, she called, "Have a good weekend." She turned to her mother. "I don't think we've seen the last of them."

Jewel had her right hand over her heart, patting her chest in a continuous beat. "We're doing the right thing being here," she declared. "If your daddy were here, he'd be wearing a pink hat, too. So would your Grandmother Cutterbuck, for that matter. Remember that old black and white photo of her holding your daddy when he was an infant? I found it the other day when I was sorting through photos. I don't know how she did it, being single and so young when Shep came into the world."

Glancing sideways, Trudy said, "I know the one. I memorized her inscription on the back of it."

Jewel leaned back, tilting her head. "Did you really?"

Trudy nodded and began to recite, "My little shepherd boy,

come to show me the way." She paused. "I remember the pride in Daddy's voice when he'd talk about how she went back to school and earned her GED."

The whole time they were talking, Jewel's middle finger and ring finger kept tap-tap-tapping against her heart. Watching her mother, Trudy got the feeling Jewel was tapping some silent code to her beloved: a silent code like the ones prisoners of war tap in captivity when that's their only means of communication.

Even her mom's right knee bounced up and down to the same rhythm as her fingers, along with the heel of her foot as if one side of her body was marching in place. "Daddy would be proud of you, Momma. You took charge and held our family together, even after we lost Bogey."

Slowly, Jewel turned, her eyes watery. "It took me a while, but I pulled myself together. And as the wife of a fallen warrior, I never thought I'd see the day when a fellow American would call me a traitor for fighting back against a bully. That woman who called us traitors, she thinks *we're* the enemy. What's wrong with people? No wonder Star is fed up and hanging her flag upside down."

Jewel picked up the thermos and unscrewed the lid. "And I keep thinking about that poor girl Vivian, raped at twelve. I'm sorry for what I said about her at the nursing home. Making a snap judgment like that. It's a good thing Dub's dead. Or I'd kill him myself."

Trudy almost choked as she downed the last spicy drops of cocoa and reached for the thermos. As she went to pour her mother another cup of cocoa, her mind drifted back to that cold November night two months ago when Georgia reassured her, "Sis, just 'cuz you took down a monster didn't turn you into one."

Later, after the protestors left, an older Latina approached the trailer, a tote bag slung over her shoulder. "Hello, ladies. I'm Mary Ortiz." Trudy jumped up to offer her a seat. Mary thanked her and sat down while Jewel raved about the snow cones she'd enjoyed over the years at their snow cone hut.

Mary thanked Jewel then opened the tote bag and took a deep breath. "Several women at Our Lady of Assumption are knitters.

We've been fighting our own causes for years, and we wanted to help out." With a quiet smile, she began pulling out one pink hat after another.

Trudy watched as her mother cupped her hands with reverence and received the hats like a woman taking communion.

Mary glanced over her shoulder and gestured at something behind her. "Thank you for displaying that flag. My Albert is a Vietnam veteran. He wanted me to relay that he's proud of you for being so brave. He drove by here earlier and saw the protestors. He said he's sorry he didn't stop. They reminded him too much of the antiwar protestors who spit on him when he came home."

CHAPTER 29

Bullies, Bricks, and Good People

Sunday, January 15, 2017

TRUDY'S CELL pinged at seven a.m. She rolled over and reached for her phone on the nightstand. Zia stirred next to her, thumping her tail on the coverlet.

Groggy from sleep, Trudy rolled back against the pillow and squinted at the screen, half expecting a text from Clay. On those mornings when they didn't wake up together, he usually sent a text with some cheerful endearment or a photo of Hercules being goofy or something his daughter sent him that he wanted to share.

But the text was from Lupi, not Clay, and it jostled Trudy out of bed. On wobbly feet, she began to read the message: Diner hit by vandals. Police here now. Nasty graffiti painted all over outside of my building, stuff like faggot lover, build the wall, eat at Lupi's pussy: authentic Mexican. WTF! My grandmother doesn't deserve this. She built this business from scratch. An editor from the *Pardon Gazette* called me shortly after the police arrived. Story's already online, too late for today's print edition. Benny posted a call for volunteers on Facebook so please share. How much you bet it was those mean girls from high school? Coffee made. Have several cases of water to pass out to whoever comes to help. Benny checked trailer. Thank God they didn't touch it. Hell of a way to get publicity!

Zia sneezed and rolled around on the bed, wanting to play.

Trudy rubbed Zia's belly then bent over her phone and began texting: I'm so sorry this happened to you. Sounds like something those mean girls might do, but it could be anybody pissed off by your activism. You're working your butt off, keeping your grandmother's legacy alive. You don't deserve this either, Lupi. I'll share Benny's post. We'll head your way shortly.

As soon as she hit *send*, her mother appeared in the doorway.

"Was that Clay? I just saw online where Lupi's place got vandalized." Jewel gripped the doorframe, teetering in her chenille bathrobe and slippers.

Trudy glanced at her mother, her face etched in new worry lines. "No, Momma. It was Lupi. Police are there now. I'm forwarding her text to Georgia and Aunt Star."

"I'm surprised the vandals didn't slash the tires or bash in the windows on the trailer." Jewel scratched her brow. "I'll go make coffee and set Zia's food out."

After her mother shuffled down the hall, Trudy called to Zia. "Come on, girl. Let's go potty."

Zia jumped off the bed and they cut through the breezeway filled with natural light and ceramic pots overflowing with greenery. As Zia trotted into the sunroom, Trudy glanced over her shoulder where Bogey once dreamed of flying in the dark. "You'd like my secret agent," she whispered. "She's yellow like the stars."

At the French doors, Trudy breathed in the crisp morning air and watched Zia shoot out across the yard like a rocket. Her phone pinged with a text from Georgia: Sis, that's awful about Lupi. She's a strong woman. She'll bounce back. I'll see you chicks Thursday. I'm leaving right after work. Should arrive by suppertime. Got my pink hat for the march. Gil was hoping to come, but he's overseeing auditions for a new production at the theater. Can't wait to meet Zia and see all the changes to the house.

While Zia raced across the yard, Trudy snuck through the narrow archway to capture a photo of their mom admiring her updated kitchen. Coffee brewed in the same coffeepot on the Talavera tile countertop their dad installed decades ago. The conquistador and poppy-red desk guarded the east wall with its fresh coat of chalk-white paint. Bogey's red and yellow God's eye hung once again next to the turquoise phone because some things were meant to stay. Stainless steel appliances complemented the creamy white cabinets with new doors and hardware.

Jewel stood at the large island, its Spanish-style wooden base painted the same red as the desk and topped by an off-white quartz counter. Two poppy-red pendant light fixtures hung from the ceiling. Running her hands over the new surface, Jewel looked up and smiled. "Hector sure brought new life to this house."

Zia barked at the back door.

"He's not the only one," Trudy pointed out as she went to let Zia in. Tail wagging, Zia charged through the sunroom, brushed past Jewel who was pouring coffee, and nosedived into her food dish next to the new refrigerator.

Accepting a steaming mug of coffee from her mother, Trudy climbed onto a new barstool and savored her first hit of caffeine. Jewel joined her at the island, hitching her robe up a few inches as she scooted up against the stool's backrest and watched Zia eat. They both listened as the big yellow dog crunched her kibble and slurped from her water dish.

"Listening to her eat reminds me of your brother scarfing down cold cereal," Jewel said, sipping her coffee before she turned and gazed at something on the east wall.

Setting down her mug, Trudy smiled at the memory then sent photos of their mother to her sister, shared Benny's Facebook post asking for volunteers, and then pulled up the online newspaper story and began reading:

Pardon Gazette: (Note from the editor)
Pardon police are asking for the public's help identifying the person or persons responsible for vandalizing Lupi's Diner, a popular eatery located on Seven Mile Road. Police are investigating the incident as a possible hate crime. The owner, Lupi Belen, a Pardon native and graduate of Yale University, reported the incident to police early this morning when she and an employee arrived at five-thirty to open in time for the Sunday breakfast crowd. They were confronted with graffiti painted on the front and west side of the building, along with broken windows and a

floor strewn with bricks and shards of glass. The graffiti contained obscenities and racial slurs normally found in public restroom stalls.

Ms. Belen returned to Pardon two years ago to run the family business after her grandmother, Guadalupe Belen, the diner's founder, passed away from a sudden illness. As a young girl growing up in Pardon, Lupi Belen said she spent weekends washing dishes, cleaning tables, and studying her grandmother's recipes. She is an active member of the Pardon Chamber of Commerce and supports many local and national causes.

Two weeks ago, the Women's March on Pardon set up headquarters in a vintage travel trailer in the parking lot, also owned by Ms. Belen, west of the diner. The march is slated for Saturday, January 21, at ten a.m. on the south lawn of the county courthouse. Complimentary pussycat hats are available at the march's headquarters to anyone who signs up to participate. All the hats were handcrafted and donated by local knitters in New Mexico. None were factory assembled.

This past Friday, a small group of counter protestors gathered for a peaceful demonstration in front of the headquarters. Two nights later, the vandals damaged the diner but left the travel trailer unscathed. This is the second time vandals have defaced a business in Pardon since the 2016 presidential election. Let's not let a few troublemakers define our community.

Volunteers are needed to help clean up a beloved diner that's enjoyed great reviews in *New Mexico Magazine* and in this newspaper. Bottled water and coffee will be provided to all who donate their time. A Facebook page has been set up with more details.

If anyone has information about this incident, please call the Pardon Police Department.

Trudy and Lupi stood on the sidewalk chatting in front of the diner. Dozens of volunteers milled about. They stopped talking when a biker dude rumbled up on a chopper and pulled into the parking lot.

"Be glad it was bricks and not *bullets*," the burly guy growled after he climbed off his motorcycle and swaggered toward them.

"I'm here to help." He peered around at the damage, his bare arms bulging with muscles and tattoos.

"Hey, Gabe, nice of you to stop by." Lupi pointed him toward the front door. "Cleaning supplies and brushes are in there. Help yourself to water and coffee. Sorry I can't offer you more."

Nodding politely at Trudy, Gabe shook his head and pinched at his long scraggly beard. "Ladies, I think we oughta stick it to the man at Sixteen Hundred Pennsylvania Avenue. If you ask me, he's partly responsible for this mess." A chain dangled from his back pocket as he stepped inside, glass crunching under his black biker boots.

"Nice guy," Trudy said as a TV news van pulled up in front of the diner. "Looks like you're making headlines."

Lupi groaned. "My fifteen minutes of fame. Ay-ay-ay." She threw her arms in the air and went to greet the TV crew. As she walked off, she turned and called to a slim black gentleman on a stepladder with a bucket dangling in one hand. "Hello, Luther. Nice of your congregation to give you a break from preaching this morning."

Luther dipped a brush in a bucket of solution and started scrubbing. "Trying to remove the worst of it for you, Miss Lupi."

"Reverend Green, you need anything before I head next-door?" Trudy glanced over at the trailer where her mother was chatting with a couple of women who'd stopped by to sign up for the march. Three more women were walking toward the trailer, two of them pushing baby strollers.

"I'm good, but thank you kindly." Reverend Green smiled then concentrated on a lewd drawing that looked like it belonged on the back of Gabe's biker vest and not on Lupi's building.

"I still say you look like an actress," a male voice rang out behind her.

Trudy whirled. The young guy from the bank walked out of the diner, a slight limp in his gait. He had a trash bag slung over one shoulder, one very broad shoulder she noticed again. "Thanks for coming to Lupi's aid."

He paused in front of her. His blue eyes twinkled beneath his red cap. "I may not agree with Ms. Belen's politics, but I'll defend

her right to have them." He hiked around the corner of the building and tossed the trash bag into a dumpster next to the parking
lot.

Trudy followed him.

After the metal lid slammed shut, he gestured toward the
travel trailer. "If you ask me, it's those women libbers stirring up
trouble. Take that old lady in her silly pink hat. Bunch of
snowflakes and libtards." He cracked his knuckles. "And the POW-
MIA flag on the side of that trailer. That ain't right." He shook his
head in disgust.

His comments jarred her. She stiffened and straightened her
shoulders. Scratching her nose, she said quietly, "I saw you leave
the bank that day. I know you're a wounded warrior." She paused,
waiting for him to say something, but he just stared at the trailer,
a look of contempt replacing the merriment in his eyes.

Finally she said, "That older woman in the pink hat. The one
seated in the lawn chair? That's my momma. We're helping with
the Women's March scheduled for next Saturday."

The young man's mouth fell open and he glanced away, looking embarrassed. "Oh Lord. I stepped in it." His cheeks turned
crimson to match his cap.

She relaxed a bit and chuckled. "It's okay. You didn't know."

Sighing, he removed his cap and brushed a hand through his
short hair, his Celtic cross ring glinting in the morning sun.
"Please don't tell me y'all hung that flag?"

Biting the side of her mouth, Trudy nodded. "My dad flew F-
4s in Vietnam. He's been missing in action since nineteen seventy-
two."

The young man sighed again. "Man, that's tough. Air Force?"

"Yeah. He disappeared from the radar right before my thirteenth birthday."

The young veteran brushed his cap back and forth against his
thigh as if the action helped him clear his head. "She never remarried?"

Trudy shook her head. "She got a call back in November. A
team of investigators found a crash site on a remote hillside where
they think my dad's plane went down. They're testing some re-

mains. Bone fragments mostly. So now we wait for another call to see if it's him."

Pursing his lips, he squinted before he stuck his cap back on. He nodded toward the diner. "That your dad's picture in there on the wall?"

"Yeah." She started to back away, to head toward the trailer. A line was forming in front of her mother and she needed to go help her. "One thing my dad didn't tolerate...bullies, especially men who push women around."

The combat veteran stuck out his hand. "Roger that. I'm Brian, by the way. And I still say you look like an actress."

"Ha," she laughed. "I'm Trudy. Let me know if your head gets cold. I'm sure Momma and I can rustle up an extra cap for you."

His blue eyes twinkled as he turned and disappeared around the corner of the building, that slight gimp not slowing him down.

Two nights later, Trudy clopped up the hallway in her old majorette boots, her baton wedged stiffly in her fingers. Zia pranced beside her, excited by the treasures Trudy excavated moments ago.

Her tassels swinging, she laughed as she paraded into the kitchen, her once creamy legs now encased in brown leggings, the skimpy green uniform stretched over her upper body. "Momma, look what I found in the back of my closet."

Jewel was lifting a chicken casserole from her new oven. Turning, her whole face crinkled in a grin as she set the dish on a hot pad on her new island. "It still fits. A bit snug, but I always loved those green sequins. Let's get a picture." Removing quilted oven mitts from her hands, she reached for her cellphone.

"Oh, Momma, I look like a giant turtle in this thing," Trudy giggled. Zia reared up on her hind legs, her front paw reaching for Trudy as Jewel captured the moment on camera.

After Trudy clopped back to her old bedroom to change, her cellphone pinged with a text from Clay: Babe, I just cracked the case on the vandalism to Gold's Department Store. Now I can retire. Someone else in the department will solve Lupi's case. I'm ready to play. Check local news. I'll call you later. And hey, you're still the best looking twirler in the band. Your mom just sent me the photo. LOL

Trudy rushed out of the bedroom, Zia nipping at the tassels swinging to and fro as she marched toward the kitchen. "Momma...!"

While the casserole cooled, Jewel sat on a barstool hunched over her cellphone. "Darling, breaking news. It's from the *Pardon Gazette*." Jewel cleared her throat and began to read. "Arrests have been made in connection with the vandalism on Gold's Department Store back in November of 2016. According to Lieutenant Clay Cordova, a detective with the Pardon Police Department, members of a hate group based in West Texas have been charged with defacing private property. Police are still asking for the public's help in tracking down the person or persons responsible for the vandalism to Lupi's Diner on Seven Mile Road." She set her phone down and looked at Trudy. "Darling, are you going to eat supper in that getup?"

January 21, 2017

On Saturday evening, hours after the Women's March on Pardon, Trudy and Clay linked fingers and cuddled in front of a blazing fire. When Trudy had left her mom's house thirty minutes earlier with an overnight bag packed for two, Georgia was sorting through her things, tossing stuff left and right, while Jewel conked out on the gold velvet sofa, the television murmuring in the background.

Zia had chased Hercules around the room since they arrived. After a while, he jumped up on the couch next to Clay and began panting. "She wearing you out, Little Man?" Clay laughed and nudged Trudy on the chin. Zia plopped down on the floor at Trudy's feet and sighed.

Reeling back, Trudy punched Clay playfully on the arm and they started wrestling like teenagers. Because they both knew one thing would lead to another and another...right when Clay went to kiss her, Trudy's phone pinged with a Facebook notification from Lupi: "The Women's March on Pardon drew an estimated crowd of two hundred people, many wearing a variety of pussy hats and matching attire. We created a sea of pink in downtown Pardon. For a small conservative town, the turnout of two hundred women, men, children, and dogs (most on leashes) was a sight to see. According to Benny Trujillo, former mayor of Pardon and one of the cofounders of the march, the crowd size was not exaggerated. We gathered on the courthouse lawn, sang songs, chanted prayers, and held up signs demanding for women's rights and human rights for our generation and future generations to come. We listened to a variety of speakers, held hands, and pledged our allegiance to stand against oppression. Stay strong, everybody! Things may get worse before they get better. But take heart, *We Shall Overcome!*"

CHAPTER 30

Flying West

Monday, January 23, 2017

DUSK SETTLED around them as Trudy, Georgia, and Clay gathered at the patio table before dinner. Moments earlier, Lupi phoned both sisters on a three-way call to share that a reporter from the *Washington Post* called to interview her for a story she was writing about the sister marches held around the country in conjunction with the Women's March on Washington, D.C. After reading on-line about the vandalism to Lupi's Diner days before the Women's March on Pardon, the reporter was curious why the vandals didn't strike the vintage travel trailer parked next door that served as Pussycat Hat Headquarters.

Lupi told the reporter that although it was purely speculation on her part, she figured the vandals knew the camper belonged to the wife of a fighter pilot missing in action in Vietnam and that some things were off limits, even for thugs. Lupi mentioned the encouragement she received from good people in her community who rallied to clean up and repair the damage to her business, regardless of their political views. Not only that, the buildup to the Women's March helped generate new interest in establishing a women's shelter and outreach center in Pardon. A handful of anonymous donors had come forward and contributed a large sum of money to build the facility.

Trudy was grateful her daughter's name would live on. The shelter would be christened Sarah Jewel's Place. Hector Cordova would serve as general contractor for construction. Rumors had it that one of the donors was a wealthy businesswoman from Texas who'd recently lost her mother. Trudy wondered if it was Madeline T.

Moments after they hung up with Lupi, a freight train rumbled past on its way into the station a few miles to the east. Zia scrambled to race it, and now she trotted along the fence line, sniffing for new treasures. Mouthwatering aromas from the kitchen wafted through the cool air where Jewel had propped open the window over her new stainless steel sink.

"Smells good," Clay said, nursing a longneck beer. His left hand rested on Trudy's knee.

Her gaze shifted from Clay to the travel trailer. After the march on Saturday, he'd moved it back to its place behind the carport. "Mom's making green chile cheese grits and Frito salad."

Georgia stared absently at her cellphone. "I offered to help Mom prepare dinner but she shooed me away. I think she wants to *luxuriate* in her new kitchen. She's enjoying her new island."

"I overheard her thanking Aunt Star for suggesting the update," Trudy chuckled. "Like it was all Aunt Star's idea."

"Hah," Georgia snorted. "And here we've been bugging her for years."

Trudy glanced at the kitchen window. Her mother's face appeared briefly, the pointy tips of her pink cap sticking up like kitty ears. "At least she's preparing something easy. I haven't had Frito salad since we were kids. Remember how Bogey always picked out the avocado?"

The two sisters grinned at the shared memory. Georgia set her phone down and lifted her glass. "To our little brother. Avocado hater and walking encyclopedia."

"And don't forget, fierce hunter of Pecos diamonds," Trudy sighed, twirling the stem of her wine glass before she raised it in a toast. "Remember how he'd pick through the gravel in the driveway looking for those little quartz crystals?"

Georgia rubbed at something in the corner of her eye. "Yeah, and he insisted on calling them *fakeous* diamonds, even when we tried to correct him."

Trudy smiled into her wine glass. "He was a smart little booger. A lot smarter than me." She glanced up at her sister. "You heading back in the morning?"

Georgia didn't look up. She was texting like a mad woman, a sly look on her face. "Yeah, I need to check on Aunt Star and get organized for class."

Trudy leaned into Clay. "Liar," she teased. "We all know the real reason you can't wait to get back."

Georgia tilted her head and offered a coy smile. "Gil wants me to teach dance at the theater. He's says lots of underprivileged kids in town could benefit from dance lessons."

"That's wonderful, sis. You're livin' your dream." When Georgia didn't elaborate on whether she would get paid, Trudy realized her sister would do it for free...just for the chance to dance and help others.

Resting against Clay, Trudy felt the sudden urge to unpack her burden...or part of it at least. Maybe the part how they fought off Dub, not the part how he ended up on the tracks. That part would remain forever tucked inside of her. "Georgia and I have something we need to tell you." She kicked her sister under the table.

Georgia looked up from her phone, a quizzical expression on her face. "We do?"

Trudy narrowed her eyes and gave her sister a slight nod. "Sis, it's time. I can't live with the deception any longer."

Grinding her foot into Trudy's shin, Georgia stared at her bug-eyed over the rim of her spectacles, slowly shaking her head. *Don't do it,* her look implored.

Clay leaned back, a lazy grin exposing his dimples. "So you're both madly in love with me, is that it? I've known all along." His eyes danced with mischief as he gazed back and forth between the sisters.

Georgia snorted. "Hah! You're a great catch, Clay Cordova, but I've already got one hot-blooded man to deal with. I don't have the energy for two." Her foot dug deeper into Trudy's shin.

Laughing, Clay folded his hands across his midsection and continued to smirk.

Trudy tossed back the last of her wine and set her glass down.

Her fingers tap-danced on the patio table as she worked up the courage to try again. She took a deep breath and met his gaze. "Clay, a long time ago, right before we started dating —"

Before she could spit it out, the doors to the sunroom flung open. Jewel appeared, capless, waving her cellphone in the air. "Girls!" she bellowed, her voice thin and shrill. "It's the Air Force. The DNA matches your daddy's. He's coming home."

Georgia jolted up, knocking over her lawn chair as she charged toward their mother and grabbed the phone from her hands. "Hello, hello," she gasped. "This is Georgia Cutterbuck speaking. I'm Major Cutterbuck's youngest daughter. Is it true my daddy's coming home? I'm standing here with my mother, Jewel, and my sister."

By now, Trudy had scrambled to her feet and stood frozen in place. Clay wrapped his arm around her waist and she leaned into him, not quite breathing, not quite believing what she was hearing: her father's remains had finally been recovered and identified.

With her eyes trained on her sister, Trudy watched Georgia's head bob up and down, nodding as she listened intently to the person on the other end of the line. After what seemed like forever, Georgia proclaimed, "Outstanding!" sounding like their father when he heard good news. After a pause, she passed the phone back to their mother.

Seconds later, Jewel hung up and stepped out onto the patio, leaving the French doors wide open behind her.

Without warning, clouds roiled in, bringing the scent of rain. Lightning cracked and a rumble exploded in the atmosphere. Zia galloped across the yard toward them, going ninety to nothing, all three legs in fluid motion.

Thunder continued to roll in. The temperature dropped drastically and they all craned their necks skyward as the dark shadow of a pointy-nosed F-4 Phantom II roared overhead, both engines in full afterburner.

Zia yodeled and yelped and howled like a coyote.

Clay yelled over the sound of thunder, "What the heck was that?"

From the corner of her eye, Trudy saw her mother grope to-ward her sister for support. With tears rolling down her cheeks, Georgia took their mother in her arms and held her tight. Even in the waning light, Trudy could see the wide-eyed excitement in her mother's soft blue eyes as Jewel cried out into the night, "It's Shep Cutterbuck, flying west."

Gulping back the knot caught in her throat, Trudy followed the shadow until it went out of sight. There was no doubt in her mind what they'd all witnessed: her daddy's spirit soaring free.

Flashes of lightning lit up the sky over the airfield as they all gaped in wonder. When the thunder faded, the brassy notes of Herb Alpert's mega hit, "Rise," exploded from the pocket of Trudy's cardigan. Fumbling for her phone, she realized she must've hit the playlist button on her cell in her excitement.

Grabbing her phone, she waved it high in the air as every cell in her body came alive. Clay kissed her forehead, and they danced around the patio with her mother and sister, their bodies swaying in rhythm to the music. Jewel pumped her fist in the air, a sign of victory.

Trudy glanced down long enough to see Zia worm her way in, her lips peeled back in a doggy grin as if she'd been in on some cosmic secret the whole time.

∾

Pardon Gazette

Pardon, NM — Major Shepard Cutterbuck, USAF, went missing in action on October 2, 1972 when his F-4 was shot down over North Vietnam. His remains have been recovered and positively identified through DNA. He will be repatriated with full military honors in a private ceremony at Pardon Cemetery at an undis-closed time. His ashes will be interred next to his only son, Shep-ard "Bogey" Cutterbuck (age 11) who died of brain cancer a year and a half after Major Cutterbuck was declared missing. Major Cutterbuck's mother, Georgia Anne Cutterbuck, died never knowing what happened to her son.

Born and raised in Kentucky, Major Cutterbuck was the first person in his family to attend college. After graduating from pilot school at Reese AFB, Texas (closed in 1997), he married the love of his life, Jewel Hurn, a former beauty queen and Pardon native. Survivors include his wife, Jewel, of Pardon; his daughters, Gertrude Cutterbuck of Pardon, Georgia Cutterbuck of Las Vegas, NM; sister-in-law Star Hurn of Las Vegas, NM; and special family friend, Clay Cordova, recently retired from the Pardon PD.

The public is invited to an informal gathering at ten a.m. on 6 February at the former Pardon Air Force Base airfield to honor Major Cutterbuck's service and sacrifice to his country. A color guard from Pardon High School's ROTC will be on hand to post the colors. Those who wish to pay their respects are asked to arrive at least thirty minutes early to allow time to walk onto the runway where Major Cutterbuck took off in an F-4 and headed to war. Two golf carts from the Pardon Country Club will shuttle those who need special assistance.

Dress accordingly. Mother Nature is expected to arrive on a stiff wind sweeping down the High Plains.

CHAPTER 31

Three Years Later

"STAR, IN my eighty-three years on Earth, this is the first time I've been without a big sister to boss me around. It's also the first time I've felt like an orphan." Jewel paused to swipe a hanky over her nose and dab her watery eyes.

Under a deep blue New Mexico sky speckled with puffy white clouds — the kind Trudy once imagined she could tie a string to and float away — a small crowd had gathered to pay their respects to Star Hurn, the longtime activist, retired nurse, and graduate of Pardon High. Although a few men were present, the crowd consisted mostly of women. Some wore pink hats left over from the 2017 Women's March. Benny Trujillo passed out white carnations in honor of all the suffragettes who fought for women's voting rights. The flowers were Lupi's idea.

Rocking back on the heels of her leather boots, Trudy breathed in the crisp November air and gazed at her mother in gold ballet flats and navy slacks. Jewel stood in front of Bogey's tombstone and tugged at her flimsy knit cap. The first cap Star made when she took up knitting after she retired.

Star didn't want a funeral; she wanted a rally for everything she stood for.

Her wishes were to be cremated and a handful of her ashes sprinkled over her nephew's grave, the remainder over Bernie's final resting place in West Texas. Trudy and Clay would scatter "stardust" in a small town where Bernie took care of everyone's critters for decades.

Plunging her hands into the pockets of a dark wool peacoat, Jewel continued. "I'll miss your daily phone calls to check on me. Your constant grumbling about the Orange Cheese Puff you later referred to as *the traitor*. The nasty man who separates families and locks kids in cages. Every time you thought things couldn't get worse, they did." Jewel stopped to catch her breath. "I'll never forget the night you called me, crying, 'He's gone too far, Sister. He's abandoned our allies to our enemies. Bribed and extorted another country to try and get dirt on a political opponent.'"

Closing her eyes, Jewel craned her neck skyward. "Keep shining your light over all of us, Star, especially in these uncertain times. And when you bump into Bogey and Shep, tell them I'm not far behind. I love you, my sister, my friend."

The back of Trudy's throat ached at the mention of her little brother and dad. Silently, she added, *if you see my baby girl, rock her for me.*

Jewel started to wobble, exhaustion setting in. Gil offered Jewel his arm. Trudy was grateful for her brother-in-law's willingness to help anyone he saw struggling, from the elderly to disadvantaged kids. No wonder Georgia fell for him the first time they met.

Tires crunched on the gravel road beside them. Trudy looked over to see a familiar face peering out the driver's side window of a late model Lexus. *Madeline T.* She must've read about Aunt Star's death in the *Pardon Gazette* and come to pay her respects to a cousin she'd never met.

The car idled a moment as Trudy and Madeline exchanged glances. As Trudy went to motion her over, Madeline gave a polite nod and the Lexus crept forward, kicking up little puffs of caliche.

Maybe one day Madeline would change her mind about meeting them, but for now this brief exchange felt like a start. Trudy wanted to tell her sister and mother they'd had a special visitor, but Georgia was speaking now.

"Aunt Star never gave up hope that our nation would heal despite the chaos of the last four years. None of us knows what tomorrow may bring or who will be our next president. But on the eve of this 2020 election"— she stopped to fling one end of her wooly scarf over her left shoulder and pull a blue sticky note out of her pocket — "I'd like to read a quote from former President Jimmy Carter. 'Our country has lived through a time of torment. It is now a time for healing. We want to have faith again. We want to be proud again. We just want the truth again.'" Georgia looked up from her note, her fingers curling around the little square of paper.

Catching her breath, Trudy stared at the ground, at the patches of yellow grass mixed with faded weeds. It was the word *truth* that set off the tiny quake in her heart.

Clay reached for her hand, his fingers lingering a moment on the turquoise wedding band that matched his. He'd noticed her tremor.

From the moment he'd walked back into her life in 2016, part of her wanted to confess she'd been lying to him since they were teenagers. She almost told him about Dub the night Clay proposed two years ago, and later on a flight to Seattle to meet Cinda and Roxy. But every time Trudy felt the dam start to break, she thought about Aunt Star and their code of silence. But Aunt Star was gone now, and...

Her mouth dry, Trudy licked her lips and stepped forward. It was her turn to say a few words. Her mind flashed to the photo of Aunt Star and Bernie on a camping trip to the mountains.

Twirling the carnation in her right hand, she began. "I used to feel sorry for Aunt Star because she never married or had kids. I thought her whole purpose in life was to patch everybody up. Our daddy liked to call her Florence Nightingale, our family's own personal nurse. Before she started wearing scrubs, her uniform reminded me of clean sheets hanging from a clothesline, her soft embrace a cushion against pain and fear. But on her death bed, Aunt Star reminded us of the sacrifices she made to protect herself from being shunned. She hid her sexual orientation for fear she'd lose her job, her standing in the community. She told us how she and Bernice had to hide their love for each other from most people. They had to pretend they were nothing more than best friends and traveling companions."

A young woman in the crowd covered her face and sobbed.

An older woman consoled her by patting her on the shoulder and offering her a tissue.

Trudy choked up, witnessing the young woman's anguish.

Holding the carnation close, she cleared her throat to regain her composure then concluded, "After decades of advancement for individual rights, we are facing new uncertainties. Aunt Star's final request was for all of us to take care of each other and vote for human rights at the ballot box."

During a moment of silence, Trudy could feel the vibration of a freight train as it rolled along the tracks to the south.

When the moment of silence ended, a loud clanging filled the air.

On cue, Lupi rang the cowbell she'd brought from the diner. "Friends," she called out after silencing the clapper, "make believe this is the Liberty Bell, the sound of freedom ringing over our land. No matter what happens tomorrow, we must never surrender to dictators and oppressors. Star Hurn lived her life taking care of others. She believed in equality and human rights. Thank God for strong women like Star. And there are others. Powerful women like Christine Blasey Ford, Marie Yovanovitch, Fiona Hill. They stand up for all of us. And remember, you don't need a lofty title to let your voice be heard." Lupi rang the cowbell again before she set it on the ground. After Benny passed her a carnation, she inhaled the scent then lifted it high in the air and led everyone in song.

Women began to chant, "We shall overcome." Some held hands while others lifted their carnations in the air like Lady Liberty with her torch.

Trudy's heart quickened. Standing shoulder to shoulder with the women, Hector Cordova held a white carnation high in the air and sang along with them. He wasn't wearing a coat as usual, only work boots and jeans, a long-sleeved white T-shirt with the words UNITED States of America emblazoned across his chest.

Tears leaked from Trudy's eyes at this image of unity. A sign of hope. If a small group of people from various backgrounds could come together in peace, maybe the country could, too.

After Jewel scattered a handful of ashes over Bogey's grave, it was time to leave. Clay and Gil escorted Jewel toward the line of cars. Trudy and Georgia trailed closely behind. At the last second, Trudy said, "Let's ditch the crowd. There's something I need to do."

Without hesitation, Georgia linked her arm in Trudy's and they hiked across the cemetery. "Guess we're going to pay the *perv* a visit."

"The one buried in Pardon," Trudy deadpanned.

When Dub's full name came into view, Georgia clenched her jaw then leaned over and spit on the tombstone. She straightened and gave Trudy a smug grin. "I've been wanting to do that for years."

"Madeline T. was here. She drove by when you were speaking."

"I wondered if that was her. I saw a Lexus pull up then leave. I can't even imagine what it feels like to be her."

Trudy took Georgia by the elbow. "Sis, I had an epiphany while you were reading what President Carter said about *truth*. It got me to thinking. Forty-five can lie and get away with it, but there are ramifications for not telling the truth. Someone always suffers. Take Aunt Star. She died with her truth, but she paid a heavy price by living in fear. Fear of being found out she was gay. Fear that Momma would lose the house if the truth came out about Dub's death." Trudy squared her shoulders and looked her sister in the eye. "I'm tired of living in fear."

Georgia removed her eyeglasses and pinched the bridge of her nose. "So, what are you saying. You wanna come clean?"

Trudy took a deep breath and slowly exhaled. "Yeah. After we get back to Momma's. Maybe after that little ceremony she has planned around the flagpole."

Turning their backs on the tomb of a serial rapist, the sisters linked arms and headed across the cemetery to meet up with the rest of the family.

∽

Since Jewel placed the campaign sign out by the mailbox a year ago, vehicles had been pulling over left and right on Seven Mile Road. As the family assembled at the base of the flagpole, another car pulled up, the driver got out, snapped a photo, then left.

Mr. Grumples hopped up on the window sill in the living room, switched his tail, and gazed out the window at all of them. Zia sat on her haunches on the front porch, tilted her head, and stared up at this new fluffy friend who'd come to live with them. Hercules had died a year ago in Trudy's arms while Clay was mowing the lawn.

Reaching to kiss her mother, Trudy stepped back to let Jewel pass.

"Clay and Gil, will you two do the honors?" Jewel held the American flag folded in a triangle; the same flag displayed upside down in front of Star's pink adobe since the day after the 2016 election.

Both Jewel's sons-in-law strode forward with the precision of honor guards, Clay in a charcoal suit, Gil in jeans and a black T-shirt, his forearms covered in tattoos.

After the men unfolded the flag and clipped it to a rope, Clay slowly hoisted the red, white, and blue up the pole, right side up.

The flag unfurled and snapped in the breeze.

Trudy and Georgia helped steady Jewel as she gazed upward. In a voice thinning but full of conviction, Jewel said, "Star was a true patriot. Her whole life was one of service to others. Each of us must keep fighting for freedom, the very freedom Shep died defending."

Trudy signaled Georgia that she was ready to speak her truth. Georgia squeezed her hand, lending her sister full support.

Heat fired through Trudy, giving her courage. "Clay, Momma, there's something I need to tell you ..."

≈

Acknowledgments

A HEARTY thank you to my publisher, Nancy C. Cleary, and the team at Wyatt-MacKenzie Publishing, Inc. for believing in my story and launching it into the world. Gratitude to my agent, Diane Nine, President of Nine Speakers, Inc. for taking me on based on a one paragraph premise, a promise, and a client's referral. Your support means the world to me.

To Joyce Gilmour for helping me polish my final draft. You keep me on my toes.

Special thanks to longtime friends, Gene and Sherry Christian, for your help in explaining eastern New Mexico agriculture.

To the late Joan Searcy for telling me stories about your days as a flight attendant. And to Flight Attendant Jenny Mack Quinn, for spending one whole afternoon on the phone with me, sharing your stories and also memories of what it was like to grow up as the daughter of a fighter pilot.

A huge thanks to Steve Bradshaw, a forensic scientist, who helped me with DNA tracking information.

Clasping my hands in appreciation to Reverend Grayce O'Neil Rowe. You not only took the time to explain your calling as a female priest with the Episcopal Church, but you helped me find my courage to write an important scene.

To friends Fred Johnson and Mary Dirickson Johnson, who know firsthand what it's like to have a family member still missing in action in Vietnam.

Thanks to Kathy Hendrickson of Southwest Detours for the private tour of the Castaneda Hotel before renovation. To learn more about the history of Harvey Girls and Harvey Houses, look for books by Lesley Poling Kempes and Rosa Walston Latimer.

A special thanks to all my author friends who helped me along the way. You all know who you are. Once in a while, a reviewer comes along who says she can't wait for your next book. Sharon Salituro, thank you for being you.

To all of my friends and family who've supported me on this writing journey, bless you.

Eternal love and thanks to my hubby, Tom, my long-suffering saint!

And to all of us who are hanging on to hope for a better future...

Book Club Discussion Questions

for *The Flying Cutterbucks* by Kathleen M. Rodgers

1. In chapter 26, Aunt Star says, "Sometimes love crosses all boundaries... Sometimes we must do things to protect those we love." Have there been times in your own life where you've crossed boundaries in order to protect someone else? Are the consequences worth the risks?

2. Throughout the novel, Trudy hears her Dad's voice in the form of pilot radio calls. Do you think her dad was trying to communicate with her from the other side? Or do you think bits and phrases of his speech were simply stored in her memory bank and she conjured up her dad's voice as a form of comfort and reassurance?

3. How would Trudy and Georgia's life have turned out if Aunt Star had called the police after Dub hit the floor instead of covering up his death? How would this have affected Jewel when she returned from recuperating from a nervous breakdown?

4. Clay Cordova is a detective. He's a smart guy. Do you think he suspected Trudy was keeping something from him? If so, why didn't he push her to confess her secret since he was a good cop?

5. At the end of chapter 12 when Trudy phones Clay that she's leaving Dallas to head back to Pardon, why does she think of her mother's place on Seven Mile Road as *the little house of shrines?*

6. Even though Major Shep Cutterbuck is missing in action throughout the narrative, did you feel like you had a sense of who he was as a person when he was alive? Why or why not?

7. When it comes to some of the animals in the story, how did you feel about Hercules, Zia, and Mr. Grumples? Did their characters add to the story? Did the author embed any hidden or obvious meanings in their physical descriptions?

8. When Trudy has a chance encounter with a female priest late in the book, how did this scene affect your feelings about women clergy? Were you offended or encouraged when Trudy suggested that a female priest be depicted in art?

9. Lupi Belen is a successful Latina businesswoman who has returned to Pardon to run the diner her grandmother founded decades ago. How does Lupi's outspoken activism help Trudy and Jewel find their own courage to speak out against oppression?

10. When Lupi's Diner is vandalized, the wounded warrior Trudy encounters at the bank shows up and offers his support even though he disagrees with Lupi's politics. How does his second encounter with Trudy affect the story overall?

11. When Aunt Star hangs the American Flag upside down as a form of national distress, how did this make you feel?

12. In the chapter titled "Demolition Day," Clay's cousin Hector arrives at Jewel's house to tear down a wall on the day after the 2016 presidential election. Discuss the author's intent here.

13. Near the end of the book, on the eve of the 2020 presidential election, why does Jewel want her sister's flag flown right side up over her house on Seven Mile Road?

14. Why did the author place Clay's cousin Hector in the middle of a group of women at Aunt Star's memorial service?

15. If you were in Trudy's shoes and you were burdened by a secret, would you confess the truth or take it to your grave like Aunt Star?

16. The author opens the novel with a quote by Toni Morrison who passed away in 2019. The quote is from an essay Ms. Morrison penned in 2015, titled, "No Place for Self-Pity, No Room for Fear." Do you think artists and authors have a moral obligation to use their platforms to speak out against aggression and fear?

Want Kathleen to talk to your Book Club? Contact us: bookclub@wyattmackenzie.com with your request!

CPSIA information can be obtained
at www.ICGtesting.com
Printed in the USA
FSHW010009250720
71820FS